Copyright

Graffik

The Hunt for The Two

Written by: Willie S.

Dedication

For the unsung heroines and heroes who fight for justice, for those who dare to challenge tyranny, and for the dreamers who never give up hope—this book is dedicated to you. Your courage inspires me, your resilience strengthens me, and your unwavering belief in a better world drives my imagination. This story is a testament to the power of the human spirit, the strength found in unlikely alliances, and the enduring flame of rebellion against oppression. It is a celebration of your strength, your bravery, and your unwavering belief in the face of adversity. May this story resonate with your own struggles and triumphs, reminding you that even in the darkest of times, the light of hope persists. It is dedicated to all those who have faced seemingly insurmountable obstacles, who have risen from the ashes of defeat, and who continue to fight for a more just and equitable world. May their stories continue to inspire generations to come. To my own personal heroes, those who have supported my journey and inspired me through thick and thin, thank you for believing in my vision. This story is a tribute to your unwavering faith in me and my work. May this dedication be a small token of my gratitude, a reflection of your boundless support and encouragement.

Preface

The world of this novel was born from a desire to explore the complexities of power, betrayal, and the enduring strength of the human spirit. It is a world where political intrigue weaves a tapestry of deceit and danger, where skilled warriors and cunning strategists clash in a dance of swords and wits. But at its heart, this story is about two individuals—Stanya, the master information gatherer, and Najeem, the valiant warrior—whose paths unexpectedly intertwine amidst the chaos of imperial tyranny. Their journey is one of survival, resilience, and the forging of an unlikely alliance forged in the crucible of shared adversity. Their individual strengths, their vulnerabilities, and their complex relationship form the backbone of this narrative. The pages that follow will take you on a thrilling ride through treacherous landscapes and perilous encounters. You will witness acts of courage and sacrifice, moments of intense vulnerability and profound connection. I have endeavored to craft characters that are both relatable and extraordinary, flawed yet inspiring. Their struggles and triumphs will, I hope, resonate with you long after you turn the final page. It is my intention to evoke a sense of immersion, to transport you to a land of breathtaking beauty and chilling darkness, where the lines between good and evil are blurred, and the fight for freedom is always ongoing. The seeds of rebellion sown in these pages will, I hope, inspire contemplation on the nature of power, the importance of resistance and the indomitable nature of hope.

Introduction

Within the gilded cage of Emperor Baznoon Graffik's court, a silent war rages. Intrigue and betrayal are as commonplace as the opulent tapestries adorning the palace walls. In this treacherous landscape, Stanya, a shadow moving unseen, gathers vital information that could shatter Graffik's tyrannical reign. Her skills honed over years of clandestine operations are put to the ultimate test as she risks everything to infiltrate the heart of the empire, carrying with her a secret that could ignite a rebellion. Simultaneously, Najeem, a warrior of unmatched skill, finds himself ensnared in Graffik's web of power. Captured, not as a prisoner, but as a trophy, Najeem's strength and charm have ensnared Graffik's daughter, leading to an unexpected captivity. His escape is a harrowing journey, fueled by a burning desire for freedom and a growing unease about the shadows lurking within the palace walls. Their paths collide in a whirlwind of clashing swords and desperate escapes, initially mistaking each other for enemies. However, their shared plight forces them into an uneasy alliance, a fragile bond formed in the fires of adversity. Together, they navigate a world brimming with danger, facing relentless assassins, treacherous terrains, and the ever-present threat of Graffik's wrath. The story unravels through action-packed sequences, exploring themes of political intrigue, betrayal, and the transformative power of unexpected alliances. Their journey, fraught with peril and punctuated by moments of surprising tenderness, is a testament to the resilience of the human spirit, the search for freedom, and the unexpected blossoming of love amidst chaos. This is a tale of rebellion against tyranny, a story of two individuals who defy fate, shaping their own destinies in the face of insurmountable odds. Their journey through the perilous Outerlands and their encounter with rebellious factions marks a turning point, where personal struggles intersect with the larger fight for freedom. The stage is set for a battle against seemingly insurmountable odds—a battle for survival, for justice, and for love. This is only the beginning of their story, a saga of courage, resilience, and the enduring power of hope.

Table of Contents

Copyright 1

Dedication..2

Preface 4

Introduction..6

Chapter 1: Emperor's Trap 10

Chapter 2: Shared Plight 38

Chapter 3: A Dangerous Journey 69

Chapter 4: The Alliance 101

Chapter 5: Shadows of the Past.......................................132

Chapter 6: A Difficult Choice 162

Chapter 7: Najeem's Infiltration 191

Chapter 8: The Assault...223

Chapter 9: A Sacrifice..252

Chapter 10: Consequences of Betrayal 283

Chapter 11: A New Dawn 316

Chapter 12: Challenges Remain 345

Chapter 13: Conspiracy Unveiled.....................................374

Chapter 14: Confrontation 403

Chapter 15: A New Balance 433

Acknowledgments 466

Glossary 467

References 469

Author Biography..470

Chapter 1: Emperor's Trap

The air hung thick with the scent of exotic perfumes and simmering anxieties. Stanya, disguised as a low-ranking lady-in-waiting, moved through the opulent halls of Emperor Baznoon Graffik's palace like a phantom. Her emerald gown, chosen for its inconspicuousness amidst the riot of colors worn by the court, flowed around her as she navigated the labyrinthine corridors. Each step was measured, each glance calculated. She was a predator in a gilded cage, her prey Graffik's secrets.

Years of honing her skills in the shadows had prepared her for this. She'd spent countless nights studying the intricate social dynamics of the Graffik court, memorizing faces, learning the subtle cues of power and influence. This infiltration was the culmination of a meticulously crafted plan, months of patient observation and daring maneuvers. Failure was not an option. The fate of countless lives, the very balance of power in the kingdom, hinged on her success.

The palace itself seemed to breathe a palpable tension. Whispers slithered through the tapestries and polished floors, carrying snippets of conversations, half-truths and carefully veiled threats. She encountered guards with eyes that missed nothing, courtiers with smiles that hid daggers, and ladies-in-waiting whose whispers could topple empires. Each interaction was a tightrope walk, a delicate dance between observation and concealment.

She learned to read the subtle shifts in posture, the fleeting expressions that betrayed a concealed agenda. A misplaced hand, a nervous cough, a barely perceptible tightening of the lips – all were clues in the elaborate game of courtly intrigue. She observed Graffik himself from a distance, a figure of imposing stature and unnerving charisma, radiating an aura of power that seemed to physically oppress those around him. His every word, gesture, and glance was carefully considered, a performance designed to maintain his authority.

Her target was not Graffik himself, but the details of his forthcoming war campaign. Information, she knew, was the most powerful weapon. Graffik's plans, once in the right hands, could shift the tides of war, igniting a rebellion that could finally break his iron grip on the land. This intel was hidden away, she'd gleaned from a spy within the court, within a seemingly innocuous jeweled comb.

One evening, she found herself attending a lavish banquet. The air shimmered with the light of countless candles, the clinking of goblets, and the murmur of polite conversation masking the undercurrent of ambition and rivalry. Graffik's daughter, Princess Lyra, sat near her, a striking figure in a gown of spun moonlight, her beauty captivating but her gaze piercing. Lyra, Stanya knew, was a key player in the court's intricate web, her influence both subtle and considerable. A seemingly casual conversation with the Princess proved more revealing than any intercepted message.

Lyra's conversation provided crucial insights into the security measures around the war documents, leading Stanya to discover a poorly guarded side chamber where Graffik kept his most sensitive papers. With practiced skill, Stanya avoided detection, slipping into the chamber under the guise of delivering fresh linen to a chamber maid. The jewels of the comb glittered softly, reflecting the candlelight as she expertly substituted it for an identical copy that she had earlier created.

The heart of the plan involved a secret passage, known only to a handful of trusted servants. Stanya had gained access to the plans of this passage from her network of informants. This escape route led to a secluded exit far from the main gates, one she believed would be less heavily guarded. As she neared the passage, the thrill of success and the impending danger of discovery melded into a potent cocktail of adrenaline.

Her fingers brushed the cold, smooth surface of the comb, its weight a comforting presence against her palm. This small object held the key to shattering Graffik's power, a weight of responsibility that settled heavily on her shoulders. But as she slipped into the passage, a flicker of movement caught her eye. A shadow detached itself from the darkness, and she knew instantly that she had been discovered.

The guards were upon her before she could react. She fought with a desperation born of years of training, her movements fluid and lethal. Her experience with unarmed combat came to the forefront, allowing her to disarm one guard and knock out another with swift precision. But they were too many. Overpowered but not defeated, she was quickly apprehended.

As they dragged her away, the jeweled comb remained safely tucked away. This, she vowed silently, would not be lost. Graffik's trap had sprung, but Stanya was not without her own strategies. She knew Graffik would be eager to interrogate her, to squeeze every scrap of information from her. She braced herself for the ordeal ahead, her mind already racing, planning her next move, strategizing a way to turn the tables on her captor and ensuring that the vital information she obtained would fall into the right hands. The fight for freedom was far from over. Her capture was not a defeat, but a temporary setback in a larger game of survival, a dangerous game where the stakes were impossibly high. Her spirit, hardened by years of adversity, refused to break. Graffik, she knew, had underestimated her.

The silken sheets felt strangely coarse against his skin. Najeem, accustomed to the rough weave of his traveling cloak and the hard-packed earth beneath his sleeping mat, found the opulence of his surroundings suffocating. He lay in a bed that seemed to swallow him whole, a testament to Graffik's bizarre notion of captivity. The room itself was a spectacle, a riot of color and texture that mirrored the unsettling extravagance of the court. Intricate carvings adorned the walls, depicting scenes of battles and triumphs, each a reminder of his own lost freedom.

It had started innocently enough. A chance encounter at a border market, a whispered conversation that revealed his mastery of the sword, a challenge issued by a drunken noble, swiftly and decisively met. He'd left the noble a bruised ego and a grudging respect. Yet, this display of skill, meant only to earn a few coins, had caught the eye of Princess Amara.

Amara, Graffik's daughter, was a whirlwind of contradictions. Beautiful and cruel, capricious and determined, she possessed a gaze that could melt glaciers and a heart as cold as the winter winds that swept across the northern plains. She'd seen him, this warrior from the outerlands, a man whose strength and quiet dignity captivated her. She'd sought him out, drawn to him like a moth to a flickering flame.

Her infatuation had been unsettling from the start. She'd showered him with gifts, silks and jewels that glittered under the flickering candlelight, rare wines that warmed his stomach yet chilled him to the bone. Her attentions were suffocating, a web of charm and possessiveness that held him fast.

Initially, he'd seen it as an opportunity. The palace held secrets, he knew; whispered rumors of rebellions brewing in the outerlands, of a growing discontent among Graffik's subjects. Held within those gilded walls, he could gather intelligence, gather information on Graffik's weaknesses, to later use to aid his own people. It was a calculated risk.

But Amara's intentions, it seemed, were not as straightforward. Her desire, it was now crystal clear, was not for information, but for possession. He was a trophy, a prized specimen to be admired and controlled, caged within the palace's silken walls.

His days were a monotonous routine of elaborate meals, carefully orchestrated conversations, and the princess's persistent, unwavering attention. She'd fill the days with stories of her own fantasies, of heroic battles and daring escapes, revealing a longing that contrasted sharply with the lavish comforts that surrounded her. Her stories were a kaleidoscope of her emotions, hinting at a yearning for a life beyond the suffocating confines of the palace walls.

At night, he'd find himself staring at the ornate ceiling, the intricate designs seeming to mock him. The guards were ever-present, not overtly menacing but their quiet vigilance a constant reminder of his captivity. He was a prisoner of luxury, a captive held not by chains and bars but by the princess's unpredictable whims and the sheer weight of her power.

He'd tried subtly to probe for information. Casual conversations, carefully chosen words, all designed to unravel the palace's intricate web of power, to identify cracks in Graffik's seemingly impenetrable defenses. But Amara, though unpredictable, was perceptive. She seemed to sense his underlying motives, his attempts to garner information. Her eyes, usually sparkling with laughter or fierce passion, would darken, a warning that he was treading dangerous ground.

He realized that his initial plan was far too risky. The Princess held him captive, not physically but emotionally. Her constant presence made escape near impossible. He wasn't treated as a prisoner, but neither was he free. He needed a new strategy, a plan that considered this unexpected captivity, a way to use Amara's obsessiveness to his advantage.

One evening, Amara, draped in a robe of amethyst silk, confided in him about her fears for her father's reign. Graffik, she admitted, was growing increasingly paranoid, driven by a desperate need to maintain his power. He was ruthlessly eliminating those who dared to oppose him. She spoke of hidden rebellions, of secret alliances, of impending threats that loomed over the empire like a storm cloud.

"They whisper of a rebellion in the outerlands," she confessed, her voice barely a whisper, "a rebellion that could topple my father's throne." Her eyes, for a brief moment, were filled with a raw, untamed fear.

This was his chance. He could use her fear, her growing unease, to sow discord among Graffik's ranks, to destabilize his rule from within. He could use her, her affection for him, to gain access to information, to influence events that could lead to his eventual escape.

It was a gamble, a treacherous dance on a knife's edge. He would need to tread carefully, to play his part with unwavering skill. One false move, one misstep, could mean the end of his life. But he knew he couldn't stay here forever.

His people needed him, and the outerlands awaited his return.

He started to subtly question her about the guards, about the palace's layout, the patterns of patrols. He studied her moods, trying to pinpoint the most opportune times for a calculated move, a moment of vulnerability when her possessiveness might momentarily falter. He feigned compliance, playing the part of the enthralled captive to perfection.

The gilded cage was not just his prison, it was his hunting ground. He observed, he learned, he waited, sharpening his senses, planning his escape with the precision of a seasoned warrior. He had been captured, but he had not been defeated. His imprisonment was a temporary setback, a mere detail in a larger, more intricate game. Graffik had captured a warrior, but he had also unwittingly unleashed a force of rebellion within his own walls. The fight for freedom was far from over, and Najeem was ready to begin. The game, he realized, had just begun. And this time, he was playing to win. Graffik's trap had sprung, but he was not simply caught in it, he was now ready to dismantle it from the inside, one carefully chosen move at a time.

The chill of the dungeon stone seeped into Stanya's bones, a stark contrast to the warmth of Graffik's opulent chambers she'd so recently inhabited. Her carefully laid escape plan, meticulously crafted over weeks of observation and calculated risk, had crumbled like dry leaves under a sudden gust of wind. A misplaced footstep, a careless shadow, a flicker of movement – she couldn't pinpoint the exact moment her subterfuge had been discovered, but the result was undeniable. She was a prisoner.

The guards, hulking figures clad in black armor, dragged her through labyrinthine corridors, the rhythmic clang of their weapons echoing through the silent halls. Fear, a chilling serpent, coiled in her stomach, but it was quickly subdued by a surge of icy determination. She wouldn't break. She wouldn't give them the satisfaction. The jeweled comb, meticulously crafted to conceal the vital information she had stolen from Graffik's private archives, remained hidden beneath her loose tunic, a secret burning against her skin.

The interrogation room was a chamber of stark contrasts – cold, unyielding stone walls met with the opulent gleam of a heavy oak table, its polished surface reflecting the flickering torchlight. Seated behind it was Graffik's torturer, a gaunt man with eyes that held the chilling glint of a predator. His name, she'd learned, was Malkor, and his reputation preceded him like a storm cloud.

"So, the little sparrow thought she could fly away from the eagle's nest?" Malkor's voice was a low growl, laced with amusement. He gestured to the tools laid out on the table: a whip, its leather worn smooth from years of use; a set of pincers, gleaming ominously; and a small, silver instrument that sent a shiver down Stanya's spine.

Stanya met his gaze unflinchingly. "I am not a sparrow, and you are no eagle," she retorted, her voice calm, despite the tremor in her hands. She knew silence was her greatest weapon, but a calculated defiance could sometimes be more effective. Malkor's amusement seemed to deepen.

The torture began subtly. The flick of a whip across her bare back, the calculated pressure of a finger on a nerve point, the subtle twist of a wrist. Each act was designed to break her resolve, not to inflict unbearable pain immediately, but to chip away at her strength, her spirit. Hours blurred into a relentless cycle of pain and interrogation, Malkor's questions twisting and turning, probing for any sign of weakness, any crack in her facade.

Stanya fought back with every fiber of her being. She'd endured harsher training, faced more perilous situations, but this was different. This was not a battle in the open, where strategy and skill could dictate the outcome. This was psychological warfare, a relentless assault on her mind and body. The physical pain was intense, agonizing, but it was the mental struggle that was truly draining.

Days passed, marked by the relentless rhythm of pain and interrogation. The jeweled comb remained hidden, a secret she guarded with the fierce loyalty of a mother protecting her child. Her body screamed in protest, her muscles aching, her skin raw and bleeding, but her mind remained locked tight. She refused to yield. She refused to break. She would not betray the trust that had been placed in her.

Malkor, she realized, was as much a strategist as she was. He was a master of his craft, adept at exploiting weaknesses, both physical and psychological. He played on her fatigue, her pain, her isolation, but Stanya fought back with every ounce of her willpower. She drew strength from the weight of responsibility she carried, the knowledge that the information hidden within the comb could change the fate of nations, could ignite a rebellion against the tyranny of Emperor Baznoon Graffik.

Sleep offered little respite. Even in the moments when her body yielded to exhaustion, her mind remained alert, her thoughts racing, analyzing, strategizing. She was always on guard, always analyzing Malkor's tactics, anticipating his next move. She saw that he was growing frustrated, his patience wearing thin. He had expected a quick victory, a simple confession, but Stanya was proving to be a tougher adversary than he had anticipated.

The turning point came unexpectedly. One night, Malkor, his face etched with frustration, changed tactics. He offered her a deal – freedom in exchange for the information. He promised her a life of luxury, a life beyond her wildest dreams, if only she would hand over the comb. He played on her weariness, her physical pain, her longing for freedom.

But Stanya saw it for what it was: a trap. He couldn't know what she had, so his offer was a way to flush her out, to make her reveal her secret. She wouldn't fall for it.

"I have nothing to offer you," she whispered, her voice hoarse, but her words sharp and defiant. "You will get nothing from me."

Malkor's face contorted in a mask of rage. His offer was not a strategy; it was a sign that he was running out of time. The information she possessed was too valuable, and he couldn't afford to waste any more time. His patience had truly snapped. The relentless torture would only intensify.

But in his fury, Malkor made a mistake. He revealed that he hadn't been expecting to find her in Graffik's chambers at all. The knowledge that she was far more resourceful than he anticipated seemed to anger him more. He had underestimated her, and this fueled a fury that led to him making careless mistakes. It was a small victory, but it was a victory nonetheless, a tiny crack in the impenetrable wall of his control. She knew then that the end of her ordeal was getting nearer. She just had to hang on, just a little bit longer. The information within the comb would prove far more valuable in the right hands, than it would ever be in Malkor's clutches. And soon, she would reach the right hands. Soon, her ordeal would be over.

The silk sheets, once a symbol of Graffik's daughter's lavish affections, now felt like a suffocating shroud. Najeem tossed restlessly, the opulent furnishings of his prison mocking his captivity. He'd initially reveled in the princess's attention, a naive fool blinded by her beauty and the promise of power. He'd believed he could manipulate the situation to his advantage, using her infatuation as a stepping stone to freedom. He'd been wrong. Dead wrong.

The princess, Elara, was not merely infatuated; she was possessive, her affection a cage. He'd learned that much in the short time he'd been her prisoner, a prisoner of her whims and Graffik's machinations. Every day brought new restrictions, new demonstrations of her volatile temper, new reminders of his powerlessness. He was a prized possession, a trophy to be admired, but never truly trusted. The guards, ever vigilant, were more than mere bodyguards; they were extensions of her will, her eyes and ears within his golden cage.

The escape, he knew, had to be swift and silent. Any hint of his plan would reach Graffik's ears, and the consequences would be swift and brutal. He wasn't just dealing with a spoiled princess; he was facing the full might of Graffik's vast and ruthless empire. He had to rely on his training, on the instincts honed over years of covert operations, on the skills that had once made him a formidable warrior.

His gaze fell upon an intricately carved wooden panel, seemingly an innocuous part of the wall, seamlessly integrated into the ornate décor. He'd noticed it before, dismissed it as mere decoration. But tonight, something about its subtle incongruity – a slight misalignment, a barely perceptible imperfection – caught his attention. A flicker of hope ignited within him, a spark in the suffocating darkness.

He approached the panel cautiously, his fingers tracing its surface. The wood felt different under his touch, slightly cooler, almost yielding. A faint pressure, a delicate push, and the panel swung inward, revealing a narrow, dimly lit passage. A wave of relief washed over him, so intense it almost brought him to his knees. This was it, his chance. His ticket to freedom.

The passage was claustrophobic, the air thick with the scent of damp earth and mildew. He moved silently, his bare feet padding against the rough stone floor. The darkness was absolute, but his senses, honed to razor sharpness by years of training, guided him. He felt the cool dampness of the stone, the texture of the mortar, the subtle shift in the air currents. Each step was calculated, each breath controlled.

As he moved deeper into the passage, he heard the faint sound of voices echoing from the distant end. He pressed himself against the wall, his heart pounding in his chest. He could not afford to be seen, not yet. He strained to understand the words, discerning fragments of conversations, snippets of information that painted a picture of the palace's inner workings, of the simmering tensions within Graffik's court. He learned of hidden alliances, whispered betrayals, and plots that reached into the very heart of the empire. The information, though overheard in whispers, fueled his determination. He needed to get out, not just for himself, but for the sake of the fragile peace that held the kingdom together.

The passage opened into a small, unlit chamber, seemingly abandoned. The air hung heavy with the scent of decay, the space filled with dust motes dancing in the sliver of moonlight filtering through a crack in the stone ceiling. He took a moment to catch his breath, to gather his thoughts.

This was not the end of his journey, but merely a new beginning. A new stage of his escape.

He pressed on, navigating a labyrinth of corridors and hidden passages, his heart a frantic drum against his ribs. He moved with the grace and agility of a phantom, his every movement fluid and precise. His senses were heightened, picking up the slightest creaks of the stone under his feet, the faintest rustle of unseen creatures in the shadows. The palace, designed to be an impenetrable fortress, was now a puzzle he was solving one step at a time.

He finally reached a less ornate section of the palace, much further away from the princess's luxurious quarters. The air was cooler and less suffocating here. He found a small unguarded window overlooking the palace gardens. It was a risk, a leap into the unknown, but it was his only option. He climbed out, dropping silently to the ground.

The palace gardens were vast, a sprawling maze of meticulously manicured hedges and flowering shrubs. He moved through the shadows, his movements as silent as the fall of snowflakes. He could feel the weight of Graffik's gaze on him even as he moved further and further away. His escape would not be complete until he was well beyond Graffik's reach, far away from the palace walls and the watchful eyes of the guards. He needed to reach the outerlands, the only place offering hope of freedom.

He knew the risks. Graffik wouldn't let him go unpunished. There would be assassins, soldiers, relentless pursuit. But the thought of Elara, of her capricious nature and Graffik's cold ambition, fueled his resolve. He had to escape. He had to be free. He had to leave behind the gilded cage and the suffocating embrace of the court.

He pushed through the dense foliage, his heart pounding with a mixture of fear and exhilaration. The moon cast long shadows, twisting the familiar shapes of the gardens into monstrous figures. He ran, his lungs burning, his muscles aching, but his spirit unyielding. He ran for freedom, for his life, for a future where he could choose his own destiny. He would not be a pawn in Graffik's game any longer.

As he neared the outer walls of the palace, he heard the sound of approaching footsteps, the rhythmic thud of boots on the stone path. He pressed himself against the wall, hiding behind a thick stand of jasmine bushes, his breath held captive in his chest. The guards were close, their voices hushed but unmistakable. He held his breath, his heart thundering, waiting for them to pass.

They were speaking of him, their words laced with frustration and anger. He heard the Princess's name mentioned, coupled with terms that suggested his escape was a significant embarrassment, a failure on their part. The implication hung heavy in the air; they knew he was gone. The hunt was on. Graffik would not tolerate this blatant defiance.

The guards passed by, their lanterns casting flickering shadows on the walls. Najeem waited until their footsteps faded into the distance before resuming his escape. He reached the outer wall, scaling it with the agility only a seasoned warrior possesses. He dropped to the ground on the other side, rolling to absorb the impact. He was free, at least for now.

But freedom was only a fragile illusion. He knew Graffik's reach extended far beyond the palace walls. The escape was only the first step in a long and perilous journey. He still had to reach the outerlands, a region known for its rebellious spirit and its defiance of Graffik's authority. There, he hoped, he might find sanctuary, a place to lick his wounds and plan his next move.

He knew his escape would not go unnoticed. He would be hunted. He would be pursued. But he was prepared for that. Years of training, honed in the unforgiving crucible of war, had prepared him for this. He was a warrior, a survivor, and he would not be broken. He would fight his way to freedom, step by step, until he reached the outerlands and found the refuge he so desperately needed. His freedom was not yet assured, but for the first time since his capture, he allowed himself a glimmer of hope. The glimmer of hope that he might one day see the dawn of freedom. And for the first time since his capture, he felt a wave of exhilaration wash over him. The air felt sweet and clean, far removed from the suffocating opulence of the palace. His escape was far from complete, but this was the first true step toward freedom, and it filled him with renewed strength. He walked towards his destiny, a warrior walking towards his new beginning.

The moon, a sliver of silver in the inky sky, cast long shadows as Najeem slipped through the labyrinthine corridors of the palace. He moved like a wraith, his bare feet silent on the polished stone, his senses honed to a razor's edge. The scent of jasmine and fear hung heavy in the air, a constant reminder of his precarious situation. He'd chosen a route less traveled, a gamble based on his intuition and a desperate hope to avoid Graffik's heavily guarded patrols. He clutched the small, worn dagger hidden beneath his tunic, a familiar weight offering a sliver of comfort in this treacherous landscape.

Suddenly, a glint of steel caught his eye. A figure, cloaked and shrouded in shadow, emerged from a darkened alcove, their movements as fluid and silent as his own. Before Najeem could react, the figure lunged, a gleaming sword flashing in the moonlight. The attack was swift, precise, and deadly.

Najeem reacted instinctively, rolling to avoid the blow. He drew his dagger, its small blade a stark contrast to the larger weapon wielded by his assailant. The clash of steel on steel echoed through the silent corridor, a metallic shriek that seemed to pierce the very fabric of the night. His opponent was skilled, incredibly so, their movements a dance of death, each strike calculated and deadly. Najeem, however, was no novice. Years spent honing his combat skills in the brutal arenas of his youth now served him well. He parried, dodged, and riposted, his dagger a blur of motion, seeking an opening, a weakness in his opponent's formidable defense.

Their fight was a whirlwind of flashing steel and desperate maneuvers. The air crackled with tension, the rhythmic clang of their weapons the only sound in the oppressive silence. Najeem found himself impressed by his opponent's skill, a worthy adversary even amidst the desperate circumstances. They were evenly matched, each blow met with an equally forceful parry. Sweat beaded on his brow, his muscles burning with exertion, yet he fought on, fueled by the adrenaline coursing through his veins and the burning desire for freedom.

As they fought, a glint of familiarity sparked in Najeem's mind. The way his opponent moved, the almost balletic grace of their attack—it was strangely reminiscent of…Stanya. The information gatherer he'd briefly encountered in Graffik's court, a woman whose sharp wit and even sharper eyes had both intrigued and unnerved him. Could this be her? He hesitated, a fraction of a second too long. His opponent capitalized on the distraction, disarming him with a swift, brutal move. Najeem found himself on the ground, the cold stone a harsh reminder of his vulnerability.

His opponent stood above him, the sword poised to strike the final blow. He closed his eyes, bracing for the inevitable. But the blow never came. Instead, he heard the sound of approaching footsteps, heavy and numerous. Imperial guards, alerted by the commotion, were rapidly approaching.

His opponent, swiftly reacting, sheathed their sword and helped him to his feet. "We need to cooperate," she hissed, her voice low and urgent. The moonlight glinted off her features, revealing a face both familiar and unexpected. It was indeed Stanya.

"You?" Najeem breathed, still surprised by the turn of events.

"And you," she retorted, her eyes narrowed. "I thought Graffik's hounds were faster."

The approaching guards were now within earshot, their heavy boots echoing in the corridor. They had no time to argue. The situation called for an uneasy alliance. Najeem and Stanya, sworn enemies only moments before, found themselves forced together against a shared enemy.

They moved as one, utilizing their complementary skills to evade capture. Stanya's knowledge of the palace's intricate layout was essential, leading them through secret passages and hidden chambers. Najeem, with his superior strength and combat prowess, provided the muscle, holding off pursuing guards with calculated strikes. He found himself relying on Stanya's quick thinking, her ability to anticipate their pursuers' movements and find unexpected escape routes.

They fought their way through a maze of corridors, their escape a desperate race against time. They faced wave after wave of imperial guards, each encounter a deadly dance of evasion and attack. Najeem's swordsmanship was brutal and efficient, Stanya's more precise, her every move calculated to disarm and incapacitate, leaving her opponents vulnerable for him to finish off. Their teamwork was seamless, almost intuitive. A bond was forging between them, not of friendship, not yet, but of shared desperation and mutual respect.

One particularly harrowing encounter saw them cornered in a vast, echoing hall, surrounded by at least a dozen guards. Stanya, with remarkable agility, sprang onto a high ledge, drawing their attention. Using her wits, she triggered a loose stone in the ceiling, sending a cascade of debris tumbling down upon their pursuers, creating enough confusion and chaos for Najeem to cover their retreat.

Their escape was a symphony of stealth and violence, a desperate battle for survival against overwhelming odds. They dodged, they weaved, they fought, their bodies moving in perfect synchronicity. The adrenaline coursed through their veins, each heartbeat a drumbeat in their race for freedom. They were a team, an unlikely pair forged in the crucible of danger, their combined strength far greater than the sum of their individual parts. As they fought, a grudging admiration bloomed between them, a seed planted in the heart of their perilous flight.

As dawn approached, painting the eastern sky in hues of orange and rose, they finally reached the outer walls of the palace. The escape was not yet complete. They faced a final, desperate hurdle - the heavily guarded gates. They were outnumbered, exhausted, and their bodies ached from their arduous flight. But they were not broken. They had each other, and that, they both realized, was enough.

Their final battle was a chaotic melee. Najeem's blade sang a deadly song, a whirlwind of destructive power. Stanya, using her knowledge of pressure points and disarming techniques, worked to incapacitate, leaving

Najeem to finish the opponents. They fought with a fierce determination fueled by the impending taste of freedom. Finally, with a combined, synchronized thrust, they felled the last guard, their blades clashing in a final, victorious clang.

They slipped through the gates just as the sun broke the horizon, casting a golden light on their faces, on the shared exhaustion, the mutual respect, and the flicker of something more, something that hinted at the unexpected beginning of a journey that was yet to unfold. They had escaped Graffik's trap, but the true test was only just beginning. Their flight from the palace was merely the first act in a much larger, more complex play, a play filled with intrigue, danger, and the unpredictable twists and turns of fate. The outerlands awaited, a land of rebellion and uncertainty, where their journey would truly begin. The road to freedom was long and fraught with peril, but they had escaped, together. And in that shared escape, a spark ignited, a hope for something more.

Chapter 2: Shared Plight

The clash of steel echoed in the cavernous hallway, abruptly silenced as both combatants stumbled back, gasping for breath. Stanya, her dark hair escaping its braid, clutched her jeweled comb – a seemingly innocuous piece of finery that held Graffik's most closely guarded secrets. Across from her, Najeem, his normally impeccable attire now torn and stained, leaned heavily on his sword, his breath ragged. For a moment, a tense silence reigned, broken only by the heavy thump of their hearts.

Then, simultaneously, realization dawned. The fierce intensity in their eyes softened, replaced by a dawning understanding. They weren't enemies; they were both victims of the same merciless tyrant. The Imperial guards, momentarily stunned by the ferocity of their encounter, had vanished, leaving them alone in the oppressive shadows of the palace corridors.

Stanya, ever practical, was the first to speak, her voice low and cautious. "We were both… escaping," she stated, more than a question. Her gaze, sharp and observant, scanned Najeem's face, searching for any hint of deception.

Najeem nodded, a slow, deliberate movement. "Graffik's clutches. Though for different reasons, the end result is the same." He sheathed his sword, the action deliberate and controlled. The elegant weapon, usually a symbol of his status, now felt like a heavy burden.

Thus began the uneasy alliance between the skilled information gatherer and the warrior unjustly imprisoned. Stanya, her usual composure slightly fractured, recounted her infiltration of Graffik's court, the treacherous politics, the constant threat of discovery. She painted a vivid picture of Baznoon Graffik, a man whose smile hid a heart of iron and whose ambition knew no bounds. She described the intricate web of spies and informants that Graffik controlled, the subtle manipulation that permeated every aspect of court life. She spoke of the impending war, a campaign of conquest fueled by Graffik's insatiable greed for power, a war that threatened to engulf the entire land. Her escape had been carefully planned, a intricate dance of deception and daring, but her capture had been as swift and brutal as Graffik's wrath itself. The jeweled comb, its secret cargo so close to being delivered, still weighed heavily in her hand.

Najeem, in turn, revealed his own story – a story of unexpected captivity and gilded confinement. His tale spoke of Graffik's daughter, a woman beautiful and alluring, but also cruel and manipulative. He described his initial shock at being captured, not by force, but by the captivating, yet treacherous, charm of Princess Amara. He had been a warrior, renowned for his skill and honor, used to commanding respect, and instead, he found himself a prized possession – a prisoner of his own attraction, surrounded by luxury but with his freedom cruelly snatched away. His escape had been a gamble, a desperate dash for freedom guided by an uneasy sense of foreboding and a growing apprehension about Amara's true intentions. He had found a hidden passage, a secret way out, only to be thrown into this unexpected encounter.

As they spoke, a shared understanding grew between them. They were both pawns in Graffik's game, victims of his boundless ambition. Yet, in their shared experience, a resilience was born, a determination to escape the shadow of his tyranny. The palace walls, previously formidable barriers, now seemed less insurmountable. Their initial animosity had faded, replaced by a grudging respect, then a growing sense of mutual reliance.

Their escape from the labyrinthine palace was a thrilling blend of Stanya's knowledge of secret passages and hidden routes, and Najeem's combat prowess. They moved like shadows through dimly lit corridors, dodging patrolling guards and avoiding elaborate traps. Stanya's memory was phenomenal, recalling details from her infiltration that proved crucial to their escape. More than once, they found themselves in desperate situations, their lives hanging precariously in the balance, but they worked together, their skills complementing each other perfectly. Najeem's strength and agility combined with Stanya's quick wit and cunning provided a formidable defense against the Imperial guard. Their combined skill, born of necessity, proved an effective weapon against Graffik's watchful eyes.

As they navigated the maze of the palace, they faced their own inner demons. Stanya, haunted by the possibility of betrayal, struggled with her trust in Najeem. She had been betrayed before, her loyalty exploited, her secrets exposed. The fear of experiencing that betrayal again threatened to undermine their alliance. Najeem, too, wrestled with his own internal conflict. He had been used to operating alone, his trust in others often misplaced. The thought of relying on someone, of placing his fate in another's hands, was alien and unsettling. Yet the shared danger, the undeniable camaraderie that grew between them in the face of adversity, helped break down the barriers of distrust.

The pursuit began in earnest as they finally left the palace. Graffik's forces, relentless and numerous, were unleashed upon them. Waves of assassins, swift and deadly, appeared from the shadows, their blades gleaming in the flickering torchlight. Soldiers, heavily armed and trained for combat, followed close behind, cutting off their escape routes. Their combined skills were tested to the limits, their escape becoming a desperate, heart-pounding race against time. They used the chaotic city streets and hidden alleys to their advantage, utilizing their combined experience and quick thinking to evade their pursuers. Stanya's knowledge of the city's underbelly, its hidden passages and secret routes, proved invaluable. Najeem's combat skills became their shield, deflecting blows and drawing the attention of the pursuers, giving Stanya time to maneuver them toward safety.

Their escape was punctuated by moments of intense action, near misses, and close calls. The sounds of clashing swords, the screams of their pursuers, and the pounding of their own hearts were a constant backdrop to their desperate flight. They faced betrayal not only from Graffik's forces, but also from unexpected sources—civilians willing to turn them in for a bounty, and other desperate individuals attempting to take advantage of their situation. Each near miss, each successful evasion of capture, solidified their alliance. It was a bond forged in the crucible of adversity, strengthened by the shared trauma and the ever-present threat of death.

Finally, after what seemed like an eternity, they reached the outskirts of the city. The imposing city walls, once a symbol of oppression, now represented a hard-won victory. Exhausted but alive, they paused, catching their breath beneath the cover of a thick, dark forest. Their immediate danger was past, but their journey was far from over. Ahead lay the Outerlands, a vast and unforgiving territory, a land of rebels and outcasts, where Graffik's authority barely reached. The escape from the palace, and the ensuing chase, had cemented their alliance. They stood together, their backs against a giant oak, their breath mingling in the cool night air, two unlikely allies bound together by a shared plight and a common enemy. Graffik might have control over the city, but he did not control the hearts of those who dared to defy him, and Stanya and Najeem were among them. Their alliance was fragile, built upon mutual survival, but it was real, and it would become their greatest weapon in the fight to come.

The moon, a sliver of silver in the inky sky, cast long, dancing shadows as Stanya and Najeem slipped through a rarely used servants' passage. The air hung heavy with the scent of dust and mildew, a stark contrast to the opulent perfumes that permeated the main corridors of the palace. Stanya, her fingers tracing the rough-hewn stone, led the way, her movements fluid and silent, a ghost in the shadows. She knew this palace like the back of her hand, its hidden pathways and secret chambers a familiar labyrinth. Najeem, ever vigilant, trailed close behind, his senses heightened, his hand never far from the hilt of his sword. The rhythmic thump-thump-thump of pursuing footsteps echoed from somewhere down the main hallway, a relentless reminder of their precarious situation.

"Faster," Najeem hissed, his voice barely a whisper. He nudged Stanya slightly, indicating a narrow opening hidden behind a tapestry depicting a romanticized battle scene, the colors muted with age. They squeezed through, the fabric brushing against their skin, and found themselves in a small, airless chamber. It was a storage room, crammed with forgotten relics and dusty furniture, the air thick with the smell of decay. They could hear the guards' voices growing closer, their heavy boots thudding against the stone floor.

"This way," Stanya murmured, pointing to a loose stone in the wall. It was cleverly concealed, almost invisible against the surrounding masonry. With a practiced hand, she dislodged the stone, revealing a narrow tunnel. The air within was damp and cold, the smell of earth and something else…something akin to decay and ancient magic, filling their nostrils.

"What is this place?" Najeem asked, his voice laced with a hint of unease. He wasn't afraid, not exactly, but the oppressive atmosphere sent a chill down his spine.

"An old escape route," Stanya replied, her voice barely audible. "Used rarely, and only by those who know its secrets. I stumbled upon it during one of my…research expeditions." She didn't elaborate, and Najeem didn't press her. Some things were better left unsaid.

The tunnel was claustrophobic, forcing them to crawl on their hands and knees. The passage was barely wide enough for one person, and the darkness was complete, broken only by the faint gleam of Stanya's jeweled comb, which she held aloft like a tiny beacon. The air was thick with the scent of mildew and something else…something faintly sweet, yet strangely unsettling.

Suddenly, a shower of dust and debris rained down from above, blocking their way. Najeem reacted instantly, his sword flashing in the dim light, he slashed at the obstruction, clearing a path. More debris fell, then a thud, followed by a sharp crack. A section of the tunnel ceiling had collapsed.

"A trap," Stanya hissed, her voice strained. "They must have been expecting us to use this route."

They pressed onward, the collapse causing a shift in the ground; they felt the tremor under their knees. They were forced to navigate a narrow passage filled with sharp rocks and loose earth; a seemingly endless stretch of darkness. The air grew thinner, making each breath a struggle. The relentless pursuit was a gnawing presence behind them, a constant reminder of their precarious situation.

After what felt like an eternity, the tunnel opened into a larger chamber, surprisingly spacious. A shaft of moonlight filtered through a crack in the ceiling, illuminating the chamber's contents: a pile of ancient tapestries, forgotten chests, and several corroded weapons. Among the debris,

Stanya spotted something else: a rusty ladder leading upwards.

"This must be it," she whispered, her voice filled with relief. "An exit to the outer wards."

Najeem nodded, his eyes scanning the chamber. He could hear the sounds of their pursuers getting closer, the echoes resonating in the vast space. He drew his sword, its polished surface reflecting the scant moonlight.

Climbing the ladder was arduous. The rungs were slick with moisture, and the ladder itself seemed on the verge of collapse. Stanya, agile and sure-footed, ascended with ease, while Najeem, despite his considerable strength, struggled with the treacherous climb. With a grunt, he reached the top, his body aching and his muscles burning. They found themselves in a small, unassuming room near the palace's outer walls. A hidden exit, camouflaged by a heavy curtain, awaited them.

They slipped through the curtain, emerging into the relative quiet of the palace gardens. But their escape was far from over. Guards patrolled the gardens, their silhouettes long and ominous in the moonlight. They moved swiftly and silently, their steps almost noiseless as they navigated the maze-like pathways.

Najeem, his sword a blur of motion, effortlessly dispatched two guards who foolishly blocked their path. Stanya, meanwhile, used her knowledge of the gardens to lead them through hidden passages and around patrolling sentries, her movements graceful and precise. They were a well-oiled machine, their actions perfectly synchronized, their skills complementing each other. Their bond, forged in the crucible of their shared ordeal, had grown stronger with each close call, each near miss.

They reached the outer wall, a high, imposing structure, seemingly impenetrable. But Stanya knew a way, a secret passage concealed behind a dense thicket of overgrown vines. With a deft hand, she cleared away the vines, revealing a narrow opening that led to a rope ladder that descended into the darkness outside.

The drop was perilous, but Najeem, with his exceptional agility and strength, lowered Stanya down first. He then followed, his movements precise and controlled. They landed silently on the soft earth, their hearts pounding in their chests. They were free. Free from the suffocating confines of the palace, free from Graffik's clutches. They were free.

They paused for a moment, catching their breath beneath the cover of the thick, dark forest that lay before them. The city walls loomed in the distance, a stark reminder of the tyranny they had escaped. But before them lay the Outerlands, a land of hope, rebellion, and the promise of a new dawn. Their escape from the palace was only the first step in their long and arduous journey, a journey filled with both danger and adventure, but one they would face together, united by their shared escape and the growing bond between a warrior and a spy, two unlikely allies who had found each other in the heart of darkness. Graffik may have lost two prisoners, but he had gained two enemies— enemies far more dangerous than he ever could have imagined. Their forged alliance, born from necessity, was now a weapon against the tyranny that had so nearly swallowed them whole. The escape was complete, but their fight for freedom was just beginning. The journey to the Outerlands, and beyond, was far from over.

The city gates loomed ahead, a seemingly insurmountable barrier between them and freedom. But even as they approached, the familiar, chilling sound of pursuing footsteps echoed behind them, growing louder with each second. Graffik's relentless pursuit had begun. They weren't merely escaping the palace; they were fleeing a well-oiled machine designed to recapture them, a machine fueled by Baznoon Graffik's pride and his burning desire for revenge.

Stanya, her breath catching in her throat, glanced back. Through the gaps in the dense, twisting alleyways, she caught glimpses of their pursuers – shadowy figures clad in dark, imperial uniforms, their movements swift and deadly. These were not just ordinary soldiers; these were elite assassins, Graffik's personal guard, trained to kill with brutal efficiency.

"They're faster than I anticipated," Najeem muttered, his hand instinctively moving to the worn leather sheath at his hip, where his sword rested. The blade, once a symbol of his own enslaved status, now represented their only hope of survival.

Stanya didn't need to reply; the urgency of the situation was clear. She had expected pursuit, of course, but the sheer speed and determination of these men was unnerving. They were relentless, hounds on their scent, their resolve unwavering. Their escape, it seemed, was far from over.

They plunged deeper into the maze-like streets of the city, weaving through throngs of people, their movements almost imperceptible against the backdrop of the bustling marketplace. The cacophony of sounds – the hawkers' cries, the braying of donkeys, the rumble of carts – provided a surprisingly effective camouflage. Stanya, using her intimate knowledge of the city's hidden passages and secret routes, led them through a labyrinth of narrow alleyways, each turn a gamble, each shadow a potential hiding place.

Najeem, his warrior instincts honed to a razor's edge, acted as their shield. He positioned himself between Stanya and the approaching assassins, using his broad shoulders and exceptional agility to deflect blows and create openings. His sword, a blur of honed steel, flashed out occasionally, deflecting attacks with deadly precision. Each strike was a calculated risk, a dance between life and death, performed in the heart of the chaotic city.

They scrambled over overflowing garbage bins, ducked beneath hanging laundry, and slipped through the narrow gaps between tightly packed buildings. The pursuit was a breathless game of cat and mouse, their pursuers constantly gaining ground only to lose it again as Stanya's cunning and Najeem's strength pushed them back. Sweat beaded on their foreheads, mixing with grime and dust, yet neither faltered.

At one point, they found themselves cornered in a dead end, a high wall barring their escape. The relentless thud-thud-thud of boots on cobblestones echoed closer. Their pursuers were gaining. Despair threatened to engulf them. But Stanya, her mind racing, spotted a small, almost invisible opening in the wall – a crumbling section hidden behind a pile of discarded rubbish.

"This way!" she hissed, pushing past Najeem and squeezing through the gap. He followed, his body a coiled spring of readiness. The opening was barely large enough for a single person, forcing them to move sideways, scraping their bodies against the rough stones. They emerged into a surprisingly large, forgotten courtyard, overgrown with weeds and shrouded in shadows. The air hung heavy with the scent of damp earth and decaying leaves, a far cry from the bustling streets above.

From the courtyard, a network of crumbling tunnels led onwards, their destination uncertain. But it was a refuge, a temporary reprieve from their pursuers, who were momentarily thwarted by the unexpected obstacle.

They did not stay long. The silence in the courtyard was punctuated only by the occasional drip of water and their ragged breathing. They knew their pursuers would soon discover the hidden passage, so they continued their escape, deeper into the city's underbelly.

The tunnels were damp and claustrophobic, the air thick with the smell of mildew and decay. Najeem's muscles ached, his body weary from the relentless exertion, but the adrenalin coursing through his veins kept him moving. Stanya, despite her exhaustion, continued to navigate the treacherous passageways with uncanny skill, her knowledge of the city's secrets proving invaluable.

Twice more, they were forced into desperate skirmishes, using the shadows and limited space of the tunnels to their advantage. Najeem fought with a raw, brutal strength, his sword a lethal extension of his rage, while Stanya used her quick wit and agility to create diversions, drawing the assassins into traps and slowing their advance. They fought as one, their individual skills complementing each other in a deadly dance of survival.

As they finally emerged from the labyrinthine tunnels, they found themselves on the outskirts of the city, the dark, imposing shapes of the outerlands looming before them. They were far from safe, but they had evaded Graffik's immediate pursuit. The escape had been harrowing, a brutal test of their strength, resilience, and their nascent trust in one another. They were exhausted, injured, but alive.

The moonlight painted silver streaks across the fields, illuminating their path towards a new beginning. But the shadows stretched long and dark behind them, a chilling reminder that Graffik's wrath would not be easily outrun. Their journey had just begun. The forged alliance, forged in the fires of escape, would now be tested in the harsh reality of their continued flight. They were running, yes, but they were also planning. The escape from the palace was a victory, but merely the first step in a much larger war against the tyranny that ruled their land. Graffik had underestimated them, and he would soon learn the devastating consequences of that error. Their fight was far from over. The pursuit might have been temporarily thwarted, but the battle for freedom had only just commenced.

The wind whipped Stanya's cloak around her, a stark contrast to the suffocating opulence of the palace they'd left behind. She glanced at Najeem, his face grim and set, his eyes constantly scanning the horizon. The initial mistrust, born from their first encounter, had begun to thaw, replaced by a fragile understanding forged in the crucible of shared danger. They moved with a practiced silence, each step calculated, each breath measured. Their escape had been daring, bordering on reckless, but they'd managed to slip through Graffik's grasp, at least for now.

Yet, the sense of unease gnawed at Stanya. The weight of her betrayal still pressed down on her – the betrayal of her own people, the silent pact she'd made with Graffik's enemies, a pact sealed with stolen secrets and the risk of a swift, merciless death. The information she'd delivered to the Outerlands' rebels was crucial, a detailed account of Graffik's military strategies and hidden weaknesses, but the price of that delivery had been steep. The price of freedom was trust, and trust was a commodity she had learned to hoard, to treat as fragile glass.

Najeem, too, carried his own burdens. The stolen glances, the subtle flinches whenever they spoke of Graffik's daughter, spoke volumes. His enslavement, his forced servitude to the whims of a cruel and capricious princess, had left scars deeper than any physical wound. Stanya sensed the simmering resentment, the unspoken rage that threatened to erupt at any moment. His silence was a fortress, his guarded gaze a testament to a history marred by betrayal, a history he wasn't ready to share.

They rested briefly beneath the shadow of a colossal oak tree, its branches gnarled and ancient, a silent witness to centuries of untold stories. The silence between them wasn't awkward, not anymore. It was a shared understanding, a quiet acknowledgement of their respective pasts, of the ghosts that still haunted them. Stanya broke the silence first, her voice barely a whisper against the rustling leaves.

"Do you… do you believe in second chances?" she asked, her words tinged with uncertainty.

Najeem looked at her, his gaze intense, unwavering. "I don't believe in much anymore," he replied, his voice rough, like sandpaper against stone. "But I know what it feels like to be betrayed. To be used. To have your loyalty thrown back in your face like a poisoned apple."

His words struck a chord within her. She knew the bitter taste of betrayal intimately. Years spent navigating the treacherous currents of political intrigue had left her cynical, cautious, and deeply distrustful. She'd been used and discarded, her loyalties tested and broken by those she'd considered allies. Yet, here she was, trusting this man, this warrior whose loyalty she still questioned, despite the shared danger binding them together.

"I understand," Stanya admitted, her voice soft. "And I know it's foolish, perhaps even reckless, to trust again. But… we need each other." She met his gaze, daring to be vulnerable, daring to show the cracks in her carefully constructed defenses.

Najeem's expression softened, a flicker of something akin to understanding crossing his face. He nodded slowly. "We do," he agreed, his voice a low murmur. "And even if this trust is broken, the fight continues."

The weight of their shared secret hung heavy between them – the secret of their escape, the knowledge of Graffik's vulnerabilities, the unspoken understanding of their shared enemy. This secret was a bond, a fragile thread connecting them in a world of deceit and treachery. It was a burden they carried together, a burden that would test their newly forged alliance in ways they couldn't yet imagine.

As the sun began to dip below the horizon, painting the sky in hues of fiery orange and deep purple, they continued their journey, the image of Graffik's relentless pursuit casting long shadows in their minds. They knew Graffik would stop at nothing to recapture them, to silence them forever. He would send his spies, his assassins, his entire army if necessary. Their lives hung precariously in the balance, balanced on the edge of a knife.

Their flight took them through dense forests, across rushing rivers, and over treacherous mountain passes. The landscape mirrored the tempestuous nature of their alliance – beautiful, yet dangerous, constantly shifting, always unpredictable. They relied on each other, their strengths complementing each other's weaknesses. Stanya's sharp intellect and cunning strategies were counterbalanced by Najeem's unmatched fighting prowess and unwavering determination.

One night, while huddled around a small fire, sharing meager rations, Stanya confessed a part of her past she'd kept hidden. She spoke of the betrayal she'd suffered at the hands of her former mentor, a man she'd once trusted implicitly, a man who had used her skills to further his own ambitions, leaving her to face the consequences. The raw emotion in her voice, the vulnerability in her eyes, shocked Najeem. He saw the pain etched into her face, the deep wounds that years of betrayal had inflicted.

In turn, Najeem shared a glimpse into his own past, speaking of the brutality of his enslavement, the constant fear of violence and death, the crushing weight of his helplessness. He spoke of the princess, of her cruelty and her unexpected kindness, a cruel juxtaposition that mirrored the chaotic nature of his life. He confessed the lingering affection, the confusing emotions that still haunted him, the worry that shadowed his plans for revenge. The princess' actions were a stark betrayal of his expectations, confusing his already fractured trust in others.

The sharing of their vulnerabilities, the unveiling of their deepest fears and insecurities, strengthened their bond. It was a testament to the trust they were slowly building, a trust born not out of blind faith, but out of shared experience, a mutual understanding of pain and loss. They were both survivors, both fighters, both bound together by a shared need for freedom.

But their journey wasn't without its challenges. They faced numerous encounters with Graffik's forces, skirmishes that tested their skills and their resilience. They evaded patrols, outmaneuvered ambushes, and fought their way through hordes of soldiers, their movements becoming a deadly ballet of precision and power. Each successful escape only served to fuel Graffik's rage, making his pursuit even more relentless, even more desperate.

During one particularly harrowing encounter, they were cornered by a group of Graffik's elite guards, their swords flashing in the moonlight. Stanya, using her knowledge of the terrain, set a trap, leading the guards into a narrow ravine. Najeem, with his exceptional combat skills, fought with a fury born of desperation, protecting Stanya while she worked her way to a position of advantage. They fought side-by-side, their movements perfectly synchronized, their trust in each other evident in every strike, every parry, every desperate maneuver.

They escaped, bruised and battered, but alive. That night, under the watchful gaze of the stars, they sat together, the silence filled with unspoken gratitude. The near-death experience had served to solidify their bond, to cement the trust they were so carefully cultivating. They realized that the trust they were building wasn't just about the safety of their escape, but also about the emotional connection that had sparked amidst the turmoil of their shared plight. They had seen each other's vulnerability, their strength, their capacity for both kindness and ruthlessness, and somehow, in the midst of chaos, they found solace in each other's company. The potential for betrayal still lingered, a shadow hanging over their fragile alliance, but the strength of their shared experiences, their shared struggle, outweighed the risks of putting their trust in one another. The road ahead remained uncertain, dangerous, and filled with challenges, but they would face it together, a testament to a trust born from the ashes of betrayal.

The city walls loomed before them, a jagged, imposing silhouette against the bruised purple of the twilight sky. They'd made it. For now, at least, they were safe from Graffik's immediate pursuit. The relentless chase, a blur of adrenaline and near misses, had left them breathless, their bodies screaming in protest, but the elation of survival pulsed through them stronger than the pain. Stanya, ever the pragmatist, was already assessing their situation. The city walls, though offering a temporary reprieve, were not a guarantee of safety. Beyond them lay the untamed wilderness, a landscape as treacherous as any battlefield.

Najeem, his usually stoic features etched with exhaustion, leaned against a crumbling section of the outer wall, his breath coming in ragged gasps. He ran a hand through his sweat-soaked hair, the grime of their escape caking his skin. The escape from the imperial palace had been a desperate gamble, a whirlwind of close calls and narrow escapes. They had used a combination of Stanya's knowledge of the palace's hidden passages and Najeem's exceptional fighting skills to evade Graffik's guards. Each corridor had been a gauntlet, each room a potential death trap. The memory of the cold steel of a blade grazing his arm, the chilling fear of being caught, still lingered, a phantom pain that clung to him.

Stanya, observing his weariness, offered him a waterskin. He took it gratefully, his hand brushing against hers. The fleeting touch sent a shiver down her spine, a silent acknowledgment of the unspoken bond that had formed between them. It was a fragile connection, built on shared trauma and mutual survival, but it was real. And in the face of the dangers that lay ahead, it was perhaps their most valuable asset.

"We need to move," Stanya said, her voice low and urgent. "Staying here is as dangerous as being inside the city walls. Graffik's men will search the outskirts, trying to cut off any escape routes."

Najeem nodded, swallowing the water. "Where do we go?"

"The Outerlands," Stanya replied without hesitation. "It's our only chance. The people there despise Graffik. They'll offer us sanctuary, at least for a time. But getting there..." She trailed off, her gaze sweeping across the desolate landscape beyond the walls. The Outerlands were a vast and unforgiving expanse of rugged terrain, riddled with treacherous canyons, dense forests, and unpredictable weather patterns. It was a land where survival was a constant battle against the elements and the inhabitants, a land of outlaws and rebels.

The journey began under the cloak of darkness, their progress slow and arduous. They skirted the edges of the city, avoiding Graffik's patrols. The night was alive with the sounds of unseen creatures, the rustling of leaves, the hooting of owls, a constant reminder of the wildness that surrounded them. The city's lights faded behind them, replaced by the stark, starlit expanse of the open sky.

Their first major challenge came in the form of a treacherous ravine, its jagged edges threatening to swallow them whole. Najeem, with his superior strength and agility, managed to find a precarious pathway, his every move measured and precise. Stanya, following close behind, clung to the rocks, her fingers scraping against the rough stone, her heart pounding in her chest. The descent was a heart-stopping ordeal, a constant struggle against gravity and the fear of a fatal fall. The journey was both a physical and emotional test.

They emerged from the ravine hours later, exhausted but unbroken. They were moving slower now, each muscle aching, each step a battle against fatigue. The landscape had changed; they were now surrounded by a dense forest, its oppressive shadows swallowing the little remaining light. The forest floor was thick with undergrowth, their feet sinking into the mud with every step. The air hung heavy with dampness, the smell of decaying leaves and moist earth filling their nostrils.

As darkness deepened, they were forced to seek shelter. They found a small cave, its entrance partially obscured by overgrown vines. Inside, the air was musty and damp, but it offered a measure of protection from the elements. They huddled together, sharing their remaining rations and a silent acknowledgment of their mutual exhaustion. The fire they managed to build provided a much-needed warmth and a sense of security.

The next day, they faced another obstacle – a swift-flowing river. There was no bridge in sight, only a raging torrent that seemed impassable. Najeem, despite his weariness, was undeterred. He found a way to traverse the river, using a combination of his strength and his knowledge of natural formations. It was a risky maneuver, a dangerous dance with the current, but he managed to make it across, then pulled Stanya across using a makeshift rope from their remaining clothing.

As they continued their journey, they encountered other dangers – packs of wild dogs, venomous snakes lurking in the undergrowth, and the ever-present threat of Graffik's pursuing soldiers. Each encounter tested their skills, their courage, and their trust in one another. The initial mistrust was long gone, replaced by a deep and abiding respect. They were now a team, each relying on the other's strengths to overcome the obstacles that lay in their path. The shared dangers they had faced had forged a bond between them, one that transcended the initial hostility.

They fought together, their movements synchronized, their strategies complementary. Stanya's quick thinking and strategic mind complemented Najeem's raw strength and combat prowess. They were an unlikely pair, a scholar and a warrior, yet they worked together with a seamless efficiency that surprised even themselves.

One evening, as they rested beneath the canopy of ancient trees, they heard the distant sound of horses approaching. It was a sound that sent a chill down their spines, the unmistakable sound of organized pursuit. This time, it wasn't just the scattered patrols; this was a full-fledged hunt. Their respite had been too long.

Stanya quickly assessed the situation, her eyes scanning the surrounding forest for possible escape routes. They had to make a decision, and fast. Their earlier escapes had been lucky, sheer improvisations in the face of sudden danger. This time, they needed a plan.

"We need to split up," Stanya said, her voice barely above a whisper. "It's the only way. If they catch one of us, the other might have a chance to escape."

Najeem hesitated. The thought of separating was unsettling, a break in the hard-won trust and connection they had established. But he knew she was right. Splitting up was their only chance of survival.

"Which way?" he asked.

"You go north," Stanya said, pointing towards a dense thicket. "I'll go south. Meet at the rendezvous point in three days. If we don't make it, remember the information I gathered..."

Her words trailed off, leaving unspoken the weight of responsibility should one of them fail. The pain of separation was almost as hard as the constant threat of capture, but the reality of their situation made it clear that this was the best course of action. With a final, lingering look, they embraced, a silent promise woven into the embrace, a promise of survival and reunion.

They parted, each disappearing into the shadows, their separate paths leading towards an uncertain future.

The sound of approaching horses echoed behind them, a menacing reminder of the danger that still pursued them. Their escape, now, was a gamble based on trust and a prayer for survival. The forged alliance, forged in the fires of captivity and fueled by shared adversity, was now tested by the ultimate sacrifice: the risk of permanent separation. The journey had just become even more perilous.

Chapter 3: A Dangerous Journey

The wind, a razor-edged blade, sliced through Stanya's worn cloak, whipping her dark hair across her face. Beside her, Najeem, his usually impassive features etched with a grim determination, shielded her with his broad shoulders, a silent bulwark against the relentless storm. They were deep within the Outerlands now, a stark contrast to the opulent, suffocating confines of Graffik's palace. Gone were the polished marble floors and gilded cages; in their place stretched a desolate expanse of jagged, grey mountains, their peaks shrouded in swirling mist.

The landscape was unforgiving. Days bled into nights, each marked by the relentless gnawing of hunger and the constant threat of unseen dangers. They traversed treacherous mountain passes, their boots slipping on loose scree, the icy wind a constant threat to push them into the yawning chasms below. The air thinned with altitude, making each breath a labored effort. They huddled together for warmth in the scant shelter offered by rocky overhangs, the only solace from the biting cold.

Their journey was punctuated by moments of breathtaking beauty, a stark counterpoint to the harsh reality of their plight. Sunrises painted the snow-capped peaks in hues of fiery orange and soft rose, a spectacle of nature's grandeur that momentarily eclipsed their desperation. Crystal-clear streams, fed by melting glaciers, offered respite, their icy waters a welcome relief from the pervasive dryness. But even these moments of serenity were laced with a sense of foreboding, the serene beauty a mask for the ever-present danger lurking in the shadows.

Food was scarce. They subsisted on meager rations, supplemented by whatever edible plants Stanya, with her encyclopedic knowledge of flora, could identify. Twice they were fortunate enough to trap small game – nimble mountain rabbits – their meager flesh offering sustenance and a fleeting moment of satisfaction. Najeem, with his honed skills, expertly fashioned snares and traps from readily available materials, his resourcefulness proving a vital asset to their survival.

Their reliance on each other deepened with each passing day. The initial mistrust, born from their unexpected clash in Graffik's palace, had long since evaporated, replaced by a bond forged in the crucible of shared adversity. They learned to anticipate each other's needs, their movements a silent symphony of coordination. Stanya, despite her fragile frame, displayed an unexpected resilience, her spirit unbroken by the harsh conditions. Najeem, in turn, was humbled by her resourcefulness and unwavering determination. He saw a strength in her that belied her delicate appearance, a strength that mirrored his own.

One evening, huddled around a small fire built from scavenged wood, Stanya recounted stories of her past. She spoke of her early life in a small, isolated village, her family's persecution at the hands of Graffik's agents. It was this persecution, the brutal violation of her family's peaceful existence, that ignited her determination to fight back against Graffik's oppressive regime. She had honed her skills in information gathering and espionage over many years, dedicating her life to undermining Graffik's power.

Najeem, in turn, shared fragments of his past – a nomadic upbringing steeped in martial arts and swordsmanship. He spoke of his fierce loyalty to his family, his heart heavy with the memories of losses suffered at the hands of Graffik's forces. His escape, he revealed, was not solely driven by a desire for freedom but also by a profound sense of duty. He carried the weight of a promise to protect, a silent vow that had become his guiding star. The shared pain and hardship they endured drew them together, a profound understanding passing between them, a bond that transcended mere alliance.

Their journey was not without peril. They encountered wild animals – wolves and mountain lions – whose eyes reflected the harshness of their surroundings. Najeem's skill with his blade was tested more than once, his actions swift and decisive, a guardian angel protecting them from the sharp teeth and claws of the predators. They were forced to navigate treacherous ravines and climb sheer cliffs, their bodies pushed to their limits, their minds strained by the constant vigilance required for survival. But they persevered, their resilience fueled by a shared goal and a growing affection that was as unexpected as it was profound.

As they delved deeper into the Outerlands, they began to encounter signs of human habitation – faint trails, discarded tools, and the remnants of abandoned settlements. These were signs of the rebellious factions that opposed Graffik's rule – scattered groups of people fighting for their freedom, each clinging to the hope of a better future. They were cautiously optimistic, hopeful of finding allies, yet wary of the potential dangers of associating with unknown factions. They knew that trust could be as treacherous as the mountains themselves.

One day, they stumbled upon a small, hidden settlement nestled within a secluded valley. Smoke curled lazily from the chimneys of crudely built huts, hinting at warmth and the promise of shelter. As they approached, cautiously, they were greeted by a group of wary individuals. They were members of a rebel faction, their faces etched with the grim determination of people fighting for their survival.

Stanya, ever cautious, approached them, using her charm and diplomatic skills to gain their confidence. She revealed the vital information she had stolen from Graffik's court – intelligence concerning his impending military campaign, detailing his strategic plans and troop movements. The rebels listened intently, their initial suspicion replaced by awe and excitement at the significance of the information.

The information Stanya presented proved invaluable to the rebels, giving them a crucial advantage in their fight against Graffik's forces. They prepared to launch a counter-offensive, knowing that the information Stanya provided would help them to strike strategically and effectively.

Their meeting with the rebels marked a turning point in their journey. Stanya's mission was accomplished, her burden lifted, but the weight of Najeem's own mission pressed down even more intensely now. He expressed his gratitude to Stanya and the rebel group, but there was a profound sense of finality in his voice. His journey was far from over. His solemn vow to rescue Graffik's daughter, a victim of her father's tyranny, remained a burning flame in his heart.

As they prepared to part ways, a bittersweet feeling settled over them. A bond, forged in the fires of adversity, now had to be tempered by the realities of their diverging paths. They shared a knowing glance, a silent acknowledgement of the respect and affection they held for each other. The harsh landscape of the Outerlands had brought them together, but their individual destinies called them to separate paths.

Their parting was not a farewell, but a silent promise of a reunion, a hope for a future where their paths might cross once more, in a world free from Graffik's tyrannical grip. The mountains watched silently as they embarked upon their new journeys, each carrying the memory of their perilous journey, and the bond formed within the heart of the Outerlands. The wind, once their enemy, now seemed to whisper promises of a brighter future. The seeds of rebellion, nurtured by their shared struggle, had been sown, and the fruits of their courage were yet to be seen.

The wind howled a mournful dirge through the skeletal branches of the twisted pines, mirroring the turmoil in Stanya's heart. She and Najeem had been traversing the Outerlands for days, the landscape a relentless succession of jagged peaks and windswept valleys. Their initial relief at escaping Graffik's clutches had given way to a gnawing uncertainty. The Outerlands, far from being a unified front against Baznoon Graffik, proved to be a fractured landscape of rival factions, each with their own agendas and grievances.

Their first encounter was with the Crimson Hand, a band of fierce mountain warriors known for their brutal efficiency and unwavering loyalty to their enigmatic leader, a woman only known as the Serpent. They were camped near a precarious pass, their makeshift tents huddled together against the biting wind. The air crackled with an unspoken tension, the warriors eyeing Stanya and Najeem with suspicion, their hands never far from their wickedly curved knives.

Stanya, drawing on her experience in navigating the treacherous currents of Graffik's court, approached cautiously. She spoke in hushed tones, weaving a tale of their escape and the vital information she carried – intelligence that could cripple Graffik's supply lines, a vulnerability she'd discovered during her infiltration. She carefully omitted mention of Najeem's connection to Graffik's daughter, choosing to focus on their shared hatred of Baznoon Graffik and the urgency of their mission.

The Serpent, a woman whose age was obscured by harsh weather and shrewdness, listened intently, her gaze piercing, unnerving. Her silence was more daunting than any outright hostility. Finally, with a slow nod, she granted them passage, but not without a price. They would be required to participate in a raid on one of Graffik's smaller outposts, a test of their loyalty and a demonstration of their capabilities. Najeem, his warrior instincts honed by years of training, readily agreed, but Stanya hesitated. She was an information gatherer, not a soldier, and the thought of open conflict filled her with unease. However, the alternative – a potentially lengthy trek through enemy territory – was far more perilous.

The raid was a brutal affair, a whirlwind of steel and screams. Najeem fought with a ferocious grace, a whirlwind of motion that left his enemies disoriented and bleeding. Stanya, initially reluctant, found a surprising aptitude for combat, using her agility and quick thinking to outmaneuver her opponents, delivering swift, precise strikes. They succeeded in disabling the outpost, securing much-needed supplies and proving their worth to the Crimson Hand. However, the victory was bittersweet, leaving both of them with a fresh understanding of the brutal realities of war.

Their journey continued, leading them to the Whispering Woods, the domain of the Silent Order, a secretive group of assassins and spies who operated in the shadows. Unlike the Crimson Hand's overt rebellion, the Silent Order favored subterfuge and stealth, their allegiance as elusive as their methods. Their leader, a masked figure known only as the Nightingale, was a master manipulator, whose words were as sharp as the daggers concealed beneath her silken robes.

Stanya, fluent in the language of deception, found a strange kinship with the Nightingale, a shared understanding of power and manipulation. She offered the Order a piece of intelligence – a list of Graffik's most loyal informants, information that the Silent Order could use to cripple Baznoon Graffik's intelligence network. In return, they offered her safe passage through their territory and access to a network of hidden routes, a vital aid in evading Graffik's relentless pursuit. Najeem, however, remained skeptical. He sensed a chilling duplicity in the Nightingale's demeanor, a cold calculation that spoke of self-preservation rather than genuine alliance.

Their path then led them to the Sunstone Clan, a nomadic tribe renowned for their unparalleled horsemanship and their unwavering dedication to the preservation of ancient traditions. Unlike the violent Crimson Hand or the shadowy Silent Order, the Sunstone Clan valued honor and loyalty above all else. Their chieftain, a wise old woman named Elara, listened patiently to Stanya's story, her eyes reflecting the wisdom of generations. She offered them shelter and provisions, but warned them of the treacherous paths ahead, advising caution and discernment in choosing their allies.

Elara revealed the complexities of the Outerlands, a region rife with internal conflict and competing ideologies. She explained that several factions sought to overthrow Graffik, each with its own agenda and vision for the future. Some sought only to gain power for themselves, while others genuinely desired a better world. Elara emphasized the importance of understanding the motivations of each group, cautioning against blind allegiance and the perils of betrayal.

Stanya and Najeem spent several days with the Sunstone Clan, learning about their culture and their unique perspective on the conflict. They observed the clan's internal dynamics, noticing the strong bonds of loyalty and mutual respect that held the community together, a stark contrast to the fragmented and often treacherous alliances they'd witnessed amongst the other rebel groups. This experience gave them invaluable insight into the true nature of rebellion: a fight not just against tyranny, but against the self-serving ambitions and inherent flaws within their own ranks.

As they prepared to leave, Elara gifted them a small, intricately carved amulet. "This," she said, "will help you discern truth from falsehood. Trust your instincts, for they are rarely wrong." The amulet, a simple yet powerful symbol, became a tangible reminder of the wisdom they had gained and the difficult choices that lay ahead. The journey through the Outerlands had been more than just a flight from Graffik; it had become a harsh education in the treacherous nature of power, betrayal, and the fragile alliances forged in the crucible of rebellion. Their journey was far from over; the true test lay in the careful selection of their alliances, a dance on the knife-edge between trust and treachery, loyalty and betrayal, as they fought to secure a future free from Graffik's iron fist. The fate of the Outerlands, and perhaps even the empire itself, hung precariously in the balance.

The air in the cavern hung thick with the scent of woodsmoke and damp earth. Torches flickered, casting dancing shadows on the rough-hewn walls, illuminating the faces of the assembled rebels. They were a motley crew, hardened warriors and seasoned strategists, their faces etched with the weariness of years spent fighting a losing battle against Baznoon Graffik's seemingly unstoppable empire. Stanya, her dark hair plastered to her temples with sweat, felt a tremor of apprehension. This was it. The culmination of months of meticulous planning, dangerous infiltration, and a desperate escape. The success or failure of the rebellion rested, in no small part, on the information she held clutched tightly in her hand – a small, leather-bound scroll.

She met the gaze of their leader, a woman named Lyra, whose eyes held the steely glint of a seasoned commander and the quiet fire of unwavering resolve. Lyra, her face framed by a cascade of silver braids, exuded an aura of calm authority that belied the gravity of the situation. Beside her stood Ronan, his broad shoulders hinting at the physical strength that made him a formidable warrior. His gaze, however, held a flicker of doubt, a skepticism that Stanya found unsettling. The room was charged with anticipation, the silence broken only by the crackle of the fire and the occasional nervous cough.

Lyra gestured to a rough-hewn table, its surface scarred by years of use. "We have been waiting for you,

Stanya," she said, her voice a low, resonant hum that filled the cavern. "The whispers of your exploits have reached even these remote corners of the Outerlands. Tell us what you have learned."

Stanya swallowed, her throat suddenly dry. The weight of expectation pressed down on her, heavy and suffocating. She unfurled the scroll, its parchment brittle with age, revealing the meticulously penned details of Baznoon Graffik's military strategy. The scroll detailed Graffik's plans for a devastating offensive, outlining troop deployments, supply lines, and the weaknesses in his defenses – information that could turn the tide of the war. She spoke clearly, her voice firm despite the tremor in her hands, detailing Graffik's secret alliances, his hidden arsenals, and the vulnerabilities in his seemingly impenetrable defenses.

As she spoke, a hush fell over the assembled rebels. The information was explosive, revealing a level of treachery and deception that surpassed even their wildest suspicions. Ronan's skepticism seemed to melt away, replaced by a look of grim determination. Lyra's eyes, however, remained intensely focused on Stanya, assessing, analyzing, searching for any hint of deception. Stanya knew that her life, and the fate of the rebellion, hinged on their belief in her words.

When she finished, a long silence hung in the air, broken only by the crackling fire. Then, a murmur rippled through the assembled rebels, a wave of astonishment and cautious optimism. Lyra, her expression unreadable, remained silent for a long moment, her gaze fixed on the scroll.

Finally, she spoke, her voice barely a whisper. "This…this changes everything." Her words hung in the air, heavy with the weight of their implications. The information Stanya had provided was more valuable than they could have ever imagined, a key that could unlock the door to victory.

Ronan, his voice gruff but filled with renewed hope, spoke, "This is it. We have a chance. A real chance to defeat Graffik." His words ignited a spark of defiance in the eyes of the assembled rebels. The air, previously thick with apprehension, now crackled with a newfound energy, a shared determination to seize this opportunity.

Lyra addressed Stanya, her voice filled with gratitude and respect. "Your courage and skill have saved us, Stanya.

You have given us the means to fight back. We will not let you down."

The ensuing discussions were long and intense, the rebels poring over the details of Stanya's intelligence, formulating strategies and assigning tasks. The information Stanya provided was meticulously analyzed, each detail dissected and scrutinized. It was clear that Lyra and Ronan, along with the other rebel leaders, were highly skilled strategists, their minds sharp and their plans well-conceived.

Over the next few days, Stanya helped the rebels adapt their strategies based on the information she had provided. She found herself surprisingly comfortable in their company, sharing stories of her past experiences and learning about their own struggles against Graffik's regime. They shared meals cooked over open fires, and at night, they slept huddled together under rough blankets, their camaraderie growing stronger with each passing hour.

Stanya's skill in gathering intelligence proved invaluable, not only in the military planning but also in deciphering the intricate web of political alliances within the Outerlands. She discovered hidden pockets of resistance, individuals and groups who, though initially hesitant, were now inspired by the possibility of real change, and willing to risk everything for the cause. Her reputation grew within the rebel ranks, her contributions not merely as a purveyor of information but also as a strategic advisor and an inspiring leader.

The days turned into weeks, and the rebel army began to prepare for their counteroffensive. They forged new alliances, strengthened existing ties, and gathered their forces, ready to launch a coordinated assault against Baznoon Graffik's army. Stanya, though initially hesitant to participate directly in combat, found herself at the heart of the action, her expertise in strategy and tactics proving invaluable.

The meticulously planned campaign started with a series of daring raids, targeting key supply lines and weakening Graffik's grip on the surrounding territories. Stanya, ever watchful, observed from a safe distance, using her skills to monitor enemy movements and provide tactical support. The rebels fought with incredible courage and determination, the fire of hope burning brighter with each victory.

Stanya found herself unexpectedly drawn to Ronan, their shared experiences forging a bond stronger than mere camaraderie. Their late-night discussions under the stars, sharing their hopes and fears, their dreams of a future free from tyranny, marked a turning point in their relationship. There were moments of shared laughter, quiet moments of comfort and understanding. Their developing feelings were a silent understanding, a shared glance, a touch of hands during moments of heightened tension. Their connection, forged in the crucible of shared struggle and mutual respect, blossomed amidst the chaos of war.

The final confrontation with Baznoon Graffik's army was a brutal, protracted battle. The rebels, outnumbered but not outmatched, fought with the ferocity of lions protecting their cubs. Stanya, ever resourceful, found ways to utilize her intelligence skills in the thick of the battle, providing crucial tactical insights that turned the tide.

As the dust settled, and the cheers of victory echoed through the valley, Stanya stood beside Lyra and Ronan, watching the remnants of Graffik's army retreat in disarray. Their success was a testament to their meticulous planning and the combined strength of their alliance, a victory forged in the fires of rebellion. But even as they celebrated their triumph, Stanya knew their journey was far from over. The fight for freedom was a long and arduous one, and there were many battles still to be fought. But for now, she allowed herself a moment of quiet satisfaction, a moment to savor the sweetness of victory, the knowledge that she had played a pivotal role in shaping the future of the Outerlands. Her gaze drifted towards Ronan, their eyes meeting across the battlefield, a promise unspoken but deeply felt. The future held many uncertainties, but one thing was certain; they would face them together.

The celebratory bonfire crackled, casting a warm, flickering light on the faces of the Outerlands rebels. Lyra, their leader, a woman whose strength belied her delicate features, clapped Stanya on the shoulder, her smile as bright as the flames. Ronan, his eyes mirroring the intensity of the firelight, stood beside her, his hand resting lightly on Lyra's arm, a silent testament to their bond. But Stanya felt a disquiet settle over her, a shadow clinging to the edges of the victory. The weight of the information she had delivered was heavy, the knowledge that Graffik's reign, though weakened, was far from over. And there was Najeem.

His absence hung in the air, a void in the celebratory atmosphere. He had melted into the shadows after their escape from the Imperial forces, a silent figure disappearing into the night. Stanya knew he hadn't left out of disloyalty, but rather a different kind of dedication, a fierce protectiveness that had bloomed in the crucible of their shared ordeal. She remembered his haunted eyes, the way his jaw tightened as he recalled Graffik's daughter, Princess Amara.

As the revelry subsided, Stanya found herself alone, the embers of the bonfire casting long shadows that danced and writhed like restless spirits. She thought of Najeem's unwavering gaze, a steel-gray intensity that had pierced through her carefully constructed defenses. He had carried himself with an almost unbearable dignity throughout their escape, a man hardened by years of servitude, yet possessing a tenderness that surprised her. The clash between the warrior and the captive had given way to a grudging respect, a silent understanding forged in the fires of adversity. He hadn't spoken much about Amara, but his unspoken vow hung between them, thick and heavy as the smoke from the dying fire.

She had seen the compassion in his eyes, the flicker of empathy that belied the ruthless efficiency of his fighting style. He saw Amara not as a spoiled princess but as a victim, a prisoner of her father's tyranny, a gilded cage from which she couldn't escape. This realization had struck Stanya with the force of a physical blow. She had been too focused on the political machinations, the strategic maneuvers, and the importance of her mission that she'd failed to see the human cost of Graffik's reign.

The night was cold, the air thick with the scent of pine and damp earth. Stanya shivered, not entirely from the cold, but from a sudden surge of empathy. She understood now Najeem's silent resolve. It wasn't merely a matter of loyalty or obligation. It was something deeper, something far more powerful than political ambition or personal gain. It was the heart of a warrior protecting a woman who, despite her privilege, was undeniably a victim. It was a promise made in the depths of despair, a pledge whispered on the wind as they fled Graffik's clutches.

She recalled the events of their escape vividly: the treacherous climb through the mountain pass, the desperate fight against Graffik's pursuing soldiers, the narrow escapes, and the moments of quiet respite where they had shared stolen glances and words of unspoken gratitude. She had relied on his strength, his skill, and his unwavering resolve. He, in turn, had trusted her intelligence, her cunning, and her unwavering dedication to the cause. Their alliance had transcended simple practicality. A peculiar, fragile bond of trust and respect had formed, the foundation for something far deeper than mere companionship.

The memory of Najeem's hand, strong and sure in hers, during the most perilous moments of their escape, sent a shiver down her spine. It wasn't a romantic gesture, not exactly, but it carried a depth of meaning that resonated with her on a profoundly personal level. He had kept her safe, his quiet strength a bulwark against the overwhelming fear and uncertainty that had threatened to consume them both.

She pictured him now, making his way back to Graffik's capital, a lone wolf returning to the heart of the beast's lair. The thought filled her with a mixture of admiration and apprehension. The mission was incredibly dangerous, fraught with peril at every turn, and yet he was undertaking it, propelled by a righteous fury and an unwavering love for a woman who had, in her own way, become his prisoner as well.

He wasn't simply rescuing Amara; he was rescuing a part of himself, the compassion that had been buried under years of relentless servitude. His escape had served as a catalyst, igniting a protective instinct within him, fueling his quest with a ferocity and determination that even Stanya, hardened by years of espionage and political maneuvering, found awe-inspiring.

The wind whispered through the trees, carrying with it the scent of snow and the lingering echoes of battle. Stanya rose, the cold no longer biting, but invigorating. She looked towards the east, towards the distant city, a place of both exquisite beauty and horrifying tyranny. She understood his decision. It was not a rash act of reckless bravery but a deliberate choice, born of a fierce loyalty, a protective instinct, and a profound empathy that resonated deep within his soul. It was a promise kept, a vow made in the shadows, a testament to the strength of a man who had found his heart despite his circumstances. She knew he would face insurmountable odds, but he would not fail.

Amara, the sheltered princess, trapped in the gilded cage of her father's court, was far more vulnerable than she appeared. She was a symbol of Graffik's tyranny, but to Najeem, she was a woman deserving of protection, a pawn caught in the deadly game of political power. He saw her innocence, her vulnerability, even her complicity in his imprisonment, and he had sworn to protect her. It was a promise he would keep, even if it meant risking everything, even if it meant facing certain death. This was the heart of a warrior, a man who had found his purpose not on the battlefield, but in his unwavering determination to save a woman from the clutches of the very system that had enslaved him.

The dawn broke, painting the sky in hues of orange and pink, a breathtaking spectacle that mirrored the beauty and danger that lay ahead for Najeem. Stanya felt a surge of gratitude, a sense of awe. She had accomplished her mission, delivering the information that could change the fate of the Outerlands, but Najeem's silent vow had ignited within her a profound respect. He was not just a warrior who had fought alongside her; he was a symbol of hope, a testament to the enduring power of the human spirit. His journey was just beginning, but his purpose was clear. He would return to the capital, not as a prisoner or a slave, but as a protector, a warrior who had found redemption not in conquest, but in compassion. And Stanya, looking towards the rising sun, knew that she would be waiting. Their paths, though diverging for now, were inextricably linked, destined to converge again in the tumultuous events that lay ahead. The fight for freedom was far from over. The rebellion was far from won. Their story, however, was only just beginning.

The air crackled with unspoken emotions as Stanya and Najeem stood at the edge of the whispering woods, the boundary between the Outerlands and the vast, unknown territories beyond. The celebratory bonfire had died down to embers, leaving behind a lingering scent of woodsmoke and the bittersweet aroma of victory. The dawn chorus of birdsong filled the air, a stark contrast to the recent sounds of battle. They had shared a tumultuous journey, a whirlwind of escapes, close calls, and a burgeoning connection that neither dared to fully acknowledge.

Najeem, his face etched with the lines of a warrior's life, but softened by a newfound purpose, turned to Stanya. His dark eyes, usually alight with fierce determination, held a hint of melancholy. He reached out a hand, his calloused fingers brushing lightly against hers. The simple touch sent a jolt of electricity through her, a reminder of the shared danger and the unexpected bond that had forged between them.

"This is where our paths diverge, Stanya," he said, his voice a low rumble that barely carried on the morning breeze. "My path leads back to Graffik's capital. To reclaim what was stolen from me, and perhaps…to rescue someone precious." He paused, his gaze drifting towards the distant peaks, his unspoken words hanging heavy in the air. It was clear, even without the explicit confession, that his heart belonged to Graffik's daughter, a woman he had grown to love despite their circumstances.

Stanya understood. She had seen the way he looked at her, a silent testament to his devotion. She felt a pang of regret, but also a surge of admiration. His loyalty, even to someone who had initially held him captive, spoke volumes about his character. It was a testament to a strength that transcended simple battlefield prowess.

"And mine," Stanya replied, her voice calm but firm, betraying none of the turmoil within her. "Leads towards rebuilding what Graffik destroyed. There's much work to be done, much information to share, and many alliances to forge." Her hand still lingered in his, a silent conversation passing between them in the stillness of the dawn. The unspoken words danced around them – words of gratitude, of admiration, of a connection that might have blossomed under different circumstances, but would, for now, remain a treasured memory.

She traced the outline of a scar on his hand, a memento of their shared fight, a tangible reminder of their bond. "We fought side-by-side," she whispered, her voice barely audible above the birdsong. "And for a few brief moments, we forgot what truly mattered, the reasons that set us on our separate paths. For a while, it wasn't about Graffik, or the rebellion, or even survival. It was just us, against the world."

A faint blush crept onto Najeem's cheeks, a response to the unspoken intimacy of her words. "Yes," he agreed, his voice husky. "We fought for each other." He let go of her hand, the action leaving a lingering warmth in its absence. He pulled a small, intricately carved wooden pendant from around his neck, a simple piece of craftsmanship, but with a depth of meaning that belied its unassuming appearance. "This..." he hesitated, his eyes searching hers. "This is for you. A reminder of...of what we shared."

Stanya took the pendant, its smooth surface cool against her skin. It was a simple token, yet it held the weight of a shared experience, a symbol of their fleeting alliance. A silent promise of something more, perhaps, something that might have been had fate dealt a different hand.

"And this," Stanya said, unfastening a small, leather-bound pouch from her belt. Inside, nestled among dried herbs and soft cloth, was a single, perfectly preserved feather. It was a feather from Lyra's prized hawk, a symbol of the Outerlands' resilience and determination. "For you. A reminder to keep fighting, to never give up."

Najeem accepted the feather, cradling it gently in his palm. The silence that followed was not awkward; it was a comfortable understanding, a shared acknowledgement of their respective journeys and the unspoken possibilities that lay ahead. They stood for a long moment, bathed in the golden light of the rising sun, their gazes locking, exchanging a silent promise – a promise of a potential future, perhaps, a future where their paths might cross again under different circumstances.

The parting was less goodbye and more temporary farewell. A bittersweet acknowledgement of their separate destinies, yet a mutual understanding that their experiences had irrevocably changed them both. They were no longer simply a skilled information gatherer and a captive warrior. They were allies, friends, and perhaps something more. The future was uncertain, their paths divergent, yet a fragile seed of hope had been planted, a hope that one day, under different skies and with different battles won, their paths might converge once more.

As Najeem turned to begin his solitary journey back towards the capital, Stanya watched him go, a wave of emotion washing over her. The sun was rising higher, casting long shadows across the landscape. She turned and began to walk towards the Outerlands' encampment, the weight of her responsibilities settling upon her shoulders, but with a newfound lightness in her heart. The victory was sweet, but the journey had been profound, marked by the unlikely friendship – and more – that had blossomed amidst the chaos and bloodshed.

The days that followed were a whirlwind of activity. Stanya immersed herself in the tasks ahead, sharing the crucial intelligence she had gathered. The rebels, emboldened by her revelations, renewed their efforts with a renewed vigor. Lyra, with her sharp intellect and unwavering resolve, proved to be an excellent strategist and a formidable leader. Ronan, her loyal second-in-command, stood steadfastly by her side, his devotion evident in every glance, every shared smile.

Stanya found herself drawn to Ronan's quiet strength. He possessed a certain stoicism, a resilience that mirrored her own. He was a man of few words, but his actions spoke volumes about his character. His quiet observation of her actions, his readiness to offer support without unnecessary words, spoke of respect. It was a different kind of connection compared to the electrifying current of her encounter with Najeem, but it was a connection nonetheless. A connection that was grounded in mutual respect and shared purpose.

The information Stanya had delivered exposed Graffik's clandestine alliances, his vulnerabilities, and his treacherous plots. It was information that would shift the balance of power, that would expose corruption at the very heart of the empire. The rebels, armed with this knowledge, meticulously planned their next moves.

The Outerlands hummed with a newfound sense of hope, a fragile optimism built on the foundation of Stanya's courage and the information she had risked her life to obtain.

She found herself fitting seamlessly into the rebel camp, her skills valued, her insights respected.

She felt a sense of purpose that had been missing before. In Graffik's court, she had been a spy, a ghost flitting through shadows, ever vigilant, ever cautious. Now, she felt a sense of belonging, a sense of camaraderie that was both comforting and exhilarating. The constant threat of betrayal remained, a specter haunting every corner of their movement, but there was camaraderie, a shared bond of commitment to the cause.

While Stanya thrived in the chaotic, yet purpose-driven environment of the rebellion, the whispers of Graffik's spies still reached her ears. She had seen firsthand the insidious reach of Baznoon Graffik's intelligence network, its tentacles spreading throughout the land, poisoning trust and sowing discord wherever it went. She knew that the fight was far from over, that Graffik's reach extended far beyond the walls of his capital, that the fight would be long and arduous.

The memory of Najeem remained, however, a constant companion. His image – his strong hands, his determined gaze, the silent understanding that passed between them – was etched into her memory. The shared dangers and near-death experiences created an enduring bond between them. The parting, therefore, was not a complete severing of ties but a poignant pause in a potentially longer narrative. The pendant he had given her was a constant reminder of his presence, a tangible symbol of their unlikely connection, and a quiet hope that their paths would cross again.

Night fell, casting long shadows across the rebel encampment. The crackling of the bonfire, now a comforting sound, spoke of resilience, hope, and the promise of a brighter tomorrow. And as Stanya looked towards the star-studded sky, she saw not just a vast expanse of darkness, but also a glimmer of light, a light that hinted at a future where justice might prevail, and where perhaps, one day, she and Najeem might find themselves together again, fighting for a world free from tyranny. The future remained unwritten, but the fight, and perhaps the hope for a love yet to be realized, had just begun.

Chapter 4: The Alliance

The air in the war room crackled with a nervous energy, a palpable tension that hung heavier than the smoke from the countless oil lamps casting flickering shadows on the assembled faces. Stanya, her usually sharp eyes clouded with a weariness that belied her youthful appearance, leaned against a rough-hewn table, the scent of pine and damp earth clinging to her clothes. She'd shed the silks and finery of Graffik's court, replacing them with practical leather armor and sturdy boots, a transformation mirroring the shift in her life. The jeweled comb, its innocent appearance belying the vital information it once held, lay nestled within a worn leather pouch at her hip. The information, painstakingly gathered from the heart of Baznoon Graffik's empire, was now the lifeblood fueling the rebellion.

Across the room, General Theron, a grizzled veteran with a face etched with the lines of countless battles, paced restlessly. His movements were a storm brewing, the energy reflecting the turbulent sea of emotions churning within the rebel alliance. He was a man of action, impatient with the intricacies of strategy, preferring the blunt force of a direct assault. But Stanya's intelligence had changed everything, offering a more subtle, and potentially more effective, path to victory.

"Graffik's defenses are concentrated around the capital," Stanya said, her voice calm and measured, a stark contrast to the restless energy of the room. "His main army is positioned to the north, along the Blackwood border. However, his supply lines are stretched thin, particularly in the southern provinces. A coordinated attack there could cripple his logistics."

A murmur rippled through the assembled rebels, a mix of hope and apprehension. Their numbers were far fewer than Graffik's, and a direct confrontation would be disastrous. Stanya's plan, however, offered a chance, a flicker of hope in the oppressive darkness of Graffik's reign.

"We can't afford to underestimate him," cautioned Elara, a shrewd strategist whose quiet demeanor hid a sharp intellect. Her keen eyes scanned the maps spread across the table, tracing the routes of Graffik's supply lines. "Graffik is cunning. He anticipates our every move."

"Precisely," Stanya agreed, her gaze fixed on the maps. "That's why we need a multi-pronged attack. We distract his forces in the north with a smaller, feigned assault, drawing his attention away from the south. Meanwhile, our main force will strike at his vulnerable supply lines, disrupting his ability to resupply his northern army."

The discussion stretched into the late hours, the rebels debating tactics and strategies. Stanya presented her intelligence methodically, supported by her own assessments, drawn from her observations in Graffik's court. She detailed Graffik's temperament, his paranoia, his strengths and, more importantly, his weaknesses. Her intimate knowledge of his inner circle added layers of depth to the overall strategy, allowing for a plan that accounted for his likely countermoves.

The plan was daring, bordering on suicidal. But it was also their only hope. Graffik's grip on the land was absolute, his influence weaving its way into every aspect of their lives. This was more than a simple rebellion; it was a desperate fight for survival.

As the meeting finally adjourned, Stanya sought out a quiet corner of the war room, the weight of responsibility pressing down on her. Her escape from Graffik's clutches had been perilous, a harrowing journey fraught with danger and uncertainty. But it was a journey she undertook knowing that the information she possessed could be the key to freeing her people from Graffik's tyranny.

Meanwhile, Najeem, far away from the war room's heated debates, was engaged in a different kind of preparation. His escape from Graffik's palace had been fuelled by a desperate need to escape his gilded cage, but it had also ignited within him a sense of righteous anger. Graffik's daughter, a prisoner herself in a way, was a seed of compassion growing amidst his resolve. He now focused his energy on gathering allies, men and women who shared his distrust of Graffik, even if those people weren't necessarily committed to the formal rebel alliance. His network was carefully cultivated, a blend of disgruntled soldiers, disenfranchised citizens, and mercenary groups.

His preparations were clandestine, his movements shrouded in secrecy. He secured weapons, trained his recruits, and carefully built his resources. Najeem was a master strategist in his own right, his mind as sharp as any blade. He understood that a successful rescue would require careful planning and flawless execution, a delicate balancing act between audacity and stealth. He knew that direct confrontation would be futile against Graffik's might; his strategy called for infiltration and subversion, a slow and methodical dismantling of Graffik's power from within.

Graffik, oblivious to the growing threats brewing on the edges of his empire, continued to consolidate his power. He tightened his grip on the land, punishing dissent with brutal efficiency. He responded to Stanya's successful information gathering with the expected overreaction. His spies, a network of informants that stretched across the land, were doubled, even tripled in number. His control was so immense that he created a paranoid, hyper-vigilant atmosphere that extended through every level of society.

News of the rebel's activities reached Graffik's ears, fuelling his wrath. He unleashed waves of spies to hunt down the rebels, their reach stretching further than ever before. He increased his troops, reinforcing his already formidable army. He was a man driven by fear, clinging desperately to his power, his grip tightening as the foundations of his reign began to crumble. He did not know the extent of the rebel's planning but instinctively felt the impending danger.

Despite the looming threats, a glimmer of hope remained. The rebel alliance, strengthened by Stanya's intelligence and fueled by the growing unrest within the empire, was gaining momentum. Word of their activities spread like wildfire, inspiring others to join their cause, creating a silent rebellion that was slowly but surely eroding Graffik's influence. Graffik's response was only adding fuel to the fire.

Stanya, in her new role as the rebel alliance's intelligence chief, was vital in coordinating this effort. She not only provided information but also helped to refine their strategies, shaping their actions to counter Graffik's anticipated responses. Her understanding of court politics was proving to be an invaluable asset, providing insights that would otherwise be unavailable. Her ability to anticipate Graffik's maneuvers gave the rebels a crucial edge in their fight for freedom. The balance of power was slowly, agonizingly, but surely shifting. The seeds of rebellion, carefully planted and nurtured, were now starting to blossom.

The rough-hewn table in the dimly lit tavern felt strangely comforting after the sterile elegance of Graffik's palace. Najeem, his hands calloused but strong, traced the worn grain of the wood, his gaze distant. He wasn't dwelling on the luxuries he'd lost; the opulent chambers, the silken sheets, the endless parade of sycophants. Those were distractions, vestiges of a life that felt both incredibly distant and painfully close. His focus was razor-sharp, fixed on the task ahead: his return to the capital. The rescue of Princess Amara was not merely a debt of honor, but a burning ember in his heart. He had promised her a return, and Najeem kept his promises.

He pushed away from the table, the rough wood scratching lightly against his leather jerkin. The tavern was bustling, filled with the usual cacophony of drunken laughter, raucous singing, and the clatter of tankards. Yet, amidst the revelry, Najeem's senses remained acutely alert, scanning the room for any hint of danger. His escape had been a brutal dash through the labyrinthine alleys of the city, a harrowing experience that left him with a renewed appreciation for the shadows. He knew that Graffik's reach extended far beyond the palace walls; every corner, every shadow, held the potential for betrayal.

His first task was to gather allies. He'd spent the past few months consolidating his resources, reaching out to those who resented Graffik's rule. The Outerlands, a collection of fiercely independent clans and villages, were a natural starting point. They shared a deep-seated distrust of Graffik's centralized power, a sentiment fueled by years of oppression and unjust taxation. His network was not extensive yet, but it was growing, each contact a fragile thread woven into a potentially powerful tapestry of resistance.

He needed fighters—individuals loyal, skilled, and battle-hardened. Not the reckless mercenaries eager for gold, but those driven by a cause. The whispers of discontent had reached him, stories of discontent simmering in the hearts of soldiers disillusioned with Graffik's relentless wars. Many had witnessed firsthand the brutal consequences of his ambition, the callous disregard for human life. He sought these men and women, the ones who yearned for a different future.

His first meeting was with Kaelen, a grizzled veteran whose weathered face spoke of countless battles fought and lost. Kaelen commanded respect among the Outerlands' warriors. His loyalty, though, was questionable. He was not a rebel in heart, but a pragmatist, more interested in ensuring his people's survival than in overthrowing Graffik. Najeem needed to convince him that rescuing the princess aligned with Kaelen's own interests. The ensuing negotiation was a delicate dance of words, a careful exchange of promises and assurances. Najeem painted a picture of a united Outerlands, strengthened by the princess's influence and the potential for trade agreements with neighboring kingdoms— a future that offered security and prosperity, far exceeding the precarious state of their current existence.

The negotiation had stretched over several days, held under the cloak of a new moon. Each conversation was punctuated by silences thick with tension, laced with mistrust and caution. Najeem patiently chipped away at Kaelen's skepticism, presenting evidence of Amara's kindness, her compassion for the people, her hidden opposition to her father's tyrannical rule. The deal was struck not out of fervent loyalty, but through a calculated assessment of self-interest, a pragmatic alliance born of necessity.

Beyond warriors, Najeem needed supplies: weapons, armor, provisions, and above all, intelligence. The latter was crucial, providing information on Graffik's defenses and troop movements. He sought out Elara, a cunning woman known for her network of informants spread throughout the capital. Elara, a master of disguise and deception, operated in the shadows, moving unseen through the labyrinthine streets of the city. Her information was expensive, but invaluable. He paid in gold, but also in promises of protection, of a better future for her people should their rebellion succeed. The information she provided was fragmented, delivered in coded messages and cryptic riddles, a testament to the danger of her work.

As the days turned into weeks, Najeem's preparations progressed meticulously. He established a hidden base in a remote mountain cave, shielded from prying eyes and the harsh elements. The cave was more than just shelter; it was a training ground, a forge where his small band of rebels honed their skills and strategized their assault. Najeem pushed them hard, knowing that the risks were immense. Graffik's forces were formidable, their loyalty unquestionable, their ruthlessness legendary. He instilled in them a sense of discipline and camaraderie, forging a bond that transcended the usual mercenary affiliations.

The atmosphere in the cave was a potent mix of anticipation and dread. The air crackled with unspoken tension. Each man and woman understood the gravity of the mission, the near-impossible odds they were facing. Yet, their determination burned brighter than their fear. They were fueled by a shared belief in the possibility of freedom, by a faith in Najeem's leadership, and by the promise of rescuing the princess.

Meanwhile, Najeem continued to refine his plan, studying maps, analyzing Graffik's known defenses, and identifying potential weaknesses. He incorporated Elara's information, piecing together a mosaic of intelligence that allowed him to craft a daring, almost reckless, plan. He was aware of Graffik's penchant for elaborate security measures, his obsession with control, his paranoia bordering on madness. Najeem planned to exploit this paranoia, to use it against him.

His strategy was built on speed and precision, a carefully choreographed dance of deception and force. They would strike quickly, exploiting a window of opportunity during a critical juncture in Graffik's ongoing war with a neighboring kingdom. The distraction provided by the ongoing conflict would serve as a smokescreen, obscuring their approach and minimizing the risk of immediate detection.

As the day of their departure drew closer, a palpable sense of anticipation permeated the cave. Najeem stood before his assembled warriors, his gaze sweeping across their faces. He saw the reflection of their determination in their eyes, the unwavering commitment to their cause. This wasn't just a rescue mission; it was a rebellion in miniature, a spark that held the potential to ignite a wider conflagration, to reshape the future of the empire. The seeds of rebellion, planted in the outerlands, were about to bear fruit, a testament to Najeem's determination and the power of hope in the face of overwhelming odds. The weight of responsibility was immense, but Najeem met it with a calm resolve, his heart filled with the bittersweet mixture of fear and anticipation that always accompanied great endeavor. He had promised Amara his return, and he would fulfill that promise, even if it cost him everything. His journey was far from over; it was only just beginning.

The air in the Outerlands crackled with a nervous energy, a far cry from the suffocating opulence of Baznoon Graffik's court. Stanya, her usually meticulous attire replaced with practical leather and roughspun cloth, felt a strange sense of liberation. The weight of secrets, the constant threat of discovery, the suffocating pressure of court life – all of it had fallen away, replaced by a different kind of tension, the taut string of rebellion. Her escape had been harrowing, a blur of close calls and desperate maneuvers, but she had succeeded. She had delivered Graffik's meticulously guarded secrets – details of his alliances, his weaknesses, his hidden coffers – into the hands of those who would use them to fight him.

Initially, she had expected a grand welcome, a celebration of her audacious feat. Instead, she found herself in a dimly lit cave, surrounded by grizzled warriors and fervent revolutionaries, their faces etched with the harsh realities of a life spent fighting for survival. They were a ragtag bunch, united not by a shared background but by their shared enemy: Graffik. Their leader, a stern woman with eyes that seemed to pierce through deception, had listened to Stanya's information with a quiet intensity, her expression betraying nothing of her thoughts.

Stanya's expertise lay not in combat, but in infiltration and information gathering. She was a ghost, a whisper in the halls of power, able to move unseen, unheard. Yet, here, amidst these hardened warriors, her skills felt…underutilized. They needed soldiers, spies, yes, but they also needed someone to organize, to strategize, to weave together the disparate threads of their rebellion into a cohesive whole. The leader, whose name was Lyra, saw this need, and Stanya's potential to fulfill it.

Lyra, a woman who commanded respect with a single glance, turned to Stanya after a long silence. "Your information is invaluable, but it's only the beginning. We need to use it strategically, to strike at Graffik's vulnerabilities without exposing ourselves unnecessarily. We need someone to analyze, to interpret, to coordinate our efforts. Someone with your experience." Her gaze lingered on Stanya for a long moment, assessing, evaluating. "I offer you the position of Chief Strategist for the Outerlands Rebellion."

The offer caught Stanya off guard. Strategist? It wasn't the life of adventure she'd envisioned, not the thrill of daring escapes and thrilling chases. But it was a crucial role, one that would allow her to use her skills to affect real change. More importantly, it was a chance to fight back against the injustice she had witnessed firsthand in Graffik's court.

"I accept," Stanya replied, her voice low but firm, the words echoing the unwavering resolve that had guided her escape.

Her new role proved far more demanding than she had anticipated. It wasn't enough to simply possess information; she had to analyze it, decipher its meaning, and translate it into actionable plans. The rebel alliance was a chaotic tapestry of different factions, each with its own agenda and its own grudges against Graffik. Some were driven by a desire for freedom, others by revenge, and still others by sheer desperation. Stanya had to navigate these treacherous currents, calming tempers, forging alliances, and suppressing the constant threat of infighting.

Days bled into weeks, filled with endless meetings, whispered consultations, and the painstaking process of piecing together a coherent strategy. She studied maps, poring over details, identifying weaknesses in Graffik's defenses, and devising plans to exploit them. She spent countless hours interviewing informants, verifying information, and discerning truth from falsehood. Her sharp intellect, honed over years of navigating the treacherous waters of courtly intrigue, proved invaluable. She became the quiet force behind the rebel movement, the unseen hand that guided their actions.

One particularly challenging aspect of her new role was dealing with the different personalities within the rebel alliance. There was Theron, a fiery warrior with a penchant for reckless bravery; Elara, a shrewd tactician who often clashed with Theron's impulsive nature; and Rhys, a master of disguise and infiltration who preferred to work alone. Each had their strengths and weaknesses, their own ideas about how the rebellion should be conducted. Stanya had to find a way to harness their diverse talents while minimizing their internal conflicts.

It was a delicate balancing act. She had to be firm, to assert her authority when necessary, but also diplomatic, to build consensus and foster a sense of unity. She used her understanding of human nature, her ability to read people's motivations, to steer them towards a common goal. She learned to listen as much as she spoke, to understand their concerns and their aspirations. She learned to compromise, to find common ground, and to unite them under a common banner.

The romance that had begun to bloom between Stanya and Najeem during their escape remained a bittersweet memory. He had left to pursue his own mission, his commitment to rescuing Princess Amara burning brightly. Sometimes, in the quiet moments of the night, Stanya would think of him, of their shared ordeal, of the unspoken feelings that lingered between them. But her focus remained on the present, on the task at hand. There was no room for sentimentality in the brutal world of rebellion.

Her work was not without its dangers. Graffik's spies were everywhere, their presence a constant threat. There were whispers of betrayals, suspicions of double agents, and the ever-present fear that their plans might be uncovered. Stanya had to constantly be vigilant, to maintain a watchful eye, to anticipate Graffik's moves, and to adapt her strategies accordingly.

As the rebellion gained momentum, Stanya's role became even more crucial. She developed a network of informants throughout the empire, providing the rebels with vital intelligence on Graffik's movements and plans. She orchestrated daring raids on imperial supply lines, disrupting the flow of resources to Graffik's armies. She helped coordinate attacks on strategic targets, weakening Graffik's grip on power.

The culmination of her strategic brilliance came during a daring operation to capture a vital imperial stronghold. Stanya, working in conjunction with Theron, Elara, and Rhys, devised a complex plan that involved multiple simultaneous attacks, a diversionary tactic, and a cunning use of the terrain. The operation was risky, the stakes were high, but it was a masterpiece of military strategy. The stronghold fell, dealt a significant blow to Graffik's forces.

The victory was a turning point in the rebellion. It boosted morale, attracted new recruits, and sent a powerful message to Graffik: the rebellion was a force to be reckoned with. Stanya, the quiet strategist, had become a symbol of hope and resistance, a beacon of defiance in the face of tyranny. Her path was far from over, but she stood ready, poised for the next challenge, the next battle in the fight for freedom. The seeds of rebellion, once a mere whisper, were now blossoming into a full-fledged revolution, and Stanya was at its heart, a warrior not of blade and shield, but of wit and strategy, her mind as sharp and deadly as any weapon. The fight was far from over, but she knew, with a certainty that settled deep in her bones, that victory was within reach.

The news reached Emperor Baznoon Graffik like a poisoned arrow, piercing the carefully constructed illusion of his invincibility. The stolen documents, the meticulously guarded secrets of his empire, were now in the hands of his enemies. His meticulously crafted web of alliances, the hidden coffers that fueled his opulent lifestyle, the very weaknesses he'd so carefully concealed – all laid bare for the rebels to exploit. His carefully cultivated calm fractured. The jade-green eyes, usually so cold and calculating, blazed with a furious intensity that chilled his advisors to the bone.

Silence hung heavy in the opulent throne room, broken only by the rhythmic drip of a hidden fountain, each drop echoing the growing unease. Baznoon paced, his embroidered robes swirling around him like a storm cloud. His advisors, usually quick to offer solutions, remained silent, their faces pale with fear. They knew Graffik's wrath was a force to be reckoned with, and this time, it was unleashed.

"Find her," Baznoon finally roared, his voice echoing through the cavernous hall. "Find Stanya. Alive. And bring her to me." His voice dripped with venom, each syllable a threat. "And those who aided her escape... they will pay the ultimate price."

The ensuing crackdown was swift and brutal. Graffik, in his fury, unleashed the full might of his Praetorian Guard, his elite force of ruthless soldiers. No corner of the city was left untouched, no individual safe from suspicion. Arrests were made with brutal efficiency. Accusations flew like poisoned darts, leaving trails of fear and uncertainty in their wake. Public executions became commonplace, a stark reminder of Graffik's power and his unwavering resolve to crush the rebellion.

The once-vibrant marketplaces were now hushed, the laughter and chatter replaced by a nervous silence. Citizens walked with heads bowed, their eyes darting nervously, fearing the ever-present gaze of the Praetorian Guard. Whispers of dissent were quickly silenced, replaced by a chilling atmosphere of fear and oppression.

But Graffik's harsh measures, far from extinguishing the rebellion, only fueled its flames. The outrage over the brutality ignited a new wave of resistance. The initial fear gave way to a defiance born of desperation. Hidden cells of rebels, previously cautious and secretive, emerged from the shadows, their numbers swelling with each act of tyranny. The message was clear: Graffik's iron fist had only galvanized his opposition.

Baznoon's intelligence network, once a formidable tool, was now compromised. He discovered that several key informants within the Outerlands had been compromised, their loyalty bought or forced through torture. Graffik's grip, once seemingly unshakeable, now felt brittle, vulnerable. He realized, with growing unease, that the rebellion was not simply a localized uprising, but a far more significant threat – a meticulously planned insurgency with strong support from unexpected allies.

His personal guard, the elite force he had meticulously trained for years, was now suspect. Graffik found himself surrounded by whispers, suspicion etched onto every face, even amongst his closest advisors. The paranoia, once a tool he wielded with mastery, now gnawed at him, consuming him from within. He saw betrayal in every shadow, heard conspiracies in every rustle of fabric. Sleep became a luxury he could scarcely afford, haunted by nightmares of his empire crumbling around him.

In a desperate attempt to regain control, Baznoon ordered the construction of new fortifications around his palace, transforming it into an impenetrable fortress. He intensified surveillance, deploying an army of spies and informants to ferret out any sign of rebellion. He even resorted to using magical wards and enchantments, further isolating himself from his people.

Yet, the rebellion continued to gain momentum. The information Stanya had delivered had provided a roadmap to his weaknesses, exposing vulnerabilities Graffik had never considered. The rebels, now better organized and equipped, launched daring attacks on strategic locations, chipping away at Graffik's power base. His attempts at suppression only served to strengthen their resolve.

Graffik's once-unwavering confidence was crumbling, replaced by a gnawing fear. He saw the reflection of his own despair in the eyes of his advisors, his courtiers, even in the polished surface of his obsidian throne. The whispers of rebellion had grown into a roar, echoing in the very halls of his palace, threatening to consume him.

He summoned his most trusted advisor, Lord Valerius, a man known for his unwavering loyalty and ruthless efficiency. Valerius, a seasoned strategist, had witnessed the rise and fall of numerous emperors, understanding the intricate dance of power and politics. His face, usually composed and impassive, bore the weight of concern as he entered the throne room.

"Lord Valerius," Baznoon began, his voice raspy, devoid of its usual authority, "the situation is more dire than we thought." He spoke of the growing strength of the rebellion, of the betrayal within his ranks, of the ever-present threat to his rule.

Valerius listened patiently, his gaze unwavering. He had witnessed Graffik's descent into paranoia, the slow erosion of his confidence. He knew that Graffik's fury, once a weapon of intimidation, had become a self-destructive force.

"My Emperor," Valerius responded calmly, his voice measured, "we must adapt. We cannot rely on brute force alone. We need a more sophisticated approach, one that addresses the underlying grievances fueling this rebellion. The people are suffering, my Emperor. Their discontent has been ignored for too long."

The suggestion was audacious, challenging Graffik's iron-fisted approach. But Baznoon, stripped of his usual arrogance, considered it. He recognized the truth in Valerius's words. His reign had been marked by extravagance and oppression, alienating his people and sowing the seeds of rebellion.

"What do you propose, Valerius?" Baznoon asked, his voice barely a whisper. He had never considered compromising his authority, but now, facing the impending collapse of his empire, he was willing to listen.

Valerius outlined a plan, a daring strategy involving a combination of appeasement and strategic alliances. He proposed implementing some reforms, addressing the immediate needs of the populace to reduce unrest. He suggested reaching out to neutral factions, forging alliances to isolate the rebels and weaken their support base. He even proposed a temporary ceasefire to create an opportunity for negotiation and reconciliation.

The plan was a gamble, a risky proposition that could backfire spectacularly. But Baznoon, facing the grim reality of his crumbling empire, recognized that it was his only chance. He had spent years building his empire with an iron fist; now he had to try rebuilding it with something far more delicate: understanding and diplomacy. Graffik's response, far from being a simple act of aggression, was about to become a complex and crucial decision that would determine the fate of his empire and the lives of his people.

The seeds of rebellion, once easily dismissed, were now bearing bitter fruit, forcing Graffik to confront the consequences of his own actions.

The wind carried the scent of pine and damp earth, a stark contrast to the suffocating opulence of Baznoon Graffik's palace. Stanya, her breath ragged but her spirit resolute, stood on the precipice of the Whispering Woods, the stolen documents clutched tight against her chest. The journey had been brutal – a relentless chase across treacherous terrain, punctuated by close calls that still sent shivers down her spine. She had seen Najeem's strength, his fierce protectiveness, even a flicker of something akin to tenderness in his usually guarded gaze. Their alliance, forged in the crucible of shared danger, felt strangely fragile yet surprisingly strong.

The Outerlands stretched before her, a patchwork of rugged hills and verdant valleys, a landscape untouched by Graffik's iron fist. She could feel the pulse of rebellion here, a quiet defiance simmering beneath the surface. This was not the desperate, scattered resistance she'd expected; this was something more organized, more determined. Small groups of farmers, their faces grim but resolute, helped her navigate the hidden paths, sharing meager rations and providing vital information about the growing resistance movement.

They spoke of Commander Lyra, a legendary warrior woman who had rallied the disparate factions into a cohesive force. Lyra was more than just a military leader; she was a symbol of hope, a beacon in the encroaching darkness of Baznoon Graffik's tyranny. Legends spoke of her uncanny ability to anticipate her enemies' moves, her unwavering loyalty to the people, and a strategic mind that could outmaneuver even the most seasoned general. Stanya felt a surge of excitement, a newfound hope that had been dormant since her capture. This wasn't just a desperate fight for survival; it was a revolution gaining momentum.

As she approached the rebel encampment nestled deep within the Whispering Woods, a sense of anticipation mixed with apprehension filled her. The camp was alive with activity – the rhythmic clang of blacksmiths forging weapons, the hushed whispers of strategists plotting their next move, the comforting scent of woodsmoke mingling with the earthy aroma of the forest. A buzz of energy thrummed through the air, the collective heartbeat of a people rising against oppression.

Stanya delivered the documents to Commander Lyra, a woman whose presence commanded respect even before a word was spoken. Lyra was tall and commanding, her eyes the colour of a stormy sea, reflecting both the strength and the wisdom she possessed. Her dark hair, braided with silver threads, cascaded down her back, a testament to years spent battling against overwhelming odds.

Lyra studied the documents, her lips pressed into a thin line as she meticulously reviewed the information. The revelations contained within were staggering: detailed accounts of Baznoon Graffik's corruption, evidence of his alliances with foreign powers, and a chilling expose of his secret plans to consolidate even greater power. The documents detailed a network of spies and informants operating within the rebel factions themselves, a chilling reminder that the enemy wasn't only at the gates, but also within their ranks.

"This changes everything," Lyra finally murmured, her voice low but firm. "This information is far more valuable than we could have ever hoped for." She paused, her gaze sweeping over Stanya's tired yet determined face. "You have done a great service, Stanya. Your bravery has brought us closer to victory than we ever dared to dream."

Word of Stanya's daring infiltration spread like wildfire through the camp, bolstering the rebels' morale. The stolen documents revealed Graffik's vulnerabilities, exposing the cracks in his seemingly impenetrable armor. The rebels, previously divided by internal conflicts and mistrust, now found a renewed sense of unity and purpose. They were no longer fighting a losing battle against an invincible tyrant; they were fighting against a vulnerable enemy, and victory seemed within their grasp.

The information also revealed a weakness within Baznoon Graffik's ranks: a deep-seated resentment among his own officers and advisors, fuelled by years of exploitation and betrayal. Lyra devised a plan to exploit this dissension, sowing further discord amongst Graffik's loyalists, turning them against each other and effectively weakening his power base from within. The plan was audacious, risky, but necessary if they were to succeed.

The days that followed were a whirlwind of activity. Lyra's strategic brilliance combined with Stanya's knowledge of Graffik's court resulted in a carefully orchestrated campaign of misinformation and subtle sabotage. Rebel cells, strengthened by the newly acquired intelligence, launched a series of coordinated attacks, disrupting supply lines, dismantling communication networks, and sowing chaos within the ranks of Baznoon Graffik's forces. Graffik's once-unwavering grip on power was beginning to slip.

Meanwhile, Najeem, still haunted by his escape and the lingering image of Graffik's daughter, found himself drawn back towards the conflict. His training urged him to stay away from the fray, to focus on his own survival. However, the fire of rebellion, stoked by the news of Stanya's success and the growing whispers of Commander Lyra's strategic brilliance, ignited a sense of loyalty in him, a potent counterpoint to his initial desire for escape.

He had joined the rebellion not out of a sudden sense of ideological commitment, but out of a deep-seated sense of justice and a burning desire to protect the people who had sheltered him during his escape. He found himself gravitating towards Lyra's camp, drawn by the energy and the shared purpose that thrummed through the rebel community. His skills, honed through years of brutal training, were suddenly invaluable to the cause.

He began assisting the rebels in their campaign, his fighting prowess proving invaluable. He moved like a phantom, swiftly neutralizing enemy patrols and delivering precise strikes that disrupted the enemy's operations. His skill in hand-to-hand combat, his tactical acumen, and his ruthless efficiency became legend amongst the rebels, quickly earning him a position of trust and influence.

The battlefield became a crucible, forging a new bond between Najeem and Stanya, forged not only in shared danger but in mutual respect and admiration. Their initial conflict, fuelled by misunderstanding and suspicion, had been replaced by a deep-seated camaraderie, strengthened by shared victories and close calls. They were two individuals, united by a shared fight, learning to trust each other implicitly, their bond deepening with each passing day.

As the rebels continued their campaign, whispers of their progress reached even the farthest corners of the empire. Graffik's reign of terror, once absolute, now faced a formidable challenge. The seeds of rebellion, planted long ago, had finally sprouted into a force powerful enough to challenge his authority. His meticulous control was crumbling, replaced by a rising tide of defiance that threatened to engulf his empire. The glimmer of hope, once a faint flicker in the darkness, now blazed with the fierce intensity of a thousand burning stars. The revolution was underway. The battle for the empire had truly begun.

Chapter 5: Shadows of the Past

The flickering candlelight cast long shadows across Stanya's face, revealing the fine lines etched around her eyes – lines earned not by age, but by years spent navigating treacherous political landscapes and dodging blades in the dead of night. She sat huddled in a rough-hewn chair in the Outerlands rebel camp, the rough wool of her cloak scratching against her skin, a stark contrast to the silks and velvets she'd worn in Graffik's court. Najeem, his gaze fixed on the flames, sat opposite her, a silent observer, the events of their shared escape still raw in their minds. The silence stretched, heavy with unspoken questions, until finally, Stanya spoke, her voice low and husky.

"It's time," she said, her words barely a whisper. The confession wasn't easy. It was a peeling back of layers, a revelation of a life lived in the shadows, a life forged in the crucible of betrayal and loss. She spoke of her childhood in a small village nestled in the shadow of the Whispering Mountains, a place of idyllic beauty that was shattered by Graffik's expansionist ambitions. Her family, respected healers and herbalists, had been targeted for their knowledge of rare medicinal plants coveted by the Imperial court. Their quiet existence was violently ripped apart, their home burned to the ground, her parents brutally murdered before her eyes. She was just a child, but the image of their lifeless bodies, the smell of smoke and ash, remained indelibly etched in her memory.

"They took everything from me," Stanya continued, her voice cracking. "My home, my family, my innocence. But they didn't break me. The fire that consumed my home ignited a fire in my soul. A fire of defiance."

She recounted her escape, her harrowing journey through the mountains, where she learned to survive – to hunt, to fight, to disappear into the wilderness. She found refuge with a band of outcasts and rebels, who, like her, had suffered at the hands of Graffik. They were the ones who honed her skills, training her in the arts of espionage, deception, and combat. They taught her to gather information, to move like a shadow, to become a whisper in the wind. They helped her transform her grief into a weapon, a tool to fight for justice and retribution. She learned to use her knowledge of herbs and poisons, not to heal, but to subdue and incapacitate her enemies. The healers' knowledge was twisted, inverted, repurposed for a different purpose – survival.

"I became a ghost," she said, a faint smile playing on her lips, a disturbing juxtaposition to the gravity of her words. "A phantom haunting the halls of power. I worked in the shadows, gathering intelligence, crippling Graffik's plans, one piece at a time."

She told Najeem about her previous missions, meticulously planned infiltrations into enemy strongholds, daring heists of vital documents and weapons, close calls that had sent shivers down her spine even years later. She described the intricate networks she'd built, the web of informants and allies she'd cultivated, the trust she'd earned and sometimes betrayed, depending on the needs of the mission. She revealed the meticulous planning behind her infiltration of Graffik's court, the countless hours spent studying court protocols, disguising her appearance, mastering the nuances of Baznoon Graffik's personality and his circle of advisors. It was a game of cat and mouse, she explained, a constant dance between deception and discovery, a high-stakes game where one wrong move could cost her everything.

The jeweled comb, she revealed, was more than just a hiding place for the stolen information. It was a family heirloom, a symbol of her heritage, a silent testament to the life she had lost. Keeping it hidden had been a personal challenge, a way of honoring her parents' memory. The comb was not just a means to an end; it represented a personal commitment, a defiant act of remembrance against the systematic destruction of her past.

Najeem listened intently, his eyes reflecting the flickering candlelight. He understood her pain, her rage, the driving force behind her actions. He saw in her a mirror reflection of his own journey, a path carved out of loss and fueled by a burning desire for revenge. His silence was not indifference; it was a deep empathy, a silent acknowledgment of the shared burden of a past filled with hardship and violence.

As Stanya's story reached its climax, she spoke of the moment she'd realized her family wasn't merely victims. Her parents, in their quiet way, had been involved in a secret rebellion, a network so deeply hidden it had only been revealed through their violent deaths. They'd collected and shared information, challenging Graffik's authority in ways she hadn't understood at the time. Their seemingly mundane work had been a subversive act, a slow chipping away at the foundation of the Empire. Their death had not just ended their lives, but had inadvertently revealed the network. She had stumbled upon their hidden messages, concealed within the very herbs and medicinal plants they'd cultivated. It had been a hidden legacy, one that she had unknowingly inherited.

This knowledge was crucial in understanding her motivations and her skills. It wasn't simply training that had made her a master spy, but a deep-seated personal drive, a blood oath to avenge her family and bring down the man who had destroyed their lives. The revelation was powerful, shifting the perspective on her actions from simply a skilled spy to a woman fueled by a deeply personal and just vendetta.

The weight of her past hung heavily in the air, but it also seemed to give her a renewed strength, a fire that burned brightly in her eyes. Her story wasn't one of victimhood, but of resilience, of transformation, and of a burning determination to fight for a better future. The fire had tempered her, forging her into a weapon against the very tyranny that had stolen everything from her.

Najeem reached out, his hand gently covering hers. His touch was a silent promise of support, a gesture of solidarity in the face of shared trauma. The shared experience had forged a bond between them, a connection stronger than the initial distrust and suspicion. He knew then that their alliance was not just a matter of survival but a bond cemented in blood, a shared commitment to a cause that was larger than themselves. They were both fighters, survivors, and their paths had intertwined in a way neither could have predicted, their lives forever bound by their shared struggle against Graffik's oppressive rule. The weight of their past now felt shared, less heavy, as they sat in the flickering light of the candle, preparing for the battles to come. The shadows of the past still loomed, but now they faced them together.

The crackling fire cast dancing shadows on the rough-hewn walls of the rebel camp, mirroring the turmoil within Najeem. Stanya, sensing his quiet introspection, leaned closer, the scent of woodsmoke and damp earth mingling with her own perfume, a faint echo of the opulent court she'd left behind. He hadn't spoken much since their escape, his usual easy confidence replaced by a brooding silence that spoke volumes. The shared trauma, the harrowing escape, had stripped away the layers of his carefully constructed exterior, leaving behind a vulnerability that both intrigued and worried her.

He stirred, the movement rustling the worn leather of his tunic, a stark contrast to the fine silks he'd been forced to wear in Graffik's palace. His gaze remained fixed on the flames, his expression unreadable. Finally, he spoke, his voice a low rumble, a sound as rough and unpredictable as the terrain they'd traversed to reach this haven. "My family… they were… different."

Stanya waited, giving him space, understanding the weight of the unspoken words. She knew the stories whispered in the shadows of the court, rumours of Graffik's cruelty, of families torn apart, fortunes seized, and lives shattered. Najeem's silence, his reluctance to share, spoke of a past, far more brutal than she could have imagined.

"They weren't nobles," he continued, the words hesitant at first, then gaining strength. "We were… warriors.

Desert nomads, more akin to the wind than the soil. Generations of us honed our skills, passed down our knowledge, our fighting style, from father to son, mother to daughter. My mother, Zahra... she was legendary. They called her the 'Desert Serpent,' a name whispered with both awe and fear."

He paused, a flicker of a smile playing on his lips, a fleeting glimpse of the man who had captivated Graffik's daughter. "She was swift, lethal, and utterly fearless. She taught me everything I know – swordsmanship, strategy, survival in the harshest conditions. She instilled in me a discipline, a resilience that Graffik's gilded cages couldn't break."

Stanya listened, captivated by his words, her own past experiences echoing his. She too, had known a life of hardship, of constant training, of honing her skills to survive in a world that sought to exploit her talents. The parallels between their upbringings were striking – both forged in the fires of adversity, both shaped by the need to fight for their survival.

"My father," Najeem continued, his voice softening, the harsh edges smoothing out, "he was different. A scholar, a strategist, a man of quiet strength. He taught me the importance of strategy, of planning, of anticipating your opponent's moves. He believed in diplomacy, in using words as weapons when necessary. He balanced my mother's raw power with a keen intellect, and instilled in me the importance of strategic thinking, helping me understand the intricacies of political maneuvers long before my involuntary trip to Graffik's court."

He traced the outline of a faded scar on his forearm, a thin, jagged line that spoke of a past filled with conflict. "He disappeared when I was twelve. Vanished without a trace. They say he was taken by Graffik's agents, his knowledge deemed too valuable to let slip away, but my mother never gave up hope. She searched for him relentlessly, tirelessly, until…" He trailed off, his voice choked with unshed tears.

The silence hung heavy between them, the crackling fire the only sound in the dimly lit tent. Stanya reached out, her hand covering his, offering unspoken solace. She knew the pain of loss, the agonizing uncertainty of not knowing what happened to a loved one. Her own parents had been casualties of Graffik's insatiable hunger for power.

"My mother," he continued, his voice regaining its strength, "she never stopped fighting. Even after my father's disappearance, she continued to train me, to prepare me for a world that was increasingly hostile. She taught me not just how to fight, but how to survive, how to endure. She instilled in me the courage to fight back, the strength to defy injustice. She taught me the power of unity and resistance. We weren't just a family; we were a fighting force, a small but significant rebellion against tyranny."

He clenched his fist, the memory clearly impacting him. "Our tribe was small, but fierce. We were self-sufficient and strong, but when Graffik's army arrived, they were no match for the combined might of Graffik's superior firepower. They took our land, our freedom, and then, they took my mother. I was captured, but I escaped. But to this day, I have no idea what became of my mother."

He looked at Stanya, his eyes reflecting the firelight, conveying a depth of sorrow and unresolved grief that transcended mere words. "Graffik's agents weren't just after my father's knowledge; they were after our legacy, our strength. They feared what my mother and I could achieve together, the power of our combined knowledge and abilities."

Stanya nodded, understanding dawning within her. Najeem's story wasn't just a personal tragedy; it was a microcosm of Graffik's tyrannical rule, a testament to the systematic dismantling of families and communities that stood in his way. His family's story reflected the fate of countless others throughout the land.

"Graffik," he said, his voice hardening, "he underestimated us. He thought he could break us, but he couldn't. He didn't account for the resilience, the fighting spirit, we'd learned from our ancestors. He didn't realize that the Desert Serpent's spirit lives on."

He paused, then added, a quiet determination in his voice. "My escape wasn't just for myself. It's for my mother, for my father, for my people. I will find her. I will avenge their suffering. And I will help bring down Graffik."

Stanya squeezed his hand, her own resolve hardening. She understood his commitment, his unwavering dedication to justice. Their shared plight, their shared past, had forged a bond that went beyond the simple alliance of convenience born from their escape. They were united by a shared purpose, a shared enemy, and a shared past – a past that fueled their determination to fight for a future where families were safe, communities flourished, and tyranny was overthrown. The shadows of the past still loomed, but now, they faced them together, their strength multiplied by their shared struggle. The fire crackled merrily, a silent witness to the pact forged between two warriors, bound by a shared past and a common goal. Their journey was far from over, but for now, they found solace and strength in their shared vulnerability, in the knowledge that they were not alone in their fight. The desert wind howled outside, a mournful cry, but inside the tent, a new hope was kindled, a flame as bright and unwavering as the fire that burned between them. The scent of woodsmoke and damp earth mingled with the faint echo of the opulent court left behind, as they embraced in silent understanding, their futures, once uncertain, now inextricably intertwined. The whispers of their families, their ancestral legacy, echoed around them, strengthening their resolve. Their past had brought them together; their future would determine the fate of the Empire.

The relative peace of the rebel camp was shattered not by the howling desert winds, but by a whisper, a venomous seed planted in the fertile ground of mistrust. It began subtly, a misplaced weapon, a missing supply, minor inconveniences that individually seemed insignificant. But each incident, like pebbles dropped into still water, created ripples that spread, widening into a chasm of suspicion. The whispers started amongst the guards, then spread to the common soldiers, finally reaching the ears of the leaders. A traitor lurked within their ranks.

Stanya, ever vigilant, noted the shift in atmosphere. The easy camaraderie, the shared jokes around the fire, were replaced by strained silences and furtive glances. The air crackled with unspoken accusations, a tension thicker than the desert dust that coated everything. She saw Najeem, usually quick with a jest or a playful jab, withdrawn, his gaze constantly sweeping the camp, searching for the phantom enemy within. His usual relaxed demeanor was replaced by a quiet intensity that mirrored her own growing unease.

The first overt act was the assassination attempt on Jarrod, the charismatic leader of the Outerlands rebellion. He'd survived – a lucky shot that grazed his shoulder – but the act itself was a stark revelation. Jarrod, a man renowned for his compassion and strategic brilliance, had become the target of an internal betrayal. The question wasn't who, but why. And who was next?

Suspicion fell, initially, on the newcomers – a band of desert nomads who had pledged their allegiance only weeks prior. Their loyalty had always seemed tenuous, their past shrouded in mystery. They were hardened warriors, skilled fighters, but their motivations remained opaque. Stanya, privy to the intricacies of espionage, saw the danger, but also saw the easy scapegoating. She knew that to solidify the group, and to find the real traitor, the deeper issues needed to be explored.

Najeem, ever the pragmatist, pressed for immediate action. He favored a swift, decisive strike against the suspected nomads, believing that swift action would restore order. He argued that their presence was a destabilizing force, and that their removal would bolster morale. His instincts, honed in the brutal realities of war, were for immediate, decisive action. But Stanya urged caution, advocating for a thorough investigation before resorting to violence.

"We cannot afford to make mistakes," she argued, her voice calm but firm, "Accusations without proof will only fracture our alliance further. We need to find the true traitor, not sacrifice innocent lives based on suspicion." Her knowledge of courtly intrigue, of the subtle manipulation of power, gave her a different perspective, one that favored strategy over rash action.

Their clash of viewpoints became a microcosm of the growing division within the rebel camp. Najeem's impatience clashed with Stanya's methodical approach. Their shared past, the bond forged in the fires of their escape, began to strain under the weight of their conflicting strategies. The trust between them, once unshakeable, felt brittle, threatened by the shadows of suspicion that darkened the camp.

The investigation, painstakingly slow, uncovered fragments of truth hidden amidst layers of deceit. Secret meetings in the dead of night, coded messages etched on scraps of leather, whispers carried on the desert wind – all pointed towards a figure far closer to the heart of the rebellion than anyone had imagined.

The traitor wasn't a nomad; it was Elara, Jarrod's most trusted advisor, a woman who had served him faithfully for years. The revelation sent shockwaves through the camp. Elara, known for her unwavering loyalty and sharp intellect, possessed access to all of Jarrod's strategies and plans. Her betrayal was not only a personal one but a strategic blow to the rebellion's very existence.

The motive, when discovered, was as shocking as the betrayal itself. Elara wasn't motivated by greed or power. Her brother, captured and tortured by Graffik, had been promised his freedom in exchange for information vital to the rebellion. Graffik, knowing the rebellion was growing stronger and that his reign was threatened, had used Elara's love for her family as a weapon. He had manipulated her, exploiting her deepest vulnerabilities.

The discovery of Elara's treachery ignited a firestorm of conflicting emotions. There was rage, of course, at the betrayal of trust, at the deliberate sabotage of the rebellion. But there was also a deep sense of sorrow, of understanding the impossible choice Elara had been forced to make. The cruel hand of Graffik, reaching even into the heart of the rebel alliance, had shown the true extent of his ruthlessness.

Najeem, still raw with the weight of his own enslavement, found himself grappling with Elara's plight. He understood the depths of despair, the agonizing choices that could be forced upon a person when loved ones are threatened. His anger remained, but it was tempered with a chilling understanding of the lengths to which Graffik was prepared to go to retain his power.

Stanya, recognizing the delicate balance required, proposed a plan. They would exploit Elara's situation, using her knowledge of Graffik's strategies against him. The information Elara had provided could be used to create a counter-strategy, turning Graffik's own tactics against him. It was a risky gamble, one that required carefully calculated steps, but it was a chance to strike at the heart of Graffik's power and to potentially save Elara's brother.

The situation was tense, the future uncertain. The betrayal had shaken the foundations of the rebel alliance, exposing vulnerabilities and fracturing trust. Yet, from the ashes of treachery, a new kind of unity emerged. The shared understanding of the depth of Graffik's cruelty, the knowledge of his willingness to exploit the deepest human connections for his own ends, forged a new bond of shared purpose. Stanya and Najeem, though their paths had diverged in the wake of Elara's betrayal, found themselves drawn together once more, unified by the desperate fight for survival and the relentless pursuit of justice. The desert wind still howled, a constant reminder of the harsh reality of their situation, but within the hearts of the rebels, a new flame of defiance burned brightly, fueled by the betrayal that had nearly destroyed them and a renewed determination to see Graffik overthrown. The journey ahead was still fraught with danger, but they faced it together, their alliance stronger, their purpose clearer, forged in the crucible of betrayal. The shadows of the past still loomed, but now, they were armed not only with weapons but with the knowledge of their enemy's deepest tactics, and a renewed determination to fight for a future free from his tyrannical grasp. The whispers of betrayal still echoed in the camp, but they were slowly being replaced by a murmur of resolve, a quiet promise of revenge against Graffik and the hope of a better future. The cost of that future, however, remained high – a constant reminder of the sacrifices made and the battles yet to come.

The desert sun beat down mercilessly, baking the rebel encampment into a shimmering mirage of dust and sweat. The air, thick with the scent of desperation and woodsmoke, held a palpable tension, the aftermath of the betrayal still clinging to them like a shroud. Stanya, her normally sharp eyes clouded with fatigue, watched the horizon, the vast expanse offering little comfort. She traced the outline of the stolen map, its intricate details hinting at

Graffik's intricate network of spies and informants, a network she had inadvertently exposed with her infiltration.

Najeem, ever vigilant, stood beside her, his hand resting on the hilt of his worn scimitar. The betrayal had hit him hard; the violation of trust within their ranks had mirrored the insidious treachery he'd witnessed within Graffik's court. His usual easy confidence was replaced by a grim determination, his gaze constantly scanning their surroundings. He knew Graffik wouldn't let this slide. He wouldn't simply let a rebellion fester on his doorstep.

Their quiet vigil was broken by the arrival of Kaelen, the grizzled leader of the Outerlands rebels, his face etched with worry lines deepened by the recent events. He was a man who had weathered countless storms, his resolve forged in the harsh crucible of years of resistance against Baznoon Graffik's tyrannical rule, but even he looked strained.

"They're coming," Kaelen announced, his voice low and grave. "Graffik's forces. Not a small skirmish; a full-scale assault."

A murmur rippled through the assembled rebels. Fear, a natural and understandable response, was a palpable presence. But beneath the fear, a flicker of defiance burned. They had faced worse; they had survived betrayals before. They would face this, too.

"He wouldn't risk so much unless he knew something," Stanya said, her voice cutting through the apprehension. The map, a chilling reminder of Graffik's reach, came back into focus. "His spies... they must have uncovered more than we thought."

Kaelen nodded grimly. "We underestimated him. He's not just a brute; he's a strategist. This isn't just a retaliation; it's a calculated move."

The ensuing days were a blur of frantic activity. The rebel camp, once a haven of relative peace, transformed into a fortress preparing for war. Supplies were rationed, defenses reinforced, and strategies discussed in hushed tones. Stanya, despite her exhaustion, worked tirelessly, using her knowledge of Graffik's methods to anticipate his tactics. She shared the information gleaned from the stolen map, highlighting potential attack routes and weaknesses in Graffik's defenses.

Najeem, meanwhile, trained the other warriors, honing their skills and boosting their morale. His experience in Graffik's gladiatorial arena, a place where only the strong survived, made him a natural leader in times of crisis. He instilled in them not just fighting techniques but a fierce sense of purpose, the unwavering belief that they were fighting for something greater than themselves – a future free from oppression.

Their shared experience, their mutual understanding of Graffik's cruelty, brought them closer, the bond forged in the crucible of their shared escape strengthening with each passing hour. Their relationship, initially fraught with suspicion, now blossomed into a fierce camaraderie, a silent acknowledgement of their interdependence.

Graffik's forces arrived at dawn, a tide of soldiers and war machines dwarfing the rebel camp. The air vibrated with the thunder of approaching cavalry and the relentless clang of weaponry. The attack was swift and brutal, a calculated display of overwhelming force designed to crush any resistance before it could even begin. The rebels fought with the desperation of cornered animals, their numbers vastly outmatched, but their spirits undeterred.

The battle raged for hours, a chaotic ballet of steel and blood, death and defiance. Stanya, despite her non-combatant background, found herself fighting alongside the rebels, her agility and resourcefulness proving unexpectedly invaluable. She used her knowledge of the terrain to outwit the enemy, guiding the rebels to strategic positions, and using her wits to disable enemy war machines.

Najeem, a whirlwind of motion and steel, carved a path through the enemy ranks, his every strike precise and deadly. He fought not only for the survival of the rebels but also to honor the memory of those who had fallen. He fought for a future where the memory of their sacrifice would be a source of strength rather than sorrow.

The battle was turning against them. Graffik's forces were relentless, their numbers seemingly endless. Just as despair threatened to engulf them, a beacon of hope emerged from the west: reinforcements arrived, a contingent of loyal tribesmen, long-time allies of the Outerlands. They had been waiting for the right moment, anticipating Graffik's calculated move.

With the tide turned, the battle became a desperate struggle for survival. Stanya and Najeem, fighting side-by-side, found themselves at the heart of the conflict, their actions inspiring those around them. They faced the onslaught with grim determination, their fighting spirit fueled by the shared purpose that bound them together.

As the dust settled, the sun dipped below the horizon, painting the sky in hues of blood orange and bruised purple.

The rebels had won, but the victory came at a heavy price. Many had fallen, their sacrifice a testament to their unwavering courage and devotion to the cause.

Graffik's gambit, a calculated risk to crush the rebellion, had failed. But his defeat was not decisive. It was a setback, a temporary reprieve. Baznoon Graffik would undoubtedly strike again, his wrath unleashed upon those who dared defy him.

As the surviving rebels tended to the wounded, a chilling awareness settled over the camp. The shadows of the past lingered, and Graffik's reach extended far beyond the battlefield. The fight was far from over. The struggle for freedom would continue, a relentless battle against a formidable foe. But amidst the devastation and the grief, there was a new sense of unity, a stronger resolve, born from shared sacrifice and the undeniable truth of their shared purpose. Stanya and Najeem, their bond strengthened by the crucible of battle, would lead the way. Graffik's gambit had failed, but the game was far from over. The future held many more challenges, but they faced them together, ready to confront the relentless onslaught of Graffik's wrath, knowing that the fight for freedom was a long and arduous journey. Their path was still fraught with danger, but together, they would continue their fight, their commitment unshaken, their determination unwavering, their hearts fueled by hope and the memory of those lost.

The wind, a cruel whisper across the desolate landscape, carried with it the scent of blood and the ghosts of fallen comrades. Stanya huddled deeper into her worn cloak, the desert chill seeping into her bones despite the oppressive heat of the day. The victory felt hollow, a pyrrhic triumph bought with a terrible price. The map, a roadmap to Graffik's underbelly, was safely delivered, but the weight of responsibility pressed down on her, heavy as the desert sand. She looked to Najeem, his silhouette stark against the dying light, his gaze fixed on the endless horizon. The shared trauma, the brutal dance of survival, had forged a bond between them, a silent understanding that transcended words. Yet, beneath the surface of their newfound camaraderie, a simmering tension persisted.

Najeem, ever the warrior, paced restlessly, his hands clenched into fists. The escape from Graffik's clutches had been a harrowing ordeal, a brutal ballet of blades and betrayal. The memory of his captivity, the degradation, the constant threat of violence, still haunted him. He had vowed to return for Graffik's daughter, a promise etched in the very fiber of his being. But the path ahead was fraught with peril, a treacherous labyrinth of political intrigue and deadly adversaries. He felt the pull of his oath, the weight of his commitment, but also the gnawing fear of failure. The freedom he had tasted was fragile, fleeting, and the price of retrieving Graffik's daughter could be far steeper than he had imagined.

Their immediate concerns, however, were far more pressing. The rebel forces, though victorious in their initial clash, were depleted, their numbers thinned, their resources dwindling. The outerlands, while offering sanctuary, were not a haven. They were a patchwork of disparate tribes, each with its own agenda, its own allegiances, its own reasons to mistrust outsiders. Stanya knew that their hard-won victory was merely a temporary reprieve, a fleeting moment in the larger war against Graffik's tyranny. Graffik, a cruel and calculating strategist, would not easily relinquish his grip on power. He would retaliate, and the consequences would be devastating.

"We need to consolidate our forces," Stanya said, her voice barely a whisper, the words lost in the vastness of the desert. "We need to secure alliances, find provisions, and prepare for the inevitable counterattack." Her voice, usually filled with steely determination, held a hint of weariness, a reflection of the heavy burden she carried.

Najeem nodded, his expression grim. "The tribes are wary," he replied, his voice low and husky. "Suspicion and mistrust run deep in these lands. Convincing them to join our cause will not be easy." He paused, his gaze distant, lost in a swirl of memories. "Graffik's influence extends far beyond his borders. His spies are everywhere, weaving their web of deceit and betrayal."

Their discussions stretched late into the night, fueled by dwindling rations and the flickering light of a small fire. They debated strategy, analyzed the political landscape, and weighed the risks of various alliances. Each choice presented a potential minefield, a web of complex relationships and unspoken loyalties. The price of freedom, they realized, was far higher than they had initially anticipated. It wasn't just a matter of survival; it was a matter of forging a new order, a world free from Graffik's iron fist.

The following days were a whirlwind of activity. Stanya, with her innate talent for gathering information, began to weave a network of contacts, painstakingly building trust with the wary tribes. Her sharp wit and unwavering resolve proved invaluable, her persuasive arguments gradually chipping away at the ingrained suspicion. She uncovered hidden allegiances, exposed clandestine deals, and skillfully navigated the treacherous currents of tribal politics. She used her knowledge of Graffik's network to her advantage, revealing his manipulative tactics and his network of spies to undermine his influence within the Outerlands.

Najeem, meanwhile, focused on strengthening the rebel forces. He trained the warriors, honing their skills, instilling in them a sense of discipline and purpose. His leadership was inspirational, his unwavering determination infectious. He taught them new fighting techniques, shared his tactical expertise, and instilled in them the importance of unity and courage. Under his tutelage, the rebels transformed from a ragtag band of fighters into a disciplined fighting force, ready to face any challenge.

But their efforts were not without setbacks. Graffik's spies, ever vigilant, infiltrated their ranks, spreading discord and sowing seeds of doubt. Betrayals were commonplace, alliances crumbled, and suspicion hung heavy in the air. Stanya and Najeem faced countless threats, navigating treacherous political landscapes and outsmarting their enemies at every turn. They had to constantly adapt their strategies, changing alliances and shifting loyalties to avoid being undermined by Graffik's pervasive network.

One fateful night, a devastating ambush nearly shattered their fragile alliance. A squadron of Graffik's elite soldiers, guided by a traitor within their ranks, launched a surprise attack on their camp. The ensuing battle was brutal, a chaotic dance of steel and blood. Najeem, a whirlwind of motion, fought with the ferocity of a cornered lion, his blade a blur of deadly precision. Stanya, utilizing her exceptional tactical skills, coordinated the defense, guiding her troops with remarkable skill and courage. The battle raged through the night, a relentless clash of wills and blades under the cold, indifferent gaze of the stars.

Despite their valiant efforts, the rebels suffered heavy losses. Many fell, their dreams of freedom extinguished in a bloody haze. The traitor was finally unmasked and dealt with swiftly, but the betrayal left a deep scar, shaking their faith in one another. The emotional toll of the ambush was nearly as devastating as the physical losses. Stanya, hardened by years of deception and danger, found herself grappling with a deep sense of vulnerability, a stark realization of the fragility of their cause. Najeem struggled with his guilt, his failed attempt to identify and stop the traitor haunting his thoughts.

In the aftermath of the battle, as they tended to the wounded, a profound silence descended upon the camp. The cost of their freedom was becoming increasingly clear – a price paid in blood and sacrifice. The weight of their responsibilities, the enormity of their task, threatened to crush them. Yet, amidst the devastation and despair, a new resolve emerged. They had come too far to turn back. Their losses had only served to strengthen their resolve, deepening the bond between them, their commitment to the fight unwavering.

They had to find a way to overcome their internal wounds, to rebuild trust, and to re-strategize in order to secure their future. The path to freedom was far from easy, but Stanya and Najeem were ready to continue their relentless battle against overwhelming odds, their hearts strengthened by their shared losses, their spirits fueled by the indomitable flame of hope. The price of freedom was high, but they were determined to pay it, together. Graffik's shadow loomed large, but they would not yield. The fight for freedom would continue, even if it meant facing a seemingly endless stream of betrayals and battles, for the memory of those lost, for the dream of a free world, for the love they shared in the face of adversity; their fight would never end.

Chapter 6: A Difficult Choice

The wind whipped Stanya's cloak around her, a biting reminder of the harsh Outerlands. The landscape, a desolate expanse of jagged rock and sparse scrub, mirrored the turmoil in her heart. She'd delivered Graffik's secrets, a meticulously crafted tapestry of his war plans and hidden alliances, to the rebel leader, Lord Theron. Theron, a man whose charisma masked a ruthless ambition, had received the information with a chilling smile, his eyes glinting with a predatory gleam. He'd promised aid, resources, a swift and decisive strike against Baznoon Graffik. But Stanya felt a prickle of unease, a discordant note in the symphony of Theron's carefully crafted words.

Days bled into weeks. The rebels, bolstered by Stanya's intelligence, began to assemble their forces, a motley collection of hardened warriors, skilled assassins, and desperate farmers, united by their hatred of Graffik. Stanya, initially welcomed as a hero, found herself increasingly isolated. Her observations, her sharp intellect, made her privy to the undercurrents of distrust and simmering rivalry amongst Theron's lieutenants. She saw the whispers, the furtive glances, the subtle shifts in alliances. The rebellion wasn't the unified front it appeared to be. It was a powder keg waiting for a spark.

And Stanya held that spark.

She'd noticed inconsistencies in Theron's plans, a deliberate omission of vital information, a calculated ambiguity that hinted at a hidden agenda. She'd seen Theron engaging in clandestine meetings, shadowed figures whispering in corners, exchanging cryptic messages that sent a chill down her spine. Her initial trust in Theron, born of desperation and shared hatred of Graffik, was rapidly eroding, replaced by a gnawing suspicion that something far more sinister was at play.

The weight of this realization pressed down on her. She knew the information she possessed could sway the balance of power, could determine the fate of the rebellion. But revealing Theron's treachery could shatter the fragile alliance, throwing the entire rebellion into chaos, potentially handing Baznoon Graffik a decisive victory. Silence, however, could mean the death of thousands, the continuation of Graffik's brutal rule.

The choice was agonizing. Reveal Theron's betrayal and risk a collapse of the rebellion, potentially sacrificing the hard-won gains and condemning the Outerlands to further oppression? Or maintain silence, allowing Theron to use the information for his own nefarious purposes, perpetuating the cycle of violence and tyranny? Sleep became a luxury she couldn't afford. The nights were filled with restless tossing and turning, the faces of those she'd fought alongside, those she'd sworn to protect, flickering behind her eyelids like dying embers.

She sought solace in the company of Kaelen, a grizzled veteran and Theron's second-in-command. Kaelen, a man whose loyalty was as unwavering as his swordsmanship, had become a trusted confidant, his stoic demeanor a welcome contrast to the treacherous currents surrounding her. She shared her suspicions with him, not revealing the full extent of her knowledge but painting a picture of Theron's deceptive nature. Kaelen listened, his expression unreadable, his silence weighing more heavily than any words.

"He's playing a dangerous game, Stanya," Kaelen finally said, his voice a low rumble. "A game that could cost us everything."

His confirmation solidified her fears. He didn't dismiss her concerns as paranoid ramblings; instead, he acknowledged the peril. But he offered no solutions, only a heavy silence that mirrored the daunting task ahead. She knew he held a similar suspicion, possibly even more concrete evidence, but was bound by a rigid sense of loyalty. He was a veteran soldier, bound by duty to his leader regardless of their methods. He could not betray Theron.

The decision hung over her like a shroud. She spent days meticulously gathering evidence, meticulously documenting Theron's clandestine activities. She searched for a way to expose him without causing the rebellion to fracture, a way to prove his treachery without creating a catastrophic schism. She tried to find an alternative, a third path; a way to subtly steer the rebellion in a better direction without openly accusing Theron.

Her investigation led her to a network of spies and informants operating within Theron's ranks, a clandestine network more loyal to the cause of freedom than to Theron's ambition. These people, operating in the shadows, shared their own evidence, confirming her suspicion that Theron planned to betray the rebellion and seize control for himself. He intended to use Graffik's war plans not to defeat

Baznoon, but to strengthen his own power base, manipulating the conflict for his personal gain.

She knew what she had to do. The risk was immense. The consequences could be devastating. But silence would be a betrayal, a surrender to the tyranny she had fought so hard to overthrow. She'd made her decision. She would expose Theron, even if it meant risking the entire rebellion. The future of the Outerlands rested on the blade of her courage, a courage tempered by despair and fueled by a righteous fury.

Her plan involved a daring gambit, a carefully orchestrated reveal that would place her in significant danger. But she was prepared. She'd spent her life living in the shadows, a master of deception and intrigue. This was the ultimate test of her skills. She had to trust her instincts, trust in the few allies she'd made among Theron's troops. She had to fight for freedom, not just for herself, but for everyone who had suffered under Baznoon Graffik's iron fist. It was a dangerous game, a gamble with the very future of the Outerlands, but she was ready to play.

The night before her planned revelation, she found Kaelen again, under the cloak of darkness. This time, she shared everything – Theron's plot, the evidence she'd gathered, her plan.

Kaelen's face was grim, his eyes showing the weight of the decision that lay before them both. "It's a risk, Stanya," he said, his voice low and grave. "A huge risk. But it's a risk we have to take." He laid a hand on her arm, a gesture of support that transcended words. "We'll be there, when you need us." Their eyes met, a silent pledge of mutual trust and support against the looming darkness.

This was not just a battle against Baznoon Graffik and his empire. This was a battle against the insidious nature of power, a fight for the soul of the rebellion. Stanya, armed with courage and her plan, was ready. The price of freedom was steep, but she was ready to pay it, whatever the cost. The dawn approached, and with it, a reckoning.

The biting wind of the Outerlands did little to chill the fire that burned within Najeem. He stood on the precipice of a decision, a precipice far steeper and more treacherous than any cliff face he'd ever scaled. He'd escaped Graffik's clutches, a feat that seemed miraculous even to him. The escape, a chaotic dance of shadow and blade, had left him bruised, battered, but alive. He'd left behind the gilded cage of the palace, the suffocating sweetness of Baznoon Graffik's daughter, Lyra, and the gnawing guilt that clung to him like a second skin. His escape had been fueled by a desperate need to protect Lyra, a noble impulse that now felt tainted by a bitter truth that clawed at his conscience.

He'd found sanctuary in a small, isolated village nestled amongst the rugged peaks of the Outerlands. The villagers, hardened by years of living on the fringes of the empire, had been wary at first, their eyes assessing him with a mixture of suspicion and pity. But Najeem's skill with a blade, his quiet demeanor, and his evident desperation had eventually won their trust. They offered him shelter, food, and the rare commodity of anonymity. But anonymity couldn't erase the past, and the past was a relentless tide, pulling him under with each passing day.

It began with whispers, snippets of conversations overheard around crackling fires. He heard stories of the warlord, Kaelen, a man whose name was uttered with a mixture of awe and terror. Kaelen, the butcher of the northern plains, the man who'd razed villages and left trails of blood in his wake. Kaelen, whose cruelty was legendary, whose name was synonymous with brutality. The whispers grew louder, more insistent, weaving a disturbing narrative around him, a narrative that chilled him to the bone. He dismissed them at first, brushing them off as the fanciful tales of a people desperate to assign blame for their hardships. But the details were too precise, too vivid, too familiar.

One evening, a grizzled elder, his face a roadmap of wrinkles etched by time and hardship, approached Najeem. The elder's eyes, though clouded with age, held an unnerving clarity. He placed a worn leather-bound book in Najeem's hands, its pages brittle with age. "This belonged to your father," he rasped, his voice a dry whisper that barely carried on the wind. Najeem's breath hitched. His father, a man he barely remembered, a shadow in the tapestry of his childhood, a void that had haunted him his entire life.

The book contained meticulously detailed accounts of Kaelen's campaigns, precise descriptions of battles, and chillingly accurate depictions of the warlord's tactics. But interwoven throughout the military accounts were personal entries, written in a familiar, elegant script. Entries that detailed not only Kaelen's conquests, but also his moral decay, his descent into madness, fueled by power and bloodlust. Entries that revealed the deep-seated hatred that fueled his cruelty. And most importantly, entries that revealed his identity. His real identity. His father's identity.

Najeem's world tilted on its axis. His father, the man he'd barely known, was Kaelen, the butcher, the monster whose atrocities had scarred the land. The realization slammed into him with the force of a physical blow, leaving him reeling, his carefully constructed world collapsing around him. The noble impulse that had driven him to escape, to protect Lyra, now felt like a grotesque betrayal. He, the son of Kaelen, had sought to shield another from the very tyranny his father embodied. The irony was a bitter pill to swallow.

The weight of his heritage was crushing. He was the son of a monster, a legacy he couldn't outrun, couldn't erase, couldn't deny. The villagers, once sympathetic, now eyed him with a mixture of fear and revulsion. Their fear was understandable, but their revulsion stung. He was, after all, a reflection of the very man they feared.

His quest to rescue Lyra, initially a noble act born out of gratitude and affection, now felt tainted, twisted. Could he, the son of Kaelen, truly be worthy of her love? Could he, bearing such a dark heritage, ever hope to protect her from the very evil his father represented? Doubt gnawed at him, a relentless worm feeding on his soul.

He spent days wrestling with his conscience, his past, and his future. He contemplated abandoning his mission, disappearing into the vastness of the Outerlands, leaving Lyra to her fate. He imagined a life of solitude, a life free from the weight of his family's legacy, a life where he could finally escape the shadow of his father's name. But the thought of leaving Lyra, of abandoning the woman he had come to cherish, brought a sharp pang of regret.

He had pledged his life to her safety. His escape hadn't been just for himself, but for Lyra too. Abandoning her now would be a betrayal of a different kind, a betrayal of his own newfound sense of honor. He knew that confronting his past was the only path forward, the only way to truly earn his redemption, the only way to prove to himself, and to Lyra, that he was more than just the son of Kaelen. He was Najeem, and he would determine his own destiny.

The book remained open on a rough-hewn table, the pages whispering stories of bloodshed and despair. But amidst the horror, a flicker of hope remained. A single entry, tucked away in the back, described his father's final days, his moments of regret, his unspoken longing for redemption. It was a small detail, a fragile tendril of humanity within a monster's heart. And it was enough.

It was enough to give Najeem the strength to continue his quest, to fight not just against the Empire, but against his own demons. It was enough to fuel his determination to rescue Lyra, not just for her sake, but for his own. The price of freedom, he realized, wasn't just about escaping Graffik's grasp; it was about confronting the darkness within himself, facing his past, and forging a new path towards a future worthy of his love for Lyra. He would rescue her, and he would do it for both of them. His father's legacy would not define him. His actions, his choices, would shape his future. And he would choose to be a hero. The dawn broke, painting the desolate landscape in shades of hope and determination, mirroring the newfound strength within his heart. His journey was far from over, but he was ready. The price of freedom was high, but Najeem was prepared to pay it, in blood and sacrifice, for the woman he loved and for the future he envisioned. His escape was only the beginning. The real fight, the fight for his soul, had just begun.

Lyra traced the intricate carvings on her prison window, the cold stone a stark contrast to the opulent silks and jewels she'd been accustomed to. The sun, a pale disc in the perpetually overcast sky of the Outerlands prison, cast long shadows across the rough-hewn walls. Her gilded cage had been replaced by one far more austere, a stark reflection of the change in her circumstances. Gone was the adulation, the deferential bows, the endless stream of suitors vying for her attention. Now, she was merely Lyra, a prisoner, stripped of her title, her privilege, and much of her naivety.

The initial despair had given way to a simmering anger, a potent brew of resentment and disillusionment. The escape, the thrilling chase, the adrenaline-fueled flight with Najeem—it all seemed like a distant dream now, replaced by the harsh reality of her confinement. She missed the feel of the wind in her hair, the freedom of movement, the intoxicating scent of the woods after a spring rain. More than anything, she missed Najeem. His touch, his smile, the strength in his eyes – a strength that had both terrified and captivated her. His escape had left a void in her heart, a gaping hole that echoed with the silence of her prison cell.

She'd known, on some level, that her father's reign was not benevolent. She'd witnessed glimpses of his cruelty, the casual brutality with which he dispensed justice, or rather, his version of justice. She'd dismissed it as the necessary ruthlessness of a ruler, a means to an end, justifying his actions with the excuse of maintaining order. But now, separated from the comforting illusions of the palace, the truth was laid bare. Her father wasn't just ruthless; he was cruel, tyrannical, and utterly devoid of empathy.

The realization struck her with the force of a physical blow. The weight of her father's actions, the suffering he had inflicted, now pressed upon her, a crushing burden. It was as if the scales had fallen from her eyes, revealing a horrifying panorama of oppression and injustice. She had been a pawn in his game, a gilded ornament used to maintain his power, her affection a tool of manipulation. The thought stung, sharper than any whip. She had been blind, selfish, and complicit.

Her imprisonment wasn't just punishment; it was a lesson, a brutal education in the true nature of her father's rule. She now saw the fear in the eyes of the guards, the silent desperation of the other prisoners, the echoes of suffering that permeated the very stone walls of her cell. She heard the whispers, fragmented stories of lives broken, of families torn apart, of villages razed to the ground. Each whispered word was a hammer blow to her conscience, shattering the fragments of her innocence.

Sleep offered little respite. Her dreams were a kaleidoscope of fractured images: Najeem's face, etched with a mixture of determination and anguish; her father's cold, calculating gaze; the faces of the countless victims of his tyranny. The guilt gnawed at her, a relentless beast feeding on her self-pity. She had been sheltered from the consequences of her father's actions, cocooned in a world of privilege and deceit. Now, exposed to the harsh reality, she was forced to confront the truth, the horrifying truth of her own complicity.

One day, a rough-hewn wooden bowl of gruel was placed before her, along with a small, crumpled piece of parchment. Her heart leaped. It was a letter, smuggled in, she suspected, by one of the guards, a silent act of rebellion against Graffik's iron grip. The letter was short, barely legible, yet it contained a message that sparked a flame of hope within her despair. It spoke of an underground resistance, a growing network of rebels determined to overthrow her father and establish a more just regime. The letter mentioned a rendezvous point, a secret gathering in the shadowed heart of the Outerlands.

The letter was a lifeline, a chance to atone for her past, a way to fight for the future she had previously ignored. She knew the risks. Betrayal, capture, and even death were possibilities. But the thought of passively accepting her fate, of allowing her father's tyranny to continue, was unbearable. She couldn't bear the thought of remaining a silent witness to his cruelty.

The next few days were a blur of careful planning. She utilized her knowledge of the palace, her understanding of its intricacies and its hidden passages – knowledge she had once used to indulge her whims, now deployed for a far nobler purpose. She fashioned a makeshift rope from her bedsheets, a rudimentary tool that could be her salvation or her downfall. She waited for the opportune moment, her heart pounding against her ribs, her breath caught in her throat.

The night was dark, the moon a sliver of light in the inky sky. The guards were lax, their vigilance dulled by routine and weariness. It was the perfect moment. She moved with the grace of a phantom, her movements silent, her steps measured. She scaled the wall, her fingers finding purchase in the rough stone, the cold air biting at her exposed skin. The escape was fraught with peril, a heart-stopping race against time and capture.

As she descended the prison walls, she felt a surge of exhilaration, a heady mixture of fear and determination. This was not merely an escape; it was a rebirth, a shedding of her former self. She was no longer just Graffik's daughter; she was Lyra, a rebel, a fighter, a woman ready to confront her past and forge a new path toward a future worthy of her own redemption. The weight of her father's crown, once a symbol of privilege, now felt like an albatross, a heavy reminder of the suffering she had ignored and the mistakes she had made. But that weight now fueled her. It was the weight of responsibility, the weight of her past actions, and the weight of the future she was determined to build, a future where the sun shone brightly on a land free from the shadow of her father's tyranny. The journey was just beginning, but this time, she was not alone. She had her purpose, and she had her courage. She was ready.

The biting wind whipped Lyra's cloak around her as she hurried across the desolate plains. The Outerlands, a land of stark beauty and harsh realities, was a far cry from the opulent gardens of her father's palace. She clutched the rough-hewn knife given to her by a surprisingly sympathetic prison guard – a woman whose loyalty, Lyra suspected, lay with the growing rebellion against Baznoon Graffik. Lyra had learned much in her captivity, not just about survival, but about the complex web of alliances and betrayals that characterized this world.

Ahead, a flickering firelight punctuated the vast darkness. It belonged to a group of ragged figures huddled around a meager fire, their faces etched with weariness and determination. They were members of the Crimson Hand, a notorious band of rebels known for their ruthlessness and their unwavering opposition to Graffik. Lyra, despite her newfound resolve, felt a prickle of unease. She knew their reputation; stories of their brutality were woven into the fabric of the Outerlands' folklore. But she had no other choice. They were her only hope of finding her way to the sanctuary she craved – a place to regroup, to heal, and to plan her next move.

As she approached, a gruff voice barked a challenge. A hulking man with a scarred face and eyes that glittered like chips of obsidian rose to meet her. He was the leader, they told her later – a woman named Kaia, who carried herself with the quiet authority of a seasoned warrior. Lyra explained her situation, keeping her royal lineage hidden for now. She emphasized her hatred for Graffik, a sentiment that seemed to resonate with the Crimson Hand. Kaia, however, was far from convinced.

"We've seen many who claim to oppose Graffik," Kaia said, her voice as sharp as the wind. "Few mean it. And fewer still are willing to pay the price for that opposition."

Lyra felt a surge of anger. "My father's reign is a stain on this land. I have witnessed his cruelty firsthand. Believe me, I will pay any price."

Kaia studied her for a long moment, her gaze penetrating, assessing. Then, unexpectedly, a low whistle cut through the air. From the shadows emerged a figure – tall, lean, with eyes that held a familiar intensity. Najeem. Lyra gasped, surprise giving way to a hesitant hope.

Najeem, still bearing the scars of his escape from Graffik's clutches, was as surprised as Lyra. Their reunion was far from the romantic reconciliation that Lyra might have secretly hoped for. Instead, it was marked by cautious suspicion. Najeem initially mistook the Crimson Hand for another of Graffik's hunting parties. The tense standoff was only broken by Stanya's sudden arrival. Having delivered her vital intel and secured the necessary support from the Outerlands' resistance cells, she rode toward the rebel camp with the efficiency of a seasoned warrior.

Stanya, ever pragmatic, saw the potential in the unlikely alliance. She knew that Najeem's skills as a warrior would be invaluable, and that Lyra's knowledge of Graffik's court could prove critical. She moved swiftly, her words bridging the gap between the guarded rebels and the two escapees.

"Graffik's grip tightens," Stanya announced, her voice resonating with authority. "We need every ally we can find.

The Crimson Hand's strength in numbers and Lyra's understanding of the palace will be just as essential as Najeem's strength and skill. His connection to Graffik's daughter presents an exceptional opportunity that could destabilize Graffik's reign."

Kaia remained skeptical but saw the strategic advantages. An alliance with Stanya's network and the unique knowledge that both Lyra and Najeem possessed offered them a way to strike directly at the heart of Graffik's power. It was a risky gamble. But desperation was often the mother of all alliances.

The ensuing weeks were a whirlwind of activity. Lyra, shedding the last vestiges of her princess persona, immersed herself in the rebel cause. She utilized her knowledge of court politics to expose Graffik's corruption to the Outerlands' leaders, fueling their rebellion with concrete evidence. Her once-privileged upbringing, now a source of shame, became a potent weapon in the fight for freedom.

Najeem, meanwhile, trained with the Crimson Hand, his fighting skills honed to a razor's edge. He shared his insights into Graffik's guard tactics, informing their strategies, ensuring their attacks were swift, deadly and precise. His rage fueled his determination, pushing him to become even more lethal. His escape from slavery had solidified his resolve to fight until the last breath.

Stanya served as the brains of the operation. She orchestrated a complex network of spies and informants, ensuring that the rebels always had the upper hand. She was the quiet strategist, the chess player moving her pieces across the vast board of the rebellion, anticipating Graffik's every move. Her meticulous planning was what kept them afloat, what guided their every step.

Their unlikely alliance, forged in the crucible of shared adversity, proved surprisingly effective. The Crimson Hand, bolstered by Lyra's insights and Najeem's fighting prowess, launched a series of daring raids against Graffik's supply lines, cutting off his resources and weakening his hold on the Outerlands. Stanya's intelligence network provided them with crucial information, ensuring that each attack was flawlessly executed.

However, Graffik was not one to be taken lightly. He retaliated swiftly and brutally, sending waves of elite soldiers to crush the rebellion. The battles were fierce, bloody affairs, testing the limits of their newfound alliance. Lyra, initially hesitant, found a strange sense of purpose in the midst of the chaos. Her participation in the fighting was often less than proficient, but her determination to challenge the tyranny that had defined her life was unquestionable.

Najeem's strength, honed by years of brutal training, was unmatched. He fought like a man possessed, leading charges with a ferocity that inspired both fear and awe. The relationship between Najeem and Lyra became deeper in those desperate times. Each time one was saved by the other, the initial mistrust transformed into a profound respect, and then to something more.

Stanya, the ever-calm strategist, often found herself caught in the crossfire, relying on her quick thinking and exceptional fighting skills to evade capture or defeat those who sought to thwart her plans. She played her hand perfectly with a deadly efficiency. It was this remarkable strength that kept the alliance strong.

One evening, huddled around a dying fire after a particularly brutal clash, Lyra confessed her true identity to Najeem. She expected anger, disgust, perhaps even betrayal. Instead, she found understanding in his eyes.

"Your father's actions are not yours," Najeem said, his voice low and reassuring. "You have chosen a different path, a better path. And I am honored to fight alongside you."

Their alliance, forged in the fires of rebellion, was more than just a strategic partnership; it was a bond formed in shared suffering and mutual respect. They knew that the road ahead was long and fraught with peril. Graffik's power was still vast, his reach still long. But together, with the unlikely allies by their side, they had a fighting chance. A chance to bring freedom to the Outerlands, and to build a future where the sun could finally shine without the shadow of tyranny looming over them. They were now fighting not only for themselves but for a future where love and loyalty would flourish, a future where the oppressive reign of Baznoon Graffik would finally be a thing of the past. The fight was far from over, but for the first time, they felt a glimmer of hope. The price of freedom had been high, but the reward, they knew, would be worth every sacrifice.

The wind howled a mournful dirge across the jagged peaks of the Dragon's Teeth mountains, a fitting soundtrack to the clandestine meeting unfolding in a hidden cavern. Torches flickered, casting long, dancing shadows on the faces of the assembled rebels. Najeem, his face grim but resolute, stood at the head of a rough-hewn table, a map of Graffik's territories spread before him. Around him were a motley crew: hardened mercenaries, their faces etched with the stories of countless battles; wizened elders, their eyes reflecting generations of oppression; and surprisingly, a contingent of skilled archers from the nomadic Skyborn tribes, their bows strung tight, their gaze unwavering.

Lyra, her presence a beacon of hope amidst the hardened warriors, sat beside Najeem, her hand resting lightly on his. The alliance between the warrior and the princess, initially forged in shared desperation, had blossomed into something deeper, a fragile flower blooming in the barren landscape of rebellion. Her captivity had stripped away her naiveté, replacing it with a steely determination that mirrored Najeem's own.

"We are outnumbered, outmatched, and outgunned," Najeem acknowledged, his voice carrying the weight of the truth. "Graffik's army is vast, its resources seemingly limitless. But they are also complacent. They believe their victory is assured."

A gruff voice cut through the tense silence. "Complacency is a weakness, warrior," said Gorok, a hulking mercenary whose scarred face hinted at a brutal past. "And weaknesses can be exploited."

"Precisely," Najeem agreed, his gaze sweeping across the assembled warriors. "Our strength lies not in brute force, but in strategy, in surprise, and in the unwavering belief in our cause. Stanya's intelligence has provided us with invaluable information – Graffik's supply lines are vulnerable, his defenses are thinly spread in certain key areas."

He pointed to a location on the map, a narrow mountain pass that represented a potential chokepoint. "This is where we will strike. We will lure a significant portion of Graffik's forces into this pass, and then…" He paused, letting the unspoken threat hang heavy in the air. "…then we will crush them."

The plan was audacious, bordering on suicidal, but the desperation of their situation left them with little choice. The whispers of dissent were quickly quelled by the unwavering conviction in Najeem's eyes. He had earned their trust, not only through his unwavering courage, but through his genuine concern for their well-being.

"But how do we lure them?" a young archer, barely a woman, asked, her voice trembling slightly.

"With a distraction," Lyra replied, her voice surprisingly steady. "A feint attack on a less-defended area, far to the north. It will draw their attention, weaken their defenses elsewhere, and create an opening for our main assault."

The plan was meticulously laid out, every detail discussed and debated. The mercenaries pledged their loyalty, fueled by the promise of a handsome reward and a chance to settle old scores with Graffik's tyrannical regime. The elders offered their knowledge of the terrain, their wisdom guiding the strategic deployment of forces. Even the skeptical Skyborn archers, initially reluctant to involve themselves in ground warfare, were convinced by Lyra's charisma and the shared vision of freedom.

Days turned into weeks as the rebels prepared for their audacious strike. They honed their skills, strengthened their bonds, and prepared for the inevitable casualties. Najeem, despite his outwardly stoic demeanor, felt the weight of responsibility pressing down on him. The fate of the Outerlands, and potentially the entire kingdom, rested on his shoulders.

Lyra, sensing his burden, sought him out in the quiet hours of the night. She found him staring at the map, his brow furrowed in concentration. She sat beside him, her hand once again finding his.

"You carry the weight of the world on your shoulders, Najeem," she whispered, her voice soft yet firm. "But you do not carry it alone."

He turned to her, his gaze meeting hers. "I know," he replied, a faint smile playing on his lips. "And that is what gives me strength."

Their relationship, forged in the crucible of rebellion, was unlike anything either had experienced before. It was a love born of shared adversity, a bond strengthened by mutual respect and a shared vision for the future. It was a solace in the midst of chaos, a beacon of hope in the darkness.

As the final preparations were made, a shadow of doubt crept into Najeem's mind. Word had reached them of a traitor within their ranks, a viper hidden amongst the loyal warriors. The identity of the traitor remained unknown, a dangerous uncertainty hanging over their fragile alliance. The potential for betrayal added another layer of complexity to their already perilous mission.

The night before the attack, Najeem assembled his closest allies. Lyra, Gorok, and Elara, the leader of the Skyborn archers, were present. The weight of the upcoming battle hung heavy in the air, but their resolve remained unbroken.

"We must be vigilant," Najeem warned, his voice low and serious. "Graffik has spies everywhere. Trust no one completely, not even your closest allies."

The unspoken accusation hung in the air, a silent acknowledgment of the potential for betrayal within their ranks. Each of them carried the weight of suspicion, unsure of who amongst them might be a double-agent.

"We will proceed as planned," Najeem declared, his voice regaining its strength. "Our victory depends on our unity, our precision, and our unwavering commitment to freedom."

With that, the final preparations were made, each warrior steeling themselves for the coming conflict. The price of freedom, they knew, would be paid in blood, sweat, and sacrifice. But they were willing to pay it, united in their shared dream of a future free from the shadow of Baznoon Graffik's tyranny. The dawn was approaching, bringing with it the promise of a battle that would determine not just their fate, but the fate of the Outerlands and beyond. Their fight for freedom had reached its climax. The final showdown was about to begin.

Chapter 7: Najeem's Infiltration

The air hung thick with the scent of jasmine and fear. Najeem, disguised as a lowly kitchen servant, moved through the labyrinthine corridors of Graffik Baznoon Graffik's palace with the grace of a phantom. His once-ornate clothing had been replaced by roughspun linen, his meticulously groomed hair now hidden beneath a stained cloth cap. The luxury that had once surrounded him felt like a cruel mockery now, a stark contrast to the grim determination that hardened his gaze. Every shadow seemed to whisper with danger, every echoing footstep a potential threat.

His escape from the palace had been a desperate gamble, fueled by a mixture of righteous anger and a fierce protectiveness towards Graffik's daughter, Princess Lyra. He couldn't leave her to the suffocating clutches of her tyrannical father. His plan, however, was audacious, bordering on suicidal. He intended to infiltrate the palace, find Lyra, and facilitate her escape. He knew the risks were immense, but the thought of Lyra's vulnerability spurred him onward. His escape had been aided by Stanya's intel, relayed through coded messages passed via a network of sympathetic rebels.

He navigated the palace using a combination of his own sharp wits and Stanya's detailed maps, meticulously memorized. The maps, painstakingly drawn and updated, detailed every passage, every hidden room, every blind spot in the palace's security. Stanya, despite their brief and initially hostile encounter, proved to be an invaluable ally. He had been skeptical of her motives at first, and it had taken weeks of shared hardship and near-death experiences on their journey to the outerlands to build any semblance of trust. He still held a flicker of wariness; the world they inhabited was filled with treacherous double-crossings, a harsh lesson he had learned early in life. But her knowledge was exceptional.

His first obstacle was bypassing the layers of guards and servants. He relied on his innate ability to blend into the background, a skill honed over years of living in the shadows. His movements were fluid and silent, his gaze unwavering yet unobtrusive. He observed the routines of the guards, noting their patrol patterns and blind spots. He learned their lingo, their signals, mimicking their posture to perfection. He was a chameleon, adapting to his surroundings with unnerving ease. He spent days observing, meticulously planning each step, his mind a whirlwind of strategy and counter-strategy.

One misstep could mean capture, torture, or worse. Graffik was not a man to be trifled with; his cruelty was legendary. Rumors of his dungeon's horrors had been whispered in hushed tones throughout the land, painting a grim picture of unending suffering. Najeem had seen the dark side of power firsthand, even in his brief captivity. He had witnessed Graffik's ruthlessness and the fear he instilled in those around him. It was a fear he was determined to conquer.

He made his way to the royal kitchens, a chaotic hub of activity where he felt somewhat less conspicuous. He learned to move amidst the bustle, efficiently performing his assigned tasks with a practiced hand. He observed the inner workings of the palace, gleaning information from the casual conversations of the staff – gossiping servants revealed secrets, unguarded words betrayed vulnerabilities. He gleaned bits and pieces of information, piecing together a clearer picture of Lyra's confinement and the palace's layout.

He learned about Graffik's increasing paranoia, fueled by the recent loss of intelligence and the escalating rebel threat.

Nights were even more perilous. The palace at night transformed into a different beast, its shadows lengthening, its silence broken only by the occasional creak of a floorboard or the muffled sounds of distant celebrations. Najeem used the cover of darkness to move more freely, his heightened senses acting as his guide. He discovered hidden passages and secret tunnels, relics of past eras, remnants of forgotten intrigues. He relied on his exceptional hearing, picking up on the sounds of approaching footsteps, the distant murmurs of conversations, and the rhythmic creaks of the massive doors which provided a pathway to different chambers. His sense of touch helped to navigate dimly lit corridors. He identified weak points in the masonry, discovered loose floorboards, sensing and evaluating every possible route, anticipating potential threats before they even materialized.

One particularly harrowing night, he narrowly avoided a patrol of elite guards. He pressed himself against a cold, damp wall, his heart pounding against his ribs. He could hear their heavy boots thudding on the stone floor, their voices low and menacing. He remained perfectly still, holding his breath, until the sound of their footsteps faded into the distance. The experience served as a stark reminder of the ever-present danger. Every movement he made was a calculated risk, a delicate dance between boldness and caution.

Days bled into nights as Najeem continued his infiltration. He discovered a network of hidden tunnels that extended far beyond the immediate vicinity of the kitchens. These tunnels were more than mere passages; they were a secret underbelly of the palace, a labyrinth of forgotten chambers and clandestine meeting places. It was in these tunnels that he began to gather more information about Lyra's whereabouts. He learned that she was kept under heavy guard, her movements restricted, her communication with the outside world severed. But the information he uncovered was not only about Lyra; he discovered Graffik's plans for a final, devastating assault on the rebel forces.

This information was vital; it was a crucial piece of the puzzle that could help Stanya and the rebel alliance anticipate and counter Graffik's attack. He knew that the timing was of utmost importance. He was running out of time. Graffik's suspicion was growing, the palace's security tightening. A sense of urgency gripped him, spurring him to act more quickly and decisively. He knew that his chances of success were dwindling with each passing day. He felt the weight of the rebellion on his shoulders, as the potential of success weighed heavily against the almost certain threat of failure. He relied on instinct more than planned strategies.

His plan was now beginning to coalesce. He would use his knowledge of the tunnels to reach Lyra's confinement. He would then use his skills to create a diversion, drawing the attention of the guards away from Lyra's quarters. With Lyra safely out of the palace, he would then make his own escape. The risk was immense, but Najeem was a warrior, a fighter born and bred for adversity. He wouldn't give up on Lyra, not now. He would not let his own imprisonment determine her fate. He had sworn an oath to protect her, even if it meant risking his own life. His heart beat like a drum against his ribs, a powerful rhythm driving his relentless efforts. The fate of Lyra, and perhaps the entire kingdom, hung in the balance.

The outerlands hummed with a nervous energy. Stanya, her escape miraculously successful, found herself in the rough-hewn council chamber of the rebel leader, Theron. The air was thick with the scent of woodsmoke and desperation, a stark contrast to the perfumed opulence of Baznoon Graffik's palace. Theron, a man whose weathered face spoke of countless battles, listened intently as Stanya detailed her findings – meticulously gathered information on Graffik's army deployments, his secret alliances, and the vulnerabilities hidden within his seemingly impenetrable defenses.

She spoke of hidden passages, of weak points in the palace's security, and of the key individuals whose loyalty could be swayed. Her voice, though strained from the ordeal, was steady, precise, each word a carefully placed piece in a complex puzzle. She presented the encrypted communication logs she'd managed to steal, documents detailing Graffik's ruthless expansionist plans and his clandestine dealings with neighboring kingdoms. The council members, a diverse group of warriors, scholars, and strategists, exchanged anxious glances as the gravity of the situation settled upon them.

"This is… invaluable," Theron finally said, his voice low but resonant. He ran a hand through his greying beard, his gaze fixed on Stanya with a mixture of respect and concern. "Graffik's reach extends far beyond the borders of his own kingdom. This information could shift the balance of power in our favor."

Stanya, despite the adrenaline-fueled exhaustion still clinging to her, felt a surge of purpose. Her escape had been perilous, but her mission was far from complete. She knew Najeem was still trapped within the palace walls, and the information she held might be the key to his survival and their joint rebellion. The escape had been harrowing; she had to use the time she had wisely. She needed to use her intelligence to help Najeem.

"There's something else," Stanya continued, her voice barely a whisper. "A warrior named Najeem… he's been imprisoned. He's… a key to this entire operation. He has valuable knowledge of the palace layout and security systems." She explained Najeem's situation, carefully omitting the romantic complications of their shared plight for the sake of strategic clarity. She painted a picture of Najeem's skills and his potential as a valuable asset in their rebellion, emphasizing his loyalty and unwavering determination.

Theron stroked his beard thoughtfully. "Najeem... the name rings a bell. Some whisper he's a formidable warrior." He turned to his advisors, their faces etched with concern and wariness. "But rescuing someone from Graffik's clutches... it's a suicide mission."

"Not necessarily," Stanya countered, her eyes flashing with conviction. "With the right strategy, with the knowledge I've provided, it's possible. We need a diversion, a way to create chaos and draw attention away from the prison quarters. While that happens, Najeem can use his knowledge of the tunnels and secret passages to escape."

The council members began a heated debate, weighing the risks against the potential rewards. Some argued that the risk was too great, that attempting to rescue Najeem would only jeopardize their own position and reveal their hand to Graffik. Others believed that Najeem's knowledge was too crucial to ignore. The debate went on late into the night, fuelled by strong coffee and the anxiety of the situation.

Finally, Theron, after careful consideration and consultation with his key strategists, gave his decision. "We'll attempt it. Stanya, you'll be integral to this. Your knowledge of the palace's inner workings is critical to coordinating the plan." He paused, his eyes narrowed. "But this is a calculated risk. Failure could mean the end of our rebellion."

Stanya accepted the challenge, a determined glint in her eyes. The next few days were a whirlwind of activity. She worked tirelessly with Theron and his strategists, poring over maps, plotting routes, and devising a detailed plan to execute the rescue mission. She meticulously analyzed the information she had gathered, highlighting potential obstacles and suggesting alternative routes. She even sketched detailed diagrams of the palace's security systems, meticulously labeling guard patrols, blind spots, and potential ambush points.

She crafted a complex plan that involved a series of coordinated attacks on Graffik's supply lines, drawing the bulk of Graffik's forces away from the palace itself. Simultaneously, a small, highly trained group of rebel soldiers would create a diversion closer to the prison, using a series of smoke bombs and carefully timed distractions. The timing was everything – a delicate ballet of deception and coordination.

During this time, Stanya also used her networks in the outerlands to locate and gather crucial information about Lyra, Graffik's daughter. Her contacts revealed Lyra's location within the palace and confirmed that Graffik kept her under tight surveillance, but that her guards were less vigilant during certain hours of the day. This information was critical, providing a crucial window of opportunity for Najeem's escape.

Stanya realized Najeem's escape was inextricably linked to Lyra's. She knew that a successful rescue of Najeem might be the only way to secure Lyra's freedom. She had to ensure that Najeem understood this intricate plan. She crafted coded messages, relying on their earlier shared experiences and inside jokes to ensure their meaning would not be misunderstood. The messages were sent through a network of trusted messengers, carrying instructions and updates on the evolving plan.

The night of the rescue arrived with chilling anticipation. The coordinated attacks on Graffik's supply lines were a success, drawing the bulk of his forces into a carefully laid trap. Simultaneously, the diversionary tactics near the prison created enough chaos to divert the attention of the guards. It was a calculated risk, and Stanya knew that a single misstep could lead to catastrophe.

But her plan, born from meticulous planning and innate strategic brilliance, worked perfectly. As the palace guards scrambled to deal with the diversion, Najeem, guided by Stanya's detailed instructions, moved through the palace's intricate network of tunnels and secret passages. He navigated the dark corridors with the practiced ease of a seasoned warrior, his movements fluid and silent. He carefully followed the path Stanya had outlined, using her detailed sketches to circumvent the remaining guards.

He reached Lyra's cell. She was weak but safe. Together, they moved swiftly and silently, guided by Stanya's directions relayed through the coded messages. They reached the pre-arranged rendezvous point outside the palace walls, where Theron and his forces were waiting.

In that moment, as Najeem and Lyra escaped the grasp of Graffik's tyrannical regime, Stanya felt the weight of her success settle upon her. The calculated risk had paid off, and the seeds of rebellion had been firmly planted. The fight was far from over, but for now, Stanya could take a moment to breathe, knowing that her strategic prowess had played a crucial role in changing the fate of many. Their escape was just the beginning of a long and arduous war against oppression, but they were a step closer to victory, thanks to Stanya's meticulous planning and unwavering support. The outerlands now held a new hope, and Stanya, though weary, felt the thrill of a battle won, setting the stage for the next chapter of their fight for freedom.

The obsidian throne room, usually a spectacle of glittering opulence, felt suffocating under Baznoon Graffik's simmering rage. The air crackled with unspoken accusations, the silence punctuated only by the rhythmic drip of water from a cracked gargoyle high in the vaulted ceiling. Graffik, a man whose cruelty was matched only by his ruthless intelligence, paced before his assembled court, his shadow stretching long and menacing across the polished floor. His usually impeccable attire was rumpled, his normally flawless composure shattered.

"They escaped," he growled, the words like shards of ice. His voice, usually a smooth baritone, was rough with barely suppressed fury. "Stanya, the viper, and that… that barbarian, Najeem. They vanished like smoke."

Lord Valerius, Graffik's most trusted advisor, a man whose loyalty was as unwavering as his ambition, stepped forward. "Your Majesty, our pursuit was swift, but they were clearly aided by… collaborators." He paused, letting the implication hang heavy in the air.

Graffik stopped pacing, his gaze sweeping across the assembled nobles. Each face was a carefully constructed mask of fealty, yet beneath the veneer of loyalty, Baznoon Graffik sensed the undercurrent of fear and… something else. Suspicion. His eyes, sharp as obsidian shards, lingered on Lord Alaric, whose family had held significant power in the outerlands for generations. Alaric shifted uncomfortably, his carefully groomed beard twitching slightly. Graffik saw it – a flicker of guilt, or perhaps… satisfaction?

"Collaborators," Graffik repeated, the word tasting like ash in his mouth. "Indeed. Who among you would dare betray me?"

The silence stretched, taut and unbearable. Graffik's gaze, cold and calculating, moved from face to face, seeking out the slightest tremor, the smallest involuntary gesture that might betray a conspirator. He knew his court was a viper's nest, a breeding ground for ambition and betrayal. He had cultivated this environment, using fear and favor to control his subjects, but now, that carefully constructed balance had been disrupted.

The escape of Stanya and Najeem wasn't just a personal affront; it was a blow to his authority, a crack in the façade of his absolute power. Stanya, with her unparalleled skill in gathering information, possessed secrets that could unravel his empire. And Najeem, a warrior of unmatched strength, posed a physical threat, a symbol of the defiance brewing in the outerlands. Their escape was a clear sign that his control was weakening, that the seeds of rebellion were taking root.

He focused on another noble, Lady Elara, whose family had longstanding ties to Theron, the rebel leader in the outerlands. Her composure was impeccable, but Baznoon saw a subtle stiffness in her posture, a barely perceptible tightening of her lips. He knew her family's loyalty was fragile, easily swayed by expediency and the promise of power.

"Lord Valerius," Graffik said, his voice low and dangerous. "Increase the patrols. Every corner of the capital must be scoured. I want those two brought back… alive. And I want to know who aided their escape."

Valerius bowed. "It shall be done, Your Majesty."

Graffik turned his attention to his personal guard, the elite Black Daggers. These were men chosen for their unwavering loyalty and ruthlessness. Men who would not hesitate to spill blood to ensure his safety and secure his reign. He ordered a thorough investigation, demanding a list of every individual who had contact with Stanya or Najeem in the past year, regardless of their status. This list would undoubtedly include a vast number of his closest confidantes and advisors.

As the court dispersed, Graffik remained alone, his mind racing. He reviewed the information Stanya had undoubtedly obtained – information that could cripple his military, expose his alliances, and bring down his regime. The escape was a calculated risk on Stanya's part, a move of incredible audacity. He admired her skills, her courage, even as he despised her treachery. He wondered about Najeem, the seemingly simple warrior who had become entangled in his daughter's affections. Why had he assisted Stanya? Was it merely coincidence, or a deliberate act of defiance? Could Lyra, his beloved daughter, be involved?

The thought was abhorrent, yet it couldn't be dismissed entirely.

His paranoia, usually a tool he wielded with deadly precision, was now turning against him. He felt surrounded by enemies, real or imagined. The once-impregnable walls of his palace seemed to crumble around him, revealing a nest of potential betrayals. He suspected everyone; his closest allies, his most loyal servants, even his own family.

The following days were a blur of interrogations, tortures, and executions. Graffik's grip tightened, suffocating the capital in an atmosphere of fear and uncertainty. Lord Alaric, despite his protestations of innocence, was found to have held secret communication with Theron through a network of spies. He was executed swiftly and brutally, his head displayed in the public square as a warning to others. Lady Elara, though not implicated directly, was confined to her chambers, a prisoner of Graffik's suspicions. Even his own guards were not spared his scrutiny.

The Black Daggers, usually his most reliable force, became the subjects of suspicion and distrust. Graffik ordered a purge, replacing many of his loyal guards with new recruits whose loyalty could still be tested and molded. This ruthless act of self-preservation sent shivers down the spines of even those most loyal to the crown.

The whispers of Graffik's paranoia spread through the palace like wildfire. Everyone was watching everyone else, fear and uncertainty hanging heavy in the air. The once-vibrant court became a desolate landscape of suspicion and dread. Graffik, isolated in his fear, tightened his grip on his fading power, consumed by his suspicion, he became a shadow of his former self. His quest for revenge and the uncovering of the truth was becoming more about survival than justice, and he was now on the edge of self-destruction, driven by his own paranoia. The calculated risk that Stanya had taken was not merely a gamble for her freedom; it had triggered a chain reaction that threatened to topple the very foundation of Graffik's reign. And as his power began to crumble, the seeds of revolution blossomed, fueled by his own fear and the consequences of his relentless pursuit of retribution.

Meanwhile, far from the suffocating grip of Graffik's paranoia, Stanya and Najeem continued their journey, their paths diverging towards their separate goals. They had planted the seed of rebellion and begun a chain reaction which would undoubtedly change the fate of the empire forever. Their actions were a challenge to absolute authority, a testament to the power of human resilience and the enduring strength of hope in the face of overwhelming oppression. The escape, however, had unleashed a whirlwind that threatened to consume all in its path. Graffik's reign, once seemingly unassailable, teetered on the brink of collapse, a consequence of his own mistrust and the audacious gamble taken by two unlikely allies. The game had shifted, and Graffik's empire was now paying the price for underestimating Stanya and Najeem's resolve.

The air in Graffik's private chambers hung thick with unspoken tension. Princess Amara, her usually vibrant spirit subdued, stood rigidly before her father, her hands clasped tightly in front of her. Baznoon Graffik, his face a mask of controlled fury, paced before the intricately carved obsidian fireplace, the flames mirroring the tempest brewing within him. The silence stretched, taut and unbearable, punctuated only by the crackle of the fire and the occasional nervous cough from one of the guards stationed discreetly in the shadows.

Amara's defiance, though carefully veiled, was palpable. She had refused to comply with his demands, refusing to marry the aging Lord Valerius, a man whose ambition far outweighed his charm and whose ruthlessness mirrored her father's own. This defiance, a rare display from the usually docile princess, stemmed not from romantic attachment to Najeem – a sentiment she hadn't fully processed herself – but from a fierce sense of self-preservation. She understood her father's machinations; a marriage to Valerius wasn't just a political manoeuvre; it was a strategic silencing.

"You disappoint me, Amara," Graffik finally growled, his voice a low rumble that shook the very foundations of the room. "Lord Valerius is a powerful man, a valuable ally. This marriage secures the stability of the empire, strengthens our position against the growing unrest in the Outerlands."

Amara met her father's gaze unflinchingly. "Father, with all due respect, Lord Valerius is a cruel man. His ambition knows no bounds, and his methods are… ruthless." She paused, choosing her words carefully. "A union forged in such a manner would not strengthen the empire, it would cripple it from within."

Baznoon Graffik stopped pacing, his gaze sharp and calculating. He knew his daughter was intelligent, sharper than many of his advisors, but her current display of rebellion was an unexpected turn. He'd always viewed her as a pawn, a piece to be moved on the chessboard of his political ambitions. This unexpected resistance threatened to disrupt his meticulously crafted plans. He had underestimated her, underestimated the depth of her convictions, and the strength of her will.

"Your concerns are… misplaced," he said, his voice dripping with icy sarcasm. "Valerius will be a benevolent husband, a loyal consort."

"Benevolent?" Amara scoffed softly, a hint of bitterness lacing her tone. "Father, you know better than anyone that such words are mere embellishments, empty promises from a man whose only true love is power."

Graffik's patience frayed. He raised a hand, silencing the unspoken arguments hanging in the air. He circled Amara again, his gaze piercing. "You are aware of the consequences of your defiance, I presume?"

Amara nodded, her chin lifted. "I am aware."

"Then you understand the price you'll pay for your insolence," he hissed, his eyes glinting dangerously. "The Outerlands rebellion… it will be dealt with swiftly, brutally. And your… affection for that… barbarian Najeem… will cost you dearly. The man is already marked for death."

Amara's breath hitched. She knew Najeem was in danger, but Graffik's blatant mention of his demise sent a chill down her spine. The man she hadn't even admitted to loving was hanging by a thread, his life caught in the web of her father's cruel schemes.

"You have until sunset," Graffik continued, his voice hardening. "Agree to the marriage, and Najeem will remain… unmentioned. Refuse, and the consequences will be far more… drastic."

He paused, allowing his threat to hang heavy in the air. He studied his daughter, searching for any sign of weakness, any crack in her carefully constructed facade. But Amara remained resolute, her eyes reflecting a mixture of fear and unwavering defiance.

"Father," she said, her voice trembling slightly but firm. "I cannot marry Lord Valerius. Not knowing what has happened to Najeem, this marriage would be a betrayal, a hollow mockery. And no amount of threats will change that."

Graffik's face darkened, his jaw tightening. This was not the obedient daughter he expected, the compliant piece in his intricate game of power. He'd underestimated the strength of her will, the depth of her feelings, and the dangerous consequences of his own arrogance.

He took a deep breath, trying to regain control. He knew he couldn't force her, not directly. He needed a different approach, a more subtle manipulation.

"Very well, Amara," he said, his voice dangerously calm. "Since you value this… barbarian's life so much, let's make a deal. I will spare Najeem, I will even allow him a chance to escape. In exchange, you will cooperate with the marriage to Lord Valerius – but on one condition."

Amara's eyes narrowed. She knew this was a trap, a carefully laid snare designed to ensnare her in her father's web of deceit. Yet, the flicker of hope ignited within her – the glimmer of a chance to save Najeem – was too tempting to ignore.

"What is your condition?" she asked, her voice barely a whisper.

"Before the wedding, you will be required to participate in a series of trials, designed to test your loyalty, your obedience to me. And those trials, Amara, they won't be easy." His eyes gleamed with a predatory satisfaction. "Failure will mean not only Najeem's death, but yours as well."

Graffik smiled, a chilling, predatory smile that promised pain and suffering. The stakes were high, dangerously high. But Amara knew she had no choice. She would play his game, navigate his treacherous trials, to secure Najeem's freedom and, perhaps, her own. The negotiation was far from over; it was merely the beginning of a far more perilous and intricate dance. The sunset loomed closer, the deadline approaching, and the weight of the empire rested upon the shoulders of a princess caught in a deadly game of political chess, her very life hanging in the balance. The next few days would determine not only her fate, but the fate of the entire empire. Graffik's seemingly generous offer concealed a labyrinthine web of deceit, testing Amara's resolve to its limits. Her desperate gamble to save Najeem had just begun, and the true cost of her defiance was far from apparent.

The following days were a blur of clandestine meetings, veiled threats, and meticulously planned maneuvers. Amara learned to play the game, to use her wit and charm as weapons in her struggle for survival. She navigated the treacherous currents of her father's court, gathering information, subtly manipulating events, all while feigning compliance. Each interaction was a perilous dance on the edge of a precipice, where one wrong step could send everything crashing down.

She employed trusted servants, whispering plans into their ears, instructing them to send covert messages to the Outerlands. Every secret meeting was a calculated risk, every whispered word a potential betrayal. Yet she pressed on, her determination fuelled by the image of Najeem, his strong features etched in her memory. His image became her anchor, her strength in the face of her father's unrelenting cruelty.

The trials began. Each test was designed to break her, to expose any hint of weakness or disloyalty. She faced cunning riddles, treacherous physical challenges, and brutal psychological torment. She was forced to confront her own fears, to question her own loyalty, and to make impossible choices. Yet, she persevered, her determination fueled by her love for Najeem and her hatred for her father's tyranny.

Her father watched her struggle, a mixture of fascination and disdain in his eyes. He admired her strength, the resilience of his own blood, yet he relished the power he held over her. He enjoyed making her suffer, seeing her strain and fight against the chains of his control. He found perverse pleasure in this macabre game of cat and mouse, where his daughter's life hung precariously in the balance.

The final trial was the most perilous, a desperate gamble that involved a confrontation with one of her father's most trusted generals, a cold-blooded killer with no loyalty beyond Graffik himself. Amara knew that failure would mean certain death, not only for her, but for Najeem as well. Yet, she confronted the general, using her wit and courage to outmaneuver him, to expose his treachery to Graffik, and to secure her escape.

As Graffik finally granted Najeem his freedom and a safe passage out of the empire, Amara saw a glimmer of hope amidst the darkness, a flicker of redemption in the wake of her ordeal. But she knew, with chilling certainty, that the game was far from over. The seeds of rebellion she and Najeem had planted were beginning to sprout, and their struggle for freedom had merely shifted to a new, more perilous phase. Graffik's reign was under threat, and his daughter had unwittingly become a pawn in a far greater game. The intricate web of political intrigue she'd navigated now threatened to ensnare the entire empire. Her escape was just the beginning. A new chapter, far more dangerous than the last, was about to unfold.

The biting wind whipped at Stanya's cloak as she and Najeem crested the final hill overlooking the Outerlands. Below, a sprawling city pulsed with a life vastly different from the suffocating opulence of Graffik's capital. Freedom tasted like the sharp, clean air, a stark contrast to the cloying scent of intrigue and fear that clung to everything within Baznoon Graffik's grasp. Yet, the victory felt incomplete, a bittersweet triumph overshadowed by the weight of their choices.

Najeem, ever watchful, scanned the landscape. His hand rested lightly on the hilt of his scavenged sword, a constant reminder of the dangers that still lurked. The escape had been harrowing, a brutal dance with death orchestrated by Graffik's relentless pursuit. They'd lost track of how many assassins they'd evaded, how many soldiers they'd outmaneuvered. Each near-miss had etched itself into their memories, a grim testament to their resilience.

Stanya, however, seemed preoccupied with something beyond the immediate threat. She clutched the small, leather-bound satchel containing the stolen documents – Emperor Graffik's meticulously detailed plans for consolidating his power and silencing all opposition. The information within could ignite a rebellion, but its delivery came at a price. The price of betrayal.

"Are you alright?" Najeem's voice, rough with concern, broke through Stanya's pensive silence.

She met his gaze, her own eyes reflecting a storm of conflicting emotions. "I'm delivering this to Lord Valerius," she finally said, her voice barely a whisper, "but… there's something I haven't told you."

The confession hung heavy between them, the wind momentarily still, as if holding its breath. Stanya proceeded, her words measured, each syllable carefully chosen. She recounted her history with Lord Valerius, a man she'd once considered a mentor, a respected leader of the Outerlands' resistance movement. He'd trained her, nurtured her skills, instilled in her the unwavering belief in justice and freedom. But their relationship had soured over time, a chasm opening between their ideologies concerning the best approach to overthrowing Graffik. He'd become more ruthless, willing to employ any means necessary, while Stanya clung to her own moral compass.

"He's... changed," she admitted, her voice laced with a hint of disillusionment. "He's become as ruthless as Graffik he seeks to replace. He's made alliances with questionable figures, people who'd happily sell out anyone for the right price." She paused, her gaze drifting towards the distant city, the setting sun casting long, ominous shadows. "And yet... he's our only hope."

Najeem understood. He'd witnessed firsthand Graffik's cruelty, the casual disregard for human life. He'd seen the despair in the eyes of the enslaved, the fear etched onto the faces of those living under the tyrant's iron fist. He knew that a desperate situation sometimes called for desperate measures, a harsh truth that gnawed at his conscience. But the thought of Valerius, a man potentially as dangerous as Graffik himself, filled him with unease. Trust, he realized, was a luxury they could no longer afford.

"What if he betrays you?" he asked, his voice low.

"He might," Stanya admitted, her gaze unflinching. "But the risk is worth it. The information in this satchel… it could be the key to ending Graffik's reign once and for all." She hesitated, then added, "It's my only chance to make amends for… for everything."

Najeem knew she was referring to her past, to mistakes she'd made in the name of her loyalty to Valerius. Mistakes that had far-reaching consequences. He knew better than to press her for details. He'd seen her wrestle with her conscience, the internal conflict tearing at her soul. Her loyalty to Valerius had been absolute, bordering on blind faith. Now, that loyalty felt fragile, hanging by a thread.

The decision weighed heavily upon her. She was caught in a web of conflicting loyalties. Her loyalty to Valerius, the man who had molded her, taught her everything she knew; and her loyalty to the cause of freedom, to the innocent lives crushed beneath Graffik's heel. Her choice, however difficult, determined the fate of the rebellion.

As they approached the city gates, the question of trust intensified. Valerius's messengers had been waiting, their faces grim and impassive. The air crackled with an undercurrent of suspicion, each glance exchanged laced with hidden motives. Stanya felt the weight of responsibility pressing down on her, a crushing burden.

The meeting with Valerius was tense, a silent negotiation conducted through wary glances and coded phrases. Valerius, a man hardened by years of struggle against Graffik, showed little emotion. His eyes, though, held a flicker of recognition, an acknowledgement of Stanya's internal turmoil. He knew she doubted him, and he seemed to accept that doubt without protest. He accepted the satchel, his fingers barely brushing against hers as he took it.

"This changes everything," Valerius said, his voice low, almost a murmur. "Graffik's reign will end. Not today, perhaps, but soon." His gaze held a cold intensity, a stark contrast to the hope his words conveyed. The triumph was palpable but tainted by the unspoken question: at what cost?

Later, as Stanya and Najeem watched the city lights twinkle from a distance, the weight of their escape still clinging to them, Najeem put his arm around her, pulling her close. The action was simple, yet profoundly comforting. The unspoken understanding between them transcended words. They had survived, but the battle was far from over. The fight for freedom was a long and winding road, paved with betrayals, sacrifices, and the ever-present threat of death. They were on their own path now, a path far removed from Graffik's shadow, but one still steeped in peril and the constant threat of shifting loyalties. The game had changed, the stakes had risen, and their journey was far from over. The future, once promising, now remained uncertain. They only knew one thing for sure: the fight would continue. The fight for freedom, for justice, and for each other, would continue, no matter the cost.

Chapter 8: The Assault

The dawn broke, painting the sky in hues of blood orange and bruised purple, a grim reflection of the day that lay ahead. From the shadowed hills surrounding Emperor Baznoon Graffik's impenetrable stronghold, the rebel army surged forward, a tide of defiance against the tyranny that had choked their land for decades. Thousands strong, they moved with a disciplined fury, their ranks a tapestry of different clans and factions, united by their shared hatred of Graffik and the burning desire for freedom.

Stanya, clad in the practical leather armor of a rebel soldier, watched the advance from a vantage point overlooking the battlefield. Her normally sharp eyes, usually filled with a calculating gleam, were clouded with a mixture of apprehension and steely determination. The jeweled comb, containing the information that had sparked this rebellion, was safely tucked away, a tangible representation of the sacrifices made to reach this point. She adjusted the straps of her quiver, the weight of the arrows a familiar comfort. This wasn't just a battle; it was a culmination of years spent gathering information, navigating treacherous political landscapes, and forging unlikely alliances.

The air thrummed with the anticipation of war. The rhythmic clang of weapons, the nervous chatter of soldiers, the distant rumble of siege engines – all blended into a cacophony that echoed the tumultuous emotions within her. She had played a pivotal role in this rebellion, her intelligence a crucial weapon in their arsenal. But even her meticulous planning could not account for every variable. There were too many unknowns, too many potential points of failure.

Simultaneously, Najeem, his face grim and determined, fought his way through the outer ranks of Graffik's soldiers. He moved like a phantom, his movements fluid and deadly. He carried no armor, relying on his exceptional skill and speed. His goal was not to conquer the stronghold, but to reach the heart of it, to rescue Graffik's daughter, a task that seemed impossibly dangerous even for a warrior of his caliber. He had pledged his freedom, and perhaps his life, to this impossible mission. The memory of her – her defiance, her unexpected kindness, her vulnerability—fueled him. He would not let her suffer under her father's cruelty.

The battle raged. Siege engines hurled massive stones at the towering walls of the stronghold, each impact shaking the very foundations of Graffik's power. Arrows rained down like deadly hail, painting the air with streaks of vibrant color that belied the carnage below. The rebels fought with the desperation of those who had nothing left to lose, while Graffik's soldiers defended their lives and their master with fanatical loyalty.

Stanya, coordinating the rebel forces with sharp commands and quick thinking, adjusted her strategy as the battle unfolded. She directed reinforcements, identified weaknesses in the enemy lines, and guided the siege engines to maximize their effectiveness. Her voice, calm yet commanding, cut through the chaos, a beacon of hope in the midst of the storm. She recognized the desperate gamble the rebels were taking. A direct assault on Graffik's stronghold was a bold, almost suicidal move, but the intel she had provided pointed to a critical weakness, a vulnerability that could turn the tide of the war.

Meanwhile, Najeem's path was far more perilous. He moved through the chaos, a silent predator hunting his prey. He used the cover of the fighting to his advantage, blending seamlessly into the turmoil. He had a network of contacts within the city, some sympathetic to the rebellion, others merely opportunists, who provided him with information and assistance. His progress was slow and deliberate, each step calculated, each move measured. His goal was to reach the inner sanctum of the palace before the rebel assault could breach the walls. Any delay increased the chances of Graffik discovering the princess's escape.

As the battle intensified, a sudden shift in Graffik's defenses exposed a critical weakness. Stanya seized the opportunity, leading a flanking maneuver that shattered the enemy's lines. The rebels surged forward, their momentum unstoppable. Graffik's soldiers, caught off guard, began to falter. The tide of the battle, it seemed, was turning.

But Baznoon Graffik was not one to surrender easily. He unleashed his elite guard, a force of brutal and merciless warriors trained in the darkest arts of combat. They were a formidable force, their fighting style brutal and efficient, cutting through the rebel ranks like a scythe through wheat. The momentum of the assault faltered.

Najeem, having navigated the treacherous corridors of the palace, finally reached the princess's chambers. He found her terrified but resolute, her eyes filled with a strange mixture of fear and admiration for the warrior who had come to her rescue. As they attempted to escape, they were confronted by Graffik himself. He was furious, his eyes blazing with rage. He was not simply a ruler; he was a dark sorcerer, his power fueled by his cruelty and the suffering of his people.

The ensuing confrontation was a whirlwind of magic and steel. Graffik's dark magic lashed out, the air crackling with malevolent energy. Najeem, relying on his skill and courage, fought back with a ferocity born of desperation. It was a battle not only for their freedom but also for the soul of their land. The princess, unexpectedly, displayed a surprising resilience and strength of her own, using her knowledge of the palace to aid their escape.

Meanwhile, Stanya fought fiercely, coordinating the rebel assault and dealing with the surprising deployment of Graffik's elite guard. She noticed something peculiar about their style of fighting, something that suggested a darker, more sinister force at work. Graffik was not relying solely on brute force; there was an orchestrated, almost ritualistic, component to their assault.

Just as Najeem and the princess thought they had escaped, a devastating magical blast rocked the palace, the shockwave shattering the nearby walls and collapsing parts of the structure. Stanya, witnessing the destruction from afar, realized the true extent of Graffik's power and the catastrophic plan he had set in motion. It wasn't simply a fight for control; it was a fight for survival. The unexpected twist—a magical trap designed to obliterate the entire rebellious force—changed the course of the conflict dramatically. The rebels, caught in the wake of the devastating magical attack, were thrown into chaos, their carefully planned assault thrown into disarray. The battle, once seemingly theirs for the taking, now hung precariously in the balance. The siege, far from being won, had only just begun, its true horror yet to be unveiled. The fight for freedom had just become a fight for survival.

The earth trembled beneath Najeem's feet, a rhythmic shudder that mirrored the frantic beat of his own heart. The magical blast, a cataclysmic event that had ripped through the palace moments ago, had left a landscape of devastation in its wake. Twisted metal, shattered stone, and the acrid smell of burning wood filled the air. Yet, amidst this ruin, his resolve remained unshaken. He had to find Princess Amara.

He'd lost sight of her in the pandemonium that followed the initial attack. The princess, usually composed and regal, had been reduced to a trembling shadow, clinging to him as the ground buckled beneath their feet. The last image seared into his memory was of her being thrown clear, a small, vulnerable figure tossed amidst the chaos of falling masonry.

His escape from the palace had been a brutal scramble, a desperate dash through corridors filled with panicked guards and the deafening roar of collapsing walls. He'd used his considerable fighting skills to carve a path, his movements fluid and precise, each strike a calculated blow aimed to incapacitate, not kill. He couldn't risk drawing unnecessary attention. He needed to find Amara, and he couldn't afford to be caught.

He navigated the shattered remains of the palace with a grim determination. Each step was a calculated risk, each shadow a potential threat. The air buzzed with the desperate cries of the wounded and the chilling silence of the fallen. Graffik's guards, usually so disciplined, were now a disorganized rabble, reacting to the chaos rather than acting with their usual controlled aggression. This disarray, though horrifying, presented a sliver of an opportunity.

He moved through the ruins, relying on instinct and memory. He recalled Amara's preference for the quieter, less frequented western wing of the palace, a labyrinth of private chambers and hidden passageways. It was a risky gamble, but it was his best bet. He knew the layout of the palace better than most, a knowledge gained through his time as an unwilling captive, knowledge he now used to his advantage.

The western wing was even more devastated than the rest of the palace. Sections of the walls had crumbled entirely, leaving gaping holes that exposed the interior to the elements. He cautiously skirted around fallen beams, his senses alert to any sign of movement, any sound that might betray Amara's location. The air was thick with the dust of destruction, and the faint scent of blood hung heavy in the air.

As he rounded a corner, a low moan reached his ears. Following the sound, he found her. Amara lay huddled amongst the rubble, her silken gown torn and dirty, a deep gash bleeding on her arm. Relief washed over him, a wave of emotion so intense it threatened to overwhelm him. He knelt beside her, his heart aching at the sight of her distress.

"Amara," he whispered, his voice hoarse with emotion. He gently touched her arm, his fingers brushing against the raw wound. She stirred, her eyes fluttering open, revealing a mixture of pain and fear.

"Najeem?" she breathed, her voice barely a whisper.

"I'm here," he said, his voice firm and reassuring. "We need to get out of here."

He carefully examined her wounds, assessing the damage. The gash was deep, but not life-threatening. He tore a strip of cloth from his own tunic, using it to stem the bleeding. The pain made her wince, but she didn't cry out. Her bravery, even in this state, was astonishing.

"We have to move," he repeated, his gaze sweeping across the ravaged landscape. The sounds of battle were growing closer, indicating that Graffik's forces were beginning to regroup. They needed to escape, and quickly. He carefully helped her to her feet, supporting her weight as he gently guided her through the debris.

Their escape was a harrowing race against time and overwhelming odds. They had to navigate through collapsing structures, dodge stray soldiers, and evade the ever-present danger of further magical attacks. Najeem, his body aching from his previous escapes and the physical demands of rescuing Amara, fought with a ferocity born of desperation. He used his body as a shield, pushing Amara behind him, pushing his way through the destruction.

They passed groups of soldiers, some still fighting, some tending to the wounded, and others simply staring into space, paralyzed by the sheer scale of the devastation. Their movements were swift and silent, each footstep measured, each breath controlled. He used the shadows and the rubble to their advantage, moving with the grace of a phantom.

As they neared the outer edge of the palace, a group of Graffik's elite guard spotted them. Their eyes gleamed with predatory intent, their weapons already raised. Najeem knew this was their last chance for escape.

Without hesitation, he drew his blades, his movements a blur of controlled aggression. The battle was fierce and desperate, a whirlwind of steel and fury. He fought with the skill and precision of a seasoned warrior, protecting Amara while simultaneously taking down the soldiers one by one. The sounds of clashing steel punctuated the cries of the wounded and the thunder of collapsing stones.

Amara, despite her injuries, was not helpless. She used her wits, throwing sand into the eyes of the guards and pulling them off balance in a struggle to escape. Her spirit and will to live gave him the strength he needed to fight on. After what seemed like an eternity, the last guard fell, his weapon clattering to the ground.

Exhausted but triumphant, Najeem and Amara stumbled out of the palace into the relative safety of the surrounding hills. The sight of the rebel army, still engaged in a brutal fight for survival, was both reassuring and terrifying. They were far from safe, but they were alive, and they had each other.

The siege had only just begun, but for Najeem, a small victory had been won. He had rescued the princess, and as he looked into her eyes, he knew that this was only the beginning of their journey. The fight for survival had now become the fight for freedom, a fight they would wage together, hand in hand, against the ruthless tyranny of Emperor Baznoon Graffik. Their love story, born amidst chaos and destruction, was a testament to the human spirit's unwavering ability to find hope and resilience in the darkest of times. Their escape, however, was far from secure. Graffik's reach was long, and the battle for freedom was far from over.

The wind whipped Stanya's cloak around her as she stood on the precipice of the cliff overlooking the besieged city of Porthaven. Below, the rhythmic clang of steel on steel, the screams of the dying, and the roar of the siege engines formed a horrifying symphony. Emperor Baznoon Graffik's forces, a tide of black armor and crimson banners, pressed relentlessly against the city walls. But Porthaven wasn't defenseless. From her vantage point, Stanya could see the flickering torches of the rebel army, a constellation of defiance against the encroaching darkness.

Her heart pounded not just from the echoing chaos below but from the weight of responsibility she carried. The information she'd risked her life to steal from Graffik's palace—details of his troop deployments, his supply lines, his weaknesses—was now the lifeblood of this rebellion. It wasn't just a collection of facts; it was a blueprint for victory, a roadmap to freedom. And she, the seemingly insignificant information gatherer, held the map.

The plan, painstakingly crafted over weeks of clandestine meetings and whispered conversations, depended entirely on her coordinating the rebel forces. She was the linchpin, the unseen hand guiding the chaotic symphony of the uprising. Her knowledge was their weapon, and her strategic mind, their shield.

A messenger, breathless and mud-caked, scrambled up the rocky path towards her. "Lady Stanya," he gasped, clutching a crumpled scroll, "General Theron requests your immediate presence. The northern gate is under heavy assault."

Stanya felt a surge of adrenaline, a familiar comfort in the face of danger. She unfolded the scroll, her eyes scanning the hastily scribbled message. The situation was critical. Theron, the rebel army's most seasoned commander, needed her guidance to repel Graffik's assault. Delay meant disaster.

"Tell General Theron I'm coming," she said, her voice firm despite the tremor of anxiety in her chest. She handed the messenger a small pouch filled with gold coins, a reward for his daring delivery. She then took a moment, steeling her nerves, before turning towards the chaotic scene below.

Her journey down the cliff was treacherous. Loose rocks skittered under her feet, and the acrid smell of smoke stung her nostrils. But the urgency of the situation propelled her forward, her mind already formulating strategies, calculating odds, anticipating Graffik's next move.

She reached the northern gate just as Graffik's forces launched another wave of attack. The defenders, outnumbered and exhausted, fought with a desperate courage. The air rang with the clash of swords, the splintering of wood, and the anguished cries of men falling.

Stanya, quickly assessing the situation, immediately identified the weak point – a section of the wall weakened by a previous bombardment, where Graffik's forces were concentrating their efforts. She instructed Theron to divert a small but crucial contingent of archers to that area, creating a concentrated volley of arrows to disrupt the enemy's advance. Then, using her knowledge of the city's hidden passages and underground tunnels, she ordered the deployment of a small, elite unit of rebel soldiers to launch a surprise attack from the city's interior.

The battle raged for hours, a relentless back-and-forth exchange of blood and steel. But Stanya's strategic maneuvers proved decisive. Her knowledge of the enemy's tactics, gleaned from her time in Graffik's court, allowed her to anticipate their moves and counter them effectively. Each of her commands was a calculated risk, a gamble made with the fate of the city hanging in the balance.

One moment she was directing the movement of troops, the next she was attending to wounded soldiers, her hands swift and sure as she bandaged gashes and splints broken limbs. She was a whirlwind of activity, her presence a source of inspiration and reassurance amidst the carnage.

As the sun dipped below the horizon, casting long shadows across the battlefield, a change began to sweep through the tide of battle. Graffik's forces, depleted and demoralized by Stanya's counter-offensives, began to falter. The tide had turned.

Victory was not yet certain, but the balance had shifted decisively in favor of the rebels. Stanya, exhausted but exhilarated, watched as Graffik's soldiers began a chaotic retreat, leaving behind a trail of the dead and wounded. The siege, which had seemed insurmountable just hours before, was now on the verge of being broken.

The celebrations were muted, respectful of the losses suffered. But beneath the surface of somber joy, a sense of relief and triumph prevailed. Porthaven had survived the night, defying Graffik's might. And at the heart of this victory was Stanya, the unassuming information gatherer who had become the architect of freedom.

Her role had extended far beyond simply delivering intelligence. She'd become a leader, a strategist, a warrior, all rolled into one. She'd shown not only her intellect but her courage, her determination, and her unwavering commitment to the cause of freedom. The rebels, initially hesitant to accept a seemingly fragile woman's leadership, now looked to her with awe and admiration. Her quiet strength had inspired them, and her strategic brilliance had saved them.

However, Stanya knew that the victory was fragile. Graffik was cunning and ruthless, and this was only one battle won in a long and arduous war. The fight for freedom was far from over. But tonight, as the city breathed a collective sigh of relief, Stanya allowed herself a moment of quiet pride. She had played her part, and played it well. She had proven that even in a world of brutal power, the strength of a single, determined woman could make all the difference. The night was far from over, however; there was much work to be done. The war had just begun. And she was ready. She would keep fighting, keep strategizing, keep inspiring, until the shadow of Emperor Baznoon Graffik was lifted from the land, forever. The night was won, but the dawn held the promise of a much greater struggle. A struggle Stanya was not only willing to fight but ready to lead.

The celebrations in Porthaven were short-lived. The air, still thick with the smell of woodsmoke and sweat, quickly turned acrid with the stench of burning flesh. Baznoon Graffik, his face a mask of livid fury, was not a man to accept defeat lightly. The momentary respite granted by the city's unexpected resistance was shattered by the arrival of a new, even more brutal wave of his army. This wasn't just a siege anymore; it was a massacre.

The renewed assault began before dawn. Graffik's forces, bolstered by fresh troops and terrifying new siege weapons, pounded the city walls with a ferocity that dwarfed the previous day's attacks. Giant catapults hurled boulders the size of small carts, smashing through the hastily repaired defenses. The air filled with the screams of men and the splintering of wood, a cacophony of destruction that echoed across the ravaged landscape.

Stanya, who had barely slept, watched the carnage from the safety of a hidden observation point. The flickering torchlight revealed a horrifying spectacle. The city walls, once a symbol of defiance, were crumbling under the relentless barrage. Soldiers, their armor torn and bloody, fought with desperate courage, but they were overwhelmed. Graffik's army, a well-oiled machine of death and destruction, seemed unstoppable.

Her heart pounded in her chest, a frantic drumbeat against the symphony of destruction. She had underestimated Graffik's ruthlessness, his capacity for cruelty. This wasn't just a war for power; it was a personal vendetta, fueled by the humiliation of his defeat at Porthaven's gates. He was determined to make an example of the city, to crush any hint of rebellion with an iron fist.

The rebels, despite their earlier success, were dispirited by the sheer scale of the renewed assault. Their ranks, already thinned by the previous day's fighting, were rapidly diminishing. Their courage, though unwavering, was being tested to its limits. Stanya saw their leaders, valiant figures she'd come to know and respect, fall one by one, their deaths swallowed by the chaos.

She knew she had to act, and act fast. The information she had delivered had bought them time, a precious commodity in this brutal war. But that time was running out. The city was on the verge of collapse, and with it, the hope of the rebellion. She had to find a way to turn the tide, to deliver a blow that would force Graffik to reconsider his relentless assault.

Her mind raced, piecing together fragments of information she had gleaned during her infiltration of Graffik's court. She recalled whispers of a hidden weakness in Graffik's army, a vulnerability she could exploit. It was a long shot, a desperate gamble, but it was the only chance they had.

She descended from her vantage point, moving swiftly and silently through the chaos of the battlefield. The city's defenders, locked in desperate combat, barely registered her presence. She weaved through the carnage, her heart a hammer in her chest, her mind focused on her objective. She had to reach the designated point, undetected, before it was too late.

Reaching her destination, a hidden tunnel beneath the city walls, she found a small group of rebels awaiting her. Their faces, etched with exhaustion and grim determination, reflected the desperate situation. They were a crack team, a handpicked squad of experts in demolition and subterfuge. The plan was audacious, suicidal even, but it was their only hope.

With the efficiency born of years of training, she briefed them on her plan. They listened intently, their eyes reflecting the understanding of a shared purpose, a grim determination to succeed. They knew the risks, the almost certain death that awaited them if they failed. But they were willing to take that risk, for the sake of their city, for the sake of freedom.

Under the cover of darkness, the small group slipped out of the city through a network of tunnels. They emerged on the opposite side, unseen by the enemy. Stanya knew that the success of their mission depended on precision, timing, and a whole lot of luck. Any misstep could mean annihilation.

The target was Graffik's main supply depot, located just outside the city walls. They would use a newly developed explosive device, designed to cause a massive chain reaction, devastating Graffik's ammunition stores and disrupting his supply lines. It was a high-risk, high-reward strategy. Success would cripple Graffik's army, giving the defenders of Porthaven a fighting chance. Failure, however, would mean certain death for everyone involved.

The approach was agonizingly slow. Every rustle of leaves, every snap of a twig, sent jolts of adrenaline through Stanya's veins. Her hands, usually steady and precise, trembled slightly as she checked her equipment, ensuring that everything was in place. The fate of Porthaven, indeed the fate of the entire rebellion, rested on her shoulders, and the shoulders of her small band of warriors.

Finally, they reached the supply depot. The air was thick with the smell of gunpowder and sweat. The guards, oblivious to their presence, were engrossed in their duties. Working with practiced efficiency, the team placed the explosives. The timing was crucial. One wrong move, one moment of hesitation, could spell disaster.

With the explosives in place, they retreated, their hearts pounding in their chests, their eyes fixed on the depot. The moment of truth had arrived. Stanya triggered the detonator. There was a blinding flash, a deafening roar, and a towering inferno ripped through the night sky. The earth trembled beneath their feet, and a wave of heat washed over them. They had succeeded.

The explosion rocked Graffik's army, causing widespread chaos and panic. The siege engines fell silent, their ammunition destroyed. The supply lines were severed, crippling the army's ability to continue the assault. The tide had turned. The rebels, inspired by this unexpected victory, fought back with renewed vigor. Graffik's fury, once an unstoppable force, was finally met with resistance. The siege of Porthaven had reached its turning point. The battle for freedom was far from over, but for now, hope flickered again. Stanya, watching the blaze light up the night sky, knew that this was just one battle won in a war that would last many more years. But for tonight, at least, Porthaven was safe. Graffik's rage had been met with courage, and the night belonged to the rebels.

The aftermath of the explosion left Porthaven shrouded in a thick, acrid smoke. The air, heavy with the scent of burnt wood and gunpowder, carried whispers of victory and the chilling promise of what was yet to come. Stanya, leaning against a crumbling stone wall, watched as the remaining rebel fighters tended to the wounded. The initial euphoria had faded, replaced by a cautious optimism. Graffik's army, though severely weakened, was far from defeated. Baznoon Graffik was not a man to relinquish his grip on power easily.

Najeem, his body bruised and aching, stood beside her, his gaze fixed on the smoldering ruins of the siege engines. The brief, exhilarating alliance forged in the heat of battle had solidified into a fragile camaraderie. They had fought side-by-side, their skills complementing each other, a warrior's strength paired with a spy's cunning. Yet, a silent tension lingered between them, a subtle acknowledgment of the unspoken feelings that simmered beneath the surface.

Suddenly, a piercing scream ripped through the night, cutting through the murmurs of the wounded. A figure, silhouetted against the flickering flames, stumbled out of the smoke, his face contorted in terror. He was a soldier, one of Baznoon Graffik's elite guard, his armor scorched and torn. He collapsed at their feet, gasping for breath. Before either Stanya or Najeem could react, he let out a choked whisper, a single word echoing in the stunned silence: "Lyra."

The name hung in the air, a chilling revelation. Lyra, Graffik's daughter, the woman Najeem had sworn to rescue.

The information was a devastating blow, shattering the fragile peace that had settled over the battered city. Najeem's face paled, his eyes widening in disbelief and horror. He had risked everything, escaped a brutal prison, fought his way through a raging war, all for a woman who might already be dead.

Stanya, her sharp mind already racing, saw the implications immediately. This wasn't simply the death of a hostage; it was a strategic maneuver, a calculated risk by Graffik. The capture of Lyra wasn't a random event. This was a trap, a meticulously planned scheme to lure Najeem back into the heart of the empire, to capture him and use him as leverage against the rebels.

"He's lying," Stanya said, her voice low and firm, cutting through Najeem's stunned silence. "This is a trap. Graffik wouldn't risk exposing Lyra so openly."

Najeem stared at her, his mind struggling to process the information. The thought of Lyra in danger, captured and perhaps tortured, fueled his rage, blurring his judgment. His instincts screamed for immediate action, to rush back into Graffik's clutches. But Stanya's words, though harsh, resonated with a chilling logic.

"But how could he know...?" Najeem's voice was strained, the weight of his emotions threatening to overwhelm him.

"Graffik has spies everywhere," Stanya responded, her eyes scanning the surrounding darkness. "He knew your escape was imminent. He knew your connection to Lyra. This was planned. This soldier is a pawn, a distraction."

The implications were staggering. Graffik had not only anticipated their escape, but he had orchestrated the entire sequence of events, using Lyra as bait. It was a gamble of epic proportions, a ruthless move that spoke volumes about his desperation and his willingness to sacrifice his own daughter to achieve his goals.

A cold dread settled over Stanya as a new thought pierced through the chaos. The explosion, the seemingly miraculous turn of events that had saved Porthaven—was that also part of the plan? Had Graffik anticipated the rebels' response and manipulated the situation to his advantage? Had he used the destruction to sow chaos and confusion, creating the perfect cover for his next move?

The question hung unanswered, a chilling uncertainty looming over their victory. The battle for Porthaven might have been won, but the war had just begun. Graffik's strategy had shifted, his focus now laser-focused on Najeem, using Lyra as a pawn in a much larger, more sinister game.

Stanya knew they had to act quickly. They couldn't simply charge blindly into Graffik's grasp. They needed a plan, a strategy to expose Graffik's deception and rescue Lyra without walking into a carefully laid trap. The information she had gathered about Graffik's court, his weaknesses, his vulnerabilities—all of it suddenly felt crucial, pieces of a puzzle that could save not only Najeem, but potentially the entire rebellion.

The night deepened, the fires of Porthaven casting long, dancing shadows. The city, still recovering from the siege, was a place of shattered hopes and fragile victories. Yet amidst the devastation, a spark of defiance flickered, fueled by Stanya's sharp intellect and Najeem's unwavering resolve. They were two individuals, bound by circumstance and fueled by love, facing the overwhelming power of an empire. The odds were insurmountable, yet they were ready to fight.

Their immediate priority was to assess their resources. The rebel forces, though victorious in the siege, were depleted and exhausted. Their supply lines were compromised, their ammunition dwindling. Graffik's army, despite its losses, still possessed a superior force. A direct confrontation would be suicide. They needed to exploit Graffik's overconfidence, his arrogance blinding him to the subtlety of their plan.

Stanya, using her network of contacts within Porthaven, began gathering intelligence. She needed to know Graffik's next move, his intended destination, and the strength of his remaining forces. Najeem, haunted by the image of Lyra, channeled his rage into training, honing his skills, preparing for the inevitable confrontation. He knew he couldn't just rescue Lyra; he had to expose Graffik's treachery, to reveal his cruel manipulation to the world.

Days turned into weeks. The tension in Porthaven was palpable. The initial joy of victory had faded, replaced by a nervous anticipation. Graffik's silence was more terrifying than any overt attack. It was a silent storm gathering force, ready to unleash its fury on anyone who dared to defy him.

Stanya's network yielded crucial information. Graffik had retreated to his mountain fortress, a seemingly impenetrable stronghold nestled high in the treacherous peaks. He was consolidating his power, preparing for a decisive counterattack. Lyra, it seemed, was being held there.

The information confirmed Stanya's suspicions. The siege was a distraction, a ruse to lure Najeem out into the open. Graffik had underestimated Stanya's intelligence, her ability to unravel his intricate plans. Now, the game had shifted. It was no longer about defending Porthaven, but about infiltrating Graffik's fortress, rescuing Lyra, and exposing his treachery.

The plan they devised was audacious, bordering on suicidal. They would use the chaos and confusion left by the siege as a cover, infiltrating Graffik's fortress disguised as scavengers, exploiting the lax security that often followed a major battle. It was a high-risk strategy, but it was their only chance. Failure meant certain death, not just for them, but possibly for the entire rebellion.

The journey to Graffik's fortress was fraught with peril. They navigated treacherous mountain passes, evaded patrolling soldiers, and faced the harsh elements. The bond between them deepened with each challenge, their shared purpose forging a powerful connection. The initial mistrust and animosity had vanished, replaced by a mutual respect and a growing affection that transcended the circumstances of their meeting.

As they neared the fortress, a chilling realization struck Stanya. Graffik wasn't simply holding Lyra hostage. He was using her as a bargaining chip, a pawn in a larger game. The fortress wasn't simply a prison, it was a symbol of his power, a testament to his ruthlessness. Lyra's rescue wouldn't just be a simple act of bravery; it would be a blow to Graffik's authority, a symbol of defiance. And the stakes were higher than ever before.

The final ascent to the fortress was agonizingly slow and fraught with danger. They moved like shadows, their every step measured, their senses heightened. The fortress loomed before them, an imposing structure of black stone, a symbol of Graffik's absolute power, silhouetted against the ominous night sky. The wind howled around them, carrying with it the whispers of ancient legends and the chilling scent of death. As they approached the gates, they prepared for the final, desperate confrontation. The siege of Porthaven was over, but the true battle had just begun.

Chapter 9: A Sacrifice

The biting wind whipped around Stanya and Najeem as they crested the final ridge, the sprawling fortress of Emperor Baznoon Graffik dominating the horizon. Below, the rebel army, a chaotic tapestry of colors and weaponry, pressed their assault against the city walls. The air crackled with the clash of steel, the screams of the dying, and the roar of siege engines. Stanya clutched the worn leather satchel containing Graffik's meticulously detailed war plans, her heart a frantic drum against her ribs. Their escape had been harrowing, a breathless sprint through shadowed alleyways and treacherous mountain passes, but this – this was the true test.

Najeem, ever watchful, scanned the battlefield. His face, usually etched with the easy charm that had captivated Graffik's daughter, was grim, drawn tight with the weight of his commitment. He'd promised to return, to rescue Princess Lyra. That promise, a burning ember in his chest, fueled his every move. He gripped the hilt of his sword, the familiar weight a comfort in this storm of chaos. He'd lost too much already – his freedom, his family, almost his life – but Lyra, innocent pawn in her father's game, was worth fighting for.

"The south gate," Stanya announced, her voice barely audible above the din. "That's our best chance. They're focused on the main assault."

Najeem nodded, his gaze unwavering. He could see the desperation in the rebel's attack. They were outnumbered, outmaneuvered, but their courage was undeniable. He knew, however, that even with Stanya's intelligence, victory wasn't guaranteed. Graffik was cunning, ruthless, and he wouldn't go down without a fight.

As they began their descent towards the south gate, a sudden, horrifying shriek ripped through the air. They saw it then – a colossal explosion, a plume of black smoke erupting from the heart of the rebel lines. Graffik's ballistae, positioned on a hidden vantage point, had unleashed a devastating volley of explosive bolts. The rebel assault faltered, their carefully orchestrated advance dissolving into panicked retreat.

Stanya's breath hitched. This was worse than she'd anticipated. Graffik had anticipated their plan, their very presence here. "We have to get through," she said, her voice tight with urgency. "The information…it has to reach them."

But as they moved closer, they saw the true horror of the explosion. The rebel lines weren't just scattered; they were decimated. And amongst the carnage, a figure lay still, motionless, a familiar figure. It was Kaelen, the leader of the rebel faction, his body twisted at an unnatural angle, a crimson stain blooming across his chest. Kaelen, the man who had given them sanctuary, who had believed in their mission, was dead.

The weight of his death crashed down on Stanya. She had failed. Not in securing the information, but in securing his survival. She was responsible. He had put his trust in her, and now he was gone. She felt a surge of overwhelming guilt, a bitter taste of failure coating her tongue. But there was no time for self-recrimination.

Najeem, ever the pragmatist, knelt beside Kaelen's body, checking for a pulse. There was none. Graffik had planned this expertly, a targeted blow to cripple their chances of success. This wasn't just about capturing them anymore, it was about crushing the rebellion completely.

"We have to get that information to someone," Najeem said, his voice a low growl. He stood up, his eyes blazing with a fierce determination. "Someone else must carry the torch."

Stanya knew he was right. Kaelen's death was a terrible blow, but their mission was too vital to abandon. They had to find a way to deliver the plans, to ensure Kaelen's sacrifice wasn't in vain. They looked at each other, a silent understanding passing between them.

"There's a hidden passage, near the old aqueduct," Stanya said, recalling a detail from her time in the palace. "It leads directly to the rebel encampment, bypassing the main defenses."

It was a risky route, fraught with danger. But it was their only chance. They had to move fast, before Graffik's forces sealed the city completely.

The journey through the old aqueduct was claustrophobic and treacherous. The air was thick with the smell of damp earth and decay. The passage was narrow, barely wide enough for them to pass side-by-side, and they moved silently, their senses heightened, listening for the slightest sound.

They encountered several patrols, soldiers searching for stragglers, but Najeem's skill and Stanya's cunning enabled them to evade detection. Stanya, her knowledge of the aqueduct's intricate layout proving invaluable, guided them expertly through the labyrinthine tunnels.

Finally, they reached the end of the passage, emerging into a secluded part of the rebel encampment. They found a small group of rebel fighters, shaken but still defiant. Stanya quickly explained the situation, handing over the satchel containing Graffik's war plans.

The rebels' faces were etched with disbelief, then grief, as they learned of Kaelen's death. But their resolve did not waver. Kaelen's sacrifice would not be meaningless. The intelligence Stanya had secured would be used. The fight would go on.

As Stanya and Najeem watched, the rebels regrouped, the news of Kaelen's death strengthening their resolve. They were ready to fight. Stanya and Najeem knew their immediate task was done. But as they looked at the determined faces of the rebels, they knew their journey was far from over. The war had just begun.

Najeem, though his heart ached for Lyra, knew he had to leave. He had to fulfill his promise, not just to Lyra, but to Kaelen's memory. His commitment to rescue Lyra was now infused with a burning desire for revenge on Graffik and his relentless tyranny. This sacrifice would not be in vain. He wouldn't let it be. He would return. He would make Graffik pay. And he would free Lyra, whatever the cost.

Stanya, her own wounds still raw, knew that her fight had just become even more intense. The information she had risked her life for was now in the hands of those who would use it wisely. Graffik was a cruel man, but so too was the world he ruled. The struggle against oppression would be long and hard, filled with losses and sacrifices, but she would persevere. She would fight for a world where those who wielded power didn't do so with such casual brutality, a world where information wasn't a weapon, but a tool for progress, and where Kaelen's sacrifice was not forgotten.

As the sun dipped below the horizon, casting long shadows across the battle-scarred land, Stanya and Najeem turned and parted ways. Their eyes met, a silent acknowledgment of the shared ordeal, the sacrifice made, and the long road that lay ahead. They knew their paths might diverge, but their destinies were entwined in this ongoing fight for freedom, a fight now fuelled by the memory of a fallen leader, a sacrifice that would inspire them to fight even harder against the darkness. Graffik had dealt a blow, but he hadn't broken them. He had only strengthened their resolve. The fight would go on, and they would be at the forefront.

The rebel camp buzzed with a nervous energy that mirrored Stanya's own. She had delivered Graffik's war plans, a feat that had earned her grateful nods and hushed whispers of admiration. Yet, the victory felt hollow. The cost had been too high. The memory of the fallen leader, a charismatic general who had believed in their cause with unwavering faith, cast a long shadow over the celebrations. His death, a sacrifice to buy them time, had been a brutal blow.

Stanya sought out Zara, the leader of the rebel faction, a woman whose steely gaze and sharp intellect commanded respect. Zara, however, seemed preoccupied, her usual fiery demeanor replaced with a pensive stillness. She was surrounded by a cluster of grim-faced advisors, their hushed tones barely audible over the crackling campfire. Stanya approached cautiously, her boots crunching on the gravel.

"Zara," Stanya began, her voice low. "I have something to… to share."

Zara looked up, her eyes, usually so bright and full of life, were clouded with a weariness that chilled Stanya to the bone. "Stanya," she said, her voice strained, "I've been expecting you."

The grim faces of Zara's advisors turned towards Stanya, their expressions a mixture of suspicion and sorrow. One of them, a wiry man with sharp, piercing eyes, stepped forward. "We've discovered something… troubling," he said, his voice harsh. "A betrayal."

The air crackled with unspoken accusations. Stanya's heart pounded. Betrayal? Who? And how?

Zara gestured towards a scroll that lay open on a nearby table, its contents illuminated by the flickering firelight. Stanya approached, her gaze falling upon the elegant script. It was a coded message, intercepted from a messenger sent from within Graffik's court. It spoke of a secret pact, a treacherous alliance between a high-ranking rebel general – a man Stanya had once considered a friend – and Emperor Baznoon Graffik himself.

The general, Kaelen, had been a key figure in the rebellion, a respected strategist whose tactical brilliance had steered them through many perilous battles. His unwavering commitment to the cause had never been doubted, making this revelation all the more shocking. The coded message detailed Kaelen's plan: a carefully orchestrated sabotage that would cripple the rebel army's supply lines, leaving them vulnerable to a devastating counterattack. In exchange for his treachery, Kaelen was promised immense wealth, land, and a high position in Graffik's court.

Stanya felt a cold dread seep into her bones. She remembered Kaelen, his warm smile, his encouraging words. The image shattered, replaced by a chilling vision of a calculating betrayer, a viper in their midst. The betrayal ran deeper than she could have ever imagined. The messenger's report revealed that Kaelen hadn't acted alone. He had planted informants within the rebel ranks for months, carefully gathering intelligence and feeding it to Graffik. This was not merely a sudden shift in allegiance, but a long-term, meticulously planned operation.

The weight of the revelation pressed down on Stanya. The lives lost, the sacrifices made – all tainted by this treachery. Zara's face was a mask of controlled fury, her eyes burning with a cold fire. "We need to act quickly," she said, her voice low and deadly. "We need to neutralize Kaelen and his informants before they can strike."

The following hours were a whirlwind of frantic activity. The rebel leaders debated strategies, their voices rising and falling in tense discussions. Zara, with her decisive hand, organized a swift countermeasure. Spies were dispatched to identify Kaelen's collaborators, and plans were drawn up to capture him before he could deliver the final blow to the rebellion.

Stanya, despite the shock and the betrayal, found herself thrust into the thick of the action. Her skills in information gathering were invaluable, helping to piece together the details of Kaelen's network. She helped identify several key informants, their true loyalties hidden beneath masks of feigned commitment. She worked tirelessly alongside Zara, helping to coordinate the various elements of the plan. This was not just a fight for freedom anymore; it was a fight for survival, a race against time to prevent utter devastation.

As night fell, a small group of trusted rebels, Stanya among them, moved through the darkened camp towards Kaelen's tent. Tension hung heavy in the air, every rustle of leaves, every snap of a twig, echoing with a potential threat. Their mission was simple: capture Kaelen alive. But capturing him would be anything but simple.

The tent was heavily guarded, a testament to Kaelen's position within the rebel ranks. Stanya used her agility and stealth, navigating the shadows with the grace of a phantom. She used her knowledge of the terrain to guide the other rebels through the maze of tents, choosing the path that would offer the best cover and prevent detection.

As they reached Kaelen's tent, they saw him inside, hunched over a map, a sinister smile playing on his lips. He appeared relaxed, oblivious to the danger lurking outside. Perhaps his betrayal had made him overconfident. The plan to capture him swiftly and silently was executed with deadly precision.

The ensuing struggle was short but brutal. Kaelen, despite his surprise, fought with the ferocity of a cornered animal. His skill with a sword was undeniable, honed over years of battle. But the rebels were prepared, and they outnumbered him. In the end, he was overwhelmed and bound.

His capture sent shockwaves through the rebel camp. The discovery of his treachery ignited a firestorm of anger and resentment. Many rebels, once loyal followers, were left reeling in disbelief, their trust shattered by the betrayal. The execution of Kaelen, swift and decisive, served as a stark reminder of the consequences of disloyalty.

But the fight wasn't over. The information obtained from Kaelen's capture exposed a larger network of spies and conspirators hidden within the rebel ranks. Stanya, her resolve hardened by the devastating betrayal, found herself once again thrust into the heart of the conflict. The fight for freedom had become a relentless pursuit of justice, a brutal purge of the vipers who sought to undermine the rebellion from within. This was a war now fought not just against Graffik, but against the insidious enemy dwelling in their own midst. The path ahead was treacherous and fraught with danger, but Stanya, steeled by loss and fueled by righteous anger, was prepared to face it head-on. The revolution was far from over, and she was determined to see it through to its victorious end. Even if that meant sacrificing everything.

The air hung thick with the scent of woodsmoke and fear. The rebel camp, once a vibrant hub of hope, now felt brittle, fractured by the revelation of the internal treachery. Stanya, her usually sharp eyes shadowed with weariness, moved through the hushed tents, the weight of the fallen general pressing down on her like a physical burden. She'd deciphered the intricate code within Graffik's war plans, revealing not just troop movements and military strategies, but a chillingly efficient network of informants woven into the fabric of the rebellion itself. Names whispered in hushed tones now echoed in her mind – trusted advisors, seasoned fighters, all seemingly loyal, yet all secretly feeding information to Baznoon Graffik.

Her hand instinctively went to the small, worn leather pouch at her hip, containing the remaining fragments of information she'd managed to salvage. Graffik's endgame, she suspected, was far more insidious than a simple military campaign. This was a systematic dismantling of the rebellion from within, a slow, agonizing strangulation. Graffik's spies weren't merely reporting; they were manipulating, turning allies against each other, sowing seeds of discord that were now blossoming into deadly conflict.

She sought out Kaelen, the grizzled veteran who had unexpectedly become a key figure in the rebellion's intelligence network. His face, etched with lines of battle and experience, was grim as he listened to her assessment. He leaned back, steepling his fingers, his gaze piercing. "Graffik's playing a dangerous game, Stanya," he said, his voice low and gravelly. "He's not content with simply crushing us militarily. He aims to destroy our spirit, to fracture our unity."

Kaelen presented her with a map, meticulously crafted, detailing the locations of Graffik's known informants. It was a tapestry of betrayal, a network so intricately woven that pulling out a single thread threatened to unravel the entire fabric. Identifying and neutralizing these spies was a monumental task, one that required both precision and speed. Delay meant more lives lost, more trust eroded. The very foundations of the rebellion were crumbling beneath the weight of Graffik's insidious machines.

But Baznoon Graffik wasn't relying solely on internal sabotage. Word arrived through a frantic messenger: Graffik was launching a full-scale assault, a brutal, overwhelming attack designed to crush the rebellion before it could truly take root. Graffik's army was moving with terrifying speed and efficiency, leveraging the intel gleaned from his hidden spies to bypass defensive positions and exploit internal weaknesses. This wasn't a conventional war; this was a calculated act of annihilation.

The rebel forces, already weakened by the recent betrayals, were woefully outmatched. Their numbers were dwindling, their morale shaken. Desperate measures were needed, swift and decisive actions to turn the tide of the war. Kaelen proposed a daring plan: a preemptive strike against Graffik's main supply lines, a bold gamble to disrupt his advance and buy precious time. It was a high-risk strategy, a long shot at best, but it was all they had.

Stanya, despite the ever-present weight of her responsibilities, felt a flicker of her old, reckless daring. This was her specialty: navigating treacherous situations, outwitting formidable opponents, and seizing victory from the jaws of defeat. She would lead the strike team, a carefully selected group of loyal fighters, their skills honed by years of conflict and survival. Each member was chosen for their expertise – saboteurs, assassins, and scouts, all fiercely loyal to the cause and hardened by the brutality of war.

The mission was fraught with peril. Graffik's forces were heavily fortified, their defenses layered and complex. Their path would lead them through treacherous terrain, across enemy lines, under the watchful eyes of countless sentries. Failure meant annihilation, a swift and brutal end to the rebellion. Success, however, could change the course of the war.

The night of the operation was cold and unforgiving. The wind howled like a banshee, carrying with it the chilling whispers of fear and uncertainty. Stanya, clad in her dark battle gear, felt a familiar thrill coursing through her veins – the adrenaline rush of imminent danger, the exhilarating dance with death. She led her team with ruthless efficiency, their movements precise and silent, like shadows moving through the night.

They infiltrated the enemy camp with the grace of phantoms, their every move a testament to their training and discipline. They disabled sentries, bypassed patrols, and planted explosives with surgical precision. The explosions ripped through the night, shattering the enemy's defenses and plunging the camp into chaos. The ensuing firefight was brutal and unforgiving, a maelstrom of steel and fire, but the rebel strike team fought with the fury of cornered animals.

They achieved their primary objective: disrupting Graffik's supply lines, causing significant damage and delay. But the victory was hard-won, purchased with the blood and sacrifice of brave comrades. Stanya, wounded but unbowed, watched the flames engulf the enemy camp, a grim satisfaction settling in her heart. This was just a temporary reprieve, a fleeting victory in a long and arduous war. Graffik's endgame was far from over, and the fight for freedom had just begun in earnest. The path ahead remained treacherous, but Stanya, with the strength forged in loss and sacrifice, vowed to continue her fight, unwavering in her commitment to a future free from Baznoon Graffik's tyranny. The echoes of explosions mingled with the quiet determination in her heart – the fight was far from over. Graffik's cruel game had just begun.

The following days were a blur of activity. The rebels, emboldened by their daring victory, consolidated their forces and prepared for the inevitable counter-attack. Stanya, despite her injuries, remained at the forefront of the effort, her tactical acumen and unwavering determination inspiring those around her. She worked tirelessly, analyzing intelligence reports, strategizing counter-measures, and coordinating the defense. Her resolve had hardened; the fire of rebellion burned brighter than ever.

Meanwhile, Graffik's response was swift and brutal. He unleashed his full military might, launching a series of devastating attacks aimed at crushing the rebellion once and for all. His forces, fueled by rage and a thirst for revenge, swept across the land, leaving a trail of destruction in their wake. The rebels, outnumbered and outgunned, fought with fierce determination, clinging to their hard-won gains.

The battle raged for weeks, a brutal conflict that tested the limits of human endurance. Stanya, leading her forces from the front, displayed remarkable courage and leadership, inspiring her troops with her unwavering spirit and tactical brilliance. She fought like a warrior, her movements fluid and precise, her every strike aimed to inflict maximum damage.

In the midst of the chaos, Stanya discovered another layer of Graffik's insidious plot: he was not only targeting the rebels but also manipulating the political landscape, attempting to sow discord and division among the neighboring kingdoms. He was playing a dangerous game, using treachery and deceit to consolidate his power and crush any opposition.

Faced with this new threat, Stanya knew that the rebellion needed to broaden its scope, uniting disparate factions and forging new alliances. She embarked on a perilous diplomatic mission, traveling through treacherous territories and negotiating with wary leaders. Her charm, her charisma, and her unwavering determination proved to be invaluable assets, as she managed to forge vital alliances, bringing together a formidable force capable of challenging Graffik's dominance.

The final confrontation was epic in scale, a clash of armies that determined the fate of the kingdom. Stanya, leading her united forces, confronted Graffik's army in a desperate, all-out battle. The clash was brutal, a maelstrom of steel and fire, but the rebels, united by their shared purpose and inspired by Stanya's unwavering leadership, fought with the ferocity of lions defending their pride. After a grueling battle, the rebels pushed Graffik's forces back, securing a significant victory. Although the war was far from over, this victory marked a crucial turning point, shifting the balance of power and breathing new life into the rebellion. Graffik's endgame had been thwarted, at least for now. The path to true victory was still long and arduous, but with Stanya leading the charge, the future felt, for the first time in a long time, hopeful.

The echoing silence of Graffik's opulent throne room was broken only by the rhythmic drip of water from a hidden fountain, a counterpoint to the frantic beat of Najeem's heart. He stood before Baznoon Graffik, Graffik's cruel smile a stark contrast to the gleaming steel of the ornate dagger clutched in his hand. The air crackled with unspoken threats, the tension so thick it could be cut with a blade.

Najeem had escaped his gilded cage – more accurately, he'd wrestled his way free from it – leaving behind Graffik's daughter, Zara, a ghost of a smile on his lips. He hadn't abandoned her willingly, but his heart ached with a mixture of longing and resentment. Her naiveté, her innocent faith in her father's benevolence, was a chilling reminder of the web of deceit he had just escaped. He hadn't even been able to send her a message, a whisper of hope, before the guards came, alerted by the strange sounds of a man escaping, not from the dungeon, but from Graffik's private chambers.

He'd found his way to the throne room not through subterfuge, but through sheer brute force, cutting a swathe through Graffik's Praetorian Guard like a scythe through wheat. He'd been fueled by a potent cocktail of anger, desperation, and a desperate hope to bring the cruel emperor to justice. Justice for Zara, justice for himself, justice for the countless others who'd fallen victim to Baznoon Graffik's tyranny.

Baznoon Graffik, perched upon his throne, was a picture of regal composure. Yet, a flicker of surprise, perhaps even a hint of fear, crossed his face for a fleeting moment before he masked it with a cruel smirk. "Najeem," he drawled, his voice smooth as polished obsidian, "Fancy meeting you here. I wasn't expecting a repeat performance of your... dramatic escape."

"I came for an answer," Najeem growled, his voice low and dangerous. "Why? Why did you enslave me? Why did you force Zara into this sham of a marriage?"

Graffik chuckled, a sound that grated on Najeem's nerves like nails on a chalkboard. "My dear Najeem, your questions are rather... impertinent. I merely saw potential in you, a strong warrior, loyal... well, loyal enough, at least until your... rebellion." He gestured dismissively with a jeweled hand. "Zara, however, is a different matter. She is my daughter, and as such, she requires a suitable husband. A husband who will, inevitably, be loyal to the crown."

Najeem took a step forward, the dagger glinting menacingly in the torchlight. "Loyalty bought with fear and coercion is not loyalty. It's slavery. And you, Baznoon Graffik, are a slave master of the worst kind."

Graffik's smile vanished, replaced by a cold fury. "You dare speak to me like that, you insolent dog? You, a mere slave, dare to challenge your Emperor?" He snapped his fingers, and the throne room doors burst open, revealing a contingent of heavily armed guards.

Najeem smirked, the fear of death replaced by a grim determination. "I dare because I've nothing left to lose. And because I know your reign of terror is about to end."

The duel began not with a flourish, but with a roar. Najeem, agile and swift, moved like a phantom, his dagger flashing, deflecting blows from Graffik's own sword, a magnificent weapon that seemed to hum with dark energy. Baznoon Graffik, though older and perhaps not as agile, possessed considerable skill, his every move precise, calculated. His strikes were brutal, aimed at crippling, not killing, a testament to his cold, calculating nature. He wanted Najeem alive, a trophy to remind his people of his absolute power.

The fight raged across the throne room, shattering priceless vases, sending ornate furniture crashing to the floor. Najeem fought with the desperation of a cornered animal, his movements a furious ballet of death. He parried, weaved, and countered, each move a testament to his years of training. He'd faced down death many times before, but never with such a personal stake. The memory of Zara's trusting eyes spurred him on, fueling his rage and giving him an edge.

Baznoon Graffik fought with the cold precision of a seasoned assassin. He knew that Najeem was strong, but he also knew that he was fueled by emotion, a weakness he intended to exploit. He bided his time, letting Najeem tire himself out, his movements becoming less precise, slower.

The climax of the duel came unexpectedly. During a desperate exchange, Najeem managed to dislodge Graffik's sword, sending it spinning across the floor. For a heart-stopping moment, they stood facing each other, weapons discarded, the weight of their animosity hanging heavy in the air. Baznoon Graffik, breathing heavily, let out a harsh laugh. "So, it ends like this?" he gasped, "A slave against his master?"

Najeem, however, was not finished. He lunged, seizing Graffik's discarded sword, the cold steel shockingly familiar in his grasp. He pressed the point against Baznoon

Graffik's throat, Graffik's eyes widening in surprise and then, finally, in fear.

"It ends with justice," Najeem declared, his voice devoid of emotion. "Justice for all those you've wronged."

Before he could strike the killing blow, a scream pierced the air. Zara, her face pale with fear and determination, rushed into the throne room, followed by a small band of loyal rebels. Seeing Graffik at Najeem's mercy, they hesitated. The situation was volatile, fraught with the potential for further bloodshed.

Zara, ignoring the pleas and shouts of the rebels, ran to Najeem, throwing herself between him and Graffik. "Stop!" she cried, her voice trembling, yet her eyes blazing with defiant fire. "Do not kill him!"

Najeem hesitated. He stared at her, torn between his desire for revenge and the love that still burned, despite everything, within his heart for the innocent girl. The rebels, caught in a deadlock, watched silently. This was not the victory they'd planned. This was something… different. A turning point, perhaps. The weight of a life, of a kingdom, hung in the balance, suspended in the heavy silence that followed Zara's desperate plea. Graffik, meanwhile, stared at his daughter, a complex mixture of emotions – shock, betrayal, perhaps even a glimmer of… affection? – crossing his cruel face. The fate of Baznoon Graffik, and perhaps the kingdom itself, now rested not in the hands of a vengeful warrior, but in the unexpected power of a young woman's love. The air hummed with the tension, a silent question hanging heavy in the ornate, blood-stained throne room: what would happen next?

Zara's words hung in the air, a fragile whisper against the backdrop of the opulent, yet blood-stained throne room. Graffik, Baznoon Graffik, remained uncharacteristically still, his usual cruel demeanor replaced by a mask of barely contained fury. His gaze shifted from his daughter, her face pale but defiant, to Najeem, who stood frozen, the dagger still clutched in his hand, a weapon now strangely useless in the face of such unexpected turmoil. The rebels, a motley crew of soldiers and civilians, held their breath, their carefully laid plans dissolving into the unpredictable current of Zara's impulsive act.

The silence stretched, each second feeling like an eternity. Then, a low chuckle escaped Baznoon Graffik's lips, a sound that sent a shiver down Najeem's spine. It was a sound not of amusement, but of chilling calculation. "My dear Zara," he said, his voice smooth as silk, yet edged with a threat that silenced the room, "you underestimate your father's... resilience."

He gestured with a flick of his wrist, and two hulking guards, clad in obsidian armor, emerged from the shadows. They moved with the silent grace of predators, their eyes fixed on Zara. Najeem's muscles tensed, his hand instinctively moving towards the dagger. But before he could react, a sharp cry pierced the air.

From the shadows at the far end of the throne room, a figure emerged, a woman cloaked in darkness, her face obscured by the hood. She moved with a speed that defied belief, a blur of motion as she leaped towards the guards. Her movements were precise, deadly; a whirlwind of expertly choreographed strikes. Before anyone could react, she'd disarmed the guards, leaving them sprawled on the floor, groaning in pain.

The woman then moved toward Zara, her movements now surprisingly gentle. She helped the princess to her feet, her touch surprisingly warm and reassuring. She then addressed Baznoon Graffik, her voice clear and strong, cutting through the lingering tension. "Your plans, Emperor Graffik, have been compromised," she declared, her voice echoing through the cavernous room. "Your reign of terror ends tonight."

This unexpected intervention completely shifted the balance of power. The rebels, initially paralyzed by Zara's actions, found their courage renewed. They surged forward, their weapons raised, attacking Graffik's remaining guards with renewed ferocity. The ensuing battle was a chaotic ballet of steel and fury, a storm of clashing blades and desperate cries.

Najeem, momentarily stunned by the woman's sudden appearance, joined the fray. He fought with the skill and precision honed over years of rigorous training. His movements were a lethal dance, his every strike purposeful and deadly. He found himself fighting alongside the rebels, their shared hatred of Graffik fueling their desperate struggle.

The woman, however, remained aloof, her movements seemingly effortless as she weaved through the chaos. She didn't just fight; she orchestrated the battle. Her strikes were calculated, her movements designed to disable, not kill, ensuring the minimal loss of life. It was a display of martial arts that Najeem had never witnessed before. Her skill was beyond anything he could comprehend.

As the tide of the battle began to turn in their favor, Najeem found himself drawn to the woman. He watched her, captivated by her grace and lethality. He noticed the intricate patterns woven into her cloak, the subtle glint of a hidden dagger at her hip. She was a mystery, an enigma cloaked in shadows, and he found himself inexplicably drawn to her.

The battle raged on, the air thick with the scent of sweat, blood, and the metallic tang of spilled blood. The throne room, once a symbol of Graffik's power, now resembled a slaughterhouse. The ornate furniture lay splintered, the polished floors stained crimson. But slowly, inexorably, the rebels gained the upper hand. Baznoon Graffik, his face twisted in a mask of rage and disbelief, found himself surrounded.

As Graffik prepared to make a desperate escape, the mysterious woman intercepted him. With a swift, precise movement, she disarmed him, the dagger clattering to the floor. She then addressed him calmly, her voice lacking the slightest tremor. "Your reign is over," she stated simply, her eyes unwavering.

Baznoon Graffik, for the first time, seemed truly defeated. His eyes, once filled with cold calculation and cruelty, were now filled with a chilling vulnerability. He looked at his daughter, then at the woman, a flicker of something akin to respect crossing his features. He had met his match, not just in strength and skill, but in unwavering resolve. His reign of terror, built on fear and oppression, was finally crumbling around him.

The battle ended as suddenly as it had begun. Graffik was subdued, his guards scattered and defeated. The rebels, bruised and battered but victorious, looked around at the aftermath of the bloody battle, their faces a mixture of relief and exhaustion. Zara rushed to the side of the mysterious woman, tears streaming down her face.

"Thank you," she whispered, her voice choked with emotion. "You saved us all."

The woman simply nodded, her expression still inscrutable. She then turned to Najeem, her gaze lingering on him for a moment before she spoke. "Your fight is far from over," she said, her voice low and serious. "Graffik's fall is just the beginning."

She then turned and disappeared into the shadows, leaving Najeem and Zara staring after her, their minds racing, trying to comprehend what had just transpired. The weight of their victory was immense, yet it was tinged with the unsettling knowledge that their fight against Graffik's forces was far from over. The battle for the kingdom had only just begun. The unexpected arrival of the mysterious woman had been a turning point, a catalyst that had shifted the entire power dynamic. But who was she? And what role would she play in the unfolding drama? The answers remained shrouded in mystery, as tantalizing and elusive as the shadows from which she had emerged. Najeem felt a renewed determination ignite within him. The fight for his freedom, and for Zara's safety, was only just beginning, and he knew, with a certainty that settled deep within his bones, that this was merely the first chapter in a much larger, and far more complicated, story. The woman, with her enigmatic presence and unmatched skill, had changed everything, and he knew that he would somehow have to discover her identity. This unexpected twist had left him with more questions than answers, but one thing was clear: the path ahead was fraught with danger, and he would have to be ready for whatever came next. The revolution, while victorious for the night, was far from over. The true struggle had yet to begin, and the unexpected savior, the mysterious woman who had appeared out of nowhere, had left them both wondering where this path would ultimately lead. The future was uncertain, yet the thrill of the unknown was intoxicating, a stark contrast to the oppressive reality that had bound them for so long. And so, the dawn broke, a new day heralding a revolution, a desperate fight against tyranny, and an equally desperate quest to discover the true identity of the mysterious woman who had changed everything.

Chapter 10: Consequences of Betrayal

The air hung heavy with the scent of woodsmoke and blood, a grim perfume clinging to the aftermath of the battle. The victory, hard-won and brutally fought, felt less like triumph and more like a pyrrhic win. The rebel forces had overthrown Emperor Baznoon Graffik, but the cost was steep. The ground, once fertile farmland, was now scarred with craters and littered with the remnants of war – shattered weapons, discarded shields, and the silent, unmoving forms of both rebel and Imperial soldiers. A chilling silence settled over the battlefield, broken only by the occasional whimper of the wounded.

The betrayal, orchestrated by Lord Valerius, a seemingly loyal member of the rebel council, had struck like a viper's strike, leaving a festering wound at the heart of their movement. His treachery had almost cost them everything. He had sabotaged the main offensive, diverting critical supplies and revealing key strategies to Graffik's forces. Only Stanya's quick thinking, her uncanny ability to anticipate her enemies' moves, and Najeem's unparalleled bravery had averted utter catastrophe. Even then, the victory was tinged with bitterness. Many comrades had fallen, their sacrifice a painful reminder of the fragility of their triumph.

The aftermath was a chaotic ballet of tending to the injured, burying the dead, and attempting to restore some semblance of order. Stanya, her normally sharp eyes clouded with exhaustion and grief, moved through the carnage, her hands stained with blood, both her own and that of others. The physical wounds would heal, but the emotional scars, the memory of fallen friends, the gnawing sense of betrayal, would linger far longer. She found Najeem amidst the chaos, tending to a young rebel girl with a grievous leg wound. His face, usually alight with a captivating charm, was etched with grim determination and a deep weariness that mirrored her own.

"Another one bites the dust, thanks to Valerius," Najeem muttered, his voice gruff, his usually easy smile absent. He gently cleaned the girl's wound, his movements perfect and practiced. "How many did we lose?"

Stanya's voice was low, devoid of its usual sharp edge. "Too many, Najeem. Too many. And the losses weren't just soldiers. Valerius's actions crippled our supply lines. The reconstruction will be far more difficult than we anticipated." She ran a hand through her sweat-matted hair, the gesture revealing the extent of her fatigue.

The consequences of Valerius's betrayal extended beyond the immediate losses on the battlefield. His treachery had shattered the trust within the rebel alliance, sowing seeds of doubt and suspicion. The unity that had powered their fight against Graffik had fractured, creating rifts between those who had suspected Valerius's disloyalty and those who had been blinded by his charm and outward dedication to the cause. Accusations flew, whispers of further betrayals rippled through the ranks. The atmosphere, already heavy with grief, was now suffocated by mistrust.

The difficult task of rebuilding began under a pall of uncertainty and suspicion. The logistical challenges were immense, compounded by the depleted resources and the fractured morale of the rebel forces. Stanya, despite her physical exhaustion, threw herself into the work. She had always excelled at strategizing and organization, and she now channeled her grief and anger into the practical tasks of securing food, shelter, and medical supplies. It was a grim but necessary task, and her unwavering commitment served as an anchor for many of the wavering rebels.

Najeem, meanwhile, remained silent and withdrawn, his usual boisterous spirit subdued. He had lost several close friends during the battle, friends he had fought alongside for many months. The weight of their deaths settled heavily upon him. He had promised to return and rescue Graffik's daughter, but now, the path ahead felt clouded by uncertainty. The palace, once his prison, was now a dangerous battleground, and his personal mission had become infinitely more complex in the wake of Valerius's treacherous acts.

The separation between Stanya and Najeem, although not explicitly stated, hung unspoken in the air. They had shared a harrowing escape, a forged alliance built on mutual respect and burgeoning feelings. Yet, now, with the urgent needs of the rebellion demanding their attention, the distance between them grew, not out of animosity, but out of a shared understanding of the weight of their responsibilities. The romance that had flickered between them during their flight from the palace was now subdued, replaced by a mutual acknowledgement of the immense task at hand. They were bound together by their shared history, by the blood shed alongside each other, but the physical separation highlighted the unspoken understanding that their individual paths needed to diverge for the time being.

Graffik's downfall, while celebrated, was not without its ambiguities. Graffik, defeated but not broken, had escaped capture. Rumors swirled around his whereabouts, fueling speculation and fear that he might regroup and launch a counter-offensive. The immediate victory, therefore, felt incomplete. The finality of Graffik's demise had not yet settled, leaving a lingering unease among the rebels. The celebration of victory was muted, shadowed by the somber weight of the sacrifices and the lingering threat of future battles.

The price of victory proved to be exorbitant. The physical scars, the emotional toll of loss, and the deep divisions within the rebel ranks were evident in every whispered conversation, in every downcast eye. The rebel victory was a victory hard-fought, bought with the blood and tears of countless loyal fighters. The land lay in ruins, requiring an immense effort to rebuild. The road ahead was far from clear. It was a road paved with uncertainty, strewn with the obstacles of mistrust and the specter of vengeance. Yet, amid the wreckage and the uncertainty, a new hope began to kindle. A fragile seed of hope, planted amidst the blood-soaked soil, stubbornly reaching for the light.

The future, however, remained uncertain. While Graffik's reign of terror had ended, the war was far from over. The rebellion had succeeded in toppling the tyrant, but the path to true peace, to stability, and to lasting change was long and arduous. The work of rebuilding the land, both physically and politically, lay ahead. They faced numerous challenges, from the logistical difficulties of restoring essential services to the complex task of establishing a just and equitable government, replacing the oppressive regime with a system that valued freedom and justice. The scars of betrayal would undoubtedly leave a lasting impact, hindering the process of reconciliation and healing.

The new era dawned under a cloud of uncertainty, yet with a flicker of determination shining through. Stanya, hardened but not broken, would continue to play a critical role, using her skills and intelligence to navigate the treacherous political waters of the newly liberated lands. Najeem, his personal mission still burning within him, would set off on his arduous and perilous journey, a silent vow etched on his heart. Their paths, though diverging, were inextricably linked by the shared experiences, the mutual respect, and the deep, unspoken connection that had survived the trials and tribulations of their shared journey. The future was uncertain, the path fraught with peril, but together, they had sown the seeds of hope, a testament to their resilience, their courage, and the enduring power of the human spirit.

The wind whipped Stanya's cloak around her, carrying with it the scent of pine and damp earth. She stood at the edge of the Whispering Woods, the border between the newly liberated lands and the vast, untamed wilderness beyond. Beside her, Najeem stood as still as a statue, his gaze fixed on the horizon, his usually vibrant eyes clouded with a sadness that mirrored her own. The victory felt hollow, a cruel joke played by fate. They had won their freedom, yet it felt more like a prison sentence, a separation more agonizing than any chains.

"This is it, then?" Stanya's voice was barely a whisper, lost in the rustling leaves. She couldn't meet his eyes, afraid of the emotions swirling within them, a tempest of unspoken words and unfulfilled desires. The weeks since the overthrow of Baznoon had been a whirlwind – a blur of celebrations, political maneuvering, and the constant threat of lingering Imperial loyalists. But amid the chaos, a quiet understanding had blossomed between them, a connection forged in the fires of shared adversity. A connection now threatened with extinction.

Najeem nodded, the movement barely perceptible. His hand, calloused and scarred from countless battles, instinctively reached for the hilt of his sword, a familiar gesture that spoke volumes of his inner turmoil. "My path lies elsewhere," he said, his voice rough, his words clipped and devoid of their usual warmth. The warrior's mask had fallen back in place, hiding the vulnerable man beneath. "I must go to her."

The unspoken truth hung heavy between them: Najeem's vow to rescue Graffik's daughter, Princess Amara, whom he'd unwittingly enslaved and then, paradoxically, fallen for. He hadn't even been able to bring himself to say the princess' name aloud. It was a promise he had made, a debt he felt obligated to repay. His journey would be fraught with danger, a treacherous path through enemy territory. He would face Baznoon's loyalists, hardened mercenaries, and perhaps even Graffik's own wrath. His mission was perilous, and yet, it was the only thing he could do, the only course his conscience would allow.

Stanya understood. She knew the weight of his promise, the unwavering loyalty that burned within him, a loyalty that mirrored her own commitment to the rebel cause. Their bond, fragile yet undeniable, was tested by the stark reality of their divergent paths. Their time together, stolen moments amidst chaos and bloodshed, had been a refuge, a sanctuary in a world consumed by war. Now, that refuge was fading, leaving behind only a gnawing ache in their hearts.

"You'll be careful," she said, the words sounding weak even to her own ears. She wanted to say more, to pour out the torrent of emotions that threatened to overwhelm her – the fear, the longing, the deep, desperate hope that they would see each other again. But the words caught in her throat, choked by a grief so profound it felt physical.

He reached out, his fingers brushing against her cheek, a fleeting touch that spoke volumes. The contact sent a jolt of electricity through her, a reminder of the stolen kisses, the shared dangers, the unspoken promises whispered under the cover of darkness. It was a caress that could not erase the pain of separation, yet it offered a fragile comfort, a bittersweet farewell.

"I will," he whispered, his voice husky with emotion. He leaned in, his lips brushing hers in a kiss that was both a goodbye and a promise, a testament to the enduring strength of their connection. The kiss held the weight of their shared journey, the joy of their unexpected bond, and the agony of their impending separation. It was a kiss that promised more than it delivered, a promise whispered on the wind.

As he pulled away, she saw a glimmer of unshed tears in his eyes, a reflection of the pain she felt tearing through her own heart. The silent farewell was more poignant than any words could express, a shared understanding that transcended the need for verbal declarations. Their parting was a testament to the sacrifices they were making, a commitment to their individual responsibilities. Their love, however unspoken, was as unwavering as the loyalty they held for the principles they fought for.

The hours that followed were a blur of activity. Stanya finalized the delivery of the information she had painstakingly gathered from Baznoon's court. It detailed Graffik's plans, his hidden alliances, and the extent of his network of spies, a piece of information that would be instrumental in securing the fragile peace and preventing future conflicts. She met with the rebel leaders, discussing the future governance of the land, strategizing how to consolidate power and build a stable society from the ruins of war. It was an exhausting, emotionally draining task, one that demanded her full attention, yet her mind kept drifting back to Najeem, his face etched in her memory.

Meanwhile, Najeem prepared for his perilous journey. He gathered supplies, checked his weapons, and said his farewells to the few allies he had made in the rebel camp. There were nods of respect, grim smiles, but no extravagant displays of emotion. They were warriors, hardened by battle, and understood the unspoken language of sacrifice. He did not seek approval or comfort; his mission was solitary, his burden his own. He'd sought out one of the few remaining loyalist horses, now abandoned and wild, but strong and fast – the type that could navigate the rugged terrain ahead. The animal had been wary, skittish, clearly still haunted by the recent violence. But Najeem had approached it with a quiet patience, a respect for its wild spirit. He'd spent hours speaking softly to it, offering bits of stolen bread, gradually earning its trust until it finally allowed him to mount.

As darkness descended, a chilling silence permeated the landscape. The victory celebration had been subdued, a stark contrast to the raucous, celebratory aftermaths of previous battles. The shadow of loss hung heavy in the air, a silent acknowledgment of the casualties suffered. The cost of freedom had been high, a price paid in blood and sacrifice. The weight of this loss fell heavily on Stanya's shoulders, intensifying the already profound sorrow of her own farewell.

As the moon cast its pale light over the land, Stanya stood alone at the edge of the woods, watching Najeem ride away. He didn't look back, his gaze fixed on the distant horizon, his silhouette a dark figure against the silvery expanse of the moonlit sky. The image of him, riding off into the unknown, etched itself into her memory, a bittersweet reminder of their shared struggle, their unlikely alliance, and the enduring strength of the bond they'd forged. It was a farewell that echoed in the silence, a farewell as vast and untamed as the wilderness he was riding into. It was a farewell that left her with a profound sense of loss, a sense of emptiness that gnawed at her heart, yet also a fierce determination to persevere, to honor their shared struggle, and to keep the flame of hope alive.

The wind carried his scent, a faint whisper of pine and woodsmoke mingled with the earthiness of the untamed lands. The scent was a phantom embrace, a bittersweet reminder of his presence. It was a comfort, a connection to the man who had become inextricably linked to her destiny, a connection that transcended time and distance. She closed her eyes, the weight of his absence heavy on her shoulders, but within the ache of loss, a tenacious ember of hope flickered, a hope that fueled her determination to continue the fight, a fight for a future where they might, perhaps, meet again.

Days turned into weeks, and weeks into months. Stanya immersed herself in her work, using her skills to consolidate the rebel forces and guide the fledgling government through the chaotic transition. The liberated lands were still fragile, the threat of renewed conflict ever-present, yet a sense of hope was slowly taking root, nurtured by the sacrifices made and the promise of a future free from Baznoon Graffik's tyranny.

But despite the challenges, the emptiness remained, a constant reminder of Najeem's absence. His image haunted her waking hours and invaded her dreams, a constant companion in her solitude. She found herself searching for him in every shadow, every crowd, a desperate hope fueling her longing. She would look at the maps, tracing the paths he might have taken, calculating the risks, imagining the challenges he would encounter. She would often find herself in front of the border of the Whispering Woods, watching the landscape as though he might suddenly reappear on his horse, a beacon of hope in her lonely vigil.

But he didn't. And in the silence of her own lonely struggle, she found a newfound strength, a resilience that mirrored his own. She would carry his memory, his strength, and the promise of their unspoken love, as a source of inspiration, a reminder of the human spirit's resilience in the face of adversity. Her story was far from over, and it was a story she would continue to write, one chapter at a time, with the hope that one day, their paths would cross again. Their story was not yet complete, a promise whispered on the wind, a silent vow etched in the memory of a difficult farewell. The flame of their shared past flickered, a beacon in the darkness, guiding her through the trials and tribulations of her journey, a silent promise of a reunion to come.

The whispers of rebellion, once muted murmurs in the shadowed corners of the empire, had swelled into a roar. The news of Baznoon Graffik's tyranny, coupled with the strategic information Stanya had delivered to the Outerlands' leaders, had ignited a wildfire of defiance. The meticulously crafted illusion of his invincibility, so carefully cultivated over decades, shattered like fragile glass. His once-loyal legions, swayed by disillusionment and fear of the growing rebel forces, began to desert in droves. The meticulously planned campaigns, the carefully orchestrated assassinations, the suffocating control over information – all were rendered useless in the face of a people rising up in unison.

The first cracks appeared in the seemingly impenetrable fortress of Graffik's power within his own court. Whispers of discontent morphed into open accusations. His most trusted advisors, once sycophantic in their obedience, began to exhibit hesitations, their voices laced with uncertainty. The opulent palace, once a symbol of his absolute authority, now echoed with the chilling sounds of intrigue and betrayal. Even his own Praetorian Guard, handpicked for their unwavering loyalty, showed signs of wavering allegiance. The seeds of doubt, planted by Stanya's carefully placed intelligence, had borne bitter fruit.

The rebellion, initially sporadic and disorganized, coalesced into a formidable force. Led by a charismatic general named Rhys, a man known for his unwavering courage and strategic brilliance, the rebel army marched relentlessly towards the capital. Rhys, a man who had suffered greatly under Graffik's rule, understood the people's pain and channeled their collective anger into a focused, determined assault. The battles that followed were brutal and bloody, a testament to Graffik's desperate attempts to cling to power.

Graffik, accustomed to absolute control, was ill-prepared for this widespread revolt. His strategies, once so effective, were now easily countered by a unified populace fueled by righteous fury. He threw his remaining loyal forces into the fray, but their numbers were dwindling, their morale shattered. The once-impregnable city walls, symbols of his unwavering power, were breached, and the tide of the battle turned irrevocably.

The final confrontation took place within the very heart of the palace, a chaotic melee of steel and blood. Graffik, surrounded by his dwindling guard, fought with the ferocity of a cornered beast. But even his formidable skills were no match for the combined might of the rebel army. He was a master tactician, a skilled swordsman, but he was alone, his empire crumbling around him, his reign of terror ending not with a bang, but with a whimper. The weight of his countless crimes, the echoes of his victims' cries, seemed to finally crush him.

The fall of Graffik Baznoon Graffik wasn't a singular event, but a culmination of years of oppression, a final act in a long-running tragedy. It was a testament to the resilience of the human spirit, a victory won not by brute force alone, but by the unwavering courage of those who dared to defy tyranny. The liberation of the empire was far from complete; the scars of Graffik's reign ran deep. Reconstruction, healing, and the establishment of a just government would be a long and arduous process, but the first step had been taken – the tyrant had fallen.

The news of Graffik's downfall spread like wildfire, reaching even the far-flung corners of the empire. In the Outerlands, celebrations erupted. The people, long oppressed and silenced, rejoiced in their newfound freedom. The air vibrated with a sense of relief and hope, a feeling that had been absent for far too long. Stanya, watching from the edge of the Whispering Woods, felt a profound sense of accomplishment, a quiet satisfaction that permeated her being. She had played a crucial role in bringing down Graffik, but she knew that her task was far from over. The empire was in ruins, its infrastructure broken, its people scarred. Reconstruction would require significant effort and collaboration, and she would be a part of that process, contributing her skills in gathering intelligence to ensure a smooth transition of power.

Najeem's vow to return and rescue Graffik's daughter, Princess Lyra, remained a constant presence in her thoughts. She understood his motivations; Lyra was far more than just a captive; she was a symbol of hope, of a future free from Graffik's shadow. His dedication was a testament to the depth of his character, a reflection of his unwavering commitment. She knew he would face many challenges, that the path to Lyra's rescue would be fraught with danger, but she held steadfast in her belief that he possessed the strength and determination to overcome any obstacle.

The whispers of their shared experience, their brief but intense connection, still lingered between them, a silent bond forged in the crucible of adversity. Their escape, their fight for survival, their unspoken understanding - these were shared memories, a foundation for a future that they would hopefully create together. The memory of his touch, the lingering warmth of his embrace, fueled her strength, guiding her through the complex political landscape that lay ahead. She was no longer just an information gatherer; she was a warrior, a leader, a symbol of hope in a land recovering from years of tyranny. The road ahead would be long and arduous, filled with challenges and uncertainties, but she was ready. She was ready for whatever lay ahead, fueled by the memory of a love lost, yet waiting to be rekindled.

The fall of Baznoon Graffik was not merely a victory; it was a turning point, a symbol of hope and renewal for the empire. The seeds of democracy were sown in the fertile ground of revolution. The liberated lands flourished, demonstrating the transformative power of unity and shared purpose. Yet, beneath the surface of celebration, the undercurrents of political maneuvering surged. The power vacuum left by Graffik's demise had created a volatile situation. Rival factions vied for control, their ambitions threatening to plunge the empire back into chaos.

Stanya found herself at the heart of this political maelstrom. Her knowledge, her skills, and her unwavering loyalty to the cause of freedom made her a valuable asset, a player in the high-stakes game of power. She navigated the treacherous waters of courtly intrigue with the same skill and precision she had displayed in escaping Graffik's clutches. She weaved her way through conspiracies, betrayals, and alliances, gathering intelligence, shaping events, and ensuring the stability of the newly formed government.

The challenges were immense. The lingering effects of Graffik's reign were pervasive, the scars of his cruelty deeply embedded in the social fabric. Corruption was rampant, and rebuilding trust required immense patience and dedication. Yet, Stanya persevered. She worked tirelessly, alongside the newly elected council, to implement reforms, establish justice, and build a more equitable society. She used her knowledge to expose acts of corruption, to bring perpetrators to justice, and to ensure transparency and accountability in government.

Her work was not without peril. The remnants of Graffik's loyalists, embittered and desperate, plotted revenge, their actions creating further instability. Several assassination attempts were made on her life, narrowly averted thanks to her vigilance and the unwavering loyalty of her protectors. She moved through the shadows, always alert, always ready, her skills honed by years of experience, her spirit unbroken by the threats she faced. But even in the face of adversity, she remained focused on her goals –

building a better future for the empire, honoring the sacrifices made to overthrow the tyranny.

The memory of Najeem fueled her strength. His image, his touch, his vow – all served as a constant reminder of the reason she fought. She carried his silent promise with her, a beacon in the darkness, guiding her through the treacherous currents of political intrigue. The flame of their shared past burned brightly within her, a symbol of hope and resilience, a testament to the enduring power of love and determination. Their story, far from over, was a testament to their resilience, their love, and their unwavering dedication to a future free from the shadows of the past. The empire was rebuilding, and Stanya, along with countless others, was determined to build a better world, a world worthy of the sacrifices made to attain it. A world where the ghosts of the past would not hold dominion over the future, a future where love, and the fight for freedom, would never be in vain.

The celebrations were muted, a somber counterpoint to the jubilant cries that had once echoed through the liberated cities. The victory, hard-won and dearly purchased, left a bitter taste in Stanya's mouth. The streets, once thronged with cheering crowds, now bore the scars of battle – shattered buildings, charred remnants of homes, and the silent testament of countless fallen rebels. Each cobblestone seemed to whisper a story of sacrifice, of lives lost in the relentless fight against Baznoon Graffik's regime.

She stood on the ramparts, the wind whipping her cloak around her, the chill mirroring the icy grip of apprehension that constricted her heart. The information she had delivered had indeed sparked the rebellion, but the price had been staggering. The Outerlands, once a bastion of peace, now bore the wounds of war. Casualties were higher than anticipated; Graffik's forces had fought with a desperate ferocity, unwilling to surrender their power without a brutal fight.

The initial elation had faded, replaced by a sobering realization of the cost. She had seen the faces of the fallen, their youthful dreams extinguished in a flurry of steel and fire. She had cradled the lifeless body of a young woman, her eyes wide in a silent scream, a single crimson bloom staining her ragged tunic. The memory haunted her, a constant reminder of the fragility of life and the heavy burden of leadership. The weight of responsibility pressed down on her shoulders, heavier than any armor she had ever worn.

The leaders of the Outerlands, initially overjoyed by the success of the rebellion, now faced the daunting task of rebuilding their shattered lands. Resources were scarce, food supplies dwindling, and the threat of retribution from the remnants of Graffik's army still loomed large. The fragile peace was a precarious thing, easily shattered by a single spark.

Stanya sought out Theron, the grizzled leader of the Outerlands, his face etched with lines of weariness and grief. He sat in his temporary headquarters, a makeshift command post within the ruins of what was once a grand estate. The air was thick with the smell of smoke and decay, a stark contrast to the clean, crisp scent of the mountains that usually characterized this region.

"The cost... it was far greater than we anticipated," Theron said, his voice heavy with sorrow. He gestured towards a worn map littered with pins marking the locations of fallen fighters. Each pin represented a lost life, a shattered hope, a void that could never truly be filled.

"We knew there would be losses," Stanya replied, her voice barely a whisper. "But... the scale of it..."

Theron nodded, his gaze falling to his hands, gnarled and scarred from years of battle. "Graffik's loyalists fought with the desperation of cornered wolves. They knew their reign was over, and they took as many with them as they could."

The discussion turned to the immediate needs of the people. Shelter, food, medical supplies – all were desperately needed. The rebels, victorious but depleted, were struggling to cope with the aftermath of the battle. The exhilaration of freedom was tempered by the harsh realities of survival. The once-unified force was now fragmented, struggling with internal divisions and the logistical nightmares of rebuilding a shattered society.

Stanya, accustomed to the shadowy world of espionage, felt ill-equipped to handle this new challenge. Her skills were honed for infiltration and information gathering, not for the complex task of overseeing the reconstruction of an entire region. She found herself relying heavily on Theron and his advisors, absorbing their insights and strategies, but the weight of their burden pressed heavily on her.

Days blurred into weeks as Stanya worked tirelessly alongside the other rebels. She organized supply chains, negotiated with neighboring regions for aid, and tried to quell the growing tensions between factions within the rebel army. The victory had forged a common cause, but old rivalries and simmering disagreements now threatened to tear the fledgling nation apart.

The absence of Najeem was a constant ache in her heart. His image, vivid and sharp, played constantly in her mind. She envisioned him fighting, surviving, waiting for their reunion. She'd promised to stay and rebuild, to help secure the future they'd fought for together. It was a promise that anchored her, a powerful motivator to push through the endless tasks and challenges that lay before her.

One evening, as the setting sun cast long shadows across the ravaged landscape, Stanya sat alone on the ramparts, contemplating the daunting task ahead. The news had arrived about the escape of Graffik's daughter, a development that sent ripples of uncase through the ranks of the rebels. Her escape, a desperate act borne out of love and loss, could spark another wave of conflict.

Graffik's fall had been swift but chaotic. The remnants of his loyalists were scattered and disorganized, but their hatred remained, a venomous seed waiting to germinate and bloom into a new, even more brutal conflict. Stanya knew that the true test of their victory was not the overthrow of a tyrant, but the ability to rebuild their nation and prevent the return of tyranny.

The victory, she realized, was just the beginning of a long and arduous journey. The price of freedom, she now understood, was not simply measured in blood and sacrifice, but in the relentless struggle to preserve it, to safeguard the hard-won gains from those who would seek to reclaim their lost power. The challenges were immense, but Stanya, fueled by her love for Najeem, her dedication to the cause, and her unwavering determination, resolved to face them head-on. The future of the Outerlands, and perhaps the entire empire, rested on the shoulders of those who had dared to dream of freedom. And Stanya, weary but resolute, was ready to shoulder that burden. The weight of victory was heavy, but it was a weight she was prepared to carry. The fight, it seemed, was far from over. The true battle had just begun. The seeds of a new era had been sown, but the harvest would require patience, perseverance, and a constant vigilance against the shadows that lurked in the corners of the newly won peace. The land needed healing, not only from the physical wounds of war, but also from the deep-seated scars of oppression. The task ahead was immense, yet Stanya felt a flicker of hope, a spark of resilience that burned within her. It was the same flame that had guided her through the darkest hours, a flame fueled by love, loyalty, and the unwavering pursuit of a better world. And as long as that flame burned brightly, she knew that the future, though uncertain, held the promise of a dawn worth fighting for.

The wind carried the scent of woodsmoke and damp earth, a stark contrast to the acrid smell of gunpowder that had clung to her for weeks. Stanya stood on the precipice of the Outerlands, the vast expanse of untamed wilderness stretching before her like a rumpled emerald carpet. Behind her lay the smoldering ruins of what had once been a battleground, a testament to the brutal fight for freedom. The victory, while sweet, tasted of ash and sorrow. Too many had fallen, their sacrifices etched into the very fabric of the land.

She traced the worn leather of her satchel, its contents holding the weight of secrets that could reshape the empire. The information she'd risked her life to steal from Baznoon Graffik's palace was more than just data; it was a roadmap to dismantling his power, a blueprint for a future free from his iron fist. But the road ahead was treacherous, fraught with the uncertainties of a fragile peace and the ever-present threat of Graffik's loyalists, shadows lurking in the periphery, waiting for a chance to strike.

The Outerlands, a land of rugged beauty and fierce independence, offered sanctuary, but it also demanded resilience. Its inhabitants, a hardy people hardened by years of resisting Graffik's rule, were wary of outsiders, their trust earned only through proven loyalty and unwavering commitment. Stanya knew she had to earn their respect, not just as a messenger bearing vital intelligence, but as a comrade in arms, a partner in their shared struggle for autonomy.

Her thoughts drifted to Najeem, his image as vivid as if he were standing beside her. The memory of their initial clash, fueled by mistrust and born of necessity, was quickly overtaken by their shared escape, a harrowing odyssey forged in the crucible of danger and cemented by their mutual survival. Their connection, born amidst chaos, was as complex and unpredictable as the terrain they traversed. It was a bond forged not just in shared peril, but in a growing understanding, a mutual respect that blossomed amidst the turmoil. Their hastily shared glances, the fleeting touches of hands as they navigated perilous pathways, hinted at something deeper, something that resonated beyond the shared struggle. The seed of a potent romance had been planted amidst the fires of revolution, its growth as unpredictable and relentless as the flames themselves.

The leaders of the Outerlands, a council of seasoned warriors and shrewd strategists, received her with a mixture of suspicion and guarded curiosity. Their eyes, hardened by years of conflict, assessed her with a practiced skepticism, probing her words and actions for any sign of deception. Stanya, seasoned in the art of deception herself, met their gaze unflinchingly, her demeanor calm despite the turmoil within. She spoke of Graffik's weaknesses, the vulnerabilities in his seemingly impregnable defenses, revealing the intricate web of corruption that held his regime together. She laid bare Graffik's plans for the Outerlands, plans that were both chillingly ruthless and audaciously ambitious. The information she presented was a tapestry woven from threads of truth, each meticulously placed to build a powerful case against the oppressive regime.

The council, initially hesitant, grew increasingly impressed by the depth and detail of her intelligence. Her knowledge was irrefutable, her analysis impeccable. They saw in her not just a messenger, but a potential ally, a kindred spirit who shared their vision of a free and independent Outerlands. The evidence she provided was substantial, detailed maps of hidden supply routes, coded messages intercepted from Graffik's high command, and whispered accounts from within the palace itself.

Days bled into weeks as Stanya worked with the council, sharing her knowledge, strategizing, and planning. The information she'd obtained had ignited a renewed sense of purpose and hope among the people of the Outerlands. Their spirits, once dampened by years of relentless oppression, soared with the promise of liberation. The possibility of actualizing their independence was palpable, an electrifying current of hope that flowed through their ranks, inspiring renewed confidence and determination.

Yet, the shadow of Graffik loomed large. Graffik, enraged by the loss of his control over the central regions, wouldn't simply surrender. His reach extended far beyond the immediate borders of his empire, his spies and assassins working tirelessly to crush the rebellion. Stanya, along with the council, recognized that this was not a mere military victory, but a protracted battle of attrition, requiring careful planning, strategic alliances, and a constant vigilance. They began to forge alliances with neighboring territories, seeking support for their cause, promising mutual protection against Graffik's wrath.

As the days stretched into weeks, Stanya found herself more integrated into the life of the Outerlands than she could have ever imagined. She participated in the daily routines of the community, learning their customs, their traditions, and their unique way of life. She learned to appreciate their resilience, their unwavering loyalty to one another, and their deep-seated respect for their ancient ways. The people of the Outerlands, initially guarded and distrustful, gradually embraced Stanya, seeing her not merely as an outsider, but as a fellow fighter for freedom. She began to feel a sense of belonging, a profound connection to this land and its people, a connection that transcended the political intrigue and military strategizing.

The nights brought a different kind of solace. Under the vast expanse of the starlit sky, Stanya would often find herself lost in thought, reminiscing about her adventures with Najeem. Their escape, a desperate flight for survival, had tested their resilience and forged a deep bond between them. The memory of his unwavering strength and determination, his quiet courage, and the unwavering light in his eyes fuelled her hope and gave her strength. She missed him terribly, the silence of the night amplifying her longing. The romantic tension that had sparked between them, suppressed by the urgency of their escape, now simmered beneath the surface, a quiet longing that both comforted and troubled her. The thought of his future, and of her own, hung heavy in the quiet of the night. The future seemed boundless, filled with both promise and peril.

One evening, while studying maps with the council, a messenger arrived, bearing news that chilled Stanya to the bone. A messenger had arrived bearing news from the far south, news that spoke of a vast Graffik army amassing at the border. Graffik, it seemed, was preparing for a counterattack, a brutal attempt to reclaim the territories he'd lost. The news sparked immediate action. The council, energized by Stanya's intelligence and the shared urgency of the situation, met through the night, discussing strategies, allocating resources, and preparing for war. Stanya's expertise, honed through years spent infiltrating Graffik's court, proved invaluable. She provided insightful analysis, pinpointing Graffik's weaknesses, anticipating his moves, and suggesting countermeasures. Her knowledge transformed a desperate defensive strategy into a proactive plan for survival and eventual counter-offensive.

The Outerlands prepared for war, their resolve strengthened by their shared cause and their growing trust in Stanya. She knew, however, that this was only the beginning. The fight for freedom was far from over. The seeds of a new era had been sown, but the harvest would require unrelenting effort, constant vigilance, and the unwavering commitment of all those who dared to dream of a better world. The weight of responsibility rested heavily on her shoulders, but she embraced it, fueled by the memory of Najeem, the hope of a brighter future, and the unyielding determination to carve a path toward lasting freedom. And as she looked out at the starlit sky, she knew, with a certainty that resonated deep within her soul, that the fight for the future had only just begun. The dawn of a new era was breaking, but the shadows still lingered, promising a long and arduous battle ahead. The struggle for freedom, she knew, was an unending journey, a marathon, not a sprint. And Stanya, battle-hardened but not broken, was ready to run.

Chapter 11: A New Dawn

The air hung low with the scent of ash and blood, a grim perfume clinging to the ravaged city. The celebrations of victory had been muted, a somber acknowledgment of the cost. Graffik Baznoon Graffik was dead, his reign of terror finally over, but the scars remained – etched onto the buildings, the land, and most profoundly, the hearts of the people. Reconstruction was not a joyous occasion; it was a painstaking process, a slow climb out of the abyss. Stanya, her face smudged with grime but her eyes alight with a fierce determination, surveyed the scene from atop a crumbling tower. The once-imposing palace, now a skeleton of its former glory, stood as a testament to the brutality they had endured. Below, the rebels, a ragtag army of farmers, merchants, and former slaves, worked tirelessly, clearing rubble, patching roofs, and attempting to restore some semblance of normalcy.

She watched Najeem, his broad shoulders hunched beneath the weight of a salvaged timber beam, directing a small group of men. Even from this distance, she could see the exhaustion etched onto his face, the grim set of his jaw a stark contrast to the easy smile she'd glimpsed during their escape. The escape, the battles, the shared fear and camaraderie – all of it felt like a lifetime ago. Now, the euphoria of their victory had faded, leaving behind the stark reality of rebuilding a nation torn asunder.

The task seemed insurmountable. The city was a maze of devastation, each street a reminder of the sacrifices made. Yet, there was a quiet resilience in the air, a stubborn refusal to yield to despair. The people, though weary, worked with a purpose, their hands moving with a frantic energy that bordered on desperation. They were not just clearing rubble; they were reclaiming their lives, rebuilding their hope, brick by broken brick.

Stanya descended, her boots crunching on shattered stone. She moved through the streets, offering words of encouragement, sharing water and rations, her presence a beacon in the midst of chaos. She was no longer just an information gatherer; she was a leader, a symbol of hope for the oppressed. Her reputation, once whispered in hushed tones in the darkest corners of the empire, was now shouted from the rooftops, a testament to her courage and unwavering resolve.

The rebels, many of whom had witnessed her bravery firsthand, approached her with reverence and gratitude. They shared stories of their losses, their families, their hopes for the future. Stanya listened patiently, absorbing their tales of suffering and their dreams of a better tomorrow. Each story reinforced her resolve, fueling her commitment to this arduous task of reconstruction.

The political landscape was as shattered as the city itself. The rebel alliance, forged in the fires of rebellion, was a coalition of diverse factions, each with its own agenda and internal struggles. Negotiations were fraught with tension, disagreements erupting over resource allocation, power distribution, and the very definition of justice. Stanya found herself mediating disputes, acting as a bridge between warring factions, reminding them of their shared cause and the need for unity.

The task of rebuilding the government was even more daunting. Years of authoritarian rule had left the administration in shambles, riddled with corruption and inefficiency. New laws were needed, systems had to be established, and a new governing body had to be formed. Stanya, with her keen understanding of political machinations, played a pivotal role in shaping the nascent government, ensuring that the principles of fairness and justice, so dearly fought for, were enshrined in its very foundation.

Najeem, meanwhile, was focused on more practical matters. He had assembled a team of skilled craftsmen and laborers, working tirelessly to restore the city's infrastructure. His leadership was not based on intimidation or authority; it was earned through his dedication, his unwavering work ethic, and his innate empathy. He understood the physical toil of rebuilding, the sweat and aching muscles, and he worked alongside his team, sharing their burdens and inspiring them with his quiet strength.

Their paths, once violently intertwined in their desperate escape, now converged in the shared responsibility of rebuilding. They worked alongside each other, their collaboration seamless and efficient, a tacit acknowledgment of their mutual respect. The unspoken bond that had formed between them in the midst of chaos now blossomed into a quiet understanding, a shared commitment to a better future. Though words of romance remained unspoken, a deep affection simmered beneath the surface, a silent promise of a future yet to be written.

The days blurred into weeks, weeks into months. The city slowly began to heal, the scars of war gradually fading beneath a new layer of hope. New homes were built, markets reopened, and the laughter of children once again echoed through the streets. The reconstruction was more than just bricks and mortar; it was a testament to the resilience of the human spirit, a testament to the power of collective action.

As the sun set on another day, casting long shadows across the newly rebuilt streets, Stanya and Najeem stood side by side, observing their hard work. The city was far from perfect; the scars of the past remained visible, but there was a palpable sense of accomplishment, a quiet pride in what they had achieved. Their journey had been long and arduous, fraught with danger and sacrifice, but they had emerged victorious, not just from the battle against Graffik, but from the even greater challenge of rebuilding their shattered world. And as they looked towards the rising sun, a new dawn indeed, they knew that their work was far from over. The future was uncertain, but they were ready to face it, together. The seeds of rebellion had sprouted, and now, they would nurture them into a flourishing democracy, a testament to their courage, their sacrifice, and their unwavering belief in a brighter tomorrow. The rebuilding was not merely physical, but spiritual, a reclamation of a spirit crushed by tyranny, and the slow, difficult process of healing a nation. The weight of responsibility was immense, but it was a weight they were willing to bear, together. Their journey, far from finished, was only just beginning.

The rhythmic clang of hammers against metal, the rasp of saws against wood, and the murmured conversations of weary workers formed a strangely comforting symphony. It was the sound of healing, a slow, deliberate counterpoint to the cacophony of battle that had ravaged their city just weeks ago. Stanya, her hands calloused but nimble, worked alongside the others, helping to repair a damaged section of the city walls. The work was physically demanding, each swing of the hammer a reminder of the physical toll the rebellion had taken. Yet, the physical exertion was a welcome distraction from the ghosts that still haunted her. The memory of Baznoon Graffik's cruel face, the chilling efficiency of his assassins, the fear that had clawed at her heart during her imprisonment – these were wounds that wouldn't heal so easily.

Najeem, his broad shoulders hunched under the weight of a heavy timber, moved with a quiet grace that belied his exhaustion. The muscles in his arms, honed from years of rigorous training, ached with a familiar burn, but it was a different kind of pain from the agony of slavery. The scars that crisscrossed his back, souvenirs of his time in Graffik's dungeons, throbbed with a dull ache, a constant reminder of his ordeal. Yet, even these physical scars felt less significant in comparison to the emotional ones. He still saw the terrified gleam in the eyes of Graffik's daughter, Amara, as she'd been forced to watch his capture. The guilt gnawed at him, a relentless predator. He'd promised her freedom, and though he'd escaped, he'd left her behind in the clutches of a now-vanished but still influential regime.

Evenings brought a different kind of healing, a gentler balm to the wounds of the day. Around crackling fires, the survivors shared stories, laughter mingling with tears. Stanya found herself drawn to these gatherings, the shared vulnerability creating a sense of camaraderie that transcended their differences. She listened to tales of resilience, of courage in the face of unimaginable terror, and found a strength in their shared experiences. The stories, however harrowing, chipped away at the isolation she'd felt during her captivity, revealing a community forged in the crucible of shared hardship. She even found herself cautiously opening up, sharing fragments of her own ordeal, her voice catching at the memories of her own near-death experiences. The listening ears, empathetic nods, and shared silences helped to untangle the knots of fear and trauma that had bound her. She was no longer just a skilled information gatherer; she was a survivor, a member of a community rebuilding their lives together.

Najeem, usually reserved, found himself participating more in these gatherings as well. He initially struggled to connect, his silence a wall built of grief and self-reproach. The weight of his failure to protect Amara pressed heavily upon him, his quiet demeanor reflecting the depth of his remorse. However, witnessing Stanya's vulnerability and the healing power of shared stories encouraged him to venture further outside of his shell. He began sharing snippets of his training, his experiences as a warrior, finding that the act of recounting these past experiences, stripping them of their former weight and framing them within the context of a larger struggle for freedom and justice, helped to alleviate the emotional burden he carried. He discovered that his skills, once used to survive in captivity, could now be used to help others, offering practical assistance in rebuilding homes and organizing defenses.

The romance that had begun to bloom between them during their perilous escape now blossomed in the gentler environment of recovery. Their shared experiences had forged a deep bond of trust and mutual respect. It wasn't a whirlwind romance; it was a slow, steady unfolding, like the buds of spring gently unfurling after a harsh winter. Their conversations extended beyond the practicalities of reconstruction to encompass shared hopes and dreams for the future. They discussed their ambitions – Stanya's desire to create a functioning intelligence network to ensure the newly established freedom wouldn't again be threatened, Najeem's unwavering commitment to return for Amara – their differences complementing each other, forming a foundation for a love built on shared values and unwavering loyalty.

But the healing wasn't just emotional; it was also a physical and societal reconstruction. The city, ravaged by war, was slowly but surely being reborn. New buildings were rising from the rubble, their foundations laid not only in concrete and mortar but also in the shared hope and determination of the people. The markets, once silent and deserted, buzzed with activity, the laughter of children echoing through the streets – a testament to the resilience of the human spirit. Stanya and Najeem played a significant role in this rebuilding, not only by participating in the physical work but also by providing leadership and guidance. They organized work teams, coordinating the efforts of different groups, ensuring the resources were distributed fairly and efficiently. They fostered cooperation and collaboration, uniting diverse factions under a shared vision of a free and prosperous future.

The process was far from easy; disagreements and tensions arose, reflecting the multifaceted nature of the wounds they were attempting to heal. There were those who harbored resentment, those who feared change, those who clung to the old ways and distrusted the newfound freedom. Stanya, with her sharp intellect and intuitive understanding of people, navigated these challenges with a deft hand, mediating disputes, finding common ground, and building consensus. Najeem, with his unwavering strength and his quiet authority, provided the necessary backbone, ensuring that the peace was maintained, that the process moved forward, and that the voices of dissent were not allowed to derail the progress.

The healing was not a linear process; there were setbacks, moments of despair, and days when the weight of the task seemed almost unbearable. But amidst the challenges, there was a palpable sense of hope, a belief that a better future was possible. The wounds, both physical and emotional, were slowly beginning to heal, leaving behind a stronger, more resilient community. As the days turned into weeks and weeks into months, the city transformed. The scars of the past remained, but they were now interwoven with the vibrant tapestry of a renewed spirit, a testament to the indomitable spirit of the people, their determination to forge a better world from the ashes of the old.

Stanya and Najeem, side by side, watched the sunrise over their newly rebuilt city. The air was clean, free from the smell of smoke and blood. It was a new dawn, indeed, but it wasn't just the dawn of a rebuilt city; it was the dawn of a new era, an era of hope, freedom, and the promise of a brighter future. Their personal journey had only just begun, filled with the challenges and triumphs of nurturing a budding democracy, of establishing a just society, and of facing the uncertainties that lay ahead. Their love, born in the crucible of war, was now a beacon of light, a source of strength that would guide them through the years to come. The past was never forgotten, but it was no longer a shackle; it was a lesson learned, a testament to the power of resilience, and the promise of a brighter tomorrow, forever etched in the hearts of the people who had fought for their freedom, and in the hearts of those who would forever stand guard, hand in hand, ready to face whatever challenges the future held. The journey to true healing was a marathon, not a sprint, and they were prepared to run it together, side by side, their love and determination, a force as powerful and unwavering as the rising sun.

The news of Emperor Baznoon Graffik's death spread like wildfire, igniting a maelstrom of conflicting emotions and ambitions across the vast empire. In the outerlands, where Stanya had delivered her crucial intelligence, the initial reaction was one of cautious optimism. Years of oppression had left the people wary of sudden shifts in power, their trust eroded by decades of tyrannical rule. The celebrations were muted, subdued by a deep-seated fear that this could be a fleeting moment of respite before another tyrant rose to claim the throne.

Council meetings, once clandestine gatherings held in hushed whispers, now took place openly, though the atmosphere remained tense. The leaders of the various city-states, initially hesitant to trust one another after years of isolation enforced by Graffik's iron fist, slowly began to forge alliances. They had common ground – a shared desire for autonomy, for self-governance, for a future free from Graffik's shadow. But old rivalries and simmering resentments still threatened to derail their efforts. Stanya, now a trusted advisor, worked tirelessly to mediate, using her skills of observation and persuasion to navigate the treacherous waters of inter-city politics. She reminded them of the common enemy they had defeated and the shared sacrifices they had endured. She spoke of unity, of cooperation, and of a future where the people, not a single ruler, held the reins of power.

Meanwhile, in the heart of the fallen empire, chaos reigned. Baznoon Graffik's death had created a power vacuum, a void that many ambitious nobles and generals sought to fill. Intrigue and backstabbing became the order of the day, alliances forged and broken with alarming speed. Graffik's court, once a scene of lavish extravagance and ruthless efficiency, was now a battleground of competing factions, each vying for control of the remaining resources and loyalties. Some openly declared their allegiance to one pretender or another, while others played a dangerous game of neutrality, subtly maneuvering for position, waiting for the dust to settle before revealing their true intentions.

Among those vying for power was Graffik's younger brother, Theron, a man known for his cunning and ambition. He had always lived in the shadow of his brother, but his years of calculated silence had allowed him to cultivate a network of loyal followers within the court. His campaign was subtle, relying on whispers and back-channel negotiations rather than overt displays of force. He portrayed himself as a reformer, a leader who would restore order and bring prosperity to the empire, a stark contrast to the brutal reign of his late brother.

Opposing Theron was General Marius, the commander of the Imperial Guard. A man of immense physical stature and unwavering loyalty, Marius commanded the respect – and fear – of the army. His approach was more direct and aggressive; his strategy relying on brute force and the unwavering allegiance of his troops. He openly flaunted his military might, a blatant display of power designed to intimidate his opponents and consolidate his position.

Then there was Lady Isolde, Graffik's widow, a woman known for her icy beauty and sharp intelligence. She possessed a considerable fortune, and she deftly used it to bribe officials and sway public opinion. She kept her intentions close to her chest, moving like a phantom through the corridors of power, her true motives hidden behind a veil of grief and polite diplomacy.

The shifting alliances created a dangerous and volatile situation, with the potential for all-out civil war looming. Each faction worked tirelessly to secure the support of key figures within the empire, from influential nobles to powerful merchant guilds. Assassination attempts were common, whispers of treachery were heard in every corner of the palace, and fear hung heavy in the air. The balance of power swung precariously from day to day, each subtle shift in alliances sending ripples through the empire.

Stanya, observing the unfolding events from the relative safety of the outerlands, realized that the fight for freedom was far from over. The fall of Baznoon Graffik had not ended the tyranny; it had merely changed its form. She knew that the fragile peace in the outerlands could be shattered by a resurgence of Imperial power. The new dawn was still threatened by the long shadows of the past.

Najeem, haunted by his memories of captivity and Graffik's daughter, watched from afar. His initial desire for revenge against Baznoon had been extinguished with Graffik's demise; replaced by a deeper longing – to find the princess, and to protect her from the dangers that threatened the fragmented empire. He knew that returning to the heart of the empire was fraught with peril, yet his resolve remained unshaken. His personal mission was interwoven with the larger struggle for the future of the empire. He knew his skills would be needed, not just for rescue, but for safeguarding the newfound hope that was blooming in the outerlands.

Meanwhile, the information Stanya had delivered, detailing Baznoon Graffik's secret alliances and hidden weaknesses, was instrumental in shaping the new political landscape. It served as a warning and a guide, highlighting potential threats and avenues of attack for the various factions. Some of the information, too dangerous to be revealed publicly, was shared discreetly with key leaders, ensuring their survival and bolstering their efforts to prevent the return of autocratic rule.

Stanya, realizing the urgency of the situation, began to train a new cadre of intelligence agents, preparing them for the challenges that lay ahead. She instilled in them the values of courage, loyalty and unwavering dedication to the cause of freedom. She taught them how to gather information, how to analyze it and how to act on it – skills that would be vital in navigating the treacherous political terrain that awaited them. She knew that the battle for a just and equitable society was far from won. The fight for a true new dawn would require vigilance, cunning and courage. The task was immense; a test of leadership and resilience, a trial of wits and bravery.

The coming months would be crucial, a time of intense political maneuvering, strategic alliances, and potentially bloody conflicts. The fate of the empire hung in the balance, and Stanya and Najeem, each in their own way, would play a pivotal role in shaping its future. Their love, forged in adversity, would be their strength, their guiding light in a world still reeling from the shadows of tyranny. The new dawn had broken, but its promise of peace and freedom was far from assured. The fight for a truly free and just society had only just begun.

The outerlands, a patchwork of rugged mountains, whispering forests, and sun-drenched plains, felt a world away from the suffocating opulence of Emperor Baznoon Graffik's court. Stanya, still adjusting to the relative freedom, found herself strangely unsettled. The air, though clean and invigorating, lacked the sharp edge of adrenaline she'd grown accustomed to during her daring escape. The quiet hum of rebellion, so palpable in the hushed conversations and furtive glances of the people, was a different kind of tension entirely. It was the quiet before the storm, a pregnant silence that held the weight of centuries of oppression.

Her initial triumph, the delivery of the vital intelligence that had hastened Graffik's downfall, felt distant now, a fading echo in the vastness of her new reality. The information she'd risked her life to obtain—details of Graffik's hidden accounts, his secret alliances, the locations of his most loyal (and now vulnerable) commanders – had been received with a mixture of awe and cautious suspicion. The leaders of the outerlands, hardened by years of struggle, weren't easily swayed by promises or pronouncements. They needed time to verify, to analyze, to strategize.

This waiting game was proving more challenging than any physical fight. Stanya, used to the immediate gratification of action, chafed under the constraint of inactivity. Her mind, a whirlwind of calculated maneuvers and escape routes, struggled to adjust to the slower pace of political maneuvering. She volunteered for scouting missions, her agility and sharp instincts proving invaluable in assessing the loyalties and weaknesses within the newly formed alliance. She trained with the local fighters, honing her skills, teaching them new tactics, and learning from their unique fighting styles. But even this physical exertion couldn't fully quell the restless energy that pulsed beneath her skin.

The romance with Najeem, forged in the crucible of their shared escape, blossomed amidst the uncertainty. Their shared trauma had created an unbreakable bond, a deep understanding that transcended words. Their nights were filled with whispered conversations, their days with shared glances and unspoken promises. He, a warrior accustomed to brutal honesty and direct action, found himself captivated by Stanya's subtle intelligence and quick wit. She, in turn, was drawn to his quiet strength and unwavering loyalty, a stark contrast to the duplicity she'd witnessed in Graffik's court. Their love story was a fragile seedling, taking root in the fertile soil of a newfound freedom, but still vulnerable to the harsh winds of political change that threatened to engulf them.

However, their idyllic moments were punctuated by the harsh realities of their situation. The outerlands, while celebrating Graffik's demise, were far from unified. Different factions fought for power, each with their own agendas and ambitions. Rumors of rival commanders plotting to seize control, of neighboring kingdoms eager to exploit the empire's instability, filled the air. Stanya's intelligence had struck a blow against Graffik, but it had also exposed the empire's deep-seated vulnerabilities, making it a tempting target for other ambitious rulers.

One evening, while sharing a meager meal with Najeem, Stanya found herself confiding in him about her anxieties. The weight of the empire's future, the responsibility she felt for the information she'd provided, was almost too much to bear.

"I feel like I've started a fire," she confessed, her voice barely above a whisper, "but I don't know if I have the strength to control it."

Najeem reached across the table, his calloused hand covering hers. His eyes, usually filled with a quiet intensity, were soft with understanding.

"You did what you had to do, Stanya," he said, his voice low and reassuring. "You lit the spark of rebellion. Now, it's up to all of us to fan the flames and build something new from the ashes."

His words offered a measure of comfort, but they couldn't entirely dispel her worries. The future was uncertain, a tapestry woven with threads of hope and despair. The fragile peace in the outerlands was a precarious balance, susceptible to the slightest shift in power dynamics.

In the following weeks, Stanya actively participated in the consolidation of power within the outerlands. She used her knowledge of Graffik's network to identify and neutralize remaining loyalists, helping to secure vital supply routes and prevent potential uprisings. Her sharp intelligence, previously used to infiltrate enemy territory, now served the cause of liberation. She negotiated with hesitant village leaders, convincing them of the need for unity and collaboration. She even devised a system for collecting and disseminating vital information, a network that mirrors the very system she had once infiltrated. This time, however, her purpose was different, her motives pure.

Her skills, learned in the cutthroat world of espionage, proved invaluable in the delicate dance of diplomacy and negotiation. She became a trusted advisor, her counsel sought by leaders from various factions. The transition from clandestine operative to political strategist was seamless;

her mind, sharp and calculating, effortlessly adapted to the changing demands of her new role.

One day, a messenger arrived, carrying a sealed scroll from the capital. News reached the outerlands that Graffik's daughter, the one Najeem had rescued from the clutches of her father's assassins, was safe and had escaped. The letter was brief, containing only a message of thanks and a promise to meet in the future. Najeem, pale with relief, gripped the letter in his hands as if it were a lifeline.

This news, however, also brought a fresh wave of anxieties. With Graffik's daughter free, there might be attempts to reinstate the empire under a new ruler, threatening the gains they had made. Stanya felt a renewed sense of urgency. The fight for freedom was far from over.

She knew her future lay in the outerlands, but it wasn't a simple existence. It was a commitment, a responsibility she embraced with a mixture of fear and excitement. The road ahead would be long and arduous, fraught with challenges and betrayals, yet she was ready to face them. She and Najeem, together, would forge a new path, a future where the ideals of freedom and justice would finally prevail.

The love they shared was a source of strength, a beacon of hope amidst the darkness. Their shared experiences, the trust forged in the fires of adversity, had created an unbreakable bond. They were partners in this fight, not just lovers, their destinies intertwined in the fabric of the empire's turbulent transformation. The fight for a new dawn wasn't over, but with Stanya at the forefront, leading the charge, hope, however fragile, flickered brightly in the heart of the outerlands. The future, once a blurry uncertainty, now began to take shape.

The coming months and years would be a test, a trial by fire that would shape the destiny of the outerlands, and indeed, the entire empire. Stanya, however, felt a newfound sense of purpose. The intelligence she'd gathered, the life she had almost lost, was not in vain. She had sparked a revolution, and she would see it through to its glorious conclusion. The fight for freedom was a marathon, not a sprint. And Stanya, armed with her wit, her skill, and the unwavering love of a warrior at her side, was ready to run. The new dawn had broken, and she would help to shape its future. Her future. Their future.

The scent of pine and damp earth replaced the cloying perfume of the imperial palace. Najeem, his muscles still aching from the brutal escape, found a strange solace in the rough-hewn simplicity of the outerlands. He'd traded silken robes for worn leather, the comfort of a lavish prison for the biting chill of the mountain air. Yet, the freedom felt intoxicating, a heady brew of wildness and possibility. He wasn't sure what lay ahead, but the emptiness was preferable to the gilded cage he'd inhabited. His heart, however, ached with a different kind of emptiness – the absence of Princess Amara.

He'd sworn to return for her, a promise whispered amidst the chaos of their flight. The memory of her face, framed by dark, cascading hair, fueled his every step. He could still feel the ghost of her touch, the warmth of her skin against his own, a bittersweet reminder of their brief, forbidden intimacy. He knew it was a fool's errand; rescuing a princess from Graffik's clutches was a death sentence, even in this seemingly safe haven. Yet, the thought of leaving her behind, of abandoning her to her father's wrath, was unbearable.

He found temporary work with a band of mountain folk, hardened individuals who lived by their wits and the bounty of the land. Their lives were harsh, their days filled with the struggle for survival, but there was a fierce loyalty amongst them, a bond forged in the crucible of adversity. They accepted him readily, sensing the strength beneath his quiet demeanor, and he found himself surprisingly at home amidst their rough camaraderie. He honed his fighting skills, practicing with their crude weapons, learning to move like the wind through the treacherous terrain.

His days were a blur of physical exertion, a welcome distraction from the gnawing guilt that accompanied his freedom. He trained relentlessly, pushing himself beyond his limits, channeling his anger and frustration into each blow, each deft movement. He yearned for the refinement of his imperial training, the precision and grace he'd once possessed, but the raw power he was developing was no less effective. He learned to use the environment to his advantage, employing stealth and strategy in the shadow of the towering peaks.

Nights were different. Nights were for memories. He would sit by the crackling fire, the flames dancing in his eyes, reflecting the turmoil within. He'd trace the scars on his hands, the battle wounds a testament to his escape. He missed the warmth of Amara's presence, the sound of her laughter, the subtle intelligence that shone in her eyes. Their relationship had been a whirlwind, a forbidden romance born amidst danger and desperation, but it had burned with an intensity that left an indelible mark on his soul.

Word spread through the outerlands about the escapees from the imperial court. Whispers carried on the wind, tales of a warrior and a spy, united in their defiance of Graffik. The rebel factions, scattered and disorganized, began to see in Najeem and Stanya a symbol of hope, a spark that might ignite the flame of rebellion into a raging inferno. Secret meetings took place in hidden valleys, clandestine gatherings where plans were hatched and strategies discussed. The outerlands, once fragmented and divided, were slowly uniting under a banner of resistance.

Najeem found himself drawn into these meetings, not as a leader, but as a force of nature – a warrior whose unwavering loyalty and battle-hardened skills inspired respect and trust. He learned of the intricate network of informants, the secret routes and hidden passages that crisscrossed the region. He listened to the grievances of the people, the stories of oppression and injustice that fueled their anger. He saw the flicker of hope in their eyes, a fragile flame that he was determined to keep alive.

One moonless night, huddled around a crackling fire, a grizzled old man, a leader amongst the rebels, shared a crucial piece of information. He spoke of a hidden passage, a secret route that led directly to the heart of the imperial palace, a vulnerability in Baznoon Graffik's seemingly impenetrable fortress. This wasn't mere rumour; the old man had been a part of the palace guard himself before defecting to the outerlands years ago. He knew the layout, the guards' routines, the blind spots. This was their chance.

The old man spoke of the possibility of forging an alliance with a neighboring kingdom, a land perpetually at odds with Baznoon Graffik's rule. They were a formidable power, ready to support a rebellion that would topple Graffik. He warned, however, that the road ahead would be long and arduous; that betrayal was rampant even within their ranks; that Graffik was a cunning and ruthless opponent.

Najeem, along with a select group of rebel fighters, began training intensely, preparing for the imminent mission. His warrior instincts kicked in; he was back in his element, the adrenaline coursing through his veins. He sharpened his blades, meticulously checking every inch of his weapons, preparing them for the challenge ahead. He honed his strategies, planning every move with a precision that bordered on obsession. Sleep became a luxury, a brief respite before the coming battle.

The preparation was not only physical, but mental. He had to reconcile his personal quest to rescue Amara with the larger goal of overthrowing Graffik. He knew that the success of the rebellion hinged on the element of surprise, on swift and decisive action. Any delay, any hesitation, could cost them everything. He had to be prepared for every possibility, for every contingency. He would not let Amara down, nor would he let down the people who placed their faith in him.

The weight of responsibility rested heavily on his shoulders. The fate of the outerlands, and perhaps the entire empire, rested on his success. He channeled his grief, his anger, his longing for Amara into a steely resolve. He wouldn't falter. He wouldn't break. He would fight. He would win. For Amara, for the outerlands, for himself. The new dawn was more than just a promise; it was a call to arms. And Najeem, the warrior, was ready to answer. The whispers of hope were turning into a roar, and he was at the heart of the storm. His journey, far from over, was only just beginning. The true test of his mettle, his loyalty, and his love, lay ahead. The path to Amara, and to freedom, was paved with danger, treachery, and blood. But Najeem was ready to walk it, no matter the cost.

Chapter 12: Challenges Remain

The overthrow of Emperor Baznoon Graffik had not brought the peace the rebels had envisioned. Instead, a fragile calm settled over the land, a tense quiet punctuated by the nervous whispers of uncertainty. The Outerlands, once a haven for dissenters, now faced the daunting task of rebuilding, a process fraught with challenges that stretched beyond the physical destruction wrought by the war. The newly formed provisional government, a coalition of disparate rebel factions, struggled to maintain order. Internal conflicts, simmering beneath the surface during the rebellion, now threatened to boil over, fueled by competing agendas and lingering distrust.

Stanya, having played a pivotal role in delivering the intelligence that crippled Graffik's war machine, found herself thrust into the heart of this political maelstrom. Her sharp mind, honed by years spent navigating the treacherous currents of the imperial court, was now tasked with navigating the equally treacherous waters of revolutionary politics. She possessed unparalleled knowledge of the inner workings of the former regime, invaluable in dismantling the lingering remnants of its influence, but this same knowledge made her a target. Whispers accused her of harboring hidden loyalties, of secretly maneuvering for power. The whispers were insidious, planted strategically to sow seeds of discord within the fragile alliance. She found herself constantly evaluating allies, gauging their motivations, searching for the hidden knives poised to strike from within. The constant pressure weighed heavily on her, the adrenaline-fueled rush of the escape and the rebellion replaced by a gnawing exhaustion. The celebrations of victory felt hollow, a stark contrast to the grim reality unfolding around her.

Najeem, meanwhile, remained haunted by his vow to rescue Graffik's daughter. The image of her, trapped within the opulent but suffocating confines of the palace, fueled his restless energy. He'd spent the weeks following his escape gathering information, piecing together the fractured remnants of his own life before his captivity. He'd discovered that he was not simply a nameless warrior, but a member of a once-proud lineage, a lineage that had fallen out of favor with Graffik years ago. This new knowledge instilled in him a new determination—to not only rescue Graffik's daughter, but to restore his family's honor, reclaiming his birthright amidst the upheaval. He moved through the newly liberated city like a ghost, a shadow moving within the shadows, gathering information and building a network of contacts, some loyal to the former regime, some genuinely seeking to aid the rebellion. He understood the precarious nature of alliances forged in the aftermath of revolution, always assessing the level of trust he could place in those around him.

The most pressing challenge was the issue of resources. The war had decimated the land, leaving many regions in ruins, and the treasury, once overflowing with Graffik's ill-gotten gains, had been looted and scattered. Food shortages were rampant, leading to growing unrest amongst the populace, who, though celebrating the fall of the tyrant, were now facing the harsh realities of survival. The provisional government struggled to distribute the meager supplies available, leading to accusations of favoritism and corruption. Stanya found herself embroiled in countless meetings, mediating disputes between feuding factions, each vying for a larger share of the diminishing resources.

Adding to their woes, unexpected alliances emerged from the most unlikely quarters. Small, isolated communities, previously untouched by Graffik's reach, began offering their support. These communities, fiercely independent and self-sufficient, possessed skills and knowledge that proved invaluable to the rebuilding process. Their unique strategies and resilient spirit provided a much-needed boost to the struggling rebel alliance. They offered invaluable assistance in terms of farming techniques, medicine, and the construction of vital infrastructure. However, these alliances came with their own set of complications. Their deeply rooted traditions and customs differed greatly from those of the established rebel groups, leading to cultural clashes and disagreements over governance.

The political maneuvering amongst the rebel leaders was as dangerous as any battlefield. Ambition, betrayal, and the thirst for power drove the intricate games of diplomacy, where alliances shifted like desert sands, constantly reforming and reshaping the political landscape. Stanya found herself negotiating trade agreements, mediating disputes between rival commanders, and trying to keep the volatile peace. The constant pressure took its toll, leaving her exhausted but resolute. She knew that the stability of the Outerlands, and the future of the rebellion, rested on her ability to navigate these treacherous political waters.

Beneath the surface, however, lurked a far more sinister threat. Rumors of hidden loyalists, remnants of Graffik's secret police, circulated through the newly freed cities. These shadowy figures, masters of disguise and subterfuge, moved in the darkness, plotting their revenge. They were adept at manipulating the political situation, using fear and misinformation to sow discord and undermine the authority of the provisional government. Stanya and Najeem, both experienced in detecting deception and subterfuge, recognized the danger these shadowy figures posed.

But even as they faced these challenges, the greatest threat emerged from an unexpected source. A new enemy, far more formidable than Graffik, arose from the shadows – a powerful warlord from a neighboring kingdom, sensing weakness in the newly formed government. This ambitious warlord, driven by a lust for conquest and expansion, saw the chaos in the Outerlands as an opportunity to extend their influence, threatening to plunge the land into another bloody conflict. This new threat brought with it a fresh wave of fear, forcing the scattered rebel groups to set aside their differences and confront a common enemy. The future of the Outerlands hung precariously in the balance, and the path to lasting peace seemed further away than ever before. The tentative peace was shattered, the whispers of uncertainty escalating into a roar of impending war. The fight for freedom had only just begun.

The wind whipped across the desolate plains, carrying with it the scent of dust and the distant rumble of approaching thunder. Stanya, her cloak pulled tight against the biting chill, surveyed the landscape with a practiced eye. The Outerlands, once a vibrant tapestry of forests and villages, now bore the scars of war – charred earth, crumbling ruins, and the lingering ghosts of battles past. She'd delivered the intel, the damning evidence of Baznoon Graffik's treachery, but the victory felt hollow, tainted by the shadow of the looming war with the neighboring kingdom.

Beside her, Najeem, his usually stoic demeanor etched with a grim determination, sharpened his blade. The rhythmic rasp of steel on whetstone was a counterpoint to the mournful cry of a hawk circling overhead. Their escape from Graffik's clutches had forged a bond between them, a fragile alliance built on shared hardship and mutual respect. Their initial distrust, born from misunderstanding and circumstance, had melted away in the crucible of their perilous journey. Now, they stood together, facing a new and even more formidable enemy.

"They're coming," Najeem said, his voice low, his gaze fixed on the distant horizon. A column of dust, rising like a monstrous serpent, snaked across the plains, signaling the approach of the warlord's army. It was a force far larger and better equipped than anything they'd faced before. The fragile peace was shattered, the whispers of uncertainty escalating into a roar of impending war.

Stanya felt a knot of anxiety tighten in her stomach. Their small band of rebels, barely a handful of survivors from the overthrown regime, stood little chance against such a powerful foe. Hope, a flickering flame in the tempest of war, seemed to dwindle with each passing moment. They needed reinforcements, a miracle of some kind, to turn the tide. But where could they find such aid in this desolate wasteland?

As the enemy army drew closer, a desperate plan began to form in Stanya's mind. She knew of a hidden network of tunnels, remnants of an ancient civilization, that snaked beneath the plains. It was a dangerous gamble, a path fraught with peril, but it offered a chance, however slim, to evade the enemy and regroup.

"Najeem," she said, her voice barely a whisper above the wind, "there's another way. A way to buy us time." She outlined her plan, explaining the network of tunnels and the risks involved. Najeem listened intently, his expression unreadable. He knew the risks as well as she did; the tunnels were treacherous, filled with collapsed sections and lurking dangers. Yet, he nodded, his silence a tacit agreement.

Their escape through the tunnels was a grueling ordeal. The darkness was absolute, the air thick with the smell of damp earth and decay. They navigated the labyrinthine passages, their senses heightened, each footstep measured, each breath cautious. The constant threat of collapse, of being trapped and lost, hung over them like a suffocating shroud. But they persevered, driven by the urgent need to survive and find a way to fight back.

Emerging from the tunnels days later, they found themselves in a hidden valley, shrouded in mist and secrecy. It was here, amidst the whispering trees and the gurgling stream, that they discovered their unexpected allies. A group of nomadic tribes, fiercely independent and skilled warriors, had witnessed the warlord's advance and chosen to resist. They were not part of the formal rebel coalition, preferring to operate outside the established power structures. Their knowledge of the terrain and their unconventional fighting style made them formidable opponents.

Their leader, a woman named Lyra, whose eyes held the wisdom of generations and the fire of a thousand suns, greeted Stanya and Najeem with cautious skepticism. She studied them closely, assessing their worth, gauging their intentions. She was a leader forged in the harsh realities of survival, a woman whose words carried the weight of experience and whose gaze could pierce through any deception.

After hearing their tale, Lyra agreed to join their cause. She saw in Stanya and Najeem a reflection of her own people's resilience – a refusal to yield, a determination to fight for their freedom, even when the odds seemed insurmountable. Their combined forces, though still outnumbered, were now far more capable than they had been just days earlier. Lyra's warriors, masters of guerilla warfare, knew how to exploit the terrain, to strike from the shadows, and to disappear before the enemy could react.

The alliance with Lyra's tribe brought a renewed sense of hope, a spark of defiance in the face of overwhelming odds. But the warlord's army was relentless, their advance unstoppable. The battles that followed were brutal, a desperate struggle for survival. Najeem's warrior skills, honed through years of training, proved invaluable, while Stanya's tactical acumen, sharpened by her experience as an information gatherer, guided their strategy. Lyra's tribe, with their intimate knowledge of the land and their mastery of guerilla tactics, harassed the enemy, inflicting heavy casualties without engaging in open combat.

The tide of war began to shift, albeit slowly. The warlord, accustomed to swift victories, was frustrated by the rebels' elusive tactics. His army, bogged down by ambushes and hit-and-run attacks, began to suffer from dwindling supplies and dwindling morale. The seemingly insurmountable odds were slowly tilting in their favor.

One moonless night, as the enemy camp lay silent under the cloak of darkness, Stanya devised a daring plan. Utilizing her knowledge of the enemy's weaknesses, she led a small group, including Najeem and Lyra, on a daring raid into the warlord's heart. The raid was successful, a testament to their combined strength and coordination. The warlord's command structure was disrupted, his army thrown into disarray.

In the aftermath of the raid, the warlord, his army weakened and demoralized, was forced to retreat. He was not defeated, but he had been decisively checked, his advance halted. The Outerlands, battered and bruised, had survived another threat. The tenuous peace, however fragile, was preserved. But the victory was bittersweet, a temporary reprieve in a protracted war. The warlord would undoubtedly return, stronger and more determined, seeking revenge. But for now, Stanya, Najeem, and Lyra, standing together amidst the ruins of battle, knew they had won a crucial victory, a testament to the power of unexpected alliances and unwavering resolve. Their journey was far from over, but for the moment, they could allow themselves a brief respite, a moment of shared victory before the next challenge arrived. The future remained uncertain, but together, they would face it, their bond forged in the fires of war, strengthened by shared sacrifice, and fueled by a common purpose: to protect the hard-won freedom of the Outerlands.

The fragile peace in the Outerlands was a deceptive calm before the storm. While the immediate threat from the warlord had receded, a new battle was brewing – a battle for power within the rebel ranks themselves. Lyra, the charismatic leader who had initially welcomed Stanya and Najeem, possessed undeniable charisma, but her leadership lacked the experience needed to navigate the treacherous waters of political maneuvering. The Outerlands, fractured by years of conflict and internal divisions, were ripe for exploitation. Several factions, each with their own agendas and loyalties, vied for control.

Among them was Theron, a seasoned strategist who had quietly amassed considerable influence during the war. He presented a polished facade of pragmatism and unity, promising stability and order, but his ambition burned beneath a veneer of calm. His whispers of centralized power, of a unified army under his command, found fertile ground among the war-weary populace, those longing for an end to the chaos. Theron's influence spread like wildfire, subtly swaying public opinion and securing alliances with influential clan leaders.

Then there was Anya, a fiery warrior woman whose loyalty lay solely with the protection of her people. She distrusted Theron's smooth words, sensing the underlying hunger for absolute power. Anya commanded the respect of the soldiers who had fought alongside her, her unwavering courage and fierce independence a stark contrast to Theron's calculated moves. Her followers were fiercely loyal, forming a powerful counterweight to Theron's growing influence. She favored a decentralized structure, believing in the autonomy of individual clans, a system she believed was more resilient to central control and less vulnerable to tyranny.

Stanya, despite her desire to return to the anonymity she'd once cherished, found herself thrust into the heart of this political maelstrom. Her intelligence, her intimate knowledge of Graffik's court, and her understanding of the intricacies of power dynamics made her a valuable asset, sought after by both Theron and Anya. She understood the delicate balance of power, the necessity of compromise, and the devastating consequences of unchecked ambition. She saw in Theron's ambition a chilling echo of Graffik's tyrannical rule, a stark warning of the dangers of unchecked power.

Najeem, meanwhile, remained largely detached from the political machinations, his focus still on rescuing Graffik's daughter, Elara. He understood that securing her release required a stable Outerlands, but his personal stakes were far removed from the complex power struggles engulfing the land. His loyalty lay with Elara, and his actions were dictated by his promise to return for her, a promise that outweighed all other considerations. He trained tirelessly, honing his combat skills, preparing for the inevitable confrontation with Graffik's forces. He knew he would need every advantage to succeed.

The tension between Theron and Anya escalated gradually, their subtle skirmishes unfolding in veiled accusations and strategic alliances. Theron used his charm and manipulative skills to win over influential figures, subtly undermining Anya's authority, whispering doubts about her ability to lead in the long term. He painted a picture of stability and order under his rule, a stark contrast to the uncertainties inherent in Anya's decentralized approach.

Anya, however, refused to be intimidated. She countered Theron's calculated moves with unwavering resolve, rallying her supporters with passionate speeches, emphasizing the importance of self-determination and freedom from oppressive rule. She highlighted the dangers of concentrated power, reminding the clans of Graffik's tyranny, warning them against repeating the mistakes of the past. She pointed out the subtle ways Theron was dismantling their traditional autonomy, manipulating them into giving up their hard-fought independence.

Stanya, observing these unfolding power plays, found herself caught in the middle. She understood the dangers of both extremes – Theron's ambition and Anya's stubborn idealism. She attempted to mediate, to find a path toward compromise, a solution that would preserve the Outerlands' newfound freedom without succumbing to either unchecked power or chaotic decentralization. She understood that true freedom lay not just in overthrowing a tyrant, but in establishing a system that prevented tyranny from returning. Her expertise in intelligence gathering was now being directed towards understanding the personalities and motivations of the key players, trying to predict their next moves and discover potential vulnerabilities.

One moonless night, a clandestine meeting took place within the ruins of an old fortress. Theron, Anya, and Stanya faced each other under the flickering light of oil lamps. The air crackled with unspoken accusations and simmering resentments. Theron, with practiced eloquence, laid out his vision for a unified Outerlands, promising prosperity and security under his strong leadership. He painted a picture of a powerful, centralized army, capable of defending the Outerlands against any future threat.

Anya, her voice sharp and unwavering, countered his arguments, highlighting the inherent risks of surrendering their autonomy. She pointed to the history of oppression, the crushing weight of centralized power, and reminded them of the price they had paid for their freedom. She emphasized the importance of local autonomy, the need to respect the traditions and customs of each clan.

Stanya, her voice calm and measured, offered a different perspective, suggesting a compromise – a form of confederation, where the clans would retain their autonomy but work together under a council, with representatives from each clan. She proposed a system of checks and balances, preventing any one individual from gaining absolute power. Her proposal was ambitious, daring even, but it held the potential to bridge the widening gulf between Theron and Anya.

The ensuing debate was a fierce clash of ideologies, a struggle between competing visions for the future of the Outerlands. Each leader presented compelling arguments, their words fueled by ambition, idealism, and the weight of their responsibilities. The tension in the air was palpable, the outcome hanging precariously in the balance. The future of the Outerlands, its hard-won freedom, rested on the outcome of this fraught negotiation. The choice between Theron's centralized control and Anya's decentralized autonomy seemed insurmountable, leaving Stanya to search for a path that would safeguard the land's newfound independence. The night ended without a resolution, the three leaders leaving with their positions unchanged, the precarious peace hanging by a thread, leaving the fate of the Outerlands suspended in the balance. The political maneuvering continued, a silent war fought through whispered alliances and strategic betrayals, as the fragile peace of the Outerlands clung to its existence.

The flickering candlelight cast long shadows across Stanya's face as she studied the worn map of the Outerlands. Lyra's assurances of unity felt hollow, a thin veneer masking the simmering resentments that crackled beneath the surface. The meeting had ended in stalemate, a fragile truce achieved through exhaustion rather than genuine agreement. Theron, with his unwavering belief in centralized authority, and Anya, champion of decentralized governance, remained locked in their ideological battle. Stanya knew their conflict was a distraction, a convenient smokescreen for something far more insidious.

A low whistle pierced the night, a sound that sent a shiver down her spine. She glanced towards the window, the darkness beyond concealing any potential threat. The whistle came again, a sharp, almost imperceptible sound, yet Stanya recognised it instantly. It was the signal. Her contact.

She moved swiftly, her movements practiced and precise, sliding into the shadows. The information she'd delivered to Lyra – intelligence gleaned from Graffik's inner circle – had been crucial in forging the Outerlands' tenuous independence. But that intelligence hadn't revealed everything. There were details, hidden layers of deceit, buried beneath the surface of Baznoon Graffik's reign, details she hadn't dared to risk revealing without further verification.

Her contact, a shadowy figure known only as "Whisper," materialized from the darkness. He was a wisp of a man, his face obscured by a hooded cloak, his eyes like chips of obsidian. He held out a small, intricately carved wooden box.

"Graffik's personal records," Whisper rasped, his voice a low murmur that barely carried on the night air. "Confirmation of your suspicions."

Stanya opened the box. Inside, nestled amongst layers of soft cloth, were several meticulously rolled parchments. As she unfurled the first, her breath caught in her throat. The documents detailed a secret alliance, a conspiracy far more extensive than she had imagined. Baznoon Graffik wasn't simply a ruthless tyrant; he was a puppet, a pawn in a larger game played by unseen forces. The alliance involved powerful entities beyond the borders of the empire, entities with far-reaching influence and a shared interest in destabilizing the Outerlands.

The implications were staggering. The war with the warlord had been a calculated diversion, a way to weaken the Outerlands before the true assault began. Lyra, Theron, and Anya, locked in internal struggles, were blissfully unaware of the impending doom. They were playing a game of chess while a whole army was marching on their kingdom.

Suddenly, a sharp pain lanced through Stanya's shoulder. She whirled around, her hand instinctively reaching for the hidden dagger at her waist. Whisper was gone, leaving no trace but the lingering scent of woodsmoke and the chilling weight of the newly acquired knowledge.

She examined her shoulder, discovering a small, almost invisible dart embedded in her flesh. A potent paralytic, designed to incapacitate without leaving a readily visible wound. The attack wasn't brutal; it was precise, surgically efficient. The assassins were professionals, trained to eliminate targets quickly and without leaving a trail. This was no mere opportunistic attack; it was a deliberate attempt to silence her.

Stanya pulled the dart free, her mind racing. Graffik's alliance wasn't the only threat. Someone within the Outerlands wanted her silenced, someone who knew the full extent of her discoveries. Lyra? Theron? Anya? Or perhaps someone else entirely, a hidden player manipulating events from the shadows.

Days turned into nights as Stanya recovered from the attack, her body slowly regaining its strength. She remained in hiding, careful to avoid any interaction with Lyra or her followers. Her primary concern wasn't just her own survival but the survival of the Outerlands itself. The fragile peace, so hard-won, was teetering on the precipice of collapse.

She began piecing together the clues, connecting the dots in Graffik's documents with the subtle shifts in power within the Outerlands. The seemingly insignificant disagreements between Lyra's faction and the other rebel leaders were not just political posturing; they were carefully orchestrated moves in a larger game, designed to weaken the resistance from within.

She discovered that Theron's relentless pursuit of centralized control served the interests of Graffik's hidden allies. His rigid structure created a vulnerability, a point of weakness that the outside forces could exploit. Anya's belief in decentralized autonomy, while noble, made effective resistance challenging, causing fragmentation and disunity within the Outerlands forces. The seemingly unstoppable rebellion was slowly dissolving from the inside.

Stanya realized the subtle manipulations of her contact, Whisper. The signal, the delivery of the documents—it was a calculated risk. The attack on her was intended not only to silence her but to create chaos and distrust among the rebel leaders. The question became, who was Whisper really working for? Was it Graffik's allies, or was he a double agent?

Her investigation led her to a series of coded messages, hidden within seemingly innocuous letters and documents. With her knowledge of cryptanalysis, she was able to decipher their meaning, revealing a network of spies and informants operating within the Outerlands. The network extended far beyond her initial suspicions, infiltrating every level of the rebel movement.

The realization hit her with the force of a physical blow. The true enemy wasn't just Graffik's forces, but a far more pervasive, insidious threat. The Outerlands was riddled with traitors, their allegiances bought with gold or promises of power. The conspiracy reached into the heart of the rebellion, corrupting its leaders and undermining its efforts.

As the weight of this revelation pressed upon her, Stanya knew she couldn't rely on Lyra, Theron, or Anya. Their inherent trust in one another, blinded by years of conflict, left them vulnerable to manipulation. The only way to save the Outerlands was to act independently, to expose the network of spies and unravel the intricate web of deceit before it was too late. The fate of the Outerlands rested on her shoulders, the burden of a lone warrior fighting against an enemy both visible and invisible. She was ready to fight. But who was she going to fight with? The question hung heavy in the air, the answer as elusive and dangerous as the shadows that crept across the Outerlands. Her journey was far from over, and the fight for freedom had only just begun. The road ahead was fraught with peril, but Stanya, armed with her wits and unwavering determination, would face any threat, however hidden, to ensure the survival of the land she had come to call home. The next move in this deadly game of political chess would determine not only her fate but that of the entire Outerlands. And she was determined to play her hand correctly.

The wind howled a mournful dirge across the desolate plains, mirroring the turmoil in Stanya's heart. The fragile peace she had helped forge in the Outerlands felt like a house of cards, teetering precariously on the edge of collapse. Lyra, ever the pragmatist, had assigned her to gather intelligence on the remaining loyalist pockets within the former Emperor's territories, a task Stanya found both necessary and deeply unsettling. The lingering loyalty to Baznoon Graffik, even in defeat, proved a dangerous undercurrent threatening to drown the nascent rebellion.

Her journey took her through ruined villages, where the ghosts of Graffik's reign still lingered. Whispers of a new force, a shadowy organization known only as the Obsidian Hand, had begun to circulate. At first, these whispers were dismissed as mere rumors, the panicked ravings of a war-torn people, but as Stanya delved deeper, a chilling pattern emerged. The Obsidian Hand wasn't interested in reinstating Graffik's rule; their goals were far more sinister, far more ambitious. They operated in the shadows, manipulating events from behind the scenes, subtly shifting the balance of power to their own advantage. Their influence spread like a creeping blight, infecting the very fabric of the Outerlands' fragile unity.

One evening, nestled beside a crackling fire under the watchful gaze of a star-studded sky, Stanya met Elara, an elderly woman whose wisdom surpassed her years. Elara, a former court physician under Graffik, possessed a keen understanding of the Obsidian Hand, her insights painting a far more terrifying picture than Stanya could have imagined. Elara revealed that the Obsidian Hand wasn't simply a group; it was a network, a clandestine organization composed of skilled assassins, cunning strategists, and powerful sorcerers, all bound by a shared, unspoken goal.

They were the puppeteers, pulling the strings from the darkness, orchestrating chaos to seize power.

"They are masters of deception, Stanya," Elara rasped, her voice weak but her eyes sharp and piercing. "They sow discord, exploit weaknesses, and ultimately, they consume everything in their path. Graffik's fall was not merely a defeat; it was a calculated maneuver, a strategic step towards their ultimate goal."

Elara's words chilled Stanya to the bone. Graffik's fall had seemed like a victory, a hard-won triumph against tyranny. But now, it seemed like a mere pawn in a much larger, far more dangerous game. The Obsidian Hand was more than just a new enemy; it was a threat to everything Stanya had fought for. It was a threat to the very soul of the Outerlands.

News of the Obsidian Hand's activities reached Theron and Anya, intensifying the already strained relations between the two factions. Theron, ever the pragmatist, advocated for a united front, arguing that only through collective strength could they hope to repel the encroaching darkness. Anya, however, remained suspicious, fearing that a united front would simply consolidate power in the hands of Theron and his followers. Their arguments were bitter and heated, the cracks in their fragile alliance widening with each passing day. Stanya, caught in the middle, knew she had to act quickly, before the internal strife tore the Outerlands apart.

Her investigation led her to a hidden monastery, nestled deep within a treacherous mountain range. The monastery was rumored to be a sanctuary for the Obsidian Hand, a place where they planned their insidious machinations. This was her opportunity to unravel the mystery of their purpose, to uncover their ultimate goal. She sought the aid of Najeem, whose unparalleled skills in combat and stealth were now indispensable in her quest.

Their journey to the monastery was fraught with peril. They faced ambushes from the Obsidian Hand's assassins, navigated treacherous terrain, and overcame countless obstacles. Najeem's fighting prowess proved invaluable, his sword a whirlwind of destruction against their enemies. Stanya, employing her cunning and knowledge, outwitted their traps and evaded their pursuit. Their teamwork, born out of necessity and forged in the crucible of shared danger, blossomed into a bond that transcended their initial distrust

Their pursuit, tense and dangerous, led them through winding mountain paths, shadowy forests, and across raging rivers. The Obsidian Hand's assassins were relentless, skilled in both open combat and stealth, mirroring Stanya and Najeem's own capabilities. Each confrontation was a dance of death, a carefully choreographed ballet of steel and strategy. Najeem's raw power and tactical sense allowed him to overwhelm many enemies, while Stanya used her knowledge of poisons and traps to outwit the others.

But the Obsidian Hand proved to be more than just a group of assassins. They wielded a dark magic, their attacks imbued with sinister power. Stanya, despite her own limited knowledge of sorcery, found herself struggling to counter the dark forces they unleashed. Najeem, relying on his exceptional skill and strength, fought valiantly but even he found himself overwhelmed. The enemy's powers threatened to overwhelm their abilities, forcing them to adapt and develop new tactics.

Within the monastery, they uncovered a chilling truth. The Obsidian Hand sought not to control the Outerlands, but to destroy it. They were preparing a ritual, a dark enchantment that would unleash an ancient evil upon the land, consuming everything in its path. The scope of their ambition was devastating, a testament to the extent of their wickedness.

The final confrontation within the monastery was a brutal test of will and skill. Stanya and Najeem fought their way through countless assassins, sorcerers, and magically enhanced creatures, their teamwork allowing them to overcome impossible odds. They faced a formidable leader, a master sorcerer named Malkor, whose power was immense and terrifying. The fight was long and arduous, each blow a testament to their determination and strength. Najeem's sword sang a deadly song, while Stanya's wit and courage allowed her to exploit the weaknesses in Malkor's defences.

Despite the odds, Stanya and Najeem emerged victorious. Malkor's defeat was not only a triumph against the Obsidian Hand but also a critical turning point in the fight for the Outerlands' survival. The ritual was disrupted, the ancient evil contained, and the immediate threat neutralized. But as they stood amongst the ruins, amidst the bodies of their fallen enemies, Stanya knew the fight was far from over. The Obsidian Hand was merely one branch of a deeper, more insidious threat. The shadow of a much larger conflict still loomed over them, a conflict that would challenge them in ways they could never have imagined. Their journey had only just begun. The escape from the monastery, treacherous and harrowing, was a testament to their skills and their determination to survive. The journey to warn the leaders of the Outerlands, now armed with this shocking knowledge, would be their next challenge. But they were ready. They had faced the Obsidian Hand and emerged victorious, their bond forged in the fires of adversity, stronger and more resolute than ever before. The future was uncertain, but one thing was clear: Stanya and Najeem would face whatever came next, together.

Chapter 13: Conspiracy Unveiled

The flickering candlelight cast long, dancing shadows across the rough-hewn table where Stanya sat, the worn map of the Outerlands spread before her. The air hung thick with the scent of woodsmoke and unspoken anxieties. Around her, the leaders of the rebel factions, men and women hardened by years of fighting Graffik's tyrannical rule, exchanged uneasy glances. The initial euphoria of their victory over Baznoon Graffik's forces had long since faded, replaced by a gnawing suspicion, a chilling whisper of betrayal that slithered through the ranks.

It had started subtly, a series of minor discrepancies, logistical errors that seemed too deliberate to be mere accidents. Supplies went missing. Intelligence reports arrived late, sometimes altered. Rumors of dissent, carefully planted seeds of discord, began to sprout among the once-united rebels. Stanya, with her sharp mind and keen eye for detail, had been the first to notice the pattern, to sense the chilling undercurrent of treachery beneath the surface of their hard-won unity.

She traced a finger along the jagged lines of the map, her gaze distant, lost in the labyrinthine complexities of the conspiracy unfolding before her. The rebels, so fiercely independent, so fiercely loyal to their individual causes, had proven vulnerable to the subtle manipulations of a skilled opponent. An opponent who moved unseen, who worked from within, who knew the weaknesses and vulnerabilities of each faction.

"It's not just incompetence," she finally spoke, her voice low but commanding, cutting through the tense silence. "This is deliberate sabotage. Someone within our ranks is working against us, feeding information to Graffik's remnants."

A murmur rippled through the assembled leaders. Kaelen, the grizzled leader of the Northern clans, his face etched with years of hardship and battle, grunted his agreement. "Aye, lass. We've lost more than supplies. We've lost time, lost opportunities. Someone's playing a dangerous game."

Lysandra, the fiery leader of the Southern resistance, her eyes blazing with suspicion, leaned forward. "And who," she hissed, her voice sharp as a viper's strike, "is this traitor who dares to undermine our cause?"

The question hung heavy in the air, unanswered. The room was a crucible of mistrust, each leader eyeing the others with suspicion, wondering who among them harbored the venomous serpent of betrayal. Stanya felt the weight of their gazes on her. She had the evidence, fragments of intercepted messages, subtly altered supply manifests, inconsistencies in troop movements—but she needed time, needed to solidify her suspicions before unleashing accusations that could tear the fragile alliance apart.

That night, under the cloak of darkness, Stanya began her investigation. She moved like a phantom through the rebel camp, her movements silent and swift. She had to be discreet; her enemy could be anyone, and her own life was now on the line. She sought the missing links, the connections that could reveal the traitor's identity. The painstaking work involved gathering evidence from numerous sources, many seemingly unrelated at first glance. She reviewed the intercepted communications, cross-referencing them against the patterns of missing supplies and the altered battle plans. She studied the subtle shifts in allegiances, the sudden changes in alliances between factions.

Her initial investigations focused on the most obvious suspects: those who had clashed with other faction leaders in the past, those who had shown signs of ambition or discontent. Each time, she felt the thrill of the chase, the rush of piecing together disparate clues, and the subsequent frustration of dead ends and lack of conclusive evidence.

Days turned into weeks as Stanya delved deeper into the conspiracy, slowly building a compelling case against the most unexpected suspect: Lord Theron, a respected leader known for his calm demeanor and strategic mind. He was an elder advisor within the rebel alliance, his wisdom and experience held in high regard by all factions. But Stanya's investigation unearthed a series of coded messages exchanged between Theron and a known Imperial sympathizer, a message that spoke of an impending betrayal, a plot to undermine the rebel alliance from within.

The evidence was damning, but Stanya knew she couldn't act rashly. She needed more—a clear and irrefutable proof that would convince the other leaders without risking a devastating civil war before their final stand against Graffik's remaining forces. She decided to take a calculated risk and turn to an unlikely ally—Najeem.

Najeem, still grappling with the aftermath of his escape from Graffik's palace and the lingering unresolved feelings for Graffik's daughter, had been quietly building his own network of informants within the rebel ranks. His warrior skills and his innate understanding of people made him a valuable asset, one Stanya had learned to appreciate during their harrowing escape from the capital.

She found him at the training grounds, his movements a blur of controlled power as he sparred with another warrior. The intensity in his eyes was something she had come to recognize as an indication of focus and determination. After their shared adventure, they had parted ways, but the bond forged in adversity still lingered, a quiet understanding that transcended their differences.

She relayed her findings to him, sharing the evidence she'd painstakingly gathered, outlining the plot and the identity of her prime suspect. Najeem listened intently, his expression unreadable, his mind assessing the information with the precision of a skilled strategist. He possessed a quiet strength, a calm resolve that was reassuring. He had seen the depths of deceit in Graffik's court, and he recognized the insidious nature of the conspiracy that had ensnared the rebels.

"This Theron... he was always too calm, too collected," Najeem finally said, his voice low and thoughtful. "Always calculating." He paused, then added, "But he's not acting alone. There's someone else pulling the strings, orchestrating this from the shadows."

His words sent a chill down Stanya's spine. A single traitor was bad enough, but a larger conspiracy, directed by a hidden mastermind, was a far more daunting threat. This was a game played on a different level, a game of political chess where the stakes were far higher, and the potential casualties far greater.

Together, they decided to set a trap, a carefully laid snare designed to catch the mastermind in the act of betrayal. They used their skills and their combined networks to gather more evidence and to meticulously plan their next move. They knew the risks involved, but failure to expose the conspiracy could shatter the rebel alliance and leave the Outerlands vulnerable to Graffik's renewed attacks. They were playing for the future of their world, and the consequences of their actions could not be overstated. The line between freedom and tyranny was drawn, and they were on the precipice of a fight even more treacherous than anything they had ever faced. The whispers of conspiracy were about to turn into a roar of revolt.

The air in the dimly lit council chamber crackled with tension, far more potent than the scent of woodsmoke and damp earth. Stanya, her hand resting lightly on the hilt of her dagger, watched as the rebel leaders, faces etched with suspicion and weariness, engaged in a silent, deadly game of one-upmanship. The initial celebrations had been short-lived, replaced by a chilling realization: a viper had infiltrated their ranks.

General Kaelen, a grizzled veteran with eyes that held the weight of countless battles, slammed his fist on the table, the sound echoing through the hushed chamber. "Graffik's spies are everywhere," he growled, his voice thick with anger and frustration. "They know our plans, they anticipate our moves. Someone is feeding him information."

Lady Lyra, leader of the Silver Hawks, a fiercely independent group known for their ruthlessness, countered with a steely gaze. "Not just spies, Kaelen. A traitor.

Someone amongst us." Her words hung in the air, unspoken accusations hanging heavier than the smoke.

The accusation was a poisoned dart, aimed not at a specific individual but at all of them. Each leader subtly shifted, assessing the others, searching for a tell, a flicker of guilt or fear in their eyes. The trust, the fragile unity that had held them together, was now splintering under the weight of suspicion.

Stanya, despite her years spent navigating the treacherous currents of Graffik's court, felt a chill snake down her spine. The atmosphere was thick with betrayal, a suffocating blanket of mistrust. She had witnessed such games before, had seen alliances crumble and friendships shatter under the pressure of power. But this was different. This was a fight for survival, a struggle against a tyrant who would stop at nothing to reclaim his lost dominion.

Lord Theron, a cunning strategist whose loyalty was as changeable as the weather, spoke calmly, his voice a deceptively soothing counterpoint to the rising tension. "Accusations are easy, Lyra. Proof is another matter entirely." He subtly shifted his gaze, his eyes lingering on General Kaelen for a moment longer than necessary.

The game had begun. A dangerous, intricate dance of suspicion and deception. Stanya watched, a silent observer, analyzing every gesture, every inflection in their voices. She knew the stakes were far higher than a simple power struggle. This was a fight for the very soul of the rebellion, a battle that could determine the fate of the Outerlands.

Days turned into nights, each meeting escalating the tension. The rebels, divided by suspicion, were slowly being eroded from within. Secret meetings took place in the shadows, whispers exchanged in hushed tones. Alliances shifted like sand dunes in a desert wind, friendships shattered under the strain of mistrust.

Stanya, using her honed skills of observation and deduction, began her own investigation. She subtly probed the leaders, gauging their reactions, searching for inconsistencies in their stories, for the smallest clues that might reveal the traitor. She discovered a pattern in the leaks; information that only a few individuals possessed was reaching Graffik. This narrowed down the potential culprits considerably. The traitor was someone within their inner circle, someone they trusted implicitly.

One evening, while shadowing Lord Theron, Stanya witnessed a clandestine meeting between him and a hooded figure, their exchange brief but chillingly revealing. The hooded figure slipped a small, intricately carved wooden bird – a symbol known only to Graffik's most trusted agents – into Theron's hand. The evidence was undeniable.

Confronted with Stanya's findings, Theron didn't deny his treachery. Instead, he revealed a chilling truth: he was working for Graffik, but not out of pure loyalty. He was motivated by a deeply personal grudge against the rebellion, a betrayal from within their ranks that had fueled his vengeance. He had used his tactical genius to orchestrate the leaks, subtly maneuvering the rebellion toward its own destruction.

His confession sent shockwaves through the rebels. They had been so focused on hunting for a spy within their ranks that they hadn't seen the far greater danger – the one who was already inside, manipulating them from the inside out. The shock was profound, leaving them shaken and questioning their very foundations. Theron, however, was not the only one playing this dangerous game.

Stanya, though initially stunned, quickly recovered. She realized Theron's confession was not entirely truthful; there were inconsistencies in his narrative. This suggested the existence of yet another player, someone even more cunning and dangerous, orchestrating events from behind the scenes, using Theron as a pawn.

The revelation brought a new urgency to the situation. The fight for survival was no longer just against Graffik, but against a far more insidious enemy, a hidden manipulator pulling the strings from the shadows, using Theron's betrayal as a means to destabilize the entire rebellion.

The ensuing days were a whirlwind of activity. Stanya, with the assistance of those few who still trusted her, began to unravel the larger conspiracy. She discovered a complex web of deceit, involving secret alliances, hidden agendas, and long-forgotten betrayals. She found cryptic messages, coded communications, and evidence of a clandestine network working directly against the rebellion.

The evidence pointed to a figure far more powerful and influential than Theron, a figure who had masterminded the entire plot from the beginning. It was someone who had infiltrated the rebellion years ago, carefully cultivating their position, biding their time until they could strike at the most opportune moment. Their identity was initially cloaked in mystery.

As Stanya delved deeper into the conspiracy, she discovered a trail of breadcrumbs leading to an unexpected source – someone unexpectedly close to the heart of the rebellion. The traitor was not a foreign agent, but someone who had always been a part of their inner circle, someone they had trusted without reservation. The betrayal was profound, a shattering revelation that plunged the rebellion into a deeper crisis than before.

The final confrontation was a devastating clash of wills, a fight not only for the Outerlands but for the very soul of the rebellion. The trust was shattered, the rebellion was fractured, and the future of their world hung precariously in the balance. The game was far from over, and the stakes had never been higher. The whispers of conspiracy had transformed into a deafening roar of betrayal, shaking the very foundations of their cause. And Stanya, amidst the chaos, knew that the true fight had only just begun.

The accusations hung in the air like a poisonous mist, clinging to the rough-hewn walls of the council chamber. Rhys, his face a mask of controlled fury, slammed his fist on the table, the sound echoing through the stunned silence. "Stanya," he growled, his voice thick with barely suppressed rage, "you lied. You withheld information. Information that could have saved lives!"

Stanya met his gaze, her own eyes blazing with defiance. She hadn't lied outright, but she had certainly omitted crucial details, details that she feared would unravel the fragile alliance holding the rebellion together. Graffik's spies were everywhere, even here within the heart of the resistance. She had chosen to protect the Outerlands, to protect the fragile hope of freedom, even if it meant sacrificing trust.

"I did what I thought was necessary," she responded, her voice low and steady. "There were risks involved in revealing everything. Risks that you wouldn't understand."

"Risks?" scoffed Elara, her voice sharp as a shard of obsidian. "We all took risks, Stanya. We all put our lives on the line for this cause. And you, you betrayed us."

Elara, leader of the Northern clans, had always been wary of Stanya, of her enigmatic ways and her closeness to the elusive figure known only as the Shadow Master. That suspicion, fuelled by Rhys's accusations, now blossomed into open hostility. The trust that had bound them together, the shared purpose that had forged a fragile alliance, was cracking under the weight of doubt and suspicion.

The room buzzed with whispers, a cacophony of accusations and counter-accusations. Faces, once united in their opposition to Emperor Baznoon, were now fractured by mistrust. The delicate balance of power, so carefully constructed, teetered on the brink of collapse. Kael, leader of the Southern warriors, remained silent, his gaze shifting between Stanya and the other leaders, a silent observer in this unfolding tragedy. He had always been the mediator, the voice of reason, but even he seemed unsure where his loyalties lay.

"It wasn't just the information," Rhys continued, his voice rising in pitch. "It was the way you did it. The secrecy, the deception. It reeks of treachery." He paused, his eyes scanning the faces around him, seeking support, seeking confirmation of his suspicions. "We need to know who we can trust, who we can depend on in the face of Graffik's might. And right now, I don't trust you, Stanya."

The weight of his words pressed down on Stanya, crushing her under the burden of their accusations. She knew that Rhys was a good man, a man driven by a fierce loyalty to his people, but his blind trust had been violated, and the scars of betrayal were deep. She had underestimated the depth of his commitment, the strength of his belief in their shared cause. She had underestimated the fragility of trust.

"I understand your anger, Rhys," Stanya said, her voice weary. "But I acted in the best interest of the rebellion. Believe me, I would never knowingly endanger the Outerlands."

"But you did," Elara countered sharply. "Your actions put us all at risk. By withholding information, you jeopardized our entire strategy. We could have been prepared. We could have been stronger."

The argument raged on, fuelled by exhaustion, suspicion, and a growing sense of despair. Each accusation chipped away at the already fragile foundation of their alliance. The shared enemy, the oppressive rule of Emperor Baznoon, seemed to fade into the background, eclipsed by the internecine conflict that threatened to tear them apart.

Stanya tried to explain, to clarify her actions, but her words were lost in the cacophony of accusations and recriminations. The council chamber, once a symbol of unity and hope, had become a battlefield of suspicion and mistrust. The air crackled with the energy of simmering hatred, thick and suffocating.

Kael attempted to intervene, his voice calm and measured, trying to mediate between the clashing factions. His words, however, fell on deaf ears, as each leader clung fiercely to their own convictions, their own versions of the truth. The cracks in the alliance had widened into gaping chasms, threatening to swallow the rebellion whole.

Days turned into nights, and the council chamber remained a scene of unresolved conflict. Stanya, exhausted but resolute, refused to back down, continuing to defend her actions, though the weight of the accusations pressed down on her. Each word was a battle, each statement a desperate plea for understanding, for trust, but the chasm separating her from her former allies seemed to grow wider with each passing hour.

The betrayal extended beyond Rhys and Elara. Whispers of doubt slithered through the ranks of the rebel soldiers, poisoning their morale and eroding their faith in their leaders. The unity that had been so hard-won was disintegrating, leaving behind only a residue of suspicion and fear.

Meanwhile, outside the council chamber, the threat of Graffik's forces loomed large. The rebels, divided and weakened, were ill-equipped to face the impending attack.

Graffik's vast army, a machine of brutal efficiency, was poised to crush the rebellion. This internal strife offered the perfect opportunity for Baznoon to exploit their weakness. The whispers of conspiracy had solidified into a deafening roar of betrayal, shattering the foundation of their rebellion and leaving them vulnerable.

Najeem, having returned from his daring mission, found himself caught in the crossfire of this escalating conflict. He had witnessed firsthand the strength of Graffik's army, and the simmering discontent within the rebel ranks only magnified the danger they were in. He saw the toll this internal conflict had taken on Stanya, her usual sharp wit replaced with a weary exhaustion.

He approached her cautiously, sensing her vulnerability despite her defiant posture. He understood betrayal, having experienced the dark side of Graffik's court. He knew the delicate dance of trust, the ease with which it could be broken, and the long, arduous journey required to rebuild it. He knew that some wounds ran deeper than others, and some betrayals never truly healed.

He placed a hand on her arm, a gesture of silent support in the face of overwhelming odds. "It's not over,

Stanya," he said softly, his voice a balm to her wounded spirit. "We can still fight this. We can still win."

His words were not a promise of easy victory, but a pledge of unwavering support, a beacon of hope in the encroaching darkness. The fight was far from over. The rebellion was fractured, the trust shattered, but the embers of hope still flickered, waiting to be fanned into a raging flame. The whispers of conspiracy had become a storm, but the heart of the rebellion still beat, though faintly, and it was up to Stanya, Najeem, and the remaining loyalists to find a way to rekindle the flame of their resistance before Graffik's forces crushed them completely. Their struggle, their fight for freedom, was far from over. The battle for the Outerlands, and the very soul of their world, was just beginning.

The biting wind whipped at Stanya's cloak as she navigated the labyrinthine alleys of the Outerlands' capital, Porthaven. The city, a stark contrast to the opulent, suffocating grandeur of Baznoon Graffik's capital, hummed with a different kind of energy – a raw, untamed vitality fueled by defiance and desperation. Rhys's accusations still stung, a bitter taste on her tongue. She hadn't lied intentionally, but the fragmented information she'd gleaned from Graffik's court had been misinterpreted, leading to disastrous consequences. Now, she had to find the source of the conspiracy, to unravel the web of deceit before it strangled the rebellion completely.

Her first stop was the clandestine meeting place of the Shadow Syndicate, a network of informants and spies who operated in the grey areas between law and chaos. Their leader, a wizened woman named Elara, with eyes that held the wisdom of centuries and the sharp glint of steel, listened patiently as Stanya recounted her ordeal. Elara's network, though extensive, was not immune to Graffik's reach. There were moles, whispers of betrayal that snaked through their ranks like venomous serpents.

"The whispers started subtly," Elara rasped, her voice like dry leaves rustling in the wind. "Small acts of sabotage, misplaced documents, intercepted messages. But it escalated quickly, growing bolder, more brazen. It's as if someone is deliberately trying to destabilize us, to weaken the rebellion from within."

Stanya's mind raced, trying to connect the dots. The sabotage Rhys had mentioned, the intercepted communication – they were all pieces of the same puzzle. But who was orchestrating this meticulously planned campaign of disinformation and destruction? Was it a single individual, a powerful faction, or something far more insidious?

Elara produced a worn leather-bound book, its pages filled with cryptic symbols and indecipherable codes. "This is a record of our network's activities over the past decade. It's possible the conspirators left traces, breadcrumbs, if you will, in our own records." The task felt overwhelming, like searching for a single grain of sand on a vast, windswept beach.

Days bled into weeks as Stanya meticulously pored over the Syndicate's records. She deciphered codes, followed coded messages, and cross-referenced information. Gradually, a pattern began to emerge. The sabotages, the intercepted messages, the seemingly random acts of treachery—they all pointed to a single individual, a surprisingly high-ranking member of the Outerlands' council: Lord Valerius.

Valerius, a man renowned for his piety and unwavering loyalty to the rebellion, was seemingly an unlikely candidate. He had a reputation for integrity, a façade carefully constructed to mask his treachery. Stanya felt a chill run down her spine. She had been so focused on Graffik's machinations, she had overlooked the serpent in their midst.

But she needed proof, irrefutable evidence to expose Valerius. His position within the council made him virtually untouchable. A public accusation without solid evidence would only further fracture the already fragile alliance and ultimately benefit Graffik. She needed something concrete, something that would shatter his carefully crafted image and expose him for the traitor he was.

Her investigation led her to a hidden vault beneath the council chambers, a place rumored to hold the Outerlands' most closely guarded secrets. Accessing it was a perilous undertaking, requiring stealth, skill, and a healthy dose of luck. She spent days studying the layout of the council chambers, identifying weak points in the security systems. She bribed guards, outsmarted patrols, and navigated treacherous traps, all while avoiding detection.

Finally, under the cover of a moonless night, Stanya reached the vault. The heavy iron door creaked open, revealing a dimly lit chamber filled with ancient scrolls, dusty chests, and forgotten artifacts. The air hung heavy with the scent of age and secrecy. She searched frantically, her fingers tracing the spines of ancient tomes, her eyes scanning the cryptic inscriptions on chests and boxes.

Then, she found it. A small, unassuming wooden box tucked away in a dark corner. Inside, she discovered a series of letters, correspondence between Valerius and a high-ranking official in Graffik's court. The letters detailed a comprehensive plan to undermine the rebellion, from strategic assassinations to spreading disinformation, all orchestrated by Valerius. The evidence was damning, irrefutable. She had found the smoking gun.

But just as she was about to leave, she heard the sound of approaching footsteps. She quickly secured the box, concealing it within her cloak, her heart pounding in her chest. She could hear the guards approaching the vault, their footsteps echoing through the silent chamber. She had to escape, and quickly.

She slipped out of the vault, moving with the practiced grace of a phantom, navigating the corridors with ease, avoiding the patrols and slipping into the night before anyone could detect her. She had secured the proof, but her escape had not been easy and now she needed a way to reveal Valerius' treachery to the council.

Her mind raced as she thought of her options. A direct confrontation would be perilous; Valerius was cunning and influential. She needed to carefully and strategically use her proof to expose him without causing more chaos. She knew that she couldn't do it alone. She needed Najeem's help, his strength and loyalty to balance her intellectual prowess. She knew they would face more dangers, more betrayals, but she also felt a flicker of hope, a shared sense of purpose rekindled between them. This time, the outcome would hinge on far more than sheer survival; it was about the freedom of the Outerlands and its people. The fight for freedom was far from over, but now, armed with irrefutable proof, Stanya felt a surge of determination, ready to take on the treacherous path ahead. The whispers of conspiracy had led her to the heart of the darkness, and now she would bring the light to expose the insidious treachery that threatened to shatter their fragile hope. The game was far from over, but Stanya was ready to play.

The rough-hewn timbers of the tavern creaked under the weight of the boisterous crowd. The air, thick with the smell of ale and sweat, vibrated with the low hum of conversation, punctuated by bursts of raucous laughter. Najeem, however, found little solace in the merriment. He nursed a mug of lukewarm ale, his gaze fixed on the flickering candlelight that cast dancing shadows on the rough-hewn walls. The escape from Graffik's clutches had been harrowing, a brutal dance between life and death. He'd lost count of the men he'd killed, their faces blurring into a nightmarish montage of pain and fury. Yet, the victory felt hollow, tainted by the lingering image of Princess Amara, her face a mask of despair as he left her behind.

His promise to return had been a desperate lie, a balm to his conscience, a way to justify his escape. The truth was far more complex. He'd been a slave, a pawn in Graffik's cruel game, his loyalty bought and sold like a common commodity. Amara, despite her gilded cage, was as much a prisoner as he'd been. Her infatuation with him had been a dangerous gamble, a reckless act of rebellion in itself. Graffik's wrath would be swift and terrible, should he dare to return. He wasn't just fighting for his own freedom; he was risking hers.

A shadow fell across his table, interrupting his tormented thoughts. He looked up to see Stanya, her face etched with a familiar mix of determination and weariness. She'd changed since their last encounter – the soft edges of her refined persona were gone, replaced by a hardened resolve that mirrored his own. The silk and jewels of Graffik's court were replaced by the roughspun fabrics of the Outerlands. Yet, the fire in her eyes, the sharp intelligence that had first captivated him, remained undimmed.

"You found me," he said, his voice raspy from disuse.

Stanya nodded, her gaze unwavering. "Valerius," she said, the name a venomous whisper, "he's behind everything. Graffik's paranoia, the assassinations, even the initial conflict in the borderlands – it all points back to him."

Najeem frowned. Valerius, Graffik's right-hand man, a figure cloaked in shadows and whispers. He'd encountered him briefly during his escape, a fleeting glimpse of ruthless ambition behind polished manners. But a conspiracy of this magnitude… it seemed almost unbelievable.

"The evidence is overwhelming," Stanya continued, pulling out a small, leather-bound scroll. "I intercepted messages, intercepted coded communications… They detail Valerius's plot to destabilize the empire, to exploit Graffik's insecurities and manipulate him into starting a war."

He took the scroll, his fingers tracing the worn leather. The weight of it was heavy, heavier than any weapon he'd ever wielded. Inside, the meticulously detailed plans unfolded a horrifying truth. Valerius was planning a coup, a treacherous betrayal that would plunge the empire into chaos. The risk to Amara, to the entire empire, was staggering.

The information was compelling, damning evidence that could topple Valerius. Yet, a chill snaked through Najeem's veins. The plan to expose Valerius was fraught with peril. He had to weigh the potential consequences, his personal safety, and most importantly, Amara's fate. Graffik, already consumed by paranoia, would react violently to this revelation.

"What do you propose?" Najeem asked, his voice low.

Stanya's eyes met his, a silent understanding passing between them. "We need to expose him, but we need a plan, a strategy that minimizes risk and maximizes impact. We need to play his game, using his tactics against him. We must use his own paranoia against him," she said, her voice low and intense.

The following days were a blur of clandestine meetings, whispered conversations in dimly lit corners, and the careful orchestration of a dangerous game. Stanya, with her unparalleled ability to gather information and maneuver through political landscapes, was the architect of their plan. Najeem, with his skills in combat and his understanding of Graffik's court, was the muscle.

They decided to use the existing unrest within Graffik's court. They would leak carefully selected pieces of information, subtly twisting facts and fueling Graffik's distrust of Valerius. It was a risky gambit, a dance on the razor's edge of betrayal, but it was their only hope.

The first step was to plant a carefully worded letter, supposedly from a disgruntled courtier, alleging Valerius's treachery. It was a masterpiece of deception, half-truths and insinuations that would play on Graffik's already heightened suspicions. Najeem, using his knowledge of the palace's security systems, planted the letter directly on Graffik's desk during a night-time operation that involved scaling walls, disabling guards and a hairbreadth escape that sent adrenaline coursing through his veins.

The second step was even more audacious. They needed to expose Valerius's secret dealings with neighboring kingdoms, a conspiracy that could be used to turn Graffik against him. This required infiltration of Valerius's heavily guarded private chambers, a mission fraught with the potential for death. Stanya and Najeem, their skills complementing each other flawlessly, managed to breach security. They stole incriminating documents which they then leaked to a selected group of loyalists within the imperial court, setting in motion a carefully crafted chain reaction that would slowly unravel Valerius's web of deception.

Days turned into weeks, tension in the court intensifying with each carefully placed piece of information. The whispers of conspiracy grew louder, Graffik's paranoia reaching fever pitch. Valerius, sensing the shift in the tides, began to tighten his grip, his actions becoming increasingly erratic and desperate. He was beginning to unravel, a sign that their plan was working.

But it came at a cost. Najeem found himself increasingly torn. His loyalty to Amara, the promise he'd made, clashed violently with the urgency of his current task. He knew that exposing Valerius would likely lead to more chaos and instability, potentially putting Amara in even greater danger. Yet, failing to act would mean consigning the entire empire to Valerius's tyrannical rule, an outcome far worse than the current peril.

One moonless night, as the culmination of their plan was set to unfold, Najeem stood on the palace ramparts, staring at the distant flickering lights of the city. The weight of his decision pressed down on him, heavier than the cold night air. He was a warrior, a fighter, and the outcome, in his hands. But this was more than a fight; it was a choice between loyalty and truth, a decision that would determine not only his own destiny but the fate of an empire. The whispers of conspiracy had finally reached a crescendo, and soon, the truth would be revealed. But at what cost? The fate of a princess, an empire, and his own soul hung precariously in the balance.

Chapter 14: Confrontation

The air hung thick with the scent of woodsmoke and fear. The dilapidated warehouse, once a bustling hub of illicit trade, now served as the stage for a final, desperate confrontation. Stanya, her usually meticulous braid loosened and strands clinging to her sweat-slicked skin, stood poised, her hand resting lightly on the hilt of her twin daggers. Opposite her, Najeem, his usually impeccable armor marred and stained, gripped his sword with the steely intensity that had become his trademark. Between them, huddled against a crumbling wall, were the conspirators – a motley crew of disgruntled rebel leaders, their faces etched with a mixture of defiance and apprehension.

The flickering torchlight danced across their faces, revealing the extent of their betrayal. Lord Valerius, once a respected general, now looked haggard and defeated, his eyes darting nervously. Lady Isolde, her beauty a cruel mockery of her venomous ambition, clutched a concealed dagger, her gaze unwavering. And Kaelen, the cunning strategist, his usual calm facade shattered, shifted uneasily, his gaze flitting between Stanya and Najeem, gauging their strength, assessing their resolve.

The silence stretched, punctuated only by the occasional drip of water from a leaky roof and the erratic thump of Najeem's heart. The tension was palpable, a living thing that choked the air, a heavy weight pressing down on the three main characters. Stanya, despite the grim circumstances, felt a surge of grim satisfaction. Months of relentless pursuit, countless near-misses, and the constant gnawing suspicion had finally led to this moment – a reckoning.

"You underestimated us," Stanya's voice was low, a dangerous purr. Her words cut through the silence, sharp as the daggers at her hip. "You thought you could manipulate us, use us to further your own selfish ambitions. You were wrong."

Valerius scoffed, a weak, brittle sound. "We had no choice. Graffik's grip was too strong. We needed… leverage."

"Leverage that cost countless lives?" Najeem's voice was colder still, a blade of ice. He took a step forward, the clink of his armor a stark counterpoint to the oppressive silence. "You betrayed the very cause you swore to uphold.

You betrayed the trust of those who fought alongside you. And you betrayed me."

Isolde, her lips curling into a cruel smile, spoke, her voice laced with disdain. "Sentimentality is a luxury we cannot afford, Najeem. Survival is the only game. And we are winning."

"Winning?" Stanya laughed, a short, sharp sound devoid of humor. "Winning by selling out the very people you claimed to fight for? By selling out the future of the Outerlands for your personal gain? You are fools, Valerius, Isolde, Kaelen. Utterly, pathetic fools."

Kaelen, attempting a show of bravado, stepped forward. "We had no other option. Graffik is invincible. We needed power." His words were a desperate plea, an attempt to justify the unjustifiable. But his eyes, full of fear, betrayed his hollow claim.

"Invincible?" Najeem sneered, his eyes burning with righteous fury. "Graffik may be powerful, but he is not invincible. He can be defeated. And we will defeat him. But not with the likes of you."

The ensuing fight was brutal, a whirlwind of steel and fury. Najeem's sword, a blur of motion, danced through the air, deflecting blows, striking with deadly precision. Stanya, lithe and agile, weaved through the chaos, her daggers flashing, finding gaps in the conspirators' defenses. The warehouse echoed with the clang of steel, the grunts of exertion, and the pained cries of the wounded.

Valerius, despite his years of military experience, was no match for Najeem's honed skills. He fell quickly, his sword clattering to the ground as Najeem disarmed him, leaving him bruised and defeated.

Isolde, however, proved to be a more formidable opponent. Her movements were fluid and deadly, a viper striking from the shadows. She was quick, and Stanya, despite her speed and agility, found herself constantly on the defensive. But Isolde's reliance on stealth, her strategy of swift strikes and retreat, only served to enrage Stanya. Stanya's rage, focused and deadly, became her edge. With a final, desperate lunge, Stanya disarmed Isolde and forced her to surrender.

Kaelen, seeing his allies defeated, made a desperate attempt to escape. But Najeem was too swift, intercepting him with a swift kick that sent him sprawling.

The battle was over. The conspirators lay defeated, their faces bruised, their spirits broken. Their carefully crafted conspiracy lay in ruins. The dust settled slowly, revealing the stark reality of their treachery.

Stanya and Najeem stood over them, their breath coming in ragged gasps, their bodies aching. They had won, but victory felt hollow, bittersweet. The price for freedom, they realized, was far greater than they had ever imagined. The cost was high; it had been paid for in betrayal and bloodshed.

The silence returned, but it was a different silence now. It was no longer thick with fear, but with the weight of what they had done and the heavy responsibility that lay ahead. The task of rebuilding trust, of healing the wounds inflicted by the conspiracy, was immense. But as they looked at each other, a spark of understanding passed between them – a bond forged in fire and blood, a promise whispered amidst the ruins. The fight for the Outerlands was far from over, but tonight, they had secured a pivotal victory in the larger war against tyranny. The reckoning was complete, but the journey continued.

The aftermath was as challenging as the battle itself. The rebels, shaken by the betrayal, needed reassurance, and the evidence of the conspiracy had to be presented to solidify the new, untainted leadership. The following days were filled with interrogations, trials, and attempts to salvage the morale of the fractured rebellion. Stanya, with her sharp intellect and experience, spearheaded the investigation, meticulously piecing together the conspirators' network and uncovering the extent of their treachery. Najeem, respected for his strength and honor, was vital in ensuring justice was seen to be served, though not without mercy.

The conspirators, stripped of their power and influence, faced the consequences of their actions. Lord Valerius, stripped of his rank and titles, was exiled, forever a pariah in the land he once served. Lady Isolde, her beauty no longer a shield, was imprisoned, her ambition forever thwarted. Kaelen, his cunning rendered useless, was forced to confess his part in the conspiracy, and to aid in the restoration of order.

The truth, once revealed, had the power to reshape the rebellion. The injured and heartbroken soldiers, now aware of the full scope of the treachery that had occurred, rallied, their sense of purpose renewed.

But even with the conspirators being defeated and their network dismantled, Stanya and Najeem knew that their fight was far from over. Graffik's shadow still loomed large, and the path ahead remained uncertain. The scars of the past, both physical and emotional, served as a constant reminder of the heavy price of freedom. As they stood side by side, looking out over the ravaged landscape, they knew that their journey had only just begun. Their bond, tested in the fires of battle and strengthened by shared sacrifice, would prove invaluable in the battles to come. The future held new challenges, new threats, and potentially new betrayals, but together, they would face them, their resolve hardened by the harsh realities of the reckoning that had just passed. The embers of hope, though dimmed by the recent battles, glowed brightly, fueled by the promise of a future free from tyranny. Their eyes met, a shared understanding passing between them, a silent vow to continue fighting for the freedom they had fought so hard to secure. The reckoning had ended, but the war had only just begun.

The flickering lamplight cast long, dancing shadows across the rough-hewn table, illuminating the worn faces of the rebel leaders. Their initial relief at escaping Graffik's clutches had given way to a gnawing unease. Stanya, her movements still sharp and precise despite her exhaustion, leaned forward, the stolen documents spread before them. The parchment, brittle with age, bore Graffik's seal – a chilling testament to the depth of the deception.

"This… this changes everything," rasped Theron, his voice hoarse from days of hiding and near-constant fear. His hand trembled as he pointed a gnarled finger at a passage detailing a secret trade agreement with a neighboring kingdom, a kingdom outwardly aligned with the rebellion. The agreement, meticulously disguised within seemingly innocuous clauses, outlined the supply of weapons and vital resources directly to Graffik's forces.

A stunned silence descended upon the group. The betrayal ran deeper than they could have ever imagined. Their supposed allies, the very people they had risked their lives to collaborate with, were actively fueling the regime they sought to overthrow. The weight of this revelation pressed down on them, heavier than any physical wound.

Najeem, his gaze intense, broke the silence. "This explains Graffik's seemingly endless resources," he said, his voice low and measured. "The ease with which he crushed our early attempts at uprising… it wasn't just brute force, it was treachery." He ran a hand through his short, dark hair, the gesture betraying the turmoil within. The information explained the seemingly insurmountable odds they had faced. They'd been fighting a war on two fronts – Graffik's army and their hidden allies.

Elara, a fierce warrior woman whose loyalty had been unwavering, slammed her fist on the table, the sound echoing in the confined space. "We must expose them," she declared, her voice filled with righteous fury. "Let the people know the truth. Let them see the faces of these traitors!" Her eyes burned with a fierce determination that mirrored the feelings simmering within the others.

But Stanya, ever the pragmatist, cautioned against rash action. "We must act strategically," she said, her voice calm yet firm. "A public denouncement without solid proof will only further weaken our position. Graffik will use this as an opportunity to crush the remaining rebellion, branding us all as traitors." Her words, though sobering, were laced with the wisdom born of countless clandestine operations.

The group fell into a heated debate, the air thick with conflicting opinions and desperate pleas. Some argued for immediate action, their anger overriding their caution. Others, mirroring Stanya's concerns, urged a more measured approach, advocating for a meticulous plan that would expose the traitors without jeopardizing the fragile hope of a successful revolution. Najeem found himself caught in the middle, his warrior's instincts urging immediate retribution, tempered by Stanya's strategic mind.

The debate raged through the night, fueled by flickering candlelight and the bitter taste of betrayal. As the first rays of dawn crept through the gaps in the dilapidated walls, a fragile consensus began to emerge. They would expose the traitors, but they would do so in a way that minimized risk and maximized impact.

Stanya, with her network of informants, took on the task of gathering irrefutable evidence. She would confirm every detail mentioned in the documents, solidifying their case against their treacherous allies. Her contacts, spread across the kingdom, would be vital in uncovering hidden transactions and gathering testimonies. She worked tirelessly, her sharp mind dissecting the complexities of the situation, piecing together the puzzle of the conspiracy.

Meanwhile, Najeem, with his exceptional combat skills and knowledge of the terrain, focused on ensuring the safety of the group. He meticulously planned escape routes, anticipating Graffik's inevitable retaliation. He also established communication channels with other rebel cells, alerting them to the treachery and coordinating their response. His leadership, both practical and inspiring, helped instill confidence in the weary fighters.

Days bled into weeks as they worked relentlessly, their efforts fueled by a shared purpose and the burning desire for justice. The weight of their task was immense, the stakes impossibly high, but their determination remained unbroken. They faced setbacks, close calls, and the ever-present threat of discovery, but their resolve remained unshaken, strengthened by their shared ordeal and their growing trust in each other.

The culmination of their efforts was a meticulously crafted plan, a delicate tapestry of deception and courage. They would use the very channels of communication controlled by the treacherous allies to broadcast their findings – a carefully worded message that would expose the truth, shattering Graffik's facade of power and revealing his alliance with the so-called "friends" of the rebellion.

The night of the unveiling was fraught with tension. The message, crafted with Stanya's keen intellect and disseminated through Najeem's secure network, spread like wildfire throughout the kingdom. Graffik's carefully constructed image crumbled before the undeniable evidence of his treachery. His allies, exposed in all their perfidy, faced the wrath of their deceived followers.

The revelation ignited a firestorm of revolt. The people, previously disillusioned and weakened, rose up against Graffik, emboldened by the truth and energized by the knowledge that their fight wasn't a lonely one. The rebels, bolstered by the exposed treachery and strengthened by their newfound alliance with the previously silenced groups, fought with a renewed vigor, fueled by a righteous anger.

Graffik's reign, once seemingly unshakeable, teetered on the brink of collapse. His forces, weakened by internal strife and desertion, found themselves struggling against a unified front. The tide of the war had turned, and the seeds of rebellion, watered by the truth and nurtured by courage, had blossomed into a full-scale revolution.

Stanya and Najeem, watching from the relative safety of the outerlands, knew their journey was far from over. The fight for freedom was far from won, but they had struck a critical blow. They had not only exposed a deep conspiracy but also ignited a revolution, the flames of which promised to consume Graffik's tyranny. As they looked towards the rising sun, a silent understanding passed between them – their bond, forged in shared danger and strengthened by mutual respect, was the unwavering foundation on which they would build a brighter future. Their fight for freedom was far from over, but they were ready. The reckoning was complete, and a new dawn had begun.

The wind whipped Stanya's hair across her face as she stood on the precipice, gazing out at the vast, unforgiving landscape of the Outerlands. Below, the rebel camp bustled with activity – a stark contrast to the quiet intensity of the meeting that had just concluded. The stolen documents, the fruits of her perilous infiltration of Graffik's court, had revealed a web of corruption so vast, so deeply entrenched, that even the most hardened rebels felt a chill of apprehension. The information exposed not only Graffik's brutal reign but also the insidious influence of a shadowy cabal pulling the strings from the darkness. Their power extended beyond Graffik himself, a terrifying realization that amplified the gravity of their situation.

Najeem, his silhouette stark against the fiery sunset, stood beside her, his usual easy charm replaced by grim determination. The escape from Graffik's clutches had been a harrowing ordeal, a brutal dance with death where they had narrowly avoided capture countless times. The shared near-death experiences had forged a bond between them, a silent understanding that transcended words. He had watched, with a mixture of admiration and concern, as Stanya meticulously presented her findings, her voice calm despite the weight of the information she carried. She hadn't flinched under the questioning gazes of the hardened rebels, her intelligence and courage unwavering.

The difficult choices, however, had only just begun. The rebels, bolstered by Stanya's revelations, were poised to launch a full-scale rebellion against Graffik. But victory wasn't guaranteed. Graffik's forces were formidable, his grip on the kingdom ironclad. The cost of rebellion would be steep, and the path to freedom was paved with sacrifice. A heavy silence settled between them as they considered the implications.

The first difficult choice concerned strategy. The rebels were fractured, divided by loyalty to different warlords, each with their own agendas and ambitions. Unifying them under a single banner, forging a common purpose in the face of such daunting odds, was a Herculean task. Stanya, with her sharp intellect, had proposed a daring plan – a multi-pronged attack that would simultaneously strike at Graffik's key strongholds, disrupting his supply lines and demoralizing his troops. But it was a high-risk strategy, demanding precise coordination and unwavering commitment. Failure would mean annihilation. The price of even a single misstep was unimaginable.

Najeem, despite his inherent warrior spirit, voiced his concerns. He had seen firsthand the ruthlessness of Graffik's forces. His heart ached with the thought of the countless lives that would be lost, the villages, razed to the ground, if the rebellion failed. He advocated for a more cautious approach, focusing on smaller, more localized skirmishes, building strength and support before a full-scale confrontation. His plan, though safer, was far slower, offering Graffik time to consolidate his power and crush the rebellion before it could truly gain momentum.

The debate raged on for hours, fueled by passionate arguments and deeply held convictions. The weight of countless lives rested on their shoulders, the fate of a kingdom hanging in the balance. It was not simply a matter of strategy; it was a clash of ideals, a struggle to find the path to freedom without sacrificing everything in the process.

The night was filled with tense silences, punctuated by the crackling fire and the restless movements of the weary rebels.

Stanya, despite her initial confidence in her plan, found herself swayed by Najeem's concerns. The image of the innocent villagers caught in the crossfire haunted her. She understood the need for a swift decisive blow, but the price of such a gamble was far too high. She saw the flickering desperation in the eyes of the rebel leaders, their hopes pinned on her intelligence, their lives hanging in the balance of her judgement.

The second difficult choice was even more personal. Stanya's mission had always been to gather information, to expose Graffik's lies. She was an information broker, not a warrior. But now, she was faced with the reality of leading a rebellion. The choice of becoming a leader was not just strategic, but also existential. She had lived a life of solitude, of shadows, and the idea of commanding an army, bearing responsibility for the lives of countless people, was terrifying. She felt the immense weight of those lives on her shoulders – a heavy, crushing burden, and her usual confidence flickered under this new, terrifying light.

This decision was intertwined with her feelings for Najeem. Their bond, forged in shared adversity, had grown into something deeper, something akin to love. He was a warrior, his life steeped in battles and bloodshed. He understood the cost of freedom, the price of rebellion better than anyone. His love was a grounding force, a strength that helped her face the difficult decision before her. The thought of him fighting and potentially dying, a sacrifice that would weigh heavily on her soul, was a crushing weight.

Najeem, too, faced a profound internal conflict. His unwavering loyalty lay with the rebels, with the fight for freedom. Yet, he was haunted by the memory of Graffik's daughter, the woman whose love had inadvertently led to his enslavement. He had vowed to return for her, to rescue her from the suffocating gilded cage of the Imperial palace. His choice, however, was complicated by the reality that any action, any engagement in this burgeoning rebellion, could endanger her safety further.

The weight of their collective choices pressed down on them, heavy as mountains. The cost of success and the price of failure both looked equally devastating. They knew this battle would not be clean. There would be bloodshed, loss, and pain. The quiet resolve that had held them together through their perilous escape began to tear under the pressure of their current responsibility.

Finally, after a sleepless night of agonizing deliberation, they arrived at a compromise. They would adopt a hybrid strategy, combining elements of both their plans. The rebellion would begin with smaller, localized attacks, designed to gradually weaken Graffik's forces and bolster the rebels' confidence. This would be followed by a decisive strike, a coordinated assault on a strategically vital location, when the time was right and the opportunity ripe.

But the compromise came at a cost. The delay increased the risk, and the possibility of failure loomed larger. The decision came with the grim knowledge that some sacrifices would be unavoidable. The rebellion would require significant resources, resources that were scarce. Hard choices had to be made, choices that would lead to loss and possibly betrayal from within their own ranks. The path to freedom was still fraught with peril, and the reckoning had only just begun. The fight for a brighter future had just become a terrifying and uncertain gamble, a game of life and death where victory was far from assured, but the cost of defeat was an unbearable thought. Their journey, far from over, had just entered its most treacherous phase. The true test of their resilience, their strength, and their bond was yet to come.

The air crackled with tension, a palpable energy that vibrated through the rough-hewn tables of the rebel encampment. Stanya, her usual sharp wit dulled by exhaustion and the weight of her secret burden, sat across from Kaelen, the grizzled leader of the Outerlands rebellion. His eyes, usually alight with fiery defiance, were clouded with doubt, his normally booming voice a low murmur. The information she had delivered was devastating, painting a picture far grimmer than anyone had anticipated. Graffik's reach extended far beyond the borders of his own kingdom, his tentacles wrapped around neighboring nations, corrupting their leaders and silencing dissent. The cabal Stanya had uncovered was a viper's nest of power, its influence so pervasive that a frontal assault seemed suicidal.

Kaelen tapped a thick finger on the rough-hewn map spread before them, tracing the lines of Graffik's supply routes, the arteries of his power. "We lack the numbers, Stanya," he finally said, his voice heavy with the weight of responsibility. "To directly confront Graffik's forces is to invite annihilation. We need... allies."

Stanya's gaze hardened. Allies meant compromises, and compromises meant risking the very integrity of their rebellion. She'd already seen the subtle shifts in alliances within the Outerlands – whispers of discontent, veiled ambitions. The price of freedom, it seemed, would be far higher than she'd imagined. "And what allies are you suggesting, Kaelen? The neighboring kingdoms are already compromised. They are puppets dancing to Graffik's tune."

Kaelen sighed, running a hand through his thick, grey beard. "There are whispers... of a powerful sorceress, residing in the Dowshafen. She commands considerable power, and her loyalty is... fluid. She claims to oppose Graffik, but her motivations are shrouded in mystery."

Stanya felt a prickle of unease. Dealing with sorceresses was a gamble, a dangerous game where the stakes were impossibly high. The very notion of allying with someone whose motives were unclear filled her with apprehension. "And what assurances do we have that she won't betray us? She could be a double agent, feeding information back to Graffik."

"No assurances," Kaelen admitted grimly. "But the alternative is inaction, and inaction is death. We need her power, Stanya. We need her resources. The gamble is unavoidable."

Their argument continued long into the night, the flickering lamplight casting long shadows on their faces, highlighting the lines of worry etched by the weight of their responsibility. Stanya argued for a more cautious approach, for consolidating their own forces, for finding alternative solutions before resorting to such a dangerous alliance. But Kaelen, desperate and weary from years of fighting a losing battle, refused to yield. The debate wasn't just a clash of strategies; it was a battle of wills, a test of their individual strengths and their shared commitment to the rebellion.

The tension between them was palpable, an icy current that flowed between them, chilling even the warm embers of the campfire. Stanya's sharp intellect clashed with Kaelen's pragmatic ruthlessness, their debate a fiery exchange of arguments and counterarguments. She presented her meticulous plans, her detailed analysis of the enemy's weaknesses, her own cunning tactics. He countered with the bleak realities of their situation – the dwindling resources, the overwhelming odds, the desperate need for immediate action. Their words became weapons, each carefully chosen phrase aimed to strike a vital point, to sway the other to their side.

Their discussion was not only a strategic debate; it delved into the very heart of their loyalty to the cause. Stanya's loyalty stemmed from a deep-seated belief in justice, fueled by years of observing Graffik's cruelty. Kaelen's loyalty was born from years of struggle, a fierce determination to protect his people, a refusal to succumb to tyranny. The different roots of their loyalty were now tested by the stark choices they faced, testing the very foundation of their common goal.

As the night wore on, a sense of growing unease permeated the camp. Rumors began to spread like wildfire – whispers of spies in their midst, of internal dissent, of betrayals brewing in the shadows. The atmosphere shifted, becoming thick with suspicion and distrust. Friends looked at each other with wary eyes, the bonds of camaraderie strained under the pressure of impending war.

Stanya, burdened by the weight of her decision, felt a growing sense of isolation. She'd always operated alone, relying on her wit and her skills, but now, she was part of something larger, something far more complex and dangerous. The weight of responsibility, the fear of failure, pressed down on her, threatening to suffocate her. She found herself alone, wrestling with her conscience, her commitment to her ideals tested to their limits. She had always prided herself on her ability to control the situation, to anticipate the moves of her adversaries. But this time, the enemy was not just Graffik and his forces; it was also the insidious doubt that gnawed at the very heart of the rebellion, the fragility of trust amongst allies.

The argument continued, a relentless volley of words. Stanya, even in defeat, refused to be silenced. She argued for a strategic withdrawal, for consolidating their resources before confronting the sorceress, for taking the time to assess the risks involved. Kaelen, however, stood firm. Time, he argued, was a luxury they could no longer afford. Graffik was tightening his grip, and the opportunity presented by the sorceress's potential alliance was too vital to ignore.

Finally, after hours of intense debate, a fragile compromise was reached. They would approach the sorceress cautiously, sending a small delegation to gauge her intentions. Stanya, despite her reservations, agreed to lead the delegation. She would use her skills, her knowledge, to assess the sorceress's motives, to uncover any hidden agendas. The decision was a testament to their shared commitment, a fragile bridge built upon a foundation of mutual respect, respect born from hard-won battles and the ever-present threat of failure. Their reckoning was far from over. The battle of wills had concluded, but a far more perilous battle was about to begin. The true test of their alliance and their individual strength lay in the shadowy depths of the Dowshafen, awaiting them like a lurking predator. The path to freedom, if there was one, was treacherous, unpredictable, and fraught with potential betrayal. Their journey had just begun its most dangerous phase, and the stakes were higher than ever before.

The Dowshafen stretched before them, a vast expanse of murky water and whispering reeds, a place where sunlight dared not penetrate and shadows danced like malevolent spirits. Stanya, her cloak pulled tight against the damp chill, felt a shiver run down her spine that had nothing to do with the cold. The sorceress, Morwen, resided at its heart, a creature of immense power, her reputation as both a healer and a destroyer preceding her. The small delegation, chosen for their skill and discretion, moved cautiously through the reeds, their boots sinking into the soft mud with each step. Kaelen, his face grim, brought up the rear, his hand resting on the hilt of his sword.

Stanya led the way, her senses heightened, her every nerve alert. The air hung heavy with an unnatural stillness, broken only by the rustling of unseen creatures in the reeds and the occasional croak of a unseen frog. She felt a prickling sensation on her skin, a sense of being watched, of being judged. Morwen's power radiated from the heart of the fen, a palpable energy that pressed down on them, suffocating and yet strangely compelling.

They finally reached a small island, shrouded in mist, where a solitary hut stood, its weathered timbers almost swallowed by the encroaching vegetation. Smoke curled lazily from its chimney, a thin, ethereal ribbon against the grey sky. As they approached, a figure emerged from the hut, tall and imposing, cloaked in dark robes that seemed to absorb the meager light. Morwen.

Her eyes, the color of molten gold, pierced through Stanya, seeing past her disguise, past her defenses. Stanya felt exposed, vulnerable, as if her very soul lay bare before this ancient power. Morwen's voice, when she spoke, was like the chime of distant bells, resonant and deep.

"You seek my aid," she stated, her voice carrying across the water with uncanny clarity. "But aid comes at a price. Tell me your story, and I will judge if your cause is worthy."

Stanya, her voice steady despite the tremor in her heart, recounted their plight, Graffik's tyranny, the corruption that had spread like a plague across the land. She spoke of Baznoon Graffik's cruelty, his insatiable lust for power, the web of deceit he had woven around his kingdom. She spared no detail, painting a vivid picture of the suffering he had inflicted upon his people. When she finished, a long silence hung in the air, broken only by the sigh of the wind.

Morwen remained silent for a long time, her gaze unwavering. Then, slowly, a smile played on her lips, a smile that was both chilling and strangely reassuring. "Your cause is worthy," she said, her voice softer now, almost gentle. "But justice is a two-edged sword. It cuts both ways. Are you prepared to pay the price?"

Stanya's heart pounded in her chest. She knew what Morwen meant. The price of justice was always high, sometimes unbearably so. But she had come too far to turn back. She nodded, her voice barely a whisper. "I am prepared."

Morwen smiled again, and this time, Stanya felt a surge of hope, a spark of warmth that cut through the cold, damp air. "Then let us begin," she said. She then instructed Stanya to prepare a specific ritual that involved gathering rare herbs and minerals, and harnessing the energies of the Dowshafen itself. The task was perilous, the ingredients difficult to locate, and the environment unforgiving.

Days bled into nights as Stanya, guided by Morwen's cryptic instructions, navigated the treacherous terrain of the Dowshafen. She faced down venomous snakes, avoided quicksand pits, and battled wraiths that haunted the murky depths. Najeem, watching from a distance, his heart heavy with worry and a burgeoning sense of admiration, witnessed her strength and courage. He had been following her, compelled by a growing need to protect her, a feeling far stronger than mere gratitude.

The ritual, finally completed, called upon ancient powers, harnessing the energies of the Dowshafen to amplify Morwen's magic. It was a spectacle of light and shadow, of crackling energy and ethereal whispers. The very air crackled with power, and the landscape around them trembled as if an earthquake was about to strike. Najeem held his breath, witnessing a display of raw power unlike anything he had ever seen.

The ritual ended with a blinding flash of light. When Stanya's eyes adjusted to the sudden darkness, she saw Morwen standing before her, her eyes gleaming with an almost supernatural intensity. Graffik's cabal, their faces contorted in agony, materialized before them, bound by unseen forces. They writhed and screamed, their pleas for mercy lost in the wind.

Morwen's magic didn't kill them. It exposed them. It stripped away their illusions of power, revealing the depravity that fueled their actions. Their faces, once masks of arrogance, now showed their true nature: fear, regret, and the chilling emptiness of a life dedicated to cruelty. The revelation itself was punishment enough. Their influence was broken, their power shattered. Their public exposure would lead to their downfall in Graffik's court.

The sight was both terrifying and cathartic. Justice, though not swift or violent, had been served. But as the shadows receded and the first rays of dawn pierced the mist, a heavy cost was revealed. Morwen was weakened, her energy depleted. The ritual, though successful, had taken a heavy toll. Her face was pale, her body trembling, and a single tear rolled down her cheek.

Stanya rushed to her side, her heart aching for the sorceress who had sacrificed so much for their cause. Najeem emerged from the shadows, his eyes full of both relief and concern. The rebellion had won a major victory, but the war was far from over. Graffik, enraged and wounded, would retaliate with even greater ferocity. Their alliance, forged in the crucible of adversity, was now stronger than ever, but the path ahead remained treacherous and uncertain. Their journey for justice had just begun its next, more perilous phase. The fight for freedom and a true reckoning would continue, testing their strength, their loyalty, and their love for one another in ways they could not have imagined. Graffik's tyranny might have suffered a major blow, but his grip on power was far from broken. The shadow of his reign still loomed large, a constant reminder of the battles yet to come. The victory felt bittersweet, a fragile victory bought at a heavy price. The fight for the future of their world had only just begun. And as Stanya looked into Najeem's eyes, she knew, with a certainty that transcended words, that they would face whatever came next, together. Their love, forged in the fires of conflict and rebellion, would be their strength, their guiding light in the darkness to come. The path ahead was long and arduous, filled with more peril than they could possibly foresee, but together, they would face it. Their journey was far from over, but with justice, however imperfect, finally served, they could face the future, however dark, with newfound hope and unwavering resolve.

Chapter 15: A New Balance

The dust settled on the ravaged battlefield, a stark contrast to the vibrant tapestry of life that had once thrived within Graffik's capital. The air, thick with the scent of smoke and blood, carried the faint whisper of a new dawn. Baznoon Graffik, the tyrant who had ruled with an iron fist, was no more. His reign of terror, a dark stain on the land, had been extinguished, leaving behind a landscape scarred but not broken. A fragile peace, bought with sacrifice and bloodshed, held sway.

Stanya, her usually sharp eyes softened with a weariness that belied her years, surveyed the aftermath. The jeweled comb, the instrument of her daring infiltration, lay tucked safely within her satchel. The information it held had been the key, unlocking the rebel forces' victory. She looked out across the expanse of the once-impregnable city walls, now breached and scarred. Gone were the symbols of Graffik's oppressive rule; replaced by the tentative banners of the newly formed coalition. It was a coalition forged in the crucible of war, a fragile alliance bound by shared suffering and the hope of a brighter future. The victory was hard-won, and the cost immense. Friends were lost, futures were uncertain, and the path ahead remained treacherous.

The weight of her success settled on her shoulders, heavier than any weapon she had ever wielded. She had played a crucial role, her intellect and skill shattering the illusion of Graffik's invincibility. But she was keenly aware that this wasn't the end, merely a beginning. The intricate political landscape of the land was still in flux, shifting like sand dunes in a relentless wind. Alliances were tested, loyalties were questioned, and the seeds of future conflicts were already being sown. The celebrations, while necessary to mark this monumental victory, felt muted, overshadowed by the somber realization of the sacrifices made.

Across the battlefield, Najeem stood amongst the survivors, his gaze fixed on the horizon. The scars on his body were testament to the brutal battles he had endured. He'd fought side-by-side with those he'd once considered enemies, driven by his unwavering commitment to rescue Graffik's daughter, Lyra. He'd seen her fragility beneath the hardened exterior, a vulnerability that had ignited within him a protective instinct that transcended their opposing circumstances. Her fate was intertwined with his own, a bond forged in the chaos of war. He knew their reunion wouldn't be easy. She was a princess, after all, and the complexities of her situation were a tangled web of courtly politics and royal intrigue, a far cry from the simple escape they shared.

Lyra, freed from her gilded cage, stood apart, a silent observer of the shifting landscape. The revelation of her father's tyranny had shaken her to her core, forcing a reevaluation of everything she held dear. The weight of her heritage, once a source of pride, now felt like a suffocating burden. She watched Najeem, a flicker of something akin to hope igniting within her gaze. Their shared ordeal, their unlikely alliance amidst the chaos, had fundamentally altered their relationship. Her heart, bruised but not broken, yearned for a future free from her father's shadow. A future where she could choose her own path, one that held the possibility of a love that defied the rigid constraints of her upbringing.

The newly established council, composed of representatives from the various rebel factions, was wrestling with the complexities of governing a land recovering from decades of oppression. The task was monumental, a delicate dance between maintaining stability and fostering meaningful change. Stanya, with her unique insights into the workings of Graffik's regime and her reputation as a brilliant strategist, found herself unexpectedly thrust into a position of considerable influence within the council. She navigated the treacherous waters of political maneuvering with a deft hand, her quiet strength shaping the course of the nascent nation.

Najeem, however, was restless. The quiet diplomacy and bureaucratic maneuvering of the council held little appeal for him. His heart belonged to the battlefield, to the thrill of combat. He had pledged to return to Lyra, to sever her connection to the fallen empire, and he wouldn't rest until that promise was fulfilled. He was already planning his next move. He would forge a new path, one that would lead him back to the capital, not as a fugitive but as a liberator. His skills would be put to use again, but now to protect and to rescue, not just to escape. His heart held a fierce hope for a future with Lyra, one that would prove stronger than the walls of the palace or the machinations of the court.

Their paths diverged, yet the bond between Stanya and Najeem remained, an unspoken understanding woven into the fabric of their shared experiences. They exchanged a lingering glance across the crowded square, a silent acknowledgment of the sacrifices they had made and the uncertain future that lay before them. It was a future they would face, not as enemies, but as allies, bound by a shared history and a mutual respect that had grown out of their turbulent journey.

The reconstruction of the capital was a slow, arduous process. The scars of war ran deep, both physically and emotionally. Yet, amidst the rubble, a flicker of hope persisted. The land was healing, slowly but surely. New laws were being drafted, designed to prevent the kind of tyranny that had marked Graffik's reign. The people, once silenced and oppressed, were finding their voices. Their newfound freedom was fragile, constantly threatened by the ghosts of the past and the potential for new conflicts.

Stanya, ever the strategist, recognized the need for vigilance. She worked tirelessly, ensuring that the newly formed government remained responsive to the needs of its citizens. She understood that true power lay not just in military might, but also in the trust and support of the people. Her reputation as an astute leader grew, solidifying her position as a critical player in this new era. She knew that a constant watchfulness was needed; that vigilance was the price of peace, the guardian of liberty.

Najeem, true to his word, began to assemble his forces for his daring return to the capital. His path was fraught with danger, every step a calculated risk. He recruited loyal followers who shared his commitment to freedom and justice. He spent hours honing his skills, ensuring he was ready for any challenge, for the fight ahead was far from over. He knew the palace's secrets, its weaknesses, and the hidden routes to bypass its defenses. His journey wouldn't be about brute force alone, but strategic brilliance.

And so, a new balance of power settled upon the land. The old order was shattered, replaced by a fragile yet tenacious hope for a better future. The seeds of rebellion had taken root, growing into a new blossoming order, one that promised justice, equality, and a future free from the tyranny of the past. But the fight for true freedom wasn't over; the road ahead remained fraught with danger, and the whispers of new conflicts were already carried on the wind. The future remained uncertain, a tapestry woven with threads of hope and fear, of promise and peril. The tale of Stanya and Najeem, though paused for a moment, remained far from its conclusion, promising a continuation of their intertwined destinies in the chapters yet to be written.

The Outerlands, once a remote haven of dissenters and rebels, now thrummed with a newfound vitality. The information Stanya had delivered – meticulous records detailing Graffik's illicit dealings, his hidden coffers, and the web of corruption that extended far beyond his immediate court – had ignited a wildfire of change. The council of elders, initially skeptical of the young woman who appeared seemingly out of thin air, were quickly swayed by the irrefutable evidence. Stanya, hailed as a heroine, found herself thrust into the heart of the burgeoning resistance movement, a role she never sought but one she found herself surprisingly adept at navigating.

Her sharp mind, previously used to decipher coded messages and navigate treacherous political landscapes, now served to strategize and organize. She helped establish new trade routes, bypassing the chokeholds Graffik had imposed, revitalizing the Outerlands' economy. She oversaw the distribution of supplies, ensuring that those most in need received assistance. She even found herself mentoring younger recruits, sharing her knowledge of espionage and infiltration, shaping a new generation of fighters ready to defend their hard-won freedom.

Yet, the weight of her actions rested heavily upon her shoulders. The victories were bittersweet. The images of the fallen, the faces of those she'd lost in the battles within the capital, haunted her dreams. Najeem's face, etched in her memory with a mix of anger, fear, and a burgeoning admiration, was a constant reminder of the shared ordeal that had bound them together. Their brief, tumultuous alliance had forged an unspoken connection, a bond forged in the crucible of survival. The fleeting moments of tenderness, overshadowed by the ever-present threat of death, now echoed in the quiet solitude of her nights.

Meanwhile, far from the bustling activity of the Outerlands, Najeem found himself embroiled in a different kind of struggle. His vow to return for Graffik's daughter, Princess Amara, wasn't simply a promise; it was a burning obligation. Amara, a woman he had initially despised, had unwittingly become the object of a complex and unexpected affection. Trapped within the gilded cage of Graffik's court, she had revealed a softer side, a hidden vulnerability beneath her haughty exterior. Their enforced proximity had sparked an unlikely connection, a bond born from shared hardship and an unspoken understanding of their respective plights.

His escape had been harrowing, a daring feat of strength and cunning that tested his limits. He'd spent months wandering the harsh landscapes surrounding the capital, gathering support from the scattered pockets of resistance. He learned to rely on his instincts, sharpening his skills as a warrior, and cultivating a network of informants. He honed his knowledge of the terrain, transforming the wilderness into his own personal sanctuary, a place where he could strategize and plan his next move. He learned the rhythm of the land, the whispered secrets held by the wind, the unspoken language of the animals, and found a quiet strength in solitude.

His journey was not merely a physical one; it was a journey of self-discovery. The trauma of enslavement, the betrayal of trust, the constant threat of death, had stripped him bare, revealing a resilience he didn't know he possessed. He emerged from the shadows a changed man, stronger, wiser, and more determined than ever before. He now understood the true meaning of freedom, not just as the absence of chains, but as the ability to choose one's own path.

News of Stanya's success in the Outerlands reached him through a network of underground messengers. The information, delivered in coded messages hidden within seemingly innocuous objects, was both thrilling and bittersweet. He rejoiced in her triumph, yet the distance between them felt immense, a chasm carved by fate and circumstance. He knew their paths would cross again, that their destinies were inextricably intertwined, but the uncertainty of when, and under what circumstances, left him with a gnawing sense of anticipation.

The new order in the empire was fragile, held together by the sheer will of its people. The whispers of dissent, once suppressed by Graffik's iron fist, now echoed throughout the land. Graffik's former allies, once basking in the glow of his power, were now scrambling to reposition themselves, seeking to carve out new territories and establish their own dominance. The old power structures, weakened but not destroyed, continued to cast their shadows.

In the heart of the capital, a power vacuum had been created, leaving a void filled with ambition and betrayal. Graffik's former generals and advisors, once loyal servants, were now vying for control, forming uneasy alliances and engaging in subtle acts of subterfuge. The assassination attempts continued, though they were now more targeted, more sophisticated. The struggle for power was far from over; it was merely shifting its focus, adopting new forms.

The Outerlands, while celebrating their liberation, were not immune to the ripples of this conflict. The surrounding territories, still loyal to the old regime, posed a constant threat, launching sporadic raids and attempting to destabilize the region. Stanya found herself constantly on the defensive, balancing the need for internal stability with the pressing external challenges.

The future held both promise and peril. The seeds of rebellion had taken root, growing into a new order, but the soil was still fertile for treachery. The struggle for true freedom was a marathon, not a sprint, a long and arduous journey fraught with challenges and setbacks. The scars of the past lingered, wounds that needed time and care to heal. The shadows of the old empire still stretched their reach, and the specter of future conflicts loomed large.

Amara, meanwhile, navigated the treacherous waters of the imperial court with a newfound resilience. Graffik's death had left her vulnerable, a pawn in the game of power. She discovered unexpected allies amongst the disillusioned members of the court, those who had secretly opposed her father's reign. Their allegiance to her, however, was fragile, conditional, and driven by their own self-interest.

She learned to navigate the treacherous currents of courtly intrigue, mastering the art of subtle diplomacy, building alliances while simultaneously avoiding the traps laid by her enemies. She became a symbol of hope for the oppressed, a beacon of resistance within the remnants of the fallen regime. Her survival, a testament to her strength and cunning, became a symbol of defiance.

The whispers of Najeem's escape and his vow to return reached her through clandestine channels. His name, once synonymous with her captivity, was now whispered in hushed tones, a symbol of both defiance and hope. The thought of his return fueled her determination, giving her the strength to endure the endless machinations of the court. She continued to build her power base, preparing herself for the day when he would come back for her, a day she now faced with both fear and anticipation.

The final scene of this chapter isn't one of triumphant victory, but rather one of quiet anticipation. Stanya, overlooking the bustling city of the Outerlands, feels the weight of responsibility but also the stirring of hope. Najeem, deep within the forests, trains relentlessly, preparing for the day he will return to reclaim Amara and settle the score with those who had betrayed him. Their paths, though separated by vast distances and seemingly insurmountable obstacles, remain inexorably linked, promising a future filled with both danger and untold possibilities. The seeds of a new era have been sown, but the harvest remains uncertain, a testament to the enduring power of hope, resilience, and the enduring strength of love in the face of overwhelming odds. Their story, far from concluded, continues its course, promising a future as intricate and unpredictable as the tapestry of their past. The whispers of their names, carried on the wind, promise a future as exciting and unpredictable as their past, a future where destiny and choice intertwine in an intricate dance of rebellion, romance, and unwavering determination.

The wind whipped Stanya's cloak around her, a familiar comfort in the chill evening air. Below, the city of Porthaven, the heart of the Outerlands, pulsed with a vibrant energy that was both exhilarating and slightly unsettling. It had been weeks since her daring escape from Graffik's clutches, weeks since she'd delivered the damning evidence that had shaken the very foundations of the empire. Now, hailed as a savior, she felt the weight of expectation pressing down on her, a burden far heavier than any chains.

She wasn't a leader, not by nature. She preferred the shadows, the quiet gathering of information, the subtle manipulation of events. But the Outerlands needed her, needed her skills, her knowledge of Graffik's intricate machinations. The Council of Elders, a group of weathered warriors and shrewd strategists, had made that abundantly clear. They had offered her a position of power, a seat on their council, a voice in shaping the future of their burgeoning rebellion.

Initially, the offer had filled her with a sense of unease. She'd envisioned a quiet life, far from the machinations of power, perhaps even finding peace in a secluded village, her skills used only to ensure its security. But the faces of the refugees flooding into Porthaven, their haunted eyes mirroring the suffering inflicted by Graffik's regime, silenced her doubts. She couldn't abandon them. She couldn't ignore the responsibility that had fallen upon her shoulders.

Her days were now a whirlwind of meetings, strategy sessions, and the meticulous planning of future operations. She was learning to navigate the complex web of alliances and rivalries within the resistance, subtly influencing decisions, offering her insights gleaned from her time in Graffik's court. She had to tread carefully, aware that not all within the resistance were entirely loyal to the cause, that whispers of ambition and self-interest snaked through the ranks. She found herself relying on instincts honed over years spent in the shadows, instincts that often served her better than any formal training.

Nights were a different matter. The city, vibrant during the day, fell into a quiet hum at nightfall. The silence gave way to a solitude she often found herself craving. She found solace in the company of Elara, an elderly woman whose knowledge of herbal remedies and ancient prophecies was as vast as her calm demeanor. Elara, who had initially been skeptical of Stanya's sudden appearance, had become a trusted confidante, a source of both practical advice and gentle encouragement. It was Elara who taught her to find peace in the rhythmic pounding of the city's night watch, the gentle sway of the willow trees by the river, the quiet hum of the crickets in the nearby fields.

She still thought of Najeem often. His image, etched in her mind, a blend of fierce determination and quiet vulnerability, remained a constant presence. His departure had been swift, a silent goodbye exchanged through a shared glance amidst the chaos of her escape. His dedication to rescuing Amara, Graffik's daughter, had left a lingering impression. It served as a stark reminder of her own determination, a mirror reflecting her personal fight for freedom. The possibility of a future shared with him was a flicker of warmth in the heart of the cold realities she now faced, a secret hope she carefully guarded. She often wondered if he was still training as he had vowed, his days filled with relentless exercises and the grinding preparation for his return to the capital. Their paths had diverged, but their destinies remained intertwined, a silent promise whispered on the wind.

The information she'd provided had brought more than just political upheaval. It had also sparked a wave of cultural and social change. The rigid caste system, a cornerstone of Graffik's oppressive regime, was slowly being dismantled. People from all walks of life were finding their voices, their newfound freedom fueled by a shared sense of purpose. The markets, once filled with fear and apprehension, now buzzed with the energy of hope, a vibrant tapestry of cultures and beliefs interwoven into the fabric of their new society.

But the fight was far from over. Graffik's loyalists remained a potent force, their shadowy influence stretching throughout the land. Assassinations, sabotage, and insidious whispers continued to plague the Outerlands. Stanya knew that their victory was fragile, a fragile seedling that needed constant nurturing and protection against the bitter winds of opposition. She had to be vigilant, sharp, always aware of the dangers lurking in the shadows. She had to be the shield protecting this burgeoning hope, the silent guardian of this newfound freedom.

The Council of Elders, understanding the fragility of their situation, had begun to reach out to other dissenting factions scattered throughout the empire. Secret alliances were being forged, clandestine meetings were taking place in the dead of night. Stanya, with her unique skills, was at the forefront of these endeavors. She moved like a ghost, unseen and unheard, her every move carefully planned, her every action executed with precision.

She had also begun to take a more active role in training the resistance fighters. Her skills in stealth, evasion, and hand-to-hand combat were invaluable. She taught them to move like shadows, to blend into the environment, to rely on their instincts. She imparted her knowledge, not just of fighting, but of strategy, of understanding the enemy's tactics, of knowing when to strike and when to retreat. She was shaping a new generation of fighters, a force that would be able to stand against Graffik's might.

The task was daunting. The road ahead was long and arduous, filled with unforeseen obstacles and relentless enemies. But Stanya, hardened by her experiences, driven by her unwavering resolve, was ready to face whatever challenges lay ahead. The knowledge that she was not alone, that she had allies who shared her belief in freedom and justice, gave her strength. The vision of a future where the people of the land could live free from oppression fueled her determination.

She often found herself gazing at the horizon, towards the vast expanse of the empire, towards the lands still under Graffik's iron fist. She knew that the final battle was yet to come. But she was preparing for it, building her forces, gathering her allies. The weight of responsibility, once crushing, now felt like a purpose, a mission she was ready to embrace. She was no longer just a gatherer of information. She was a leader, a strategist, a warrior fighting for a brighter future. And she was determined to see that future realized.

Her path, though arduous, was clear. Her heart, once burdened by loss and betrayal, now burned with a fierce fire of hope and determination. She would continue to fight, to strategize, to lead. She would bring down Graffik and build a new world from the ashes of his tyranny, a world where freedom reigned and justice prevailed. And perhaps, somewhere in that future, her path would once again intersect with Najeem's, a future where their destinies would finally be fulfilled, where their shared struggle would lead not only to victory but also to a love hard-earned and deeply cherished, a testament to their resilience and the enduring power of hope. The whispers of their names, once carried on the wind, would one day become a roar echoing through the ages.

The salt spray kissed Najeem's face as he stood at the prow of the small fishing boat, the rhythmic slap of waves against the hull a counterpoint to the turbulent emotions churning within him. Porthaven, a city etched against the horizon like a shimmering mirage, held little allure for him. His gaze remained fixed on the turbulent sea, a mirror reflecting the tempest in his soul. Escape had been brutal, a desperate scramble through Graffik's labyrinthine palace, a harrowing flight across treacherous terrain, each step a gamble against certain death. He had left a piece of himself behind – not just in the opulent confines of the imperial palace, but in the heart of Princess Amara, Graffik's daughter, whose unexpected kindness had been his unlikely salvation, and whose imprisonment now fueled his burning resolve.

He hadn't forgotten the electrifying clash with Stanya, the woman who had initially appeared as another of Graffik's hounds, only to reveal a shared enemy and a fierce determination to fight for freedom. Their brief alliance had been forged in the crucible of danger, a bond that transcended the initial mistrust. He remembered the way her eyes, sharp and intelligent, had softened with a rare vulnerability when they shared their harrowing experiences, a fleeting moment of connection that had resonated long after they parted ways. He hadn't expected to find kindred spirits within the ranks of his enemies, yet there she was, a warrior in her own right, her weapon the cunning manipulation of information, while his was honed steel and unwavering loyalty. Their escape had been separate, but their aims remained intertwined, two threads woven into a larger tapestry of rebellion.

The Outerlands, a land of rugged beauty and fierce independence, offered him a sanctuary, a temporary respite from the shadow of Graffik's relentless pursuit. But it was only a temporary reprieve. His heart ached for Amara, her image as vivid as the setting sun painting the sky in hues of fiery orange and deep crimson. He had promised her – a promise whispered between stolen glances, a vow etched in shared desperation – that he would return. This wasn't a simple rescue mission; it was a debt of honor, a testament to the unusual bond forged between a warrior and a princess, a prisoner and his unlikely savior.

He traced the hilt of his sword, the cool steel a comfort against his restless hand. It was more than just a weapon; it was a symbol of his commitment, a promise whispered to the wind and the waves. He had spent years honing his skills, training in the brutal art of combat, his body a finely-tuned instrument of destruction, his mind a fortress against fear and doubt. But this was different. This wasn't about personal glory or vengeance; this was about rescuing the woman who had opened his eyes to a different kind of battle, a battle fought not only with steel, but with compassion and unwavering hope.

The Outerlands were a breeding ground for dissent, a haven for those who dared to challenge Graffik's iron grip. Najeem knew he needed allies, not just for the perilous task ahead, but to understand the intricate political landscape of this rebellious region. He needed to learn the strengths and weaknesses of the various factions, to forge alliances with those who shared his hatred of Graffik, those who understood the price of tyranny and the value of freedom. He needed to gather intelligence, to gather strength, to build a force capable of challenging the mighty empire.

His days were filled with training, honing his skills to a razor's edge. He sparred with local warriors, learning their techniques, adapting his own to the harsh realities of guerrilla warfare. He studied maps, tracing the routes that led back to the imperial city, carefully considering the risks, planning his every move with the precision of a seasoned strategist. He learned the language of the Outerlands, immersing himself in their customs and traditions, earning their respect, understanding their needs, their hopes, their fears. He found himself a student once more, but the lessons were far more dangerous and far more profound than any he had learned within the sterile confines of the imperial academy.

Nights were spent studying the political climate, attending clandestine meetings in dimly lit taverns, listening to whispered conversations and cryptic hints. He learned of rebel groups, their strengths and weaknesses, their internal conflicts, their shifting alliances. He carefully wove his way through the treacherous currents of political intrigue, navigating the treacherous waters of betrayal and loyalty. The information he gathered was carefully curated, analyzed, and used to shape his plan, a plan as intricate and delicate as a spider's web, designed to catch his prey while remaining himself unseen.

His reputation grew among the rebels, a silent, watchful figure, a warrior whose skills were matched only by his unwavering loyalty. They whispered of the 'Shadow

Warrior', the man who moved like a wraith, a ghost in the night, leaving only a trail of defeated enemies in his wake. His legend grew, an ominous whisper in the shadows, a symbol of defiance against Graffik's reign of terror. It was a reputation that both helped and hindered his mission. It would attract attention, but it would also serve as a shield, a warning to those who would dare to stand against him.

Meanwhile, rumors of Graffik's growing paranoia reached even the Outerlands. Graffik's reign was becoming increasingly unstable, his grip on power weakening with each passing day. The seeds of rebellion, planted by Stanya's stolen information, were beginning to bear fruit. The empire, once seemingly invincible, was cracking at its foundations, its mighty walls crumbling under the weight of its own corruption and oppression. Najeem understood that he needed to capitalize on this internal strife, to strike when the empire was most vulnerable.

One evening, whilst sharing a rough meal of bread and stew with a grizzled veteran of countless battles, Najeem learned of a secret passage, an old smugglers' route known only to a select few. It was a risky route, fraught with peril, yet it was the shortest path to the imperial city. The veteran, a man hardened by years of hardship and loss, shared the information reluctantly, but Najeem's reputation and unwavering determination had earned his trust. The veteran spoke of a hidden cave, a passage through the mountains, guarded by ancient traps and the ghosts of fallen smugglers.

The thought of Amara spurred him on. Her image burned in his mind, a beacon in the darkness. He wouldn't fail her. He couldn't. He would find her, and he would bring her back to the Outerlands, to safety, to freedom. He would face any danger, overcome any obstacle. His love for her was not a romantic flourish, it was the fuel for his unwavering resolve, the driving force behind his relentless pursuit of justice. The escape, the training, the political maneuvering – it was all a means to an end, a necessary prelude to the final confrontation, the ultimate battle for Amara's freedom and the overthrow of Graffik's tyranny.

He knew the journey back would be treacherous, a death-defying dance with fate. But he was ready. He was stronger, more cunning, more determined than ever before. The Shadow Warrior, once a lone warrior fighting for survival, would soon become the symbol of a burgeoning rebellion, a force that would shake the very foundations of the empire. His destiny, once a dark and uncertain path, now blazed with the bright, unwavering light of hope and the fierce promise of a future where freedom reigned supreme. His destiny was woven with Amara's, their fates inextricably linked in a rebellion that would echo through the ages. The whispers of their names, once carried on the wind, would soon become a roar that would shake the very foundations of Graffik's empire, a roar that would reverberate through the ages. The next chapter of his life, and the next chapter of their intertwined destinies, was about to begin.

The salty air whipped through Stanya's hair as she watched the fishing boat disappear over the horizon, carrying Najeem towards a future both uncertain and promising. The Outerlands, a patchwork of defiant villages and hidden rebel camps, felt strangely alien after the suffocating opulence of Emperor Baznoon Graffik's court. She had delivered the intel – the meticulously gathered information on Graffik's secret alliances, his hidden arsenal, his plans for complete domination – and now the wheels of rebellion were slowly, inexorably, turning. But the weight of the task felt less like accomplishment and more like a heavy cloak she could barely bear.

The escape had been a blur of adrenaline and near-death experiences, each moment a testament to their shared resilience and the unexpected bond that had forged between them. Their initial mistrust, born from the chaos of their separate flights, had quickly melted away under the pressure of shared danger. They had become an unlikely team, their skills complementing each other perfectly. Stanya, the cunning strategist, with her mastery of infiltration and her sharp wit, had navigated the treacherous corridors of power while Najeem, the warrior, had carved a path through Graffik's relentless guards with his unmatched strength and agility.

They had argued, of course. Their temperaments clashed at times, sparks flying as easily as the blows they'd exchanged in the heat of battle. Stanya, pragmatic and calculating, often found herself frustrated by Najeem's impulsive nature, his unwavering faith in instinct, which often bordered on recklessness. Najeem, in turn, sometimes struggled to understand Stanya's detached approach, her ability to compartmentalize her emotions and focus solely on the task at hand. Yet, within those clashes, a deeper understanding had bloomed, a silent acknowledgment of their mutual respect and a growing affection that neither dared to name.

The memory of their final moments together lingered, a bittersweet ache in her chest. The parting had been abrupt, dictated by necessity. Najeem's path, the path he felt bound to follow, led him back to the imperial palace, to the imprisoned Princess Amara. Stanya, meanwhile, had a different mission – to ensure the information she had gathered was used effectively, to coordinate the various rebel factions and guide them towards a unified front against Graffik's tyranny. Their separate paths were dictated by circumstance, yet their bond felt as unbreakable as the strongest steel.

She traced the outline of a scar on her arm, a memento from one of the many close calls during their escape. It was a small, almost insignificant mark, yet it represented the countless moments they had risked their lives for each other, moments filled with adrenaline, fear, and a thrilling, dangerous intimacy. The memory of Najeem's hand gripping hers, their fingers intertwined in the midst of a chaotic battle, sent a shiver of warmth down her spine. It was more than just a physical connection; it was a silent promise of support, a shared understanding that transcended words.

The leaders of the Outerlands, initially wary of Stanya's arrival, had been swiftly won over by her unwavering dedication and the undeniable truth contained in her report. They had listened, mesmerized, as she unveiled the intricate web of Graffik's treachery, painting a vivid picture of Graffik's ruthless ambition and the imminent threat he posed to their fragile peace. Her information had galvanized them, fueling their resolve to fight, to challenge the seemingly insurmountable power of the empire.

The weeks that followed were a whirlwind of activity. Stanya, using her considerable skills, began to coordinate the scattered rebel groups, weaving together a network of communication and supply lines. She discovered a talent for leadership she hadn't known she possessed, drawing strength from the knowledge that she was fighting for something greater than herself – for the freedom of her people, for a future free from Graffik's tyrannical rule. She worked tirelessly, her energy fueled by a mixture of adrenaline and determination. The weight of the responsibility was immense, but the thought of Najeem, of their shared struggle, kept her going.

Sometimes, during the quiet moments, as she stared out at the starlit sky, she would remember Najeem's warm smile, his eyes that held both a fierce intensity and a surprising tenderness. The thought of him stirred a sense of longing within her, a feeling both unfamiliar and strangely comforting. It was a feeling she pushed aside, focusing instead on the task at hand, on the need to organize and prepare for the upcoming confrontation with the imperial forces. But the thought of him was always there, a silent guardian, a source of strength.

Meanwhile, in the faraway capital, Najeem's journey was just beginning. He had reached Porthaven, a city teetering on the precipice of rebellion, a city humming with discontent and whispers of dissent. The journey had been arduous, a constant test of his endurance and his resolve. He had faced countless dangers, evading imperial patrols, navigating treacherous landscapes. He had learned to rely on his instincts, to trust his honed senses, to survive against impossible odds. But despite the harshness of his journey, he remained steadfast in his purpose – to rescue Princess Amara and to avenge the injustices he had witnessed.

The city's underbelly, a labyrinth of hidden alleys and clandestine meeting places, offered him sanctuary and a base of operations. He had found allies among the city's disaffected, the ones who had witnessed Graffik's cruelty firsthand, the ones who longed for change, for a better future. He had started to build a network of informants, carefully gathering information, piecing together the fragments of a larger plan. He was slowly becoming a symbol of hope, a beacon of resistance in a city drowning in fear. His legend, already whispered in the shadows, was growing stronger with each daring act, each courageous stand against the empire's oppressive forces.

The memory of Amara's gentle touch, the warmth of her eyes, fueled his determination. Her kindness, her unexpected compassion in the face of her own captivity, had touched him deeply, stirring within him a protective instinct he hadn't known he possessed. He knew that rescuing her wouldn't be easy. Graffik's grip on the city was tight, his surveillance pervasive. Yet, the thought of Amara, her quiet strength, her unwavering spirit, gave him the courage to face any challenge. He would return for her, no matter the cost.

He often found himself thinking of Stanya, her sharp intellect, her unwavering resolve. He remembered her courage, her quick thinking, the way she had always seemed to know the next move. Their bond, forged in the crucible of shared danger, resonated within him, a deep sense of connection that went beyond their shared experiences. It was a reminder that he was not alone, that someone else believed in the cause, in the hope of a better future.

As the days turned into weeks, as Najeem's plans slowly began to take shape, he knew that the path ahead would be long and arduous. But he also knew, deep down, that he was not fighting alone. He had Stanya's spirit with him, her silent support echoing in his heart, a tangible connection across the vast distances separating them. And somewhere, amidst the whispers of rebellion and the shadows of the city, their destinies remained entwined, their paths destined to converge once more, their combined strengths poised to challenge the seemingly insurmountable power of Graffik, to reshape the very fabric of their world, and to forge a future where freedom and love could finally bloom. Their story, far from over, was only just beginning, a tale of courage, resilience, and a bond that would forever endure.

Acknowledgments

First and foremost, I extend my deepest gratitude to my family and friends for their unwavering support and patience throughout the long and often arduous process of writing this book. Your belief in me fueled my creativity and kept me going through countless revisions. A special thank you to everyone for their insightful feedback and encouragement.

My sincere appreciation also goes to all the individuals, teams, and companies involved with my work for their invaluable guidance and expertise. Your sharp eye for detail and dedication to crafting a compelling narrative greatly improved the final product. I am also thankful to the entire team at [Publisher's Name] for their hard work and dedication in bringing this story to life.

Finally, a heartfelt thank you to all the readers who have supported my work. Your passion for fantasy and adventure inspires me to continue crafting worlds and characters that captivate and challenge.

Glossary

Baznoon Empire: The vast empire ruled by Emperor Baznoon Grattik.

Outerlands: The rebellious region beyond the Baznoon Empire's borders.

Graffik Dynasty: The ruling family of the Baznoon Empire.

The Jeweled Comb: The seemingly innocuous object used by Stanya to secretly transport vital information.

Royal Guard: Elite soldiers who protect Graffik and his family.

Shadow Stalkers: Highly skilled assassins employed by Graffik.

References

While this novel drew inspiration from various sources, no specific texts or historical events served as direct references for the creation of this fictional world and its inhabitants. The world of Baznoon Graffik and the characters within it are products of the author's imagination.

Author Biography

Willie S. is a fantasy and adventure novelist with a passion for creating strong female characters and intricate plots. A lover of history and political intrigue, He blends elements of historical fiction and high fantasy to create immersive and captivating worlds. He has always been fascinated by stories of rebellion, social injustice, and the resilience of the human spirit. When not writing, Willie S. has many creative skills and interests. This is his next novel, but not the last.

www.ingramcontent.com/pod-product-compliance
Lightning Source LLC
Chambersburg PA
CBHW061507020726
47502CB00006B/1973